Valpar

The Promised Mates of Monktona Wood

Vera Foxx

Foxx Fantasy Publishing

Publisher: Foxx Fantasy Publishing

Editing by: MarcEdits

CONTENTS

DEAR READER

The following book has a different type of heroine. Calliope is an adult but lacks the awareness of danger, has a child-like personality with the body and desires of an adult. At times, she often appears aloof and silly. It is part of the fae culture and of her own person. If this sort of age play bothers you, this book may not be for you.

Other warnings you may need to consider:
Size difference, monster cock, primal play, chase scene, voyeurism, language, graphic scenes, child abuse (talked in passing, no details), death, pet kidnapping, heroine kidnapping from MMC, spanking, punishments, depression.

GLOSSARY

MONKTONA WOOD- NAME OF orcs' home

Dark Forest- What everyone else called Monktona Wood before they knew of the orcs beyond the wall.

The Dark War- When Bergarian went through dark times and had to fight through a dark entity. A wall was discovered, revealing the orcs and with their help the Bergarians were able to win the war.

Orgamo- Father

Seeded orgamo- Sired father

Ogamie- Mother

Clan- A small family that holds one orc female and several males. Each male has their own cabin, while the female visits one male every night. Clans are no longer in practice because all the female orcs have died.

Tribe- The orc race as a whole

Miresa- Orc word for mates

Moon Fairy- Moon Goddess

Bassza- Curse word equivalent to *fuck*

Fattyu- Bastard

Guardard snap- Curse word equivalent to *damn it.*

Orcling- Orc child or child in general

CHAPTER ONE

Valpar

THE GLEAMING CHESTNUT COAT of my horse glistened under the warm sunlight. As I secured the leather tightly around his shoulders, I felt the tautness against his powerful muscles. A slight tension coursed through him when my claws came too close to his neck. With each stomp of his hooves, the ground reverberated beneath us. Protesting, he threw his head back, and his ears flattened against his skull, conveying his displeasure.

I relaxed my face and tensed shoulders, as my palm smoothed down his neck. The horse, whom I have named Ulam, calmed, and I could feel the thrumming of his drum beneath my large hand. My nails ran up and down his neck, his skin shivering at my touch and he leaned into me.

Horses could read an orc. They knew when an orc was sad, happy or angry, and most of the time, territorial. We had been gifted several horses by the Golden Lights' King Osirus, and a stableman to teach us how to care for them. Only a few of us wanted one to keep, as the forest wasn't ideal for these creatures, who often needed open spaces. They had seen us in war, so they knew how ferocious we were. It took months for us to gain these beasts' trust.

Most of the tribe didn't like them, they found them too jumpy. I found them to be smart and useful, if one had the patience.

Patience with animals, I had... with other creatures, not so much.

"Is that the last of it?" Alark called from behind the wagon, which was attached to my horse.

Ulam jerked his head, and his front legs stomped into the soft ground.

I sighed and ran my hand through my messy hair. "Yes, now stop barking near the horses or we won't get anywhere," I replied quietly.

The horses were used to my grunts and barks since I spent more time with them, but this fat fattyu understood nothing. His head was not completely formed.

"They fear everything. We should leave them with Osirus. You must treat them like orclings to get anything from them," Alark said, putting his hands on his hips. He was tall and covered in scars from the war. He was a fool, hot-headed, and dumber than a pixie.

I did not know how his clan could stand him. His ogamie would be sad to know the moss in his skull gets smaller each day.

"Fine, we'll do that. You can haul the cart with all the *exports,* then."

Exports was a word Osirus taught us. We 'exported' food, furs and other goods from Monktona Wood that came from nowhere else in Bergarian. In return, we gained gold or other materials such as sugar, flour and other things we could not get called *imports.*

I grunted and turned away from the male. He rolled his yellow eyes, and I didn't have time to explain simple things. Today was enough to bear.

I let out a low, guttural groan, and the sound echoed through the dense forest. Anger surged within me, causing my hand to clench into a tight fist. As my sharp claws dug into my palm, a surge of pain shot through my body, but I welcomed it, relishing in the release.

It had been an entire year since I last ventured beyond the towering trees of Monktona Wood, and the thought of leaving now filled me with an overwhelming sense of unease.

I wanted to hit something.

I could hit Alark's face.

I enjoyed staying in the Monktona Wood to look after the elders. It was welcomed; it was quiet. I didn't have to dress up in *for-mal* cloth. I did not have to smile and talk to funny-smelling fairies or shifters.

Thorn, our unofficial leader of the tribe, said he would stay behind to watch out for the elders this time. He told me that I could not stay behind for a third migration.

My chest felt like a boulder was sitting on it. It pushed heavily on my bones as I observed Thorn's slow approach. Exhaustion seeped into my body, weariness accumulating with each visit to the Golden Light or the Cerulean Moon Kingdoms, always returning empty-handed, and my hopes shattered like fragile glass that hung in those fancy castles.

It had been over ten years since the Moon Fairy came to the tribe and promised that our tribe would have females again. She called them mates, not miresas, but it was all the same to us. She said we would have one for each male and never have to share if we did not want to, and we all believed her.

I wanted one so badly. My body ached watching the last female orc pass this world and go to the stars. There were no females left and none to be given to the youngest generation. Our orgamos were withering away with no females, and they were ready for death and to meet them on the other side.

Thorn approached, his eyes trying to give us false hope. His grin stretched across his face. The warmth of his fake happiness was sickening. I could almost hear the joyous hum of his contentment, as he reveled knowing that I was assuming leadership of the tribe, while he would stay behind to rest in peace.

Stupid, ugly-faced ogre.

I grunted and grabbed my sword from the side of the cart. "Are you sure I cannot stay?" I took the sword and slid it into its sleeve behind my back. "I can be of more use here."

Thorn's disappointed gaze pierced through me, then his judging eyes looked straight toward my gut. I could almost taste the words he wanted to utter hovering on the edge of his tongue. I stood before him, distinct from the rest of the tribe, my figure softer around the midsection. Yet, my strength remained unwavering and fierce enough to protect our tribe from any enemy.

So what if my body differed from the others? I could still slaughter more than the rest.

"Valpar, it has been too many moons since you have visited either kingdom. I must push you to do this. Our ogamie would want this for you."

I furrowed my brow, clenched my teeth and pushed my jaw forward stubbornly. He knew the thought of our ogamie was a soft spot in my heart. He used it many times to manipulate me into taking action.

I sighed and rubbed my neck. "I dislike when you bring up our birth ogamie. It isn't fair."

Thorn frowned and stepped forward to put his hand on my shoulder.

None of the orcs enjoyed touch, but since he was my brother I allowed it. We were of the same clan, the same ogamie. We may be from different orgamos, but we were still close in each other's eyes. Especially since our ogamie left this world.

Thorn spouted off nonsense to ease my pain, to help me realize that this was for my own good, and to find my miresa- the female that was meant to be mine, my *soul mate or fated mate,* as many Bergarians have called it-but I could hardly pay attention.

I gazed at my horses, and the excitement of the rest of the tribe. I couldn't understand it. It had been ten years since the war and not one of us had found a miresa. I often had intrusive thoughts that the Moon Fairy was never real, when lying under the stars at night. It could have all been a lie.

Perhaps we all drank bad ale and wished for the Moon Fairy to give us miresas.

I huffed in annoyance once Thorn stopped speaking. No, I could not get my hopes up.

"The shifters smell like wet animals, and the fae and fairies smell too sweet. I don't see how I will find my miresa amongst a bunch of terrible smells," I spat.

Sugha, the youngest of our clan, came up behind Thorn and I with a frown on his face.

How long had he been there?

"Yes, and the Bergarians look at us differently too, don't they?" Sugha said, wringing his hands together.

Sugha was the happiest of all of us, and here I was making the poor, adult orcling sad.

Bassza, I couldn't do anything right.

Shifters could change from animal to human. Fae, fairies, pixies and sirens all looked human. Orcs didn't look human at all. We were green and couldn't change our appearance.

We were so different.

We were monsters in their world, and not just by the way we looked.

Orcs couldn't be around each other for long periods of time. We were very much alphas. We all lived in our own territories because of our aggressiveness toward each other. We only gathered in time of trade, when one might need help with building a new home or taking down trees.

We didn't socialize with one another unless we needed to.

Thorn sniffed the air, his mind taking him to other places. He turned, his heavy feet carrying him away from us and toward the wall. He grazed it with his fingers, and his nose flared while he traveled deeper into the Wood.

Strange male.

He was most likely faking that he had something better to do than leading the tribe.

Sugha's mood lightened. With his bag on his back and a wide grin on his face, he ran in front of Ulam, who didn't see Sugha as a threat in the slightest. "Ready to go, buddy?" Sugha reached into his pocket and grabbed a few sugar cubes.

Ulam pranced on his feet and grunted.

"Do not feed my horse sugar. It will make him jumpy!" I yelled and stomped over.

"A treat won't hurt!" Sugha waved me off, holding out his hand.

Ulam greedily took it, licking his palm until it vanished, and then my horse flicked his lips toward me to show me it was gone.

I let out a low grunt, the sound mingling with the creaking of the leather reins as I freed them from their position around his neck. My grip tightened around the worn, weathered leather, its texture comforting in my hand. Glancing back, I scanned the formidable caravan of orcs following closely behind us, their heavy footsteps creating thunderous movement along the path.

They were all talking amongst themselves, not as lively as they were the first time we had taken the journey, but everyone was accounted for. Bags, satchels of things to trade, and still odd murmurs of finding their miresas...

"Yup, got my stuff. I'm going to look around the coast this time. Maybe she's in the water," Sugha said excitedly, as I tugged on the reins for Ulam to follow.

I made a gagging sound as we trotted over the wall line, which was what separated the Monktona Wood and the Bergarian lands. "They smell like fish. You hate fish."

Sugha shrugged his shoulders. "But if she is supposed to be mine, then it won't matter. I'll love her smell no matter what."

I didn't say anything in reply. I kept my eyes on the path I'd taken over the years. Orcs still traveled by themselves and went on their own journeys to find their mates, but the big migration every six months, we all did together, for the mating balls. Except for the elders.

"Whatever you say. Just don't drown. You can't swim. And Thorn and your seeded orgamo would get angry with me. I can't watch you all the time."

Sugha stopped in his tracks and put his hand over his mouth. "You know, I forgot about that. Think she will still feel the bond from the shoreline?" Sugha placed his hand across his smooth face and scratched his cheek.

Ah, that bond everyone talks about. I see it at these mating balls. They sniff or look at each other and just know that is who their mate is.

I never stick around too long to watch the other creatures get their miresas. I became too tired and disappointed. My miresa has never shown up. No orc has ever claimed their mate. What if there was something more we needed to do? What if it wasn't a smell or a look? Do we need to touch them?

I hated touching.

"I'm sure she will come to you," I told Sugha, to appease him.

How could Sugha be so excited after all this time waiting? He was always the optimistic one, even as a young orcling.

I pulled on my messy hair, tugging at the head pain that was coming. Ulam, sensing my discomfort, nudged my arm and I wrapped it around his head.

His touch didn't bother me. Maybe it was because I spent most of my time with him. I never felt threatened by the beast. It was a new concept for orcs, caring for an animal, but amongst those in Bergarian they were called *pets*.

Once, my orgamos said they wanted to cook Ulam, and that was the first time I'd felt fear.

He has never been anywhere near my seeded orgamo or orgamos ever again after that.

"What do you think, do you think I would attract my miresa with this?" Sugha stepped in front of me and walked backwards to keep up the pace. When I gazed up at him my head reared back in shock.

Sugha was wearing a bright pink tunic, opened in the front, showing no hair on his chest at all.

I frowned and side-stepped. "It's hideous."

Moon Fairy, save me. Must I be tormented by such a clan brother?

Sugha fluffed up his tunic. Other orcs behind us barked in laughter and pointed at his ridiculous cloth.

"Hey, I don't see you having any miresas on your arm, or on your shaft! Mind your own!" Sugha shouted at the others.

I groaned and ran my hand down my face. "Take it off! You are causing a scene," I hissed and tugged on his tunic.

"No, I think my miresa will like it." Sugha ran his hand down the large ruffles in the middle of the shirt. He didn't even have pants on, just his long cloth that exposed his thighs. It looked ridiculous.

"You look like a bird. That is what you look like. A funny, skinny bird with bright colors. You want your miresa to be the most beautiful, not you."

Sugha smiled, and his cheeks turned a dark shade of green. "Ah, Valpar, do you think I am beautiful?" He blinked his eyes rapidly in my direction.

My mouth hung open, and I turned away from him, keeping my head on the path. "I, uh. No, I do not. I find you disgusting and, bassza, very annoying. Now leave me be and let me lead the caravan."

Sugha squealed, skipping up to me. "But Valpar," he said in a higher-pitched voice. "How can I ignore it when you find me so captivating." He flipped the invisible hair on his shoulder behind him and tried to intertwine his arm around mine.

I snarled, gripping his arm and putting it around his back. Instead of screaming in fear, he laughed, giggling while the other orcs watched in amusement. "Do not touch me," I growled. "And stop with your foolishness. This is serious."

Sugha calmed and nodded his head when I let go. He straightened himself as we carried on, but it was just a few minutes later when he spoke again.

"You still want to meet her, then?" He tilted his head, and I shook mine in reply.

"My job is to get the tribe there. If I meet my miresa, then great." I dropped my hand on my thigh, and it echoed through the wood.

Sugha studied me from my peripheral and, for once, I wondered what was on his mind.

"We are going to find them," he murmured.

Okay, maybe I didn't want to know what was on his mind.

"We are going to find them when we least expect it, and the wait will be worth it."

Good for him; he had hope. But my hope had run out. I was ready to accept my life to live alone. All I needed was my seeded orgamo, who still lived back in the Monktona Wood, and my horse, Ulam, who didn't argue back.

Chapter Two

Calliope

I TILTED MY HEAD, and my fingers brushed the delicate vine to make a perfect circle on the ground. It was perfect; this was the greatest trap I had ever created.

There was a pixie on the loose, who had stolen one of my cupcakes. It was a special one, too, made at the palace, and I had saved it for a rainy day.

Everyone knows cakes from the Golden Light Palace never went bad. They stayed fresh, never molded, and tasted as fresh as the day they were made. It was my favorite flavor, lemon with a lemon custard filling. It had a blueberry-swirl icing with a mint leaf on top.

I had it hidden away in a special cupcake chest under a floorboard in my roost.

My roost was a sacred place. Where I slept and kept all my belongings. No one could go there. But that little flying turd went in there and stole it!

Crumbs were over my blankets and pillows. He'd gnawed on the wood with his sharp little teeth. Then, he broke into the chest, and with the pixies being so small he couldn't eat all of it. He could have taken a few small bites and put it back at least, but no. He called all his friends to come eat it with him.

I whimpered and sat back on my heels.

That flying piece of glitter-turd was gonna pay.

I leaned forward and put a strawberry-flavored cupcake in the middle of my trap. I fastened the vine to the tree behind me while I worked. I had to keep checking on it to make sure Simon would not eat it.

Simon was in a mood, too, because he knew how much I enjoyed my lemon custard blueberry-frosted cupcakes.

"Simon, do you eat pixies? You eat everything else." I mumbled and stood up to back away.

Simon bleated and went back to eating the grass.

The trap would have to do. I had little time.

Simon's high-pitched bleat echoed in my ears as I walked ahead, his wiry chin hair gently dancing in the cool breeze.

"You best get out of here. There is gonna be blood when I'm done with him. You don't need to see it." Simon let out another bleat and trotted behind the tree, flicking his tail.

Yup, best idea ever. I couldn't wait to dunk the pixie's wings in some water, so he couldn't fly for days.

I peeked my head up from behind the tree and gripped the vine.

Maybe that was too mean.

I tapped my lip. What else could I do to him?

"What are you doing?"

I felt someone sit on my shoulder.

I hummed and let my fingers twirl the vine. I had to keep my concentration; I could not go squirrel and forget my task.

"Trying to catch Karma. The pixie stole my cupcake."

The person on my shoulder grunted and I heard their wings flutter.

"What a drag."

"Yeah, who does that? Steal a poor fairy's food?"

The person sitting on my shoulder scoffed. "You ain't a fairy. Maybe you deserved it."

I growled and jerked my head to the offender to find none other than Karma, the pixie.

"You!" I snapped. The bane of my existence.

I let go of the vine and tried to grab him, but he flew off, leaving a trail of fairy dust. I fell into the thick grass, and Karma flew above my head pulling on my wings.

"Seriously, Calliope. Still wearing these?" Karma taunted.

Simon belted out a long bleat, and I heard his little hooves vibrating on the ground. I tried to scramble up from the ground, but Simon used my body to launch himself and headbutt Karma.

Karma laughed, darting away, and Simon's body seized, falling to the ground, his body ridged.

Ah, the woes of having a pet fainting goat.

Karma laughed, his arms wrapping around his belly, yet with his impressive ability at flying, he was able to stay in the air.

I groaned and let my face rub into the thick green, blue grass, and took my defeat. That stupid pixie will get his one day.

"What is the meaning of this?" I heard a stern voice come from the distance and my head poked up immediately.

I instantly felt my sour mood sweeten, when I saw my uncle fall from the sky and land with a powerful stance.

Like one of those superheroes on Earth.

My uncle always exuded a regal and powerful presence, dressed in a royal purple ensemble with silver trimmings that glistened in the sunlight. The intricate designs of his clothing radiated luxury and commanded attention. The silver buttons on his coat were so bright that they nearly blinded me, reflecting light like tiny mirrors.

Pretty.

Today, he braided his long hair behind his back, and a few pieces fell in front of his face when he scowled. He didn't scare me though, few people did, but him least of all.

"Uncle Osirus!" I jumped up from the ground and ran toward him. He held out his arms, but his sight was still on Karma.

"I said, what is the meaning of this?" Osirus engulfed me in the hug. He held onto me tightly and I relished his cotton candy smell.

Mmm, candy.

Karma's stuttered voice made me laugh, and Osirus pulled me back by the shoulders. "Calliope, what happened to your wing? It's bent?" Uncle Osirus fiddled with the top of my hand-made wing and frowned.

"Oh." I looked back at Karma, who was shaking his head. His glitter was pouring out of his body like he was taking a pee right there.

Osirus took me by the chin with his index finger and thumb and raised a brow.

It's super hard to lie to Osirus. He had this aura of power, and he could read me like an open book. He could read my emotions, and he knew exactly what I was feeling. I didn't have to say anything at all for him to know what was going on.

He sighed and shrugged his shoulders.

"Little one, I know you are trying to do big things, but Karma is my subject, and I will not let him treat my family this way."

Osirus' features transformed, as if a shadow had cast upon his face. The wings on his back, usually resembling a delicate honeybee, now writhed with sinuous black lines, which gradually consumed them entirely.

"He just ate my cupcake." I tugged on Osirus' arm. "I can get another one at the palace, right?" I fluttered my lashes at him.

Osirus gripped my hand and pulled me with him to get closer to Karma. Karma was already on the ground, nearly covered in the tall grasses.

"I gave her the gift to speak with pixies so she can befriend all of you, and you think it is wise to pick on the King's favorite niece instead?"

"Oh, hamburgers," I whispered, covering my mouth.

Karma was in a deep poop hole.

"Get to the palace and request to be put into the dungeon, by my order. If you are not there when I return and I have to hunt you down, you will not live another day."

I held back a snort when I let my vibrant pink hair fall in front of me.

This was too good. He was getting a swat.

Karma shook and crawled away from us.

"Fly, imbecile!" Osirus barked, and I broke into sobs of laughter without letting go of Osirus' hand.

When I was done with my fit, Osirus looked down at me with a smirk on his lips. "Now, Calliope, why could you not just say he was bullying you?"

I wiped a tear from my eye and grew quiet.

Because I didn't want to look like a loser.

I lowered my head and bit my lip.

"Ahhh." Osirus kneeled and pushed my chin up with his knuckle. "Nothing to be ashamed of when you have family here. Especially in high places, hmm? Now, do you remember what today is?"

I pouted and looked up at the sky. The only thing that was on my mind was my cupcake.

"Nope."

Osirus stood up and chuckled, leading me back home. "I can't believe you forgot. I'm offended."

Well, now I really needed to remember.

It wasn't the Spring Festival or the Summer Festival, it wasn't my birthday, and it wasn't the Moon Goddess celebration. I stopped mid-stride, and my eyes widened.

"A month-long sleepover!" I screamed.

I grabbed Osirus' hand and pulled him along. He threw his head back and laughed, while I continued to pull us.

"And why are you so far away from your house? Where are your parents? Usually, they are watching you like a dragon guarding its hoard," he paused. "Even though you are twenty-five…" he muttered.

I giggled and nodded as I continued to pull him along.

"Yeah, well, they were playing the Hokey Pokey this morning. I get to sneak out when they do that."

Osirus choked and sped up to keep up with me. "Pardon? The Hokey Pokey?"

"Yeah, the Hokey Pokey. It's a game. *You put your right arm in, you put your right arm out,*" I sang and showed him how I put my arm in front of me and behind me. "But instead of their arms and legs, your brother likes to put his *thing* in between mom's legs."

Uncle Osirus said little for the rest of the trip. He just smiled, shook his head, and ran his hand down his face.

As we neared the towering tree house, nestled amongst the tallest trees to the north of the majestic Golden Light Palace, the distant sound of my mom's voice reached my ears.

It was like the piercing sound of nails scraping against a chalkboard. Instinctively, I spun around, ready to flee, only to be halted by Osirus' firm grip on my shoulders. He swiftly turned me back around.

"We are going to do this right. She was worried about you."

I groaned and pulled on the strap that held my wing in place. I felt the leather tug on one side of my shoulder where the wing was bent. It would take time to fix it since I made it with a special type of thread and tulle. Luckily, Uncle Osirus and Melina had an outstanding sewing room at the palace.

"Calliope! Where are you?" My mom's worried tone struck through my heart. It was the one where she was at her last nerve, and soon she would have Osirus' brother, Birch, my adoptive father, send out the cavalry.

The entire army of the Golden Light Kingdom.

It had only happened once, but it was a hot mess.

I waved from below and yelled, "I'm here, Mom!"

You couldn't hear my mom's feet running through the thick planks of the tree house. Now that she was a fae, a true fae, she was light on her feet.

Birch, the only father I'd known, built this tree house with his own bare hands. He built it before he went in search of his mate on Earth so long ago. He swears it is the sturdiest of all the homes of the Golden Light Kingdom. It withstood a war. The only thing missing was the furniture and a few personal items.

Since bringing my mother and me from Earth, Dad said that she truly made it a home. Birch got the help of the elves and had vines grown all around it, so it blended into nature.

The tree house was surrounded by lush green vines, creating a natural camouflage that blended seamlessly into the forest. Tiny leaves and delicate flowers add pops of color to the otherwise earthy tones. From a distance, it looks like a part of the trees themselves, hidden among the branches and leaves. Only upon closer inspection could one see the detailed workmanship of the elves Birch had hired, who had carefully intertwined the vines to create a sturdy foundation for the tree house. It was truly a hidden gem of the forest, easily missed by those who passed by.

There was one thing that stood out though, letting everyone and their mamas know there was a home here. It was the platform that helped me get up and down from our house. It was built with planks of wood and a small railing, that mom insisted on, so I wouldn't fall off.

"Get up here this instant!" Her harsh whisper let me know she meant business. I sheepishly stood on the platform and Osirus followed me.

"You can just fly up. You don't have to ride it," I said and took off my wings to make more room.

"And miss another moment standing next to you? Never." Osirus wrapped his arm around me and my face flushed.

I wish I could have a mate like Osirus.

Hamburger! I wish I could have a mate.

Mom pulled the lever at the top of the tree house before I could press mine at the bottom.

Boy, she sure is antsy.

The welded metal and vines worked together. The pullies let out squeaks and groans the higher we went. The elevator was so heavy it didn't even swing in the wind, so it was safe in all ways, just how Mom wanted it for me.

When the elevator rose to the platform, Mom stood at the entrance. Barefooted and arms crossed, wearing her favorite yellow flying dress. Her wings fluttered violently, like they always did when she was agitated, but when she saw the sight of Osirus by my side her eyebrows shot up to her hairline.

Dad strode in with just a towel around his waist from a fresh shower and ran his hand through his hair to shake off the water.

"Brother, fancy seeing you here. You're early!" Dad stepped forward and gave Osirus a big hug, all while my mom was shooting daggers at me.

I tried to scoot to the side to escape, but she stepped in front of me with her arms folded. "Where were you? Honey, I've been worried sick," her voice softened, and she pulled me into a hug. "Just anyone could have snatched you away and taken you. My sweet Calli, don't do that to me."

"She's fine, Kelsey. She's grown." Osirus pulled away from Dad. "Besides, your game of Hokey Pokey was enough incentive for little Calliope to go on a pixie hunt."

Mom paled. "A what?"

"Hokey Pokey. You know, when you go in and out? In and out?" I made my index finger and thumb into a circle with one hand, and then took my finger from my other hand and put it in the hole I made.

CHAPTER THREE

Calliope

MOM'S FACE FLUSHED, HER cheeks turning a deep shade of red. Osirus couldn't contain his excitement, his laughter filling the room with a contagious giddiness. Meanwhile, Dad's hand gently brushed through his thick beard, amusement evident in the twinkle of his eyes.

Dad had been attempting to persuade my mom to see reason that I was old enough to leave the tree house more, but she remained adamant that I always had someone with me.

This was the reason why I always caught them playing games in bed that were meant for mates.

"Calliope, why don't you go pack your bag?" Dad suggested and nodded his head to my room.

I let out a high-pitched squeal of excitement, and my voice echoed through the air. With anticipation bubbling inside me, I bounced up and down on the balls of my feet, feeling the ground beneath me spring back with each joyful movement. The wait had been agonizingly long, but today was finally the day I had been eagerly counting down to.

A whole month at the magnificent palace, with my beloved Uncle Osirus and Aunt Melina, awaited me. The grandeur and opulence of the palace would surely mesmerize my senses, from the intricate details of the architecture to the shimmering chandeliers that illuminated the halls. The air would be filled with an aura of elegance and sophistication, tinged with the faint scent of freshly cut flowers that adorned every corner.

But that wasn't all, the icing on the cake was the much-anticipated mating ball, which was a celebration like no other. The thought of attending this enchanting event sent shivers of excitement down my spine. I couldn't help but feel a rush of anticipation, imagining the vibrant colors of the ballroom, the soft melodies of the orchestra, and the rhythmic sound of dancing feet on the polished marble floor.

Melina, with her loving and caring nature, had promised to take me to the ball. I could already picture us twirling and spinning, our dresses swishing around us, as we joined in the festivities. The thought of being a part of such a grand event, surrounded by the laughter and joy of the celebration, filled my heart with giddiness.

This was a day I had been dreaming of for what felt like an eternity, and now it was finally within reach. Anticipation and excitement coursed through me.

I bounced my way into my roost and could already hear Mom starting her protests. Her complaint was that I wasn't old enough. She'd put it off every year, but Osirus said he wouldn't let her put it off any longer.

He pinky-promised. Pinky-promises were sacred!

"No, Kelsey. I won't let you talk me out of it this time. Calliope is old enough, far old enough." His tone was bored and, in my mind, I could almost see his wings flicking about.

I was old, especially by human standards. I was practically an old maid! I was going to get wrinkles, and my boobs were gonna sag.

If I had boobs.

I wrinkled my nose and looked down at my low-cut dress. They were the size of tiny apples. Wait, smaller than that. Dwarf apples. No, not even apples. Why am I obsessed with apples, right now? Did I want an apple? Am I hungry? Mandarin orange! They were the size of a mandarin orange...

"I just don't think it's wise. That spell has made her—"

I stopped and listened. Maybe this time she would finish her sentence, but she didn't.

Made me what? What was wrong with me? And what spell?

Was it my hair?

I pulled a strand in front of my face. For my sixteenth birthday, Osirus and Melina gave me a tonic that turned it pink. Forever it will be pink—my favorite color. It was awesome. I'm the only human in the Golden Light Kingdom with pink hair.

"Please, Birch, just one more year?" Mom groaned and Birch let out a huff in disagreement.

Dad was on Osirus' side. He was ready for a kid of his own blood. I understood; he hadn't experienced having a baby yet, and neither had Mom.

I picked at the cuticle on my nail with my teeth and sat on my bed of thick blankets. My bed was so large it covered almost the whole room.

I liked living here, don't get me wrong, but I knew Dad wanted to start their own family. I just wanted a little more freedom, just a little. I could live next door in my own tree house.

But Mom wouldn't let me. And I didn't know why.

"She's been through a lot; I have to protect her—" Mom urged both men.

Protect me? Been through a lot? My life has been great!

Parties, solstices, great food, traveling to the Cerulean Moon Kingdom - I have even been to Atlantis!

"And you don't think Melina and I can protect her?" Osirus mused. "Honestly, you wound me right here." I heard Osirus pat his chest.

My lip curled into a smile, and my butt wiggled on the bed.

"It's not that I don't trust you, it's just... She isn't ready for a mating ball. There are things she doesn't know," Mom hissed.

"Like the Hokey Pokey?" Dad barked out a laugh, and Osirus followed.

I snorted. *If only she knew how much I knew about all that.*

Giggling softly, I instinctively placed my hand over my mouth, and the sound muffled against my palm. Suddenly, a thump resonated from behind, causing a jolt of curiosity to course through me. The delicate tulle curtains swayed gracefully, their ethereal movements whispering across the creaking floorboards. Emerging from within, a majestic figure materialized before my eyes. With each step, the barefooted goddess exuded an aura of enchantment. Her flowing white hair, adorned with vibrant blue and green tips, cascaded down her back as she gracefully approached. Bathed in the morning sunlight, her exquisite purple dress, perfectly complementing Osirus' attire, shimmered and sparkled, casting a dazzling reflection.

"Aunt Melina!" I squealed and ran towards her.

Melina screamed, her beautiful wings, that resembled those of a butter-fly, fluttered violently and pushed the fabrics away from us. "Calliope, I haven't seen you in forever!" Melina squeezed me tighter.

"I saw you three days ago," I said, muffled into her shoulder.

"Still too long." She pushed me back and looked at my empty bag on my bed. "You forgot!" She pushed my shoulder, and I shook my head.

"No! Okay, yes, but there was this pixie and—"

"Yeah, yeah, I know all about it. The forest was laughing about how he got sent to the dungeon for messing with the king's favorite." She winked at me and pulled out my dresser drawers.

Melina packed only a few of my things and said she had a whole special room full of clothes made just for me. I was going to match her and Osirus the whole time I visited, and my heart flipped in my chest the entire time she talked.

Rough life, my butt! My life was awesome. Mom was over-protective sometimes, but awesome, nonetheless.

"Ready?" Melina chucked the bag over her shoulder and pointed to my wings on the bed.

I scooped them up, and she eyed the broken tip, but I waved her off as we stepped out of my room.

Simon bleated from the elevator entrance. Not that he needed an elevator. He could climb the tree with only three legs if he really wanted to, because Simon was a talented goat. He could climb anything.

"She's ready!" Melina gave the bag to Osirus and put her arm through mine. I waved to Mom and Dad, and pulled Melina to the elevator before Mom could say anything more.

"Hold on a second," Dad grunted when he pushed away from the door frame. He was wearing his traveling gear, now. It was actually for hunting and fighting but Mom had made him swear not to hurt the little critters from the forest anymore. Dad wasn't even allowed to hunt for food and bring dead animals home.

Thank the goddess!

I cried for two days straight when he came home with three bunnies dangling from his belt for Mom to cook one night. Now, we get our meat already skinned and precooked from the palace.

Maybe I couldn't live on my own.

I leaned my head back to sigh and stared up into the leaves of our roofless home.

Huh, the rain never gets in. I wonder how that is?

Wait, what was I supposed to be thinking about?

Oh, right.

I'm never gonna have a sleepover at Uncle Osirus' palace.

"You are allowed to go, but..." Dad said, stepping forward.

Simon bleated.

"Damn goat," Dad muttered, and I gasped and put my hands over Simon's ears.

"You can't cuss like that in front of Simon. I told you that, he is sensitive. He almost fainted when I said the word b-l-o-o-d today," I whispered.

Dad pressed his lips into a thin line, and Mom elbowed him in the gut. "What I mean is, your mother would prefer..." She elbowed him again, so he took his arm away from her and stepped away. "We prefer you do not attend the mating ball this year."

My shoulders sagged in defeat.

But balls had food, dancing and more food. They also had really handsome men there, too. Which has really, really been on my mind lately. I wanted to see what a dick looked like. I've only read about them, and I didn't want to see Dad's dick.

Ew, gross.

I wanted to see a real one.

And fae balls are freaky-deeky. At least, that was what Melina had said.

There are hot fae, fairies, shifters of all kinds, and I've heard about orcs.

I haven't seen any pictures of the monsters, but I heard through some of the gossiping fairies that they are large, can be scary, have big teeth, wear a loincloth that barely covers their...

I want to meet one.

Melina stomped her foot and crossed her arms when Osirus continued to shake his head that I couldn't go.

With Melina being a queen and all, I did the same.

"You are being unreasonable, Kelsey. Let her go. There won't be any harm in it." Melina flopped her arms by her sides. "People go years without finding—"

Osirus cleared his throat and put his hand on his mate's shoulder. "We should talk about this later, Melina. Her parents believe it is in her best interest that we wait, and wait we shall."

Melani gasped, "You promised we wouldn't take her, didn't you?"

Osirus frowned. "She is their daughter. We are not her parents."

Melina's eyes flickered with a brief glimpse of pain and a subtle shimmer of unspoken emotions.

My lower lip curled into a pout. "But why?"

"Things happen at fae balls that you should not see. Of all people, you know that, Melina." Mom raised a brow.

Melina's mood quickly changed, she snickered and nodded. "Yeah, but they are fun."

Mom sighed. "Alright, well. Calliope, do you still want to go to the palace for the month? You don't have to. Your dad and I can stay at home. Right, love?"

Dad gave a forced smile and nodded, reluctantly. This was supposed to be their anniversary month. They wanted a baby; I know they did. One that was part Mom and, part Dad. I wasn't related to either. Well, Mom said she was actually my aunt. She was my birth mother's sister.

Not that I remembered any of that. I didn't know my real mother.

"I'm certain. I absolutely want to go!" I sprinted to my mom and hugged her tightly. As I pressed against her, I felt her squeeze me tight. I inhaled her deeply and savored her familiar scent. She smelled of Dad - a crisp essence of the forest mixed with the fragrant aroma of tree sap.

"Thank the goddess," Dad groaned in relief. I peeked out from my mom's shoulder and saw Dad rub both hands down his face and tangled his fingers into his beard.

I knew that face. He wanted his Hokey Pokey time.

I pulled away from Mom, or at least tried. She held onto me and let out a whimper, until Melina and Osirus pried her off of me.

A tiny tear escaped her eye, and I almost felt bad.

Keyword was *almost*.

I was ready to go and have some fun!

"Remember, no funny business while we are away. I expect you here the day we get back," Mom said, as we all stood at the bottom of the tree house.

Osirus had his fingers on my fake wing, trying to repair it the best he could as it sat on my back. Meanwhile, Mom went through a mental list, to remind me of all the things I was supposed to do.

Like I was going to remember her long list.

Brush your teeth, take your vitamins, send clothes to the launder, don't tell jokes to the guards, don't run up and down the hallways. It's like she thought I was a child or something.

"And lastly," she leaned down and pulled me into another hug, "remember that I'm gonna miss you." She pressed a kiss to my cheek and pulled away.

I smiled and gave her one last hug before Dad pulled her into the carriage. "If you don't hurry, we won't get to the Toboki tribe by tomorrow, and I want their damn barbeque."

Mom's face lit up, and she playfully slapped Dad on the shoulder. With a swift command from Dad to the coachmen, the enormous horses sprang into action and the carriage jolted forward. The coachmen skillfully prodded the powerful beasts to pick up speed, sending the carriage careening down the winding road. The sound of hooves thundering against the ground filled the distance between us.

As soon as they were out of sight I jumped up, letting out a yell of victory, and Melina did the same.

"Now, we can really party," Melina said, pulling me away from the grove of trees.

Osirus trailed behind us, carrying my small bag of clothes on his shoulder, while Simon trotted behind us. "Now hold on there, I'm not breaking my promise to your parents, Calliope. We will not be taking you to the ball."

I whined and kicked the dirt. "It isn't fair. Everyone else gets to go when they are eighteen."

And I mean everyone. I've seen fairies and pixies who lived around here for years come and go. Some found mates, some had yet to find them. I was human. I would never find one, but at least I could go to a party.

It wasn't like I didn't know what sex was. I'd read plenty of Mom's dirty books she tried to keep hidden.

A girl gets bored on a rainy day.

So, what was the big deal?

"I told your parents I would not take you, and I will have to stand by that. I will make sure you go to the ball at some point." Osirus put his hands behind his back and leaned over me. "But for now, I will respect your parent's decision. *We* will not take you to the ball."

Melina snarled at him. "Well, it doesn't mean we can't have fun while Calli is with us. We can still have our spa days, cook and mess with the guards, right?"

I perked up at that. Melina knew how to get into trouble. It was her favorite thing.

"I have a meeting," Osirus glanced up at the vibrant sky, its hues of pink and blue blending together. The first sun ascended, casting a warm glow, while the second trailed closely behind. "I have a pixie to put in line."

I snickered. *Boo ya, Karma.*

Osirus picked me up with one arm under my legs and the other around my back. I squeaked and wrapped myself around his neck.

"Hey Melina, you wearing panties this time?" I snickered and winked at her.

Her face reddened, and she hissed at me. "Calli!"

Oops.

Osirus growled. "Darling," Osirus' voice was smooth when he turned the both of us to Melina. She was holding Simon by his collar, getting ready to attach him to his flying sling, which she used to carry him with us while we flew.

I cupped my hand and leaned into Osirus' ear. "She's been wanting a spanking, Uncle Osirus." He hummed and smiled.

"Is that so? Well, Darling, why don't you go put your underwear back on, and I will give you a punishment you won't like."

Melina tsked, dropped the sling and sashayed behind a nearby tree. "Promises, promises."

Osirus let out a chuckle, and I tilted my head up at him.

Everyone that had mates were so head-over-heels in love. The books I read, about romance and about fairy tales from the human world, just didn't compare. Mates were sacred and beautiful, and the few mated stories written by authors here in Bergarian were so... possessive. Raw.

But I was human.

Would I ever get something like that?

"Am I going to get a someone to spank me like you spank Aunt Melina?" I asked Osirus.

Osirus coughed, and his grip around me tightened. "Is that what you want, little one? A someone to spank you?" He raised a brow.

I curled my lip into my mouth and scratched at the skin. I couldn't deny that I have desires of being with a male. I had fantasized many, many times what it would be like. I've touched myself in the privacy of my bed more times than I could count, but never had a satisfied feeling afterwards. I didn't know what I was missing. I've just never been with someone. It was hard to with a mother who was so overbearing.

"I want a mate," I stated firmly. "Like you have Melina, like Mom has Birch. But—I'm human." I lowered my head, ashamed.

Being human was so boring. I couldn't fly like a fae or fairy, I couldn't swim like a siren, I couldn't shift into an animal. I had nothing. Mom used to be human, but Birch found her on Earth and when the bond snapped into place and he made her his, she turned out to be just like him.

And where did that leave me? Just a human in a supernatural world.

I was plain.

Osirus shrugged his shoulders. "So? Who says you can't?"

"No one said I could have one." I tilted my head. "Does that mean I can have a mate?"

Melina came from behind the tree and brushed her dress down. She picked up the sling and stuck Simon's legs into the holes so he would be comfortable flying.

"You see Kelsey as your mother. She has taken care of you, loved you as her own. I don't see why you wouldn't get a mate, Calliope. There are many humans who have had children before they have met their mates. Those children from other relationships have all found mates."

My smile widened. "You think it's possible?"

"Your mother isn't sure you have one, and she doesn't want to leave you disappointed." Osirus placed his forehead against mine. "For now, we will have fun and I will speak with her more on the matter. There are balls every six months, it's not like you are running out of time to meet a mate."

I nodded, and Melina pranced up to us.

"Ready?" Melina lifted up her dress to show her panties, and Osirus groaned.

"Darling, not in front of Calliope."

"I don't mind!"

Chapter Four

Valpar

I<small>T TOOK TWO DAYS</small> to arrive at the Golden Light Kingdom. With the heavy bags the tribe carried and horses that needed rest, we traveled slower than we normally would. No one complained, the tribe admired the sights along the way.

The foliage was different here than in the Monktona Wood. The trees more sparse, not as thick and healthy. King Osirus said it was a temperate forest. These trees were thick with smaller leaves, bushes abundant with flowers, and the area did not harbor as many enemies as it did back home.

We had packed our traveling tents for when we reached our final destination, but as we traveled, we all opted to sleep below the stars. We had not seen such a clear view, without the giant leaves and vines covering the sky.

It was the only good thing about traveling away from home.

For the most part, everyone kept to themselves. Only the horses trotted around the campground, occasionally pulling at the thick blue, green grasses. All except for Sugha, who kept mumbling how excited he was to see Queen Melina and King Osirus. He was ready to explore and meet fae, at the markets, who he had made friends with, in the past.

I've never seen such an orc, ready to mingle with every creature.

As we got closer to the palace, I could feel the brightness of the light sources raining down their powerful rays. I had forgotten how powerful they could feel on this side of the continent of Bergarian, and my skin prickled with heat as we drew near.

My eyes squinted as we came atop a hill, that would bring the palace into view, the light sources burning its rays into my eyes.

I groaned and put my hand above my brows to see the layout before me. *Bassza, it was too bright.*

Sugha sprinted up beside me and his body collided with mine. I grunted in annoyance and pushed him away from me. "Watch where you are going, orcling!" I snarled.

Sugha laughed and pulled his shoulders back. "It's beautiful! Just as I remembered!" He gazed down at the land before us.

Clear streams snaked their way through the lush, green landscape, cutting through fields of swaying grasses. Screaming fairies danced in and out of the tall blades, their high-pitched laughter piercing my ears as they darted playfully. With each quick movement, they shot up into the canopy of trees above, their clear, insect-like wings fluttering in the sunlight. It looked like one of those pictures from a fairy tale book I'd seen before, over in the Cerulean Moon Kingdom.

I hated it.

How could they be so happy all the time?

Sugha nudged me, and I glanced at him. He had a dark, round, thin veil over his eyes, and hooked it around his ears. I waved my hands in front of him and he laughed, pushing them to his forehead. "Sunglasses," he pointed to them. "I got them at the Cerulean Moon Kingdom last journey. Want to try? Helps with the light sources' brightness."

I scoffed and turned away, pulling on my horse's reins for him to follow. "No, you look ridiculous."

"Suit yourself," he taunted.

The orcs behind us pushed forward, not caring to wait for us to proceed. They were ready to arrive and set up their tents, so they can scout the land for their miresas.

I shrugged my shoulders, my heavy footsteps dragging along the way. I had somehow gotten stuck in the middle of the caravan while Sugha was leading the way. I let him, because there wasn't a way for him to mess this up from here.

I was not ready to make merry faces with the locals. It was going to be another disappointing trip, and I could not understand why everyone was so happy to be here, not when it was one disappointing trip after another. I huffed, watching my tribe grow more excited as the weight on my shoulders grew.

The palace stood grand and majestic in the distance, its golden spires glinting in the light sources' rays. As we made our way down the hill, the air seemed to shimmer with magic, an energy I couldn't describe thrummed through the very ground beneath our feet. The closer we got, the more vibrant the colors became, and flowers of every hue carpeted the landscape, their sweet fragrance filling the air.

There was a tickle in my nose, and I tried to rub the sudden itch I let out a sudden sneeze, my loose hair fell over my face. My eyes were itchy and watery, and fury built in my body. These scents, these sounds, it was too much.

Ugh, I hated all these smells. Too many flowers and too many fairy *sprinkles*.

The fairies gathered around the caravan, flying overhead. They used their small forms to their advantage, some planting themselves in the middle of the group. Then they grew, using their magic to grow as tall as a fae, which allowed them to walk among the taller species for a few hours of the day.

Sugha raced ahead, his excitement infecting the others, and he shouted gleefully at the fairies flitting around him. I couldn't help but smile at his orcling wonder, his joy a stark contrast to the grouchy orc I was.

All I thought about was these fairies' and fae's curiosity with orc shafts?

They have been fascinated by the idea of what lay beneath the cloth.

And since orcs arrived, we were seen as either monsters or a prize to behold.

I shook my head as I watched the tribe interact with them. The males were being nice, far better than I would be, but I could tell they were looking to find their miresas.

At least they had some form of dignity and not falling for their tricks. I guess the moss in their skulls was not so small after all.

A fairy with yellow hair jumped through the grass behind me. I could feel the heat of her body as she neared me, her hand outspread to touch my arm. I turned my full body to give her a scowl, and she gasped in fear when I bared my teeth.

"Have you no honor for the male or female who wish to claim you?" I growled.

The fairy, her ears pointed, delicate and once brimming with excitement, now had drooping wings that barely fluttered. Her shoulders sagged, weighed down by disappointment. The anger in her wide eyes burned fiercely, devoid of any hint of shame.

"Just had to look in your eyes to see if you were mine. Glad you are not." She shot out away from me, her wings fluttering quickly to the other side of the caravan and began talking to another orc.

She didn't just look into his eyes, she was touching, fluttering her lashes like there was dirt in them.

I grunted. Stupid, lying fairy.

I didn't miss the surrounding orcs who saw the confrontation. They gave me annoyed and disappointed stares for being harsh. I didn't care in the slightest. She wasn't checking to see if I was hers, she was simply a curious creature.

They all were.

I've heard far too many times how vain the fae and fairies are. They like pretty things. They want things sparkling, beautiful and stunning. The orcs were anything but. We lived in cabins far from the brightness of the light sources. We lived in the shade, beneath large leaves of the Wood, but we took care of our own.

If we lived here, out in the open, we would kill whatever male came close to our female. We would hide our female from any threat, and any other male who dared look at what was ours would surely suffer.

I don't think Osirus would care for the orcs to kill all his creatures.

Just traveling with this band of orcs agitated the alpha within us, and by the time we all went home, we would not want to see one another for months.

As we reached the palace gates leading to the courtyard, they swung open without a sound. The wind blew toward us, the bushes and groves of trees with their flower fragrance hit my face and I sneezed again.

Bassza.

It was going to be a long seven days.

The courtyard was bustling with activity. Servants scurried toward us, their uniforms clean and not a single cloth out of place. I stared down at our cloth and muddied feet, and I knew we didn't belong.

The fae had their wings fluttering behind them, helping my tribe grab things off the wagons, and orcs who rode their horses dismounted and handed their reins to the stablemen.

I reluctantly handed my reins over, and Ulam pushed at my shoulder. I rubbed his forehead and pulled oats out of my satchel to gift my friend before handing the reins over to the stableman. "Give him your best bed or I'll find you," I grumbled and shoved the satchel full of oats into his arm.

The stableman, who was tall for a fae, nodded his head and waved the satchel in front of Ulam as he followed, cart and all, with the rest of the horses.

"Can you be nicer?" Sugha hissed, pulling on my arm.

I growled and pulled my arm away. "They are touching my horse."

"That Osirus and Melina gave you. They wouldn't hurt him," Sugha argued back.

I turned my neck to crack it as I followed Sugha to the bottom of the steps that led up to the palace. The rest of the tribe had already gathered and were gazing up at the tall, regal figure with shimmering silver wings, which glowed in the sunlight. Her hair matched the dark plum-colored robes she wore, and I was thankful it wasn't some bright-colored cloth to burn the eyes out of my skull.

"Welcome to the Golden Light Kingdom," she said, her voice like music. "I am Lady Elowen, advisor to Queen Melina. Her Majesty awaits you in the throne room."

With a graceful sweep of her hand, she waved for us to climb the steps that led into the palace, where every surface sparkled and shined. Our feet dirtied the floor, but no one was behind us cleaning up like we were trouble to the palace. We were their guests.

I mean, we did help them win a war all those years ago...

The throne room was bathed in a warm golden light, that shone from large crystal rocks suspended from the ceiling. Why you needed a bunch of rocks hanging from the ceiling, I did not understand.

There were also flowers. Tons of flowers in decorated pots and I rolled my eyes. My nose was already tickling, and I could feel a sneeze coming.

Bassza!.

There, seated upon a throne of silver and gold, was Queen Melina. Her wings were a bright array of colors—the only wings in the kingdom that could do that. Melina rose to her feet as we entered.

"Oh, I'm so excited!" She jumped up from her throne and trotted down the stairs. "I thought you were never gonna get here!" She ran across the floor and gave a big hug to Sugha, who twirled her around and set her down gracefully.

"We wouldn't miss it, would we, Valpar?" Sugha nudged me in the gut.

I grunted from the pain and rubbed my belly. "No, never."

Melina tilted her head downward. "Right. I know you have been skipping out on these things. This time, you will have loads of fun! Sugha told me all your favorite foods and we replicated your ale. You won't even have to pretend to be nice, Mr. Grumpy Pants. Er—grumpy loin cloth."

Melina eyed me up and down, and the female servants giggled in the corner.

I sighed heavily and rubbed my eyebrow with my claw.

She linked her arm with Sugha and walked past me. The normal scent she carried was typically sweet, like candy, but today there was another scent lying beneath it.

Sugha and Melina continued to walk around as she pointed to a new stained-glass window, and I followed them, trying to pinpoint the smell. I took in another breath and my shoulders relaxed.

What is it?

Sugha turned around and cocked his head. "Valpar, you alright?"

I blinked several times and found myself hovering over Queen Melina, sniffing her hair. I stood up straight and realized that everyone was staring at me.

Shit. As the King of the Cerulean Moon Kingdom would say.

I cleared my throat. "Sorry, thought I saw a bug."

"I was flying today. There might be." She patted her hair. "As long as it isn't a whisp, those things will knot my hair up, and I can't get them out."

I breathed a sigh of relief when Sugha and Melina continued their conversation.

"Are you sure the tribe won't stay in the bedrooms? We have plenty of space." Melina waved over at the male servants. They were wary as they stepped forward, but followed her orders.

"No," Sugha said, waving his hand. "Orcs in enclosed spaces, still a no, I'm afraid. We like being outdoors. Besides, being able to see the moon so clearly is a treat."

Melina nodded happily while Sugha continued with the pleasantries. The other orcs murmured to each other, pointing at different paintings on the wall and the shiny jewels displayed in the windows.

It was like they had never been here before.

"Sorry, Osirus isn't here. He's with our niece, who arrived earlier this afternoon. You might see her bouncing around the palace somewhere. But please, make yourselves at home. You can go anywhere in the palace, as always. Order anything from the kitchen and I hope, this time, your mission will bring you mates!" Melina's wings fluttered, her hair flying around her head.

I nodded and without saying a word I pointed in the direction of the nearest exit so the tribe could set up their tents.

As much as I tried to push through and get the tribe settled, I couldn't help but think of the faint scent on Melina. What was it? And why could I not stop thinking about it?

CHAPTER FIVE

Calliope

THEY WERE RIGHT THERE.

I leaned over the banister of the small balcony in my room, looking at the breathtaking view. The vibrant curtains gently caressed my ankles while the cool breeze whispered against my bare thighs.

I could almost see the big, green orcs down at the courtyard-turned-campsite. They looked like little peas walking around, or cooking meat that smelled delicious. The orc camp was bustling with activity. I could see them prepping more pieces of meat to be cooked over a roaring fire. The smell was intoxicating, and my stomach grumbled in protest.

They argued a lot and when they couldn't agree on something, they settled the argument by throwing fists, clubs or swords. They swung and yelled, stomped around, and told one another they were ugly.

I found it pretty funny.

I wish I could see up close what they looked like.

Some said they were hideous, others said they were ruggedly handsome. I wanted to see for myself.

Dang it for being a human and having small, squinty eyes.

I leaned over a little more before I heard Simon bleat behind me, grabbing the ruffles of my night dress that settled on my upper thigh, and pulled me backwards.

Simon had expensive taste. He loved silk. He already ate the bottom of my silk dress last night when I tried sneaking peeks of the burly, green men.

Simon pulled harder. The threads ripped, and I swatted him away.

"Ugh, you are no fun," I grumbled, and planted my feet firmly back on the ground, with my hands fisted the golden railing.

I wish there were vines closer so I could grab hold and climb down, just so I could see them without detection, but of course Uncle Osirus would be meticulous in his directions for the gardeners and make them prune the foliage away from my window.

All the other windows and balconies had vines on them. Mine didn't.

You get caught climbing down from your room one time, and he has to have the gardener go clipping away.

I narrowed my eyes again and crossed my arms. Simon bleated, dipped his big horns and pushed them into my butt to get me moving.

"Yeah, yeah, I'm going," I said, before I looked over the railing one more time to see if the orcs were still there.

They were filing inside.

The orcs arrived yesterday, and I'd been dying to get a closer look, but Aunt Melina had kept me busy. She took me to the palace spa, where the glistening private pool was fun and relaxing. We got body scrubs and facials.

Aunt Melina was trying to keep my mind off of the ball. People who were working on the ball preparations were freaking out with flowers, decorations and food. She was trying to keep everything fun for me, but I couldn't help the longing to go.

I was old enough. I could find a mate.

So, why doesn't Mom want me to go?

"I'm sorry we can't take you," Melina continued to say, over and over during our spa days. "We promised."

Melina had to get her wings cleaned, as well as her hair and makeup done, today. She had them do the same to me, and no one said a word about my wings being fake. They even added glitter to them, smiled and told me how pretty they were.

Melina did all this so I wouldn't feel left out.

I was really lucky to be blessed with the family I had. Why was I even complaining?

Simon pulled on my nightgown again, and this time he took a chunk of the ruffle of it. His tongue fell out of his mouth to lick at the random string that hung down his chin, continuing to lick until he'd slopped it up like spaghetti. Simon's hooves clomped toward a fancy cradle where Uncle Osirus had the royal hay put inside for him. Simon twisted his nose up at that and plopped his butt on his bed.

The bedroom I always stayed in when I visited was a far cry from my small room at the treehouse. It was too big, you could get lost in it. I preferred smaller rooms; I liked to feel cozy, and so, I often made a tent in the corner.

Today, my mind had raced too much. I was obsessed with the ball. Obsessed with dancing, the food, watching fairies, fae and other creatures find their mates. And—what about me? Could my mate be down there?

I flopped on the bed, my hair spread out and I let out a deep sigh. It was then, that I could hear the faint music of the ball from here. It sounded so—fun.

I groaned and took a pillow, slapping it over my face.

I must be grateful for what I have.

Simon bleated, his hooves trotting against the wood floor and his head butted my leg. I sat up and reached behind his ear to scratch it.

"I'm being stupid. I just need to—"

"—You just need to go," a voice urged from the corner of the room.

Simon half yelled and paused before unceremoniously tipping over with a plonk on the floor.

I scrambled off the bed to check on him. He didn't have soft ground to land on, but a hard wooden floor.

"W-who in cheesus are you?" I said, as I petted Simon's head and stared up at the purple-haired woman.

She was dressed in a slim black corset and her apples looked very much like melons. She had dark leather pants and a dark cut-off leather jacket to complete her look.

So cool.

She leaned on the door frame to the closet and pushed off, her high heel boots trotting across the floor.

"Well, I am—" she started, but I gasped as I stood up.

This woman... she came out of nowhere. There are guards at the door. No one can get in or out of here without going through them. You would have to be a powerful witch or—

"Are you my fairy godmother!?" I screamed.

My fairy godmother looked back at me with wide, amethyst eyes and laid her hand on her full melons. "Pardon me?"

"You know, my fairy godmother? You've come to help me get to the ball!" I jumped up and down, clapped my hands and turned to Simon, who was just shaking off his short-term paralysis.

"I, uh, is he okay?" She pointed to Simon, and I nodded.

"Yes, he's a fainting goat. Perfectly normal, but I try to avoid his fainting spells. It worries me to death. I'm his emotional support person and, so far, I'm not doing a great job." I raised my finger to my lip and bit down on the nail.

My fairy godmother shook her head and pinched the bridge of her nose. Huh, people do that a lot.

"Listen! I am not your fairy godmother. Do I look old to you?" She waved her hand up and down her body.

"No, you look great! Cinderella just happened to have an old fairy godmother. I do have to ask, though, where is your wand?" I walked closer and padded around her body. She raised an eyebrow and watched me circle her.

"My name is Starla, and I am **not** your fairy godmother. I don't even have wings."

"Cinderella's fairy godmother didn't have wings," I stated.

Starla huffed and crossed her arms. "Then, how do you know she was a fairy?" Starla said frustratedly and rubbed her eyebrow. "Ugh, anyway. I am here to get you to the ball."

I stood in front of her and stared at her blankly.

She had to get in here through magic, and she was going to get me to the ball. Who in the heck was she?

"Fine, I'm your fairy godmother." Starla sighed, looking defeated.

"I knew it!" I squealed, jumping up again, and Simon froze, this time not falling but standing in place. "Crumbs and cheese, sorry, Simon."

I was terrible at being his 'person'.

But, as the excitement grew in my chest, I knew what I was about to do was wrong. I couldn't just go to the ball. Melina and Osirus said they couldn't take me and had done a lot for me.

Sure, I get in trouble sometimes: climb out of the treehouse when I'm not supposed to, climb out of a tower, maybe sneak some extra cupcakes, but this seemed like a really big deal. Besides, when I get there...they could just send me back to my room.

"What's going on in that brain of yours, Calliope?" Starla's face softened considerably more from how it was before. Her knuckles ran down my cheek, and I turned away.

See, she is my fairy godmother. She knows my name!

"I can't go. Uncle Osirus and Aunt Melina said they couldn't take me. My mom and dad don't want me to go either."

Starla hummed and pushed my pink, curled hair behind my back.

"Yeah, well, I have it on higher authority that you should be there." She nodded, agreeing with herself. "From a goddess that believes you are more than ready to be the woman you should be. It's time for you to grow up."

My lips parted and my confidence bloomed.

I'd wanted nothing more than to be told I was big enough to do something on my own. As much as I loved my family, I wanted to make decisions for myself.

"Really?" I whispered.

Starla nodded. "Yes and think of those words that your uncle and aunt told you. What did they keep saying when they left you in here?"

I certainly remembered before they closed the door to my room: 'We are sorry we cannot take you to the ball.'

I looked up into Starla's eyes. "They said they couldn't take me. But they didn't say they would stop me?" I pondered, and my mood lightened.

Starla laughed and walked toward my closet. "That's right. Now, let's use some of that fae logic and get you to the ball."

"And my parents?" I tilted my head and walked with her.

"For once, be selfish, Calliope. Kelsey and Birch want the best for you, little one." Starla turned to me, putting both hands on my shoulders. "But what Kelsey wants is to protect you from everything and everyone. It's okay to fall and scratch your knee. It's okay to feel pain and sadness. She cannot hold you in a bubble forever." Her finger trailed down my cheek. "The time is now."

I bit my lip and slowly nodded.

I didn't think about not having anyone to break my fall, not having someone there to help me when I fell. Would I have someone there to pick me up? I didn't want to do it completely alone, but I also didn't want to live in a bubble either.

Starla turned and continued to lead me to the closet.

This was just a ball. It was one night. Surely one night wouldn't change everything...would it?

Simon shook his head and bleated, his steps following with mine as he walked to the closet. "Hey, aren't you going to make me a dress? That's what Cinderella's fairy godmother did."

Starla put her hand on her hip and stared back at me. "Fuck. You're serious, right now? You aren't short on dresses here and you are already in the damn palace."

Oops, bad word.

Starla put her hand on the rack. "Now, you get in here and let me dress you in something pretty."

My face flushed after being reprimanded, and I let her choose a dress for me.

"You look absolutely stunning!" my fairy godmother gushed, her voice filled with excitement, as we stood on the enchanting balcony overlooking the dazzling ballroom. Soft, golden lights bathed the room, which cast a warm glow over the opulent chandelier that hung low, creating an elegant but also a fast-paced party, the way they would twinkle slow and fast. The sweet scent of desserts and flowers wafted through the air, adding to the magical atmosphere. From our hidden vantage point, we could observe the grandeur of the ball without being seen.

I could see fae, fairies, shifters, a few vampires, and even my aunt and uncle dancing on the floor, swaying to the music. It was a ball that surpassed any dream that I could think of and my eyes roamed over everything.

I could stay on the balcony and watch, and be perfectly happy up here, but my fairy godmother wasn't happy with that. She was very much wanting me to go down and mingle.

"I-I thank you." I pulled down the dress she decorated me in, feeling shy.

It was blue silk. It looked like nothing more than a short nightgown slip, but it covered more than most of what all the other fae and fairies were wearing. I wore my wings, still too shy to let everyone know I was human.

I was sure they could smell human on me, but with all the fae wine and orc ale, I hoped I would blend in at least a little.

"You are the only human at the ball," my fairy godmother pointed out. Well, crumbs!

"Why don't you take the wings off?" My fairy godmother offered. "Humans are a delicacy and I'm sure you will meet a male for the night?"

My face turned red, and I shook my head. My wings were a crutch, like a handbag you needed to carry, even if you didn't need it. I just had to have them to hold on to.

"Suit yourself. You don't need them, though. You should be proud of who you are, Calliope. You're stunning, and your personality is just perfect for him. I'll have to stay close and watch this one." She chuckled.

I tilted my head, and when I turned to face her, she was gone.

My mouth dropped open and Simon bleated at me, his head stuck in between the spindles of the balcony.

Stuck!

I'm gonna saw off his horns. That is just what I'm gonna do.

I tilted his head, trying to pull him out. He yelled again, and I could feel him panic. "Hang on a second, I'm coming." Simon would calm down when he saw me. With his head on the other side of the banister, I knew I was going to have to climb over.

I took off my shoes and lifted my leg over the golden, vine-woven balcony. It wasn't the prettiest sight leaping over, but I was able to get in front of him. "Okay, Simon. You have to calm down." His beady eyes saw me, and he stopped pushing on the rods holding his head. "Now, I'm gonna move your head." He stopped moving, and I managed to move his head to maneuver his horns and pushed him free.

He bleated a 'thank you,' as I heard a shout from a guard my fairy godmother had put to sleep earlier so we could sneak past. "Hey, what are you doing!?"

Crumbs and cheese, I was in trouble.

Simon bleated loudly and charged at the guard. I watched intently, giggling, still holding on to the handrail, when another guard was suddenly at my side said, "Here, let me help..."

As he startled me, a high-pitched yip of a scream escaped my lips. In my panic, I released my grip on the gleaming gold medal, causing it to slip from my fingers. With a sudden jolt, I fell backward into the bustling crowd.

Chapter Six

Valpar

The scent was the only reason I had decided to go to the ball.

I had intended to stay away from the party from the start of this journey. I didn't care to watch the dancing, the happy, smiling faces, and watch as all the other creatures gained *mates*.

It wasn't fair, and I hated the Moon Fairy.

She got our hopes up all those years ago, and for what? So we could fight in a war and receive nothing in return?

I snarled.

All these emotions swelled inside my body. I had no release, no tree, no mound of dirt or boulder to pound my fists in to or swing my blade at. We were staying on the palace grounds and had to keep things *nice*.

We must leave the area as we found it. We weren't monsters, and we were still trying to prove that to the many creatures that still looked at us in worry.

Sugha was the one orc they fully trusted. He was the joyous one of us all, but, he was also the one who hadn't lived the longest. He was the youngest of all of us. He wasn't bitter, yet.

I came to the party tonight because of the scent that surrounded the palace grounds. It was near and then it was far. I could not find the beginnings of it, but I could always find the trail of where the scent had once been.

After a lot of thinking, which had caused much of my distress, I realized it reminded me of a tea that Queen Clara of the Cerulean Moon Kingdom had given the orcs long ago. It was to help with sleep after the war—chamomile.

I requested the servants to bring me the tea. Maybe my body craved sleep, and the herbs would make me less on edge, but I was disappointed. This scent I craved and had smelt on the queen earlier had a sweeter smell, one that made my mouth water.

And so, I searched the palace grounds for most of my day, encountering nothing until a gentle breeze carried it straight to my lungs.

Infuriating!

"Can you at least smile a bit?" Sugha whispered to me as we stood at the entrance to the ballroom.

The largest room in the palace lacked nothing for what the king and queen had put together. Its towering walls and ceilings were filled with hanging, shining rocks, each one crafted and dripping with crystals that shimmered in the soft glow of the hanging candles. Decorated cloth, depicting scenes of creatures that lived in Bergarian meeting their mates, scenes of the land, and other kingdom pictures filled the walls, adding to the welcoming atmosphere.

As guests entered, their eyes were immediately drawn to the opulent centerpiece, a massive golden fountain overflowing with cascades of fae wine. The room buzzed with excitement as fairies and fae, their petite wings fluttering, darted through the air, offering trays laden with fancy food- barely enough to fill my tongue - and beverages.

Everyone's scents, along with the smell of food, was almost too much. I tried to block it out so I could smell only food and the scent I really craved, but I wasn't a shifter. I didn't have the skill set.

This was going to be a waste of time.

The room was alive with laughter, music and the clinking of glasses. I rolled my eyes. I scratched my backside, the *for-mal* wear itching my skin. The *pants* were too much, making me hot and my body leak fluid. I pulled on the string of the tunic and let my chest go bare. I did not mind feeling the air when a fairy flew by and gave me instant relief with a breeze.

"You shouldn't do that. Everyone is dressed up. What if you meet your miresa?" Sugha scolded.

All the people in the room were dressed in their finest clothes. Females sparkled in short cloth, and males in clothing that covered most of their bodies. Some had shiny rocks hanging on their chests, and others had extra fabric hanging around their neck dripping behind them as they walked.

The orcs were the least dressed, but it was very *for-mal* to us: White tunics with either black or brown pants. I'd rather have my shaft free than feel confined like this.

"Our miresas won't show up, anyway, why should I care?" I hissed, harsher than I would have liked, at my brother's excitement. I pulled my tunic from the ties of my pants. I despised the fact that the tunic made my soft belly more noticeable when tucked into the pants.

Sugha made a disappointed face. "At least let me pull back your hair. You don't even have a braid in it."

My lip curled, and I turned away from him, stomping over to the food. He tricked me earlier. He told me there was fungus growing in my hair and, sneakily, tried to brush it to make me look 'presentable'.

I stomped over to the food, away from the tribe. My chest rose and fell as I gazed at the enormous spread. The first time we came to one of these balls, it was nothing but finger food. Small sandwiches, fruits and vegetables, and flower salads drizzled with honey. We were all starving at the end. Later, we went out and killed deer on the king's land, then roasted it on a spit to drown our woes and fill our bellies.

Now, we can fill our stomachs in here and watch everyone else get their miresas.

At least we won't go hungry at this party.

The tribe was still mingling, sniffing and looking. They were looking for any sign, for a spark that a female or a male could be theirs, but they were coming up with nothing despite the large, crowded room.

Orcs are not meant to feel. We are meant to hit, kill and hunt. To feel is to be vulnerable. To let any of this feeling out, we are to hit, stomp and roar into the Wood to let out this—*emotion*. Unfortunately, since we are here in the palace, we cannot let out our frustrations, instead of hitting things, they resorted to drinking and hitting each other.

I filled my plate. As the years went by, King Osirus had begun to serve meats and breads to satisfy the orcs' hunger. I filled it with not just meat, but the sweets that Sugha liked to bake in his cabin.

I'd never tell him how much I cared for his pies and cakes, but I'm sure he knew I'd steal them.

I rubbed a hand over my softer belly.

Worth it.

I took my plate and sat on a *so-fa* furthest away from the crowd. I sunk into the plush cushion and watched the fae and shifters mingle. Most stayed away, but a few adventurous fae and fairy females spoke with the orcs, their hands brushing their arms, and a head tilt to a private hallway.

I bit down on a large roll and ripped it with my teeth.

No decency, these creatures.

As the night wore on, with my belly full and the mingling progressing, the lights dulled and the music grew louder. The fae and shifters danced, their bodies moving, grinding against each other to the beat of the drums. I watched from my spot on the sofa, a sense of envy creeping through me as I watched them let loose and enjoy themselves.

My eyes landed on a group of orcs in the corner, their jeering laughter filling the room. They were all drunk, talking amongst themselves, swapping war stories with other males not yet paired.

The music was loud and hit me in the chest. I was ready to escape the party and return to my tent for the night, when I smelled it.

The same scent that caught me the first day I was here.

I was too afraid to move, and my instincts told me to stay right where I was, as I took deep breaths.

Bassza, it was like a heavenly fairy blessing me.

I put my plate to the side and gazed around the room, too scared to move far, should I lose the scent. Before I could stand, I heard a scream, and something fell straight into my lap.

Soft pink tresses fell around me, cascading like ocean waves that seemed to defy gravity. Despite its almost weightless form, I felt an unusual force pressing against my legs, holding me firmly in place. The creature's touch hit me like a bolt of lightning, as if it possessed a power beyond my comprehension. As I looked down into the mess of hair, I couldn't help but feel a mix of curiosity.

Was it an animal?

I growled and almost threw the creature off me when I heard its voice.

"I am so sorry! Sorry!" she gasped.

The voice was high in a state of distress, and my instincts went on high alert.

As I gained my control, I saw legs kicking and arms waving around my body, while she tried to regain her balance. Finally, I grabbed her around her waist and held her close to me.

Heat ran through my skin as I grabbed onto her. The lighting jolted through my chest once more. The heavy burden I carried lifted, and a euphoric groan escaped my lips.

What was this magic?

She had a delicate sprinkling of freckles across her nose and cheeks, adding youthful innocence to her appearance. The strands of pink hair cascaded down her shoulders, perfectly complementing her fair complexion. Her heart-shaped face held soft, rosy lips that formed a smile as she met my gaze. Those big blue eyes held a glimmer of curiosity. The way she looked at me, with a mixture of surprise and wonder, made the drum in my chest skip a beat, and I couldn't help but be drawn to her magnetic presence.

Her small, delicate hands were placed on my chest as she steadied herself.

Her dainty features and petite stature made her appear fragile. Despite her size, there was a sense of strength emanating from her presence. The subtle curves of her body, accentuated by her wide hips, hinted at a womanhood. Her small nips, barely noticeable, added to her youthful charm.

I could carry her around all day and do my chores, and not break a sweat. That thought became more appealing as she sat there in my lap, rubbing her sweet backside against my shaft.

I let out a low groan as my shaft filled with seed and my life force. Not once have I felt it fill on its own, without me willing it.

What magic has this female cursed me with?

"I'll just get off now," she said, still staring into my eyes.

She made an attempt to leave my lap by moving her backside down my leg, but that only fueled a primal urge to keep her with me.

I did not want to let go, and I would not let her leave.

My grip tightened around her waist, and her fingers dug into my chest. The prick of pain was welcomed with those small painted talons.

"What's your name?" I rasped, trying to keep my anger at bay. I did not want to scare this female, I just simply wanted to know who she was and why she had this effect on me.

Moon Fairy...was she?

My heart pounded in my chest like large drums, echoing into my ears. Each beat was a reminder of the fierce emotions that this female had stirred within me. Her scent... the chamomile tea! It filled my lungs, made my mouth water and my cock leak with wild desire.

She continued to struggle against my hold, her eyes growing wide with confusion. I could see the questions swirling in her mind, but I needed answers just as much as she did.

"What is your name?" I asked again, my voice low and demanding.

Her lips parted as if she was about to speak, but then they closed again. She seemed to debate whether to reveal her identity to a stranger.

"Calliope," she breathed, holding still. Her hands were still on my chest, and when she tried to remove them, I let out a grunt in protest.

She quickly placed them back.

"Good, female," I hummed in appreciation, my tense body softening. Her ocean blue eyes dilated, her long lashes brushing her cheeks when she slowly closed them and opened them again.

I took my time studying her, my shaft filling by the second. She held perfectly still as I studied the cloth she wore. The blue silk cloth clung to her curves and went up her thigh.

"What is this cloth made of?" I asked, pointing to the item with a single clawed finger. I was trying to get her to talk, to hear her voice while I studied her body.

What creature was she? She did not smell like any creature I had encountered before.

Her eyebrows furrowed in confusion before she looked down at it. "S-silk," she explained with a small smile.

I had never felt cloth this soft and smooth before. My people were simple beings, wearing only what was necessary for survival. The texture means nothing. But this dress...it seemed almost magical in its appearance. It felt like the skin of this creature.

"I like it," I said honestly, my eyes roaming over her body once again.

I like it almost as much as this female's body.

She blushed at my words and fidgeted in my lap. "Thank you," she said softly.

I couldn't help but let out a low growl at the sight of her flushed cheeks and submissive posture. My possessive instincts were roaring to life within me – this female was mine to claim.

Bassza...mine.

My hand traced up her lower back and spine. She leaned into me, her breath coming in short, steady pants. Then, I felt something between her shoulder blades, and I paused.

When I pulled back, taking in her whole view, I saw none other than wings sprouting from her back.

My mouth went slack, and disappointment flared.

A fairy or a fae.

Could this female be using magic on me?

"W-what's your name?" The innocence in her voice was captivating. It took me by surprise each time she spoke. She captivated my body, the drum in my chest, my skin, and my shaft, telling me that she was the one, that she was mine, but my mind told me another.

It could be a trick. A trick from a fae or fairy trying to see my shaft, to play and toy with me.

My expression turned to a scowl, but her bright face didn't register my change in mood.

Calliope blinked several times, while her legs swung from my lap, since they couldn't reach the ground.

Why did she have to look so tempting?

"Leave." I gritted my teeth, picked her up by her tiny waist and placed her on the ground.

She laughed. "That's a weird name. Did your parents name you that? Is it a derivative of leaf or something?" She tilted her head and put her hands behind her back, rocking back and forth on her feet. "I know a couple of elves named Leaf. You match the name Leaf better because you're green. But I think I would call you Tree, or something, because you are so huge." She continued. "Hey, do you want me to get you a cupcake? They have my favorites out," She teased.

Calliope pointed over to the dessert table, and her tiny tongue swept across her lip. My shaft leaked more, and my hand covered my pants to conceal my want.

The fairy had cast a spell on me, that's all this is.

"Sure," I ground out.

"Kay, be right back! Don't go anywhere!" She hopped off, her rounded backside making me groan, but those damn wings caught my sight, again.

She is a fairy, or a fae. I never could tell which was which when they were in their larger forms. I stood, still staring at her as she gathered a plate for each of us, but I knew what I had to do. Get away from her, get my head on straight, and away from her bewitching powers.

As I turned, I smelled the sickly-sweet scent of King Osirus, and a laughing Queen Melina come closer.

"I knew she'd come," Queen Melina skipped joyfully toward me.

Osirus steadied himself after I almost knocked him over. He brushed off his arm, and his lips curled into a smile. "Indeed, but I have to say, even I did not see this little pairing coming."

CHAPTER SEVEN

Calliope

I DIDN'T TIP TOE and act like a graceful fairy when I went to the dessert table. I pranced, my bare feet slapping the marbled floors. I was too excited, my hands shaking at what had just happened.

I fell into an orc's lap. I saw one up close.

Scars littered his chest, which I imagine were from the war so long ago. His hair wasn't in a braid like most of the orcs I'd seen. In fact, his hair was rather messy, but I liked that. I wanted to run my fingers through the strands. It looked so soft, like the rest of him. Which was strange, because most of the orcs look hard and lumpy. He was so comfy.

Leave was much softer than I imagined an orc would be. His legs were large as tree trunks, his arms strong and muscular, but he was surprisingly gentle with his size.

His yellow eyes stared at me, giving me a look that I had never experienced. There was a heat in his gaze that I'd often seen Uncle Osirus give to Melina, and my dad with Mom.

It made me squeeze my thighs together, and the parts between my legs pulsed like they had never done before just looking at a male.

I bit my lip as I remembered how he looked at my dress, felt the softness between his fingers, and touched my thigh.

A shiver ran through my body. His touch had lit a fire inside me. One that I hoped never burned out. I felt like the heroine in those romance books, who finds a male to quench desires that only mates should have for each other.

And he was—handsome.

Leave was certainly different from the other orcs. He had harder lines on his brow, and he was really bossy. But I liked that he was different. I wanted to know more about the male who saved me from making a mess all over the palace floor.

It wasn't the first time I'd fallen from high places, but usually I fell in the soft grasses or even in a pond or lake. Never on an orc. I snorted when I lifted a plate and gazed over the desserts.

Though his lap was soft, I noticed that it grew harder the longer I sat. I placed a hand over my lips to hide my smile.

He liked me! Leave liked me. A male's privates get hard when they like someone, or so it said in those romance books. He liked me, maybe he wanted to kiss me.

My eyes widened.

Could a human and an orc kiss? Can we date? Can we even like each other? The orcs were looking for mates, and he didn't say I was his. He didn't claim me when he saw me.

That was how the balls worked. If you found your mate amongst the crowd, you were to hold one another in each other's arms and make a loud announcement. Well, that was what you were supposed to do: scream mine, my intended, beloved, or mate, then they'd kiss and leave the party.

Leave didn't do that.

So, he wasn't my mate.

My lips pouted as I put an assortment of cupcakes on my plate. He can like me, and I can like him. People do date, but they have to know, going into it, that their mates are out there. Wouldn't that make it messy?

I huffed and grabbed another plate.

No, I couldn't do that. No matter how curious I was about kissing, touching and... the Hokey Pokey, I couldn't do anything like that. It's kinda like cheating.

I felt a nudge at my leg, and I looked down to see Simon. He let out a bleat and nudged me again.

"You got me in trouble, kid, but I made a new friend." I shrugged my shoulders and held the two plates in my hand. Simon tilted his head in the direction of Leave, and when I turned to bring his plate, his back was to me and he was walking away.

"Leave?" I muttered and watched as he continued to walk further away.

Uncle Osirus had his lips pressed into a thin line as he followed Leave to the door. Aunt Melina came toward me instead, with a smile on her face.

"Did you make me a plate?" Her colorful wings fluttered, and I blinked back the warm tears threatening to fall.

I knew I was different. I knew being a human in the Golden Light Kingdom was rare. There were a lot of humans who lived in the Cerulean Moon Kingdom, with a parent from previous relationships, and were stuck being human while their parent changed into their mate's designation.

But here? It was rare.

And I was the king and queen's favorite. You would think other fae, fairies and pixies would want to be my friend, but they didn't.

I couldn't help it that I found everything interesting and fun. I felt like I was seeing the world for the first time every day. What was the big deal, enjoying every light source rise like it was a gift? To smile when a flower bloomed and to chase after the fireflies?

At least I had Simon.

He didn't judge me or care what species I was. He'd been there for the longest that I could remember.

The people who cared about me—my mom and dad—Uncle Osirus and Aunt Melina, I loved them to pieces, but I also knew they did too much for me. They hid me from the world and being the sensitive girl I was, I let them do it for too long.

"Uh, yeah. Here." I handed Aunt Melina the plate, and her eyes dazzled. "This just looks delicious, and I see you have your favorite here." She wiggled her eyebrows.

I took a deep breath and plastered a fake smile on my face, trying to hide the knot of discomfort in my stomach. Even though I wasn't starving anymore, I acted excited as Melina urged me to eat. The party was still going strong and would continue until dawn.

Melina continued to talk as we ate our food. She was excited that I had come down, and she and Osirus had broken no vows to my parents. I was here, on my own, and enjoying a party that I should have been coming to for years.

I forced a smile, refusing to glance back at Leave who had walked to the door. The pain was overwhelming, almost impossible to bear. The shattered remnants of the notion that a male, especially an orc, could feel any attraction towards me weighed heavily on my heart.

Maybe he just had to pee.

I wrinkled my nose.

Laughter grew louder over the music, and a rowdy group of orcs approached us, interrupting Melina's long-winded story about Karma already being let out of the dungeon because of good behavior and swearing to leave me alone.

Which was fine... Karma was just...Karma.

I would get my revenge.

"She is so small. I think this one is a fairy!" One orc raised his goblet of orc ale, and it sloshed onto the floor toward me.

"Yes, I think so, too," said another. "Her pink hair gives it away, also. I don't think the fae could create such a beautiful color with their genetics."

Heat flooded my face, and I suddenly stared at the floor.

"That's enough!" A slimmer orc pushed through the crowd. He was wearing a pink tunic with ruffles going down the middle. He stood out from the rest with the bright smile he wore. "Hello. I'm Sugha, and we need to settle a debate."

The other orcs nodded and elbowed each other in agreement.

"You see, we have a bet. We can't figure out the difference between the fairies when they are large; if they are fairies or if they are fae." Sugha nudged me with his arm. "Would you be so kind and tell us, what is the difference and what you might be?"

My heart warmed. They really thought I was a fairy? Or a fae?

I looked to Melina for help, but she stuffed a cupcake right into her mouth.

Okay...

"Well, a fae can hide their wings while a fairy can't." All the orcs nodded. "A fairy, while being in their larger form, well, there is one way to tell that they are a fairy."

All the orcs leaned closer to me. Their eyes were yellow and wide with curiosity.

"The patterns on their wings are different. If you look at a fae, their wings look like a large, winged insect's, but have deeper, darker veins going through them. They are able to withstand harsh wind." I pointed to Melina's wings and showed the dark veins of her wings that separated the color.

The orcs oohed and awed over them like they had never seen them up close.

"Pretty," one of them said, and I laughed.

"As for the fairies, the veins in the wings are much smaller. They cannot withstand windstorms and cannot fly over the coast. The sea wind is too strong for their delicate wings.

Sugha walked around me to study mine. "Yours are neither." His eyebrow raised.

"I-I, uh, well, I am neither," I said sheepishly. "I am a human."

An orc in the back spit out his ale, while his friend hit him on the back. "A hu-man?" The one in the back pushed everyone away. "I have never seen one. They have wings? Do you fly?"

I shook my head quickly and pulled down the strap on my shoulder. "No, I made these. I like to pretend I can. I am the only human living in the kingdom, right now, and I just wanted to fit in." I shrugged.

Sugha tutted and grabbed my elbow. His hand slid down my arm until it rested on my wrist. He patted it and showed off his white tusks. "A sweet cupcake like you was meant to stand out. Why cover it with cloth that doesn't shine as bright?"

My lips parted when I leaned my head back to stare up at him. He was thinner than Leave but he had some of the same facial features that reminded me of him.

"How about a dance? I have read much about dancing but never been able to practice with a partner?"

The other orcs muttered to each other and were nudging in excitement. "Yes, show us. We want to see a human and orc dance."

Melina stood behind me, gently taking off my wings. "You won't need these, I don't think." She winked and put them on the table. She kissed my cheek and squeezed my shoulders. "Now, go have some fun."

I've never danced with anyone else before, other than Uncle Osirus and my dad during solstices or festivals, so I tentatively put my hand in Sugha's. His eyes and smile grew so large, and he pulled me gently to the floor.

He was graceful, more than I ever thought an orc would be. But, I guess I needed to stop thinking that orcs were clumsy and too large, because the two I'd met were both very different from the stereotypical orcs I thought they would be.

"That's it, come on, don't be shy." Sugha wrapped his large hand around my waist, covering it entirely with his one hand. "Now, whatever happens, I want you to know that I will be alright. No need to worry about me. I have a strong skull."

I tilted my head in confusion when a roar came from the other side of the ballroom.

Leave barged into the room, his legs spread in a wide stance. His hair was a mess, his tunic was ripped, displaying a large, muscled shoulder and speckled chest hair. His eyes were wild, his bottom jaw jutted out and his large teeth gleamed in the candlelight.

So hot!

Several orcs jumped back while others stood their ground, ready to defend themselves if necessary.

"Sugha! What are you doing?!" Leave growled, his fists clenched at his sides.

Sugha stopped dancing and turned to face Leave, still holding onto my hand. "I am dancing with this lovely human girl," he replied calmly.

Leave's eyes narrowed even more, and he took a threatening step closer. "She is not yours to touch. You are not allowed to breathe the same air as her."

The tension in the room was strong, as everyone watched the exchange between the two orcs. I could feel my heart pounding in my chest, utterly confused about what was going on. Leave left...

Maybe he had to go poop?

Simon bleated during the silence.

"I didn't know she belonged to anyone," Sugha said innocently, smiling, and released my hand.

Leave's face turned red with anger and he stepped even closer to Sugha, their chests almost touching. "She is mine," Leave growled.

Wait, what?

Simon bleated and bit on Sugha's pants to pull him away.

Sugha chuckled, unfazed by Leave's aggression. "I meant no disrespect, brother. I simply wanted to dance with her."

"Brother?!" I squeaked.

Leave shook his head in disbelief and turned towards me. His eyes softened as they met mine, and he reached out to gently touch my cheek. "Are you alright? Did he hurt you?"

Warmth spread through my cheek, down my neck, and straight to between my legs.

I was taken aback by Leave's sudden change in demeanor, and I could feel everyone's eyes on us. "No, I'm fine," I replied softly.

Sweet Moon Goddess, I need to be alone and take care of the pulsing problem between my legs.

But wait, why would Sugha hurt me?

Leave nodded and then turned back to Sugha, his tone still harsh. Before I could process what was going on, Leave pulled back his arm and landed a right hook into Sugha's jaw.

All the orcs threw their goblets in the air and took hits at one another. It was a chain reaction, as all of them laughed and began to wrestle.

"Oh heckers! Sugha!" I screamed and fell to the floor to check on Sugha. The ballroom went into mass chaos, couples running away and the guards flocking toward us.

Simon licked Sugha on the cheek, but before I could check on him, I felt two large hands pick me up by my waist.

"Wait, let me go!" I screamed again, only to be thrown over a giant shoulder and be very acquainted with a very delectable butt. It was a perfect combination of muscular and soft.

Great, now I was conflicted.

"I'm fine!" Sugha yelled from the floor.

Screams and panicked shouts filled the room as people frantically tried to navigate their way to safety. Amongst the chaos, Leave remained calm and composed, effortlessly carrying me away from the frantic crowd. His strong arms held me securely as he skillfully weaved through the flying fairies, ensuring our safety amidst the pandemonium. The sound of crashing furniture and shattered glass reverberated throughout the room, but Leave's focused expression never wavered as he guided us towards the nearest exit.

"She's MINE!" he roared, and my head lifted up to scan the room, to look for my uncle and aunt.

Once I found them, I saw them holding onto each other, waving playfully as Leave carried me out of the ballroom, into the hallway and out the front doors.

CHAPTER EIGHT

Valpar

"I knew she'd come," Queen Melina skipped joyfully toward me.

Osirus stood up, steadying himself after I almost knocked him over. He brushed off his arm, and his lip curled into a smile. "Indeed, but I have to say, even I did not see this little pairing coming."

Pairing? Did he really mean it? This woman attempted to deceive me, using enchantments or a fragrance that heightened desire to seduce me. And her feigned innocence only served to further infuriate me.

I could not bear to remain in this place for even a solitary minute longer. The thought of enduring another raucous mating ball was unbearable. Instead, I would find solace in the depths of the Wood. There, amidst the earthy scent of moss and damp leaves, I would spend my days as a solitary orc, finding solace in my own company. In the quiet solitude, I would find respite, allowing my hand to caress my own shaft for pleasure.

I brushed my arm against Osirus as I passed. The king was out of his mind. Perhaps too much of his female's scent has gone to his head. I'd heard of males being consumed once mated.

I would have done the same, but there would be no light source rising that will bring me my miresa. Not then, not ever.

Melina's small gasp reached my ears and muttered that small fae's name. I could smell a faint scent of Calliope on both of the royals, and I wondered if this was the niece who was visiting?

"I'll take care of her; you take care of that—" Melina spat at my back. I didn't know a queen could spout such hatred.

I didn't care in the slightest.

Osirus's unamused hum filled the air, as the sound of his wings fluttering echoed behind me. The guards, their trembling bodies a testament to their fear, became a spectacle as I approached the door. I let out a low grunt, feeling the weight of my presence intensify their unease. They put out their swords to block me, but one glare their way, they deflated and backed away.

"Let him go," Osirus said in a bored tone. "I'll take care of the stubborn goblin."

I let out a tired sigh as I stepped into the serene hallway just outside the bustling ballroom. The echoes of laughter and chatter had faded away, leaving behind a peaceful silence.

Finally.

The air was thick with the lingering scent of fresh flowers that sat on every table, their delicate fragrance filled my nostrils. A sudden sneeze escaped me, followed by a low groan of my annoyance as I used my arm to wipe my nose, while I felt the tickle of irritation.

"I knew you to be the most stubborn of your brothers, but I didn't know you could also be the most dense," Osirus drawled.

I had spent countless hours studying ancient picture texts of my people and honing my combat skills. My mind was sharp, my strategies were fool-proof and my determination to protect my tribe was unwavering. While others may have faltered in the face of strong forces, I stood tall, ready to confront them head-on.

My ideas during the war proved tactful; I counted for every possible scenario, ensuring that no witch or warlock would escape my grasp. With precision and finesse, I dismantled their dark reign and helped bring peace back to our land. I was confident in my abilities.

Dense? He said I was dense.

I snarled, the anger flashing in my eyes, and swiftly turned to face him.

"That fae tricked me!" I balled my fists at my side. "She smells nothing like a fae. She used magic, a potion to hide her scent. She made me want her. She did things to my body!" My breath heaved and sweat beaded on my brow.

My body instantly remembered her touch, like it was supposed to be there. The drum in my chest thrummed like hundreds lived in there. My body shook, wanting to hold her body in my arms, to protect her, take her, rut her, and leave my marks on her clean, unmarked skin.

I let my fists relax, when I found a whiff of her scent on my tunic. My chest purred, a sound I had never made before, and my eyes widened as I placed my hand over my chest to feel the rumbling that I felt.

Osirus's lips curled into a smug smile, as he confidently adjusted the coat draped over his body. "You really believe magic would do that?" he taunted, gesturing towards my sturdy shaft.

I growled in warning, and he chuckled.

"Tell me, how did you help us win the war, Valpar? What was the turning point?"

I jutted out my chin, showing off my tusks. "Orcs are powerful, we have the strength of ten shifters. We can destroy anything in our way, we are immune to mag—"

Osirus perched his hand under his chin when the sudden realization hit me.

"Is that so? You are immune to magic." he said condescendingly.

Bassza!

All orcs are immune to magic, so then, why does my body react to this female? Why am I drawn to her? Why do I need her, want her? Why does my cock leak?

"She—she does not smell like a fae." I swallowed trying to keep Osirus' scrutinizing gaze away from me.

Osirus leaned on the wall, picking a flower up from a vase. "That is because she is not a fae, or a fairy, or any other creature of this realm. She is a human, Valpar."

A hu-man.

I grabbed my shaft that laid beneath the cloth I wore. I knew of *hu-mans*. All orcs were given a book, made by Queen Clara of the Cerulean Moon Kingdom. It was of each species of shifters, vampires, fae and fairy. It was to help the orcs in case we found a miresa among those creatures.

There was a chapter on humans, because humans at the time came into the Bergarian realm from another place called Earth. It had been so long I hardly remembered what was written about any creature. I gave up studying years ago. I could hardly read that book now even if I wanted to.

From what I remember, humans were weak. No powers, and no way to protect themselves.

If I was not there to catch her when she fell—she could have hurt herself!

My drum pounded in my chest, its rhythmic beat echoing like a thunderstorm. Panic surged through me, tightening its grip around my skull as I imagined her lying on the frigid floor, writhing in agony. The sheer intensity ignited a surge of my life-force, burning like a fierce flame.

What if I was not there?

My growl echoed down the hallway, my claws pulling into my thick hair.

"Valpar, are you alright?" the fae in front of me asked smugly. "You seem... distressed."

"She is mine?" I whipped my head toward the King of the Fae. "She is my miresa. This is why—" I held my hands out in front of me and the only thing I could see was her in my arms. The way her eyes turned black, when I told her she was good—

"I don't know, you tell me. How do you feel?" Osirus asked.

My body tingled with an electrifying power, coursing through me like a surge of lightning. It brought me to life, the crimson life force flowing through the branches of my body. From head to toe my body was shocked to life at the sudden realization — I had a miresa!

I was eager and possessive. My hands tingled with the desire to take her into my arms, hide her from the world and to keep her all to myself.

After years of waiting, of hoping that she would be given to me, she was dropped into my lap, and with my foolishness, I almost missed it.

I had been given the greatest gift.

I will never again be alone, and neither will she.

I clenched my fist tightly, feeling the knuckles strain against the pressure. With a fierce thud, I pounded my fist against my chest, the force reverberating through my bones. A resounding roar erupted from deep within me, echoing through the air.

My tunic ruffled as I tugged at it, frustration boiling inside me. The anger pulsated through my veins, making my head spin. I shook it vigorously, strands of hair whipping against my face.

The absence of something to strike intensified my fury. I longed to release this pent-up energy, to unleash my rage upon something, anything. But the palace's delicate treasures were off-limits, a boundary I could not cross.

Yet, amidst the turmoil, a glimmer of determination sparked within me. I knew there was one way to alleviate the pain, to make things right.

Claim my female.

I stomped away from Osirus, although I felt him closely behind my back. My vision was red, not in anger but using the instincts my orgamo had taught me as an orcling. Instincts I should only use during battles, hunts, and—claiming one's female.

I pushed in the door, my body wild with desire and my instincts on high alert.

I would take what was mine, what was gifted to me.

How could I have been so oblivious, so foolish, to just leave my miresa in a room full of unmated? The shame gnawed at me. I became determined to spend every remaining moment of my existence making amends. I would gladly press my lips against the very soil she trod upon, ready to carry her weight so she may never walk alone again. I would tenderly indulge her, even as her pleas for respite filled the air, driven by an overwhelming desire to bring her pleasure.

If she didn't want to give me my release to punish me, I would accept it. Whatever she wanted, so that I may receive her forgiveness.

I pushed the doors to the ballroom open and let out a roar as they both slammed against the walls. The room stilled and the music stopped.

Everyone stared at me in shock and horror, while I stopped myself from smiling.

This is what I craved, their fear, to show my miresa that I will be her protector.

The crowd parted and I saw my brother, Sugha, holding my mate in his arms. She was standing there, her lips parted and the sweet smell of chamomile wafting toward my nose. My nose flared and, it was then, I realized it was her arousal.

Bassza, this female, would destroy me before the night was done.

But my brother, with his smug smile, made me seethe.

"Sugha! What are you doing?!" I growled and balled my fists. I will destroy him for touching my female.

Words were exchanged, but I barely registered them.

He. Was. Touching. Touching what was mine.

After making sure my female was safe, her sweet and small voice confirming it, I pulled my arm back and landed my knuckles straight into my brother's face.

With the rest of the tribe drunk, they found it fun, and it was the perfect escape for taking my miresa away from the party. I grabbed her by her waist and threw her over my shoulder. I tried to ignore the heat that ran up my arms and straight to my shaft.

I groaned, my shaft leaking and soaking my pants as I adjusted myself. This was why we wore basic cloth instead of pants. I'd be chafing until my skin was raw.

"Oh heckers! Sugha!" my miresa screamed, and I growled, flipping a table closest to me. Food fell to the floor, and the crowd screamed, running away from me and the orcs brawling behind me.

My miresa will never speak my brother's name, not after tonight. She will only scream mine.

"Wait, let me go!" My miresa shouted as I hoisted her up and threw her over my shoulder.

"I'm fine!" Sugha shouted. I snarled and held onto my miresa's back-side. *Mine.*

I sucked in a breath and turned before I departed through the doors. I tilted my chin up, happy to claim my prize. "She's mine!" I announced to the room.

The clashing orcs abruptly halted, their bellowing cheers echoing through the air, before the resounding thud of one striking another in the face reverberated amidst the chaos. I stormed away, grasping my miresa's ass, carrying her away from the clamor, and seeking a moment of solitude to have her all to myself.

Finally, I had her and I would not let her out of my sight—ever!

Chapter Nine

Valpar

I kept one arm wrapped around her legs, the other arm free to push away anyone I needed to. The guards were compliant as I stomped down the halls and found my way to the front entrance. I didn't want anyone to think I was ashamed of claiming my mate. They needed to see that I had taken her from the ball, that I had claimed Calliope, and she was mine.

The front doors stood wide open, inviting in the soft glow of the radiant blue moon. The guards cast wary glances in my direction, and their hands gripped the hilt of their swords, ready for any potential threat.

Behind me a hoard of creatures were stampeding in either their animal forms or flying out with their wings. The vampires strode quietly, their expensive leather footwear clicking down the hallway.

I hated those blood-sucking...

"Hey! I can walk!" My miresa poked my lower cheek and took a tentative grab. "It's both squishy and muscly, and I can't decide which it is."

I tried to hide the smile that settled on my face while I carried her. I needed the other creatures to stare at me with fear. I couldn't break character while I carried my precious cargo.

The echoes of my tribe reverberated through the hallways, accompanied by the shattering of glass and the forceful slamming of food against the windows. Amidst the chaos, I'm sure Osirus didn't attempt to halt the commotion. The mischievous fae likely found delight in the spectacle.

"Where are we going?" My miresa placed her hands on my lower back and pushed away from my body to look around. "Hi, Simon! You stay there, okay! I'll come back and get you in a second! Melina might have a treat for you if you are good!"

Simon? Who the basssza is Simon?

I pulled my mate from my shoulder and carried her in my arms. Her hair fell into her face and she hastily pushed it away from her vision. "Hey, what's all with this man-, er, orc-handling? You can't be doing that, I might throw up!"

"Throw up?" I stopped in my tracks and stared down at her. "What does this mean?"

She huffed and crossed her arms. "I have a high-sugar diet. If you keep throwing me around, it might come out of my mouth and get your clothes all dirty. That wouldn't be sexy at all, and then how else are you gonna continue to like me?"

I raised an eyebrow. "There is not much you could do to make me not like you. You are mine, Calliope."

I could feel her frail drum beat faster in her chest as I held onto her. "Now, who is Simon?" I continued our walk to the courtyard that the tribe had taken over. Away from prying eyes, so I could grab my belongings and take her away from my own species.

"Simon's my best friend. I'm his person. I help protect him and he probably protects me, too. He's got this condition, and I'm there to help him as much as I can. We do everything together—"

As my miresa talked, I listened intently, but also made a list in my head. I must gather my tent, my belongings, grab Ulam and then we will make the trek back to the Monktona Wood tonight. We will sprint back to the cabin, and even if it is less than desirable for my miresa to be there, I will make it to her liking.

New furs on the bed, clean up the kitchen, I will bring flowers—fresh kills—all of it will be for her. She will not have to lift a finger and once it is all in place I will claim her—when she is ready. She is small. From what I can remember about humans, their holes are small and I must prepare her.

First step, get her out of this kingdom and away from the other orcs.

I couldn't have my miresa vulnerable here in the Golden Light Kingdom. Just anyone, like my brother, could steal her from me. What if she found one of the other orcs more desirable?

I picked up my steps at the thought.

"—We even sleep together. He has this cute little snore—"

"WHAT?" I roared and the birds, sleeping in the trees of the garden, flapped their wings and vanished into the night sky.

The thought of anyone sleeping in the same bed as my miresa brought the orc who fought in the war to the forefront of my mind. I wanted blood!

My back straightened, and I realized I was carrying my tiny miresa in my arms. One so tiny that I could have completely messed up our bonding experience. She could be afraid of me. An orc's roar is powerful, deafening.

I feared to check her state, but I had to know if she would shy away from me. But, when I finally looked down at her, she gave me a stare of bewilderment.

"Are you constipated or something?" she asked innocently.

My mouth dropped.

"I said, are you constipated? Do you need to drop some tummy dumplings? Because I get cranky when I feel a little stopped up. There is this fruit you can eat called the hinbel. I don't know if you have it over there in your wood, but here it is quite reliable in helping your digestive system. It will have you cleaned out in no time."

Did she just ask me if I needed to defecate?

"Is that why you left earlier? Because you needed to go to the restroom?" She played with her fingers and didn't look at me when she asked.

I sighed heavily, took long strides over to the courtyard's stone wall and sat her on top of it. I was still taller than her, despite its height.

"I left because I thought you had put a spell on me," I said honestly.

Her thick bottom lip pouted, and a confused look appeared on her face. "A spell? I can't do spells. I'm a human. Besides, orcs can't—"

"—Can't be affected by magic, yes, I know. You made me feel things I never thought I would ever feel, Calliope. And you were dressed as a fae, I thought you were just trying to trick me. Many fae and fairies want to know what it is like to be with an orc."

My miresa's face turned red and she bit her bottom lip.

Interesting.

"I was looking for reasons that you could not be mine. It was just too good to be true and I was also—" I scratched the back of my head, "—afraid."

She laughed. "You can't be afraid. You are too big and strong."

My chest puffed up in pride. I leaned forward and put both hands on either side of her hips. "The thought of never having you... yes, an orc can be afraid. Are you not afraid of me, little fairy?"

She shook her head. "No," she whispered. "Even when you are constipated."

I chuckled. Strange female.

My miresa would not look me in the eye, her face wandered down my body. I hoped she appreciated what she saw. I knew I was different; it wasn't a secret. I did not suck in my gut to show off my muscle underneath. I did not hide who I was. I hoped she would no longer hide who she was either.

However, she dressed like a fae earlier and I had many questions falling onto my tongue.

"Who is this Simon?" I asked as she traced a scar on my arm.

"I told you, my best friend, and why did you get mad when I said he sleeps with me?"

My fist tightened, and she put her hand on top of mine. Could she not see jealousy? Did she not understand it? Did she not understand fear at all?

An orc's roar is—powerful. She should have flinched, her drum should have beaten wildly in her chest, yet there was nothing that changed her feelings toward me after that.

My miresa continued to study my hand, touching the thick branches that protruded from my strenuous grip. I briefly remembered that humans do have relationships, multiple relationships, before they settled down. My miresa may not have known she would gain a companion from the Moon Fairy, so this Simon could have been her bed partner.

I lifted my lip in a snarl.

It wasn't fair for me to be angry. She wouldn't have known. That doesn't mean I can't kill this Simon, or anyone else who has touched her.

"Nahhhh!" A noise came from my right, and I turned to see a white goat at my side. As if the Moon Fairy knew where my mind was taking me, she distracted me with a gift. A gift to fill my miresa's belly before our long journey back to our home. I will save the extras, and we could eat it along the way.

"Calliope, I will feed you before we leave." I said excitedly, trying to rid my jealousy of this Simon.

I will come back and kill him another day.

I reached down and picked the goat up with one of my hands. "This animal will be your feast, I'm sure this will fill you up, yes?" I held him out proudly as he screamed.

Calliope's eyes filled with water and she shook her head. "No, no! You can't eat Simon!"

I jerked my head back when the goat let out a long noise again and wiggled its legs.

"This is Simon?" I pointed to the goat.

Calliope nodded, holding out her arms for the goat, and I gave him to her. She held him, cradled him more like, and petted his fur. "We would never eat you. He was only kidding." Calliope glared at me and panic ensued.

I could not have her angry with me.

"My, my miresa, I didn't mean to upset you. I did not know Simon was, a goat."

"My name is Calliope, not Miresa! Did you already forget my name, too? You think I'm a liar? You try to eat my best friend. Are you just trying to get a free pass into my no-no areas?!"

This is going horribly wrong, this is not what I intended at all.

"Calliope, miresa means mate in my tribe. I did not forget your name. I swear it to the Moon Fairy." I got on my knees and put my head on her legs, rubbing my cheek along her thigh.

Her scent bloomed between her legs, and it was all I could do to stifle back a groan. Why did she have to smell so good?

I took a tentative lick at the inside of her knee. She tightened her legs together and I moved my hands along the outside of her legs, going higher until I cupped her backside.

She fit perfectly into my palms.

My miresa's eyes fluttered, and she hid her smile behind her goat.

However, the goat yelled at me, knocking the tension from my miresa and me.

Calliope shook her head. "I-I don't know. I would like to ask your brother some questions about you, and about this miresa stuff." She gripped onto her goat. "I'm not stupid. I know I say stuff and people laugh at me, but—"

"You are not!" I growled. "I swear it to you, on my life, and the bond we will share, you are mine. Miresa means mate amongst my kind." I put my arm over my chest to swear it. "And I was foolish to think that you would trick me. I've been lonely, my little fairy," my voice softened.

I stood up from the ground, trying to get closer, but the goat snapped his teeth at me.

"It had been many years and I had lost hope. I never thought you would fall into my lap."

Calliope turned her head, biting her lip.

"Please," I begged her, grabbing her arm and letting the fire burn between us. "I will prove my worth to you."

Her breath stuttered and she nodded. "Um, I'm not ready to go, wherever you wanted to go, just yet. Can we stay here in the Golden Light Kingdom? And please, don't eat my goat, Leave."

I winced and held her hand tightly so she could not pull away. "I vow to you that we will not leave until I prove my worth. And, I have one more thing to tell you my fairy. My name is not Leave, it is actually Valpar."

Her eyes narrowed, and again it pierced through my drum.

I was in such trouble with this female.

CHAPTER TEN

Calliope

I LET SIMON DOWN. He wasn't used to being carried, especially since he weighed as much as me. I wasn't about to have Valpar carry him, either.

Valpar.

Sounds much better than Leave, even so, I wasn't overly happy about these new revelations. Don't get me wrong, I'm ecstatic to have a mate. I never thought I would have one, let alone that mine would be an orc.

The first person to get an orc!

I bet everyone is super jealous that I got the best looking one, too.

Still, it wasn't the enchanting scene I had thought in my head what my mate might do to claim me at the ball, but it was the most exciting.

Valpar picked me up as soon as I let Simon off my lap. He cradled me to his chest, and Simon jumped off the stone wall and trotted close behind.

Simon didn't like Valpar much. He was nipping at Valpar's pants as we walked through the courtyard, instead of taking a bite out of the flowers he wasn't supposed to eat.

It was hard to stay mad at Valpar. I'm sure it was the bond at work. Mom would get mad at Dad often, but it wasn't long before he was making her smile with just a touch of his hand on her arm or whispering dirty things in her ear.

Yeah, they were really dirty things, too.

That's when I would go to my room and read about other people doing dirty things.

Unfortunately, I couldn't hide from Valpar. The way he held me in his arms and scouted the area for anyone coming our way was a small hint of that. Even with his long strides and his constant alertness, he would dip his giant head to take a strong whiff of my hair, and I thanked the Goddess that I actually washed it today.

Sometimes, this girl is lazy.

Valpar continued to take us deeper into the garden until it opened up into a wide area of the lawn. The grass, meticulously cut short, lacked the presence of any trees or flowers, leaving a barren landscape. Normally, it served as a picturesque spot for picnics during parties, joyous tea celebrations, and hosting lively yard games. However, this time, it lay in a mess that would have Aunt Melina clutching her dress. Tents were haphazardly pitched and cluttered the area. The once-enormous bonfire was now smoldered, its flames on the verge of extinction, emitting a faint crackle. The air was heavy with the acrid scent of burnt wood and lingering smoke. Amongst the chaos, weapons lay strewn carelessly across the grass. The worst part was a gruesome sight when I saw a half-eaten boar that continued to rotate on a spit above the dwindling fire.

Poor piggie.

I guess the orcs were having a lot of fun while they stayed.

"We can't stay here," Valpar grumbled and had me sit on a leather chair next to a tent. It was large enough to fit Valpar and three other orcs. It was made of brown leather and the bedding looked like plush fur, giving it a cozy feel.

I leaned over and peeked inside, revealing a treasure trove of warmth and comfort - an abundance of furs and blankets adorned the interior. Soft, fluffy fur lined the walls, providing a sumptuous backdrop, while a variety of thick, velvety blankets were scattered and not yet made.

I was instantly drawn to it. It was like an invitation for me to sink in and indulge in ultimate fluffy coziness.

Instantly, I jumped off the chair and scrambled inside while he rooted for a bag on the other side of the tent.

"This is awesome!" I yelled from the inside. It was soft, and the underside of the fur blankets, where the leather was, equally so. The furs were warm, much warmer than the silky blankets I usually slept on. I rubbed my face in it and burrowed my body inside.

That's it, I'm never leaving.

"This is my burrow now, I have claimed it for my own," I whispered and took in deep breaths. It didn't smell like the wood or the stink of animals—it smelled like Valpar. And he just smelled like... a man. No, an orc. He smelled like a clean orc? No, he smelled like forest rain. Yeah, he smelled like clean forest rain. Like a fresh beasty.

"Miresa, what are you doing?" Valpar whispered.

"It's so soft. How do you get it so soft? And it smells just like you." I took a large inhale.

I groaned and wiggled deeper into the furs. Gah, this was better than Uncle Osirus' beds. Shh, don't tell him that.

"We can't stay here. The tribe will be back. I will not let them come near you—" Valpar said quickly, still packing the bag. "Come out and I will pack our bedding." He grabbed his crotch and held out his hand.

Huh.

I shook my head and huffed in annoyance. "Why? What's wrong with seeing the tribe?"

Was he ashamed of me?

Wouldn't be the first time someone hid me because they didn't want to be seen with me.

I sat up from the furs and wrapped one of them around me. I sniffed it, breathing in deeply. Why did he have to smell so good?

That cursed bond.

Just because we were mates doesn't mean I have to do everything he said. Even if he made my lower lady parts cry.

And she was crying, like a lot. I was surprised he hadn't noticed.

Then again, he had licked my leg earlier.

I decided to let him win for now, so crawled out of the tent and sat in the chair. I hunched over, resting my elbows on my knees, and rubbed my nose.

Valpar—if that was his name, could be lying about claiming me too then, couldn't he? Especially since a human can't feel the bond as strongly.

"Miresa, what is wrong?" Valpar came closer, his tunic still ripped and his pants wrinkled.

His face went soft when he kneeled. He hesitated to touch me with his gigantic hands even though he carried me from the palace down to the courtyard.

I rubbed my lips together and let my toes tickle the grass beneath my feet. "Do you not want me to meet your tribe? Why can't I meet them?"

Valpar huffed and stood, his back retreating. Then, he took off his shirt and I forgot the question entirely. His back was... nice.

I wanted to sink my fingernails into it and run them down his green skin. It was muscular, but not overly so. I liked the softness it held but there was strength there. I knew because I'd felt him hold me in those muscular arms. He turned and I saw his torso. He wasn't as defined as the other orcs I had seen from a distance, and I liked that he was different.

I licked my lips and I waited for him to remove his pants, but he ran his claws through his messy hair, opening and closing his mouth over and over again.

That was okay. I was enjoying the view I had.

As I sat there, my clit pulsed with desire, aching for attention. With a quick shift of my legs, I felt some relief. It was just enough to soothe the ache, but made me want more.

Finding moments alone had been challenging living with my parents. They were always present, their heightened senses making me paranoid about any lingering scent. But now, in this open space, a gentle breeze was moving, and it could carry away the trace of my arousal.

And I couldn't help but think... *Valpar's fingers grazing over his chest, tracing the jagged landscape of scars. Visions flooded his mind: the clash of steel against steel, the thunderous thuds of his enemy's weapons, his giant roar. The thought of him standing tall, wielding a sword or a club, braving the odds to protect the land that I could now stand on.*

Oh gods, I was getting far too... turned on.

I let out a whimper, and Valpar jerked his head toward me. I had paid so much attention to the upper part of his body I didn't look below the waist—

"My little fairy," he groaned. "Your scent."

Oopsie.

Valpar's chest heaved as he stared at me with a mixture of confusion and desire. My cheeks flushed red, and I quickly looked away, feeling embarrassed for being caught with my scent.

What do I do?

His pants were tented, revealing a hint of his *little orc*, and it was clear that he enjoyed catching my scent.

Underneath those pants, oh cheese and crumbs, it was way bigger than what I had accidentally seen of my dad.

What does he feed that thing?

I bit my lip nervously, unsure of what to do or say. Sure, I'd read books, but none of the women in there had an orc for a mate.

He had a third leg.

My lady hole can't fit that.

Does he have to put it in there, right now?

Before I could gather my thoughts, Valpar took a step towards me, his long bamboo stick aiming right at me, as he knelt down.

He reached out and gently brushed a strand of hair behind my ear, his touch sending shivers down my spine. "My little fairy," he said softly, his eyes burning into my skin. "I do not want the tribe to look at you, or even smell you. I do not want them to take you from me." He gritted his teeth.

"What?" I panted, when I felt his hands part my legs. My short dress was no match, and I knew he could see straight into my silky, damp underwear.

"You are my miresa," he took in a deep breath and lowered his head. "In your time living in Bergarian, you must know how males are possessive over females, yes?" He emitted a low, menacing growl, his hot breath caressing my skin as it traveled up my leg, igniting a fiery sensation between my thighs.

My head fell back, and I let out a soft whimper.

"Orcs are alphas." He licked the inner part of my left knee.

Oh, dragon eggs.

"My tribe will be jealous of me. Try to take you for themselves and delay our bonding. I. Will. Not. Let. Them."

Valpar's warm, wet tongue glided slowly along my bare leg, sending heat to my should-be no-no zone. I could feel the tickle of the rough skin of his cheek, as he playfully nuzzled his nose against the delicate fabric of my underwear. Inhaling deeply, he savored the scent that came from between my thighs.

"Mmm, my miresa. I want to bury my face here."

Um, please!

I was no longer thinking how angry I was before, that he almost left me because he was so stubborn, or that he wanted to hide me from everyone.

Nope, not one bit.

All I could think about was him relieving this ache that pulsed between my legs. And his face, his tongue... it was right there.

I bit my cheek so I didn't say anything embarrassing, because that would be something I would do. None of those other women in the books say anything, they just took it. Allowed a man to have their way with them, but—

I couldn't hold it in.

"Are you supposed to sniff it?" I squeaked, wiggling in his arms. "And is it supposed to feel like this?!"

Valpar's big hands engulfed my thighs easily, pinning me to my seat as held me still. He groaned, and the vibrations ran up my inner thigh.

He hummed. "How does it feel, my little fairy?"

I bit hard on my cheek, drawing blood. I felt everything. Fire, electricity, magic pricking my nipples and soaking my core.

I was so wet. What if he thought I peed?

Before I could answer, Valpar cupped my butt-cheeks and tipped my hips up like he was burying his face in a cupcake batter bowl. He rubbed his nose over my underwear, and I gripped his thick hair so I didn't fall over.

Valpar snarled into my thighs, his claws digging into my cheeks. I let out a cry that could be mistaken for pain, but deep-fried fudge, I wanted more.

Simon yelled his loud baaaa, and I heard his hooves charge across the grass and straight into Valpar's hip. He didn't move. He continued to rub his cheek, face and nose between my legs.

Simon didn't let up. He continued to back up and charge, but I was too lost in the sensations, and too excited at the new experience my body was feeling. Vapar was becoming bolder, more excited, grunting and rooting like he was a wild boar.

My grip tightened in his hair, as his large tooth caught on my dress. I heard it rip and gasped, as his hand gripped my waist to keep me in place.

Valpar's hands clenched on my hip, holding me as Simon charged towards us again. I could feel his hot breath on my skin and the sensation of Valpar's tongue flicking over my underwear, and it was almost too much to handle.

He hasn't even licked me yet.

Shouldn't we have kissed first before all this?

I closed my eyes and let out a soft moan as Valpar continued to tease me with his tongue. His hands slid up my back, pulling me closer to him. The night wind blew by, cooling my flushed skin.

Valpar lifted his head and looked at me hungrily, his yellow eyes beaming. "You smell so good, I cannot wait any longer," he growled before diving back between my legs.

As soon as his tongue touched me again, all rational thoughts flew out of my head. It was like every nerve in my body was on fire, every touch sending sparks through me.

His sharp teeth pulled at my underwear, ripping and tearing as his tongue slipped through the holes of the fabric. "You taste so good," he mumbled into my thigh and his tongue slipped over that bundle of nerves I'd been too afraid to play with.

I let out a high-pitched gasp, then my eyes widened, because I saw my uncle and aunt coming down the palace steps in the distance.

Goddess above!

"Valpar!" I breathed, tapping his head, holding back a moan. "Please!"

His tongue flattened against me, sucking onto my clit.

I slapped my hand over my mouth and used my leg to push his shoulder. That only encouraged him, moving his shoulders closer to my body.

"St-ah-ah!"

But Valpar was relentless, his grip on my waist tightening as he continued to pleasure me. His tongue flicked back and forth over my sensitive spot, sending waves of pleasure through me.

I bit down on the inside of my cheek, trying to hold back the wave of sheer bliss that was going through my body. I was...going to do something. It was the climax, the orgasm. Oh Goddess, I was going to come.

Valpar paused, his head tilted to check his surroundings, and he groaned.

He flicked my clit again and my body jolted. His lips wrapped around it and sucked, pulling and dragging while his lower teeth dug into my thighs. I thrust my chest up as I rode his face until I slumped back into the chair.

Valpar's lips caressed my quivering thighs, his warm breath tickling my skin. The sound of my rapid heartbeat drowned out any potential embarrassment as waves of pleasure washed over me. His gentle kisses trailed along my thighs. With a slow and deliberate movement, he lowered my dress, covering my hips. As he rose, he pulled my hands from his hair and ran his own fingers effortlessly through it.

My body was still putty. I was done for.

"Hi," I panted.

Suddenly, Simon let out a loud bleat and charged towards Valpar again. This time, Valpar caught him by the horns and kept him still. He pulled away from me, looking up at me with a mischievous grin before standing up and adjusting his pants.

He still had a very apparent desire for me.

Do I grab it, or —?

Valpar's head darted to the distance and the palace. "We must go," he growled and picked up a bag of his supplies.

His log brushed against my leg when he pulled me to his side, and he tore down his tent in a rush.

My heart was still pounding in my post-pleasure glow. I didn't think to question what was happening, I just watched as he quickly and efficiently packed up his tent in record time. He folded, rolled and shoved it into a large satchel and threw it over his back.

"Come, female." He lowered himself and perched me over his forearm. I wrapped my arms around his neck, and my face leaned into his.

His face was still wet from—me.

Valpar grunted, heading west of the courtyard, away from his tribe's camp, and the king and queen.

"Be my good female and keep quiet. I will reward you with my face between your legs again." My cheeks flushed at his words, but I couldn't deny the tingling sensation that spread through me at the thought of him pleasuring me again. I nodded, keeping my mouth shut.

He studied the footpath in front of him, checking the lay of the land as we passed all the tents and layout of the camp.

Orc laughter came to my left, where they were returning from the ball and my excitement rose. *I could talk to his brother.* Really make sure Valpar wasn't fooling me.

But, with my mind still muddled from the pleasure my mate had given me, and the thrill as he raced us across the yard, all my thoughts were fleeting. Because we were running out of places to escape.

He isn't gonna jump over that, is he?

Valpar held me tightly as he stepped up on the stone wall and looked briefly onto the other side. A grass slope greeted us on the other side.

"You're not gonna..."

Valpar jumped! Just moments later, he landed two-footed on the incline, perfectly balanced as he adjusted to the weight of his bag and me. His feet slid through the grass, my grip on him tightened, and then he groaned as my tiny mandarin oranges barely squished into his face.

"Miresa, I cannot see!" he growled and pulled me away from his face.

"Tree! Tree! Tree!" I chanted loudly.

The large tree came into view had pixies screaming in terror as Valpar and I went barreling towards them. We weren't slowing down, and I didn't know if that was part of his plan or—-

I screamed again, knowing very well that humans do not heal at rapid speeds like everyone else in this realm. Valpar let go of his bag and pulled me to his chest, tucking me into his body as his side skidded further down the hill.

CHAPTER ELEVEN

Calliope

VALPAR'S BODY VIOLENTLY COLLIDED with a towering tree. The impact shook my body as I found myself in his protective embrace. I was shaken up, but I didn't feel any pain. Slowly, his arms slackened, and I cautiously opened my eyes. The sight that greeted me was Valpar's eyes shut, but the rhythmic sound of his breathing reassured me that he was still alive.

"Valpar?" I bopped his nose, but he was fast asleep.

Knocked out.

I've knocked myself out a few times when I fell out of the tree house, but for me being human, it was much worse. They had to call the palace physician to mend a broken bone or two and check my head for swelling.

That's why they put the elevator in because they were tired of me falling out of the tree.

Valpar was an orc, and orcs were known to have hard heads.

I opened his eye with my thumb to check and see if they were still dilated, and the moonlight hit his pupil.

Phew, he *looked* okay. *Maybe I should go get Uncle Osirus.*

"Well, if it isn't little Calliope," a voice sneered from the top of the tree. I pushed Valpar's heavy arm off my body and he groaned. "What did you do now, drug an orc to make him think he was your mate and make the whole ball jealous? Such an attention hog."

Karma gracefully descended from the tall tree, landing with a soft thud on Valpar's head. The minuscule pants he sported were exceedingly small, even for his pixie form. They were frayed cut-offs, revealing his toned legs and well-defined chest. If he were a fairy or a fae, I guess he could be considered an attractive male, for *someone.*

But he was a pixie, and pixies couldn't be trusted. As my godfather and King of the Cerulean Moon Kingdom has once said, *never trust a fucking pixie.*

I snorted. I couldn't say that word out loud but in my head I could.

Karma scoffed and folded his arms.

"I didn't drug him. Valpar really is my mate!" I explained, pointing to the giant heap of muscles on the ground. "Orcs are immune to magic and potions." I crossed my arms in return.

Karma walked lightly across Valpar's body, jumping over the mountains of muscle. "Then you must have tricked him, with your uncle's persuasion, that he is your mate because there is no way that Calliope, a human, would get an orc."

I growled watching Karma walk over Valpar's body. There was a pressure in my chest that I couldn't explain. I didn't like him touching Valpar, and the more he walked over his body, the more I wanted to squeeze his guts out.

I wonder if he would poop glitter.

"Get off of him!" I stomped my foot and walked closer to pluck at his wings.

Karma's mischievous laughter echoed through the air as he swiftly soared away from Valpar's body, slipping through my fingers like a playful breeze. "Aw, is Calliope jealous? Jealous that someone else is touching what shouldn't be hers to begin with?"

If smoke could come out of my ears, it would have. "He's mine! You leave him alone!" I swung my arms at Karma, and he laughed again, along with the posse of pixies in the trees.

"Calliope, he isn't yours. Why would an orc have you? Orcs can have anyone they want. They are the heroes of the realm, and what have you done? Become the kings' favorite, and more like a nuisance everyone is trying to get rid of."

I tilted my head in confusion.

Nuisance?

Karma landed on a high branch. His close friends nudged him to continue while other pixies shook their heads at him. They didn't come to my rescue, though.

"Yeah, Osirus is just trying to pawn you off for a while, so his highness Birch can have his mate to himself. King Osirus and his mate can have time for themselves and not have to watch you. These poor fae can't get anything done with you around getting hurt and being weak all the time." He waved his hand in the air.

I grabbed a nearby branch to steady myself. "What are you talking about, Karma? Valpar and I are mates, chosen by the Moon Goddess herself. He told me so!"

At least, that is what I was starting to believe.

Karma scoffed and rolled his eyes. "Do you really believe that? The Moon Goddess choosing a mere human as an orc mate?"

I clenched my jaw, trying to control my anger. "Yes, I believe it. And even if it isn't true, it doesn't matter because he chose me."

Valpar came around after a while. He recognized the bond in the end, right? Then again, Uncle Osirus went to talk to him. Did Osirus have something to do with us getting together?

Karma snorted. "Choose you? More like your uncle persuaded him to be with you. Everyone saw his majesty leave the room with the fleeing orc."

My blood boiled at the accusation. I wouldn't let Karma think he won. "That's not true! Valpar and I have a connection!" *The desire in his eyes was proof enough of that, right?*

The other pixies started gossiping among themselves, some siding with Karma while others murmured. But none of them came to my aid or stood up for me. They were all too afraid of offending the popular pixie leader.

Karma continued to taunt me, getting closer and closer until he was right in front of me, his face only inches away from mine.

"Face it, Calliope, Valpar is just your babysitter," he sneered before flying back up into the tree and sitting on the branch with a laugh.

Why is he so mean?

I balled up my fists and stomped toward the tree. I was going to beat his tiny little butt into a pulp. I growled, stuck my bare foot onto the first limb and climbed.

Karma jeered, his close friends laughing along with him. "Look at her trying to climb! Where are your wings, Calliope? Why don't you fly up?"

I huffed and climbed higher, higher than I should, but I continued to press forward. I would not chicken out. I was going to catch Karma, shove a stick so far up his butt and then roast him over an open fire until he popped like a popcorn kernel.

Skittles, I've become so violent.

Karma continued to laugh. The one brave pixie who hadn't laughed flew towards me pulling my dress. "Calliope, just let it go. He's a jerk," Meadow said. "He's jealous he wasn't part of the court before you arrived and got all the attention. Come on, climb down."

I growled and continued to climb, but Meadow stayed by my side. "Calliope, you are going to fall. Don't!"

"I gotta do this, destroy him before he destroys me!" I snapped.

I wondered if Valpar would grind Karma's bones and eat him in his bread.

Wait, giants do that.

Valpar is as big as a giant.

Just like that giant thing in his pants.

As I began climbing out onto the limb, it shook and I wrapped my legs around the branch.

Uh, oh.

"Calliope can't even climb a tree!" Karma fell over the limb and flew around to get into my face.

I repeatedly swiped my hand through the air in front of me, while firmly wrapped around the tree with my legs, determined to maintain my position. With a surge of frustration, I released my grip on the tree with one arm and forcefully slapped my hands around Karma when he wasn't looking.

I caught him.

While I held Karma tightly in my hands, he struggled and became more frantic as he realized he was trapped.

Revenge was so close I could practically taste it.

"I'm gonna pop you like a pimple. Ain't so mighty now, are you pixie!?" I taunted, feeling a surge of power and satisfaction.

But then the branch beneath us cracked loudly. I looked at the side of the tree where a giant crack shot from the limb to the tree.

Oh, no.

Meadow screamed from below, "Calliope, let go!"

But I couldn't. Not now that I finally had Karma right where I wanted him. The branch gave way completely, my legs let go and we tumbled through the air.

I squeezed my eyes shut and braced for impact, but instead of hitting the ground, I felt myself being caught by a soft body.

"Female..."

Valpar

I had to get my miresa away from the tribe, from her family, especially the King and the Queen.

If I did not, they would take her, so I knew I must take action to keep her. I could not fight them on my own, because they were many and I could not leave my miresa alone in the dark. She would hurt herself trying to defend her family.

Knowing that she would defend them brought fire inside my belly. She should only want me, not them. I am her sole protector, now. She no longer needed any of them.

When I grabbed our supplies and my miresa, I did what I did best. I sunk back into my instincts, as when I was back in war time and needed to get one of the fallen away, to be protected and hidden.

And I would, I would protect her with all my being.

I didn't realize how steep the hill was, but it was no match for me. I would have evaded the tree, but when my miresa became frightened she blocked my view, and my balance was thrown.

It was my fault; I should have known better. Calliope had just met me and she was still a skittish little fairy. It most likely didn't help how I was lost in my desires to bury my face between her legs.

Her cunt.

I remembered the word from so long ago, along with many words that are of human origin. The female anatomy of many creatures had fascinated me. They all looked similar but had their own differences.

My brother Thorn hardly paid attention to the classes or even read the book that was given to us. He was too busy trying to keep the tribe's hopes up. There was a time, years past, when I studied it every night, and I had not forgotten the pleasure areas of a female—and a male.

Luckily, I have a female, because I found my little fairy's body more appealing.

I couldn't wait to see it in the daylight, couldn't wait to see the rest of her, to taste her properly and touch her.

If I wasn't so lost in my desires and didn't have to shift my shaft to avoid it getting in the way of our escape, we could be sliding down the hill towards the forest, and I could be buried into her cunt now.

Instead, I heard annoying bells in my ear and wings fluttering near my face.

I groaned and waved the flying nuisance away from me. It was a pixie. Why it was coming near me I wasn't sure.

"I'm gonna pop you like a pimple. Ain't so mighty now are you, pixie!?" I heard my miresa speak.

I didn't know my miresa could speak so harshly, but it had my cock filling with need that I could have done without, right now. I needed to keep her hidden, away from the tribe, and away from the royals.

No one would steal her from me.

I sat up, rubbing the back of my head, where a large knot was forming.

Bassza, I hit the tree. Luckily, I am a powerful male, and my skull cannot be cracked by one of the weak trees in the Golden Light Kingdom. These trees were brittle and when I looked at the base, I saw a crack at the base, leading up to the taller branches.

Some fairy or pixie can fix it.

I rubbed my hand down my face, and the ringing bells sounded again. I opened my eyes and saw a pixie flying in front of my face, pointing up into the tree.

Wait, where is my female?

"Calliope?" I got ready to stand, but before I did, the cracking of a branch sounded, and a familiar squeak came from above.

A soft, light creature fell into my lap and when I looked down, I saw the beautiful head of pink hair and the scent of chamomile fell around me.

I growled, "Female." I pushed back her hair and ocean-blue eyes stared back at me.

"I got him!" She held out her closed-cupped hands, but when she opened them, there was nothing inside. "Aw, fiddle sticks. Where'd he go?!"

Ringing bells sounded off to my right, a male pixie waving his fist near my mate. I scowled and blew wind in his direction, causing him to be caught in the draft and fly away.

"Come back here!" Calliope tried to escape my lap, but I wrapped my arms around her and held her still.

"Female, you are nothing but trouble!" I held her down as she squirmed right on my shaft. I groaned, holding her tighter until she gave up. "You will not leave my side; you hold my hand or I carry you."

"But I almost had him!" She pouted. Her thick bottom lip stuck out. "I must get my revenge!" She showed me her fist and shook it.

My little fairy was a fighter. I didn't know what sort of revenge she wanted, but now was not the time.

"Calliope!" I heard Queen Melina call from above. "Calliope! Where are you?"

My miresa opened her mouth, and I covered it with my hand. "Be my good little mate, so I can reward you." She squirmed again in my lap. "I would very much like to lick your cunt again if you will be willing." I breathed down her neck and she stilled, moving closer to my voice.

Hmm, it seemed she likes to be rewarded. I would have to remember that.

Before I stood, I was greeted with a bump in my side. When I turned, I saw none other than the white goat taking steps back to run into me again.

"Simon!" Calliope whispered. "That's not nice!"

"Are you sure you will not let me eat him?" I ground my teeth.

Simon paused, his body frozen mid-run, and then he just fell over.

Bassza! I broke him.

What will my mate think?

"Whoopsie daisy." She got off my lap, and I let her, watching her go over to the goat and pet him. "It's okay. He does that sometimes. Now, are we gonna go, so we can do more than what you did earlier?"

Moon Fairy, what is happening?

CHAPTER TWELVE

Valpar

AFTER CAREFULLY GATHERING OUR supplies, I gently scooped up Calliope, feeling her warmth against my chest. The silence enveloped us as I cradled her in my arms, our bodies melding together as we ventured deeper into the dense forest. Peering through the foliage, I spotted her worried family and my brother anxiously scanning the surroundings, their worried expressions etched on their faces. Thankfully, the distance shielded us from their searching gazes.

I huffed and turned away, determined to keep Calliope hidden until I fully claimed her as mine. I would not have them change their mind about letting me have her, or tell me how to claim my miresa, or how I should treat her.

I was chosen by the Moon Fairy to keep and protect her in all ways, and I would do just that.

As I cradled her in my arms, the rhythmic rustle of leaves and the hushed whispers of the forest enveloped us, lulling her into tranquility. The faint scent of moss and pine mingled in the air, creating a serene atmosphere. She yawned softly, her drowsy sighs blending with the gentle sway of our surroundings. It was of my own doing, I'm sure, having my face in her cunt. I also acknowledged that it was well past her time to be sleeping.

Humans were much weaker, and I knew she needed her rest after such an exciting day.

The moon was high, having moved further than halfway through the night. I continued onward, and the further we traveled, the more I could smell the salt of the ocean coming nearer. I was running out of places to run to, but it wasn't the time to get her back to the Wood, just yet. I told her I would keep her around the Golden Light Kingdom until she knew me better and I had proven my worth.

I heard the waves crashing down on the shoreline. I hadn't been here in many years, since my curiosity got the best of me. Back then, sirens lined the shore, their tails waved and baked in the light sources and even they were curious about the orcs that helped turn the war.

I hoped we weren't greeted by the sirens, but you never know since we were getting close to their territory.

They, too, were always invited to the mating balls, especially since Queen Melina was half siren. It was harder to pick them out among the bunch of more human-looking creatures. They all had pointed ears, but they also held scales in some areas of their bodies.

"Where are we going?" My miresa yawned and nuzzled into my chest. Her eyes drooped and I hurried to pick up the pace.

I was looking for anything, a shelter of some kind to keep my mate hidden until I figured out what deal I could make with her to take her back to our home. I would not break the vow I made her, but she had to know the dilemma of the alpha within me, wanting to take her away from all these creatures.

"A place to rest for a time," I mumbled into her hair, taking a deep draw of her scent. "A place where you will be comfortable."

She hummed, her eyes staying closed. My chest puffed with pride that my little fairy would be so willing to succumb to sleep in my arms and would trust me even this much after the worries she had shown earlier.

Yet, she's had a very busy night.

"There is a cave." She lifted her head and nodded to the northeast. "It hasn't been used in years; my uncle sealed it off."

I hummed and headed in that direction. The palace gradually faded into the background, but its spires remained visible above the trees. Once we reached the sandy shores it came into better view, and I didn't like how close we were to it, but it was late.

"Would your family find you here?"

My miresa yawned again and shook her head. "No, like I said, they don't use the cave anymore. Aunt Melina expects people to stay in the palace. She likes the company and expects everyone to bring their whole family to visit."

It made sense that the queen would want everyone in the palace, especially their children. In the war, the queen was stabbed in her womb with a demon sword and, even now, they say she may never bear children.

And the queen loved children and wanted nothing more than to have some of her own.

The tribe and I knew that feeling all too well.

The cave would do for now. When the light sources rise, we can find another place to hide.

As we drew closer, the waves continued to crash into the shore. The smell of fish was much better than the flowers that surrounded the palace. As I came to the boulders blocking the way to the cave, Calliope squirmed in my hold, rubbing her eyes.

"It's here," she finally spoke up, pointing to a spot between two large rocks. "You will need to move those boulders."

I nodded, feeling the weight of my supplies as I let them drop with a soft thud onto the ground. Rolling my shoulders back, I could hear the faint crack of bones readjusting. Determined, I gazed at the towering boulders ahead, ready to showcase my strength as a capable male.

I carefully placed her on a nearby rock, the rough texture scraping against my palm. Reluctantly, I had to let her sit, for she was a tenacious female who disliked being idle. Yet, a thought crossed my mind - would it be necessary to secure a rope around her waist, ensuring she never strayed from my side?

Hmm.

I flexed my arms, taking in a deep breath and getting ready to move the boulders that were blocking the entrance of the cave. I didn't want to move them too far. I planned on moving them back once we had settled in the cave. That way, no one would stumble upon us while we stayed here.

I easily rolled the large boulders away from the entrance, not even breaking a sweat.

Calliope watched intently as I worked, her eyes wide with wonder as she saw me effortlessly move the heavy stones out of our way. Soon enough, there was a clear path for us to enter the cave.

My drum beat faster in my chest as she watched. Was she proud of me? Did she find me capable? I continued to have thoughts run through my head, my mind pounding with ideas that I shouldn't have. If I thought too much, I would want to relieve the emotions that should not build within an orc.

I wanted her to find me capable, and strong.

Next to her were the supplies, and I rummaged through them to find a glass jar full of light. It was filled with mushrooms which were both tasty and useful, because they gave off light in the darkest of places. They were only found in a special cave my brothers and I traveled to once, during a deep blue moon.

I gestured for Calliope to follow me, wanting to get her inside and her scent away from any other males. I left the supplies outside in case an animal was already inhabiting the cave, and we'd need to leave quickly. She hesitated for a moment before following, and I wrapped my hand around hers as I helped her step inside, looking around cautiously.

The cave was cool and inviting, its damp walls glistening in the soft glow of our jar of light. The air was still and crisp, carrying a hint of earthiness and a touch of dew. Despite being sealed, it was still fresh and clean and would soon be filled with her scent. The cave would be perfect for refuge, shielding us from the wrath of potential storms or lurking families. As we made our way through the narrow passage, the ground beneath our feet felt reassuringly flat and smooth.

"Is this okay?" I asked Calliope as she stared at me with curious eyes.

She nodded slowly, still taking in our surroundings. "Yes..." she trailed off uncertainly.

I scanned the cave quickly before turning back to her. "I will make sure everything is secure outside before joining you." I handed her the jar of mushrooms, and she stared at them in wonder. She shook them and they glowed brighter.

Yet, they are not as bright as her smile.

She giggled and nodded again. "Okie dokie..."

I grabbed my supplies and took a moment to seal us inside. When I returned to the passage where I left my miresa...she wasn't there.

That's it, I'm going to have to tie her around my waist like most ogamies do to their orclings. It would be safer that way. That way she could not wander.

I traveled down the passage, seeing the light of the mushrooms at the far end. My vision was clear, and I could see much better than most, especially a human, in the dark. I was still worried, since my female had limited light, and she could fall if there were a cavern she couldn't see.

My drum thumped wildly in my chest. "Calliope... miresa, where are you?"

The goat cried, and I rushed forward down the passage until it opened into a large room that wasn't empty, but completely furnished with—-actual furniture. There was a bed large enough to fit me and my miresa, a cooking hearth and even another area which could be a *bath-room*.

It looked nothing like a normal cave.

"What—?"

In the vast bed, a gentle snore resonated, drawing me nearer. As I approached, a soft glow emanated from the light in my miresa's embrace, casting a warm ambiance. Nestled in the center, she lay, without any blankets to shield her from the cold.

She shivered, and immediately my protective instincts kicked in, as I rushed to pull furs from my bag to cover her with. She did not know how much I enjoyed her lying in my furs back in the courtyard. How she put her scent all over my bedding. It made me hard. My shaft had leaked, already coating the front of my pants, and I was ready to rip them off my body.

But first, I must tend to her.

Calliope stirred gently under my touch, her eyelids fluttering as she drifted between sleep and wakefulness. I carefully choose my finest furs, their texture brushing against my fingertips as I tenderly draped them over her slumbering form. Settling down beside her on the bed, I marveled at the delicate contours of her face, her ethereal beauty outshining any fairy or pixie of this realm. The room was bathed in a gentle glow from the mushrooms.

How I got to be so lucky to have such a creature to be all mine and no one else's, I wasn't sure. And to think I almost let her go!

I growled and let the back of my fingers brush against her cheek.

Mine.

Looking around the room again, I noticed there were other items besides furniture. Utensils for cooking such as pans hung above the hearth. There was also a door to the left of the bed and when I went to open it, found a full bathroom with a quartz tub, *toi-let* and *sink*.

All things I would need to build in our cabin back home to suit her. I would need to ensure she could not climb anything in my cabin, or have anything around that could hurt her.

My knives and weapons! I would need to build a room to hide all my sharp objects.

I glanced back at Calliope who was now sleeping peacefully, her long eyelashes resting gently against her cheeks. I couldn't help but wonder if she had lived this long with no sense of danger. This female had fallen from high places twice this night, luckily both times landing into my arms, and she'd wandered off into a dark cave without a care.

This female needed a keeper, and I was such an orc that would keep her safe. My miresa would not like the way I'll keep her, but it would be for both of our sakes.

Orcs had to be extremely old to be able grow white and grey hair, but I believe Calliope might make mine grow as such.

I decided to explore more of our new living quarters while she slept. There was another small room off to the side, which appeared to be a storage area, filled with supplies such as food, extra blankets and pillows. There was a large pile of furs placed neatly against one far wall, recognized instantly as fae-made pelts; warm and perfect for keeping us comfortable during chilly nights. Also, a chest that sat against the wall.

I sniffed the air and entered. There was no lock on the chest, so I opened it and inside found things I had not seen before.

Actual cocks and shafts in different colors, with no bodies!

I quickly shut the chest and stood, no longer interested in what else could be in there. I grabbed hold of my cock, backed away, and left the room, shutting the door quickly.

What sort of place was this?

We would not need the furs from this room. My furs would be fine. I grabbed a heavy chair, one that my miresa could not pick up on her own, and set it in front of the door.

No, she would never go in there.

Never!

CHAPTER THIRTEEN

Calliope

As soon as I heard the rhythmic clicking of Simon's hooves on the smooth stone floor, my eyes flew open. The sound echoed through the room, piercing the silence. I watched Simon's sleepy movements as he made his way towards the bathroom, his hooves softly tapping against the hard surface.

He was potty trained, so I didn't have to worry about taking him outside. It weirded out Dad, but let's face it, Simon climbing down a tree in the middle of the night worried me, and just dropping poo from a tree on an unsuspecting animal or person would be downright disturbing.

Simon was smart, so teaching him to use the toilet was the right thing to do.

Simon stared at the closed bathroom door and tilted his head to look back at me.

When we first wandered into the main room of the cave, I knew this place was built as a guest house for the palace. I'd been here once before when I was younger, and it looked almost exactly the same. They sealed it a few years later, after Melina complained she would rather have people come stay with her.

Simon huffed in annoyance seeing the door was shut. "I don't know, buddy, maybe Valpar is in there. Remember, he gets grumpy when he's constipated."

Simon huffed and we walked around the room. If I remembered correctly, there was a door that led deeper into the unfurnished parts of the cave. Simon could wander around back there and maybe find a corner to go in. He would just have to be like a regular goat.

As we ventured deeper into the cave, our eyes fell upon the colossal door, its hinges encrusted with rust and burdened by its weight. With a strained effort, I tugged at its handle, and the door emitted a mournful groan. A gentle gust of wind whispered through the opening, sending shivers down my spine as my dress fluttered in the cold air.

"What do you think? Can you do your business in there?" Simon sniffed and walked in. I kept the door open so he could return, but he trotted down the cave toward a light at the far end of the winding passage, which suggested there was moonlight somewhere in there.

I shrugged my shoulders, left the door cracked so he could return and headed back into the main room of the cave. That was when I heard a grunt coming from the bathroom.

Oh, maybe he ate too much meat.

I'd heard Uncle Osirus talk about orcs eating a ton of meat and not enough veggies, when they come to these balls. He always had to ask the dragon shifters to bring in the cows and steers from up in the mountains. The big boar over the fire must be an animal they caught on the way up here.

Another groan came from the bathroom, but this time, a whisper of my name was there.

Is he thinking about me while he's pooping?

I tiptoed closer to the door and leaned my ear against it. There was movement on the other side, grunts and heavy breathing.

That must be one big—

"Calliope. Yes," he growled lowly.

I stood up straight and put my hand to my chest.

Oh, oh! He was not pooping, but doing the nasty in the bathroom.

And he didn't invite me!

Aren't we supposed to be mates? Isn't that my job to help him? *You know, take care of his male parts?* I've read about women taking care of men, but my experience was non-existent.

I put my ear back up to the door, because hearing my name on his lips was doing something to my body. It gave me the tingles from my nipples down to my pussy.

Cheese and crumbs, I wish I had enough confidence to just knock on the door, better yet, open the barrier between us and demand to help him.

But I wasn't there yet.

What if it was different looking? Everyone in the realm wondered what an orc *thing* looked like.

Valpar groaned again, and I cupped my breast with one hand, while the other trailed down my hip and between my legs. This was so hot and so steamy I couldn't stand it.

Oh, to be denied for so many years, and finally I could explore my sexual desires.

Shut up, Calliope, you sound ridiculous.

"Yes, female, so tight," he whispered harshly.

I nibbled on my lip, delicately circling my finger around my clit, yearning to replicate the sensation of Valpar's tongue. But it fell short. I craved his touch, the real thing.

I let the visions come, of how he roughly handled me, grabbing my hips and pulling me into his mouth, and how he wore my thighs like earrings until I felt myself build that amazing sensation. I heard Valpar's restrained grunt, and splashes hitting the floor.

And it kept coming.

He kept coming.

Goddess, how much does an orc come?

I couldn't finish, I was too much in awe of how much I heard hit the floor.

The sink turned on, my heart pounded in my chest, and I raced away from the door. I would not get caught, not yet.

I practically ran back to the bed, with my body on fire. It was like a different type of ache, and I needed relief badly.

Goddess, how much did an orc come? Was it the same as humans? Did he produce more because he's bigger?

Darn those romance books not talking about orc come.

I threw the furs over my body, rubbing my thighs together in an effort to quell the ache. But it only seemed to make it worse.

I waited for Valpar to open the door, but he never did. Instead, I heard him groaning again.

Goddess, is he doing it again?

Maybe I should just go back and knock on the door. Maybe he'll let me help him finish. Maybe he will do things to me—like he said he would.

Then fear took over. What if Karma was right? What if he was my babysitter?

I didn't want to be someone's problem. I didn't want to force him to do things to me but—I'm so needy right now.

I was lying on the bed, my hand rubbing roughly between my legs. But it was not enough. It was never enough when I thought about Valpar. I'd never had anyone look at me the way he did, and talk to me, not treat me like I would break.

He wanted me so ferally. And I wanted more of those grunts between my legs.

Cheesus. What was wrong with me?

I rubbed my fingers over my clit, beneath the blanket, too afraid to emerge and knock on the door. I continued feeling the wetness gather on my fingers until I dipped them inside. I hadn't explored myself, and I was excited to have a chance to as I pushed a finger inside.

I bit my lip, pushing it deeper and found a slightly rougher area, and I rubbed there several times, until I arched my back and threw my breasts out.

That's the spot.

I continued to rub it, inserting another finger. It was tight, but I knew I needed to stretch myself. Valpar was big. If I was going to have him inside me one day, I needed to make some room, right? He had to claim me at some point. What if he couldn't get in?

What if he had to force it inside?

The thought of that made me impossibly wetter.

"Mmhm, Valpar."

I felt my body seize and that delightful high reached its peak. I continued to pump my fingers, using my hips to pretend I was riding his...*thing*. Whatever it looked like.

I panted, now hot under the furs. I was tired, and the door left open for Simon to get back in made it colder. To make my body temperature even, I stuck one foot out, as my eyes grew heavy.

I hoped next time Valpar would make the move again. After hearing Karma's words, I didn't know if I ever wanted to make the first move. I didn't want to be a burden. I didn't want him to be just the human-sitter because I annoyed everyone.

I really wanted to believe he was my mate, that we were meant for each other.

I sniffed, taking in the deep breaths of the blankets he wrapped me in. He was sweet, taking care of me even after I went to bed without him. I just couldn't help myself. I was just so tired... and he made me feel so safe.

I yawned, and I felt the wetness between my legs drying.

I should clean up, but that would require me to get out of bed, use the bathroom and—I wasn't about to do that.

The shower turned on and I saw steam coming out from beneath the door. I hummed and laid my head back down on the pillow.

Tomorrow, tomorrow I'll get washed up.

Valpar

I couldn't believe what I had just heard outside of my door. My little human was touching herself. The sounds she made were like music to my ears, making my cock hard again. I had just finished emptying my shaft, trying to be as quiet as possible so she wouldn't hear me. But it seemed like she was too lost in her own pleasure to notice.

Goddess, she was driving me crazy.

I wanted nothing more than to burst through that door and take her for myself. But I couldn't do that, not yet. I had to win her over, prove myself and gain the trust of the female.

But hearing her moan and knowing what she was doing to herself was too much for me to handle. My hand automatically went down to my aching cock, again as it swelled, stroking its large bumps slowly as I listened.

I could imagine her lying on the bed, her hand between her legs, fingers working furiously on that tight little pussy of hers. And all of it was because of me. It had to be. The way I licked her cunt, how I tasted her this night. How could she forget it?

It took all of my willpower not to go over there and finish her off myself. But then I heard something new, a squelching sound, that made my shaft grow even more.

She was soaked, wetting my furs, letting it all seep deeply into the leathers. I would always smell her in our bedding.

I took a deep breath, pumping my shaft furiously, and watched my seed continue to drip down my length and onto the floor.

My sack was heavy. It continued to fill, ready to fill her, to fill her womb. I wasn't ready to fill her with orclings, I wanted just her. All to myself. To not share her with the realm.

My sack slapped against my thighs as I grew harder, then my miresa let out a squeak and my body shook as I held in my roar. My seed splattered against the tub as it shot out of my body, coating the marble. It landed with a loud noise, but I was too lost in my pleasure to care.

I turned on the shower and rinsed off my seed. The only smell I wanted was my miresa, so I quickly rinsed, grabbed my cloth, and wrapped it around my waist. Normally, I would sleep with no cloth, but since my miresa has never seen an orc's shaft—at least she better not have, and I growled at that thought alone—it was best to remain covered.

I opened the door, and her soft snores filled the room—along with her arousal. I took in deep breaths and my sack fills again. It pointed straight out, moving my cloth. The cloth we wore kept our thighs open for effortless movement of our legs and was just enough to cover our shafts and backsides. When we were hard, however—

Bassza, how did one not have this thing in the way all the time?

I went to my bag of supplies and pulled out leather straps for binding wood. I took the softest ones, the most used, and tugged on them, shaking my head. I would not scare my miresa, especially as young-looking as she was.

I took my shaft and pointed it downwards. I winced and groaned as I strapped it to my leg, to keep it from sticking out.

I guess there is a reason some male creatures wear pants.

But never this male.

I made adjustments to the bindings as I approached the bed, which reeked of her scent, and I growled within my chest as I lay upon it and lifted the furs to join her.

Bassza! I bit my lip and swore to the Moon Fairy; her legs were still wet!

One lick would not hurt, just one.

I leaned down and took a taste. I moaned into her leg, trying not to bite the supple meat there. She sighed as I did so, and I had to restrain myself from doing more.

Once she has had a proper sleep, I would wake her with my face in her cunt. I had permission to do so; she let me do it before.

Satisfied with my plan, I wrapped my arms around her and pulled her on top of my chest. She was like a limp doll. So small and fragile, but since she was gifted to me, I knew she was strong and hearty. She would take my cock nicely.

My miresa's legs barely reached around my stomach when she suddenly spread them. I tried not to imagine her cunt wide open, so close to my shaft.

Good thing it is tied.

I wrapped my arms around her and nuzzled my nose into her hair.

Mmm, this was a good night.

Chapter Fourteen

Calliope

THE SMELL OF THE sizzling bacon took away the sick feeling in my tummy. When I saw the raw meat I just about threw up in the basket. With my strong determination to show Valpar I was a good mate for him and that I wasn't weak and helpless, I got the bacon sizzling in no time.

When I woke up this morning, I found myself on top of his body. I left a little pool of drool on his chest, but I was in too much shock to wipe it away.

Did I climb up on top of him in my sleep?

I needed to rein in the eagerness here. He's gonna think I'm one of those fairy hoes.

I slid off his body, and the urge was strong to look under the blankets to check out what was going on beneath them. He didn't have morning wood, as I have often heard Mom call Dad's thing through the thin walls of our tree house.

Does that mean he didn't find me attractive?

Or maybe it wasn't morning at all? *Do male appendages have a timer in them, to know when it is morning?*

I quietly slid off the bed and ran to the doorway I left ajar for Simon. The light was streaming brighter down there than the moonlight.

Hmm, it was morning.

So, he wasn't so attracted to me, then.

He might be my babysitter, not my mate. I couldn't be for sure, yet.

To show my gratitude and to prove to him I could be a fit mate, I got the great idea to make breakfast. All men like food, Aunt Melina has once told me. Especially species that do a lot of manual labor, such as shifters. Valpar wasn't a shifter, but he looked like he did a lot of manual labor.

The muscles.

I wonder what he would look like chopping down a tree?

He would look like a hot lumber*snack.*

I snorted when I flipped the bacon over, and the hot grease flung back and hit me in the eye.

"Eeeek!" I covered my eye, and Simon wailed at my sudden movement.

Simon fell to the ground with a thud. Valpar jumped from the bed with a roar and ran to shield me. What from, I wasn't really sure.

"What happened? Who touched you?!" his voice was loud and echoed into the cave walls, making it sound louder than it really was.

"No one touched me!" I slapped his arm and pointed to the frying pan over the hearth. "I just got some bacon grease in my eye. It popped out of the pan and got me. It was an accident."

Valpar looked at me and back to the frying pan several times.

"Where did you get pig fat? Why are you cooking?" Valpar gazed around the room for the first time, seeing the torches lit along the walls and the big basket of food sitting on the table for two.

"Where, where did you get this food?" He waved his hand at the table. "Did you leave the cave? I sealed it off, female!" he growled and pulled me to him, smashing my face against his man boobs.

"I didn't leave, Simon brought it back," I mumbled into his chest.

Valpar pulled me back. "How did he get out?"

Simon yelled and stumbled when he tried to get up from fainting. He shook out his fur and stood up proudly.

"Simon and I always go to the market in the mornings. The market fills up a basket and I always let him carry it. Makes him feel important," I whispered. "I didn't go with him today. When I woke up it was already sitting on the table. I sent him through the cave passage down that way last night." I pointed to the other side of the cave, with the door. "You were taking too long last night, uh, pooping—" I blushed. "So, I had to let him out to go somewhere. I didn't know he could actually get out of the cave."

Valpar's face turned a deeper shade of green, and his hand ran down his face. "Bassza, I—" he groaned, pulled out the chair and sat down in it. It moaned under his weight, while I went back to the hearth, to take the rest of the bacon from the pan and plate it up for him.

I had a lot of bacon cooked and planned on giving it all to Valpar, so I took it and placed it in front of him. "Here, I made you breakfast!"

He stared down at it and his brow furrowed.

"Female, we need to talk," his voice was raspy, and instantly my shoulders dropped. When someone said they need to talk, it meant they were unhappy.

I lowered my head in shame and Valpar leaned over in his chair to wrap his hand around my waist, pulling me between his legs. He tilted my chin up with one finger and his eyes buried into my soul.

"You do not have to burden yourself to feed me a meal. I am a grown orc, I feed myself."

"But I wanted to," I argued back. "I wanted to show..."

"It is my duty as your male to feed you while I court you. I have failed you, again. I am to feed and provide. You are a good female trying to fill my belly, but let me do this."

I tilted my head to the side. "Oh." My face flushed. "So, orcs are supposed to feed their women first?"

Valpar grunted and picked up a piece of bacon. "I will need to be quicker on my feet with you, Calliope. You are faster than any female I thought I would receive. You are testing my abilities."

My shoulders slumped again. *I was making things hard for him. Like I do for everyone else.*

"I like it," Valpar added quickly. "I like you to test me, but you will not like it when I prevent you from besting me." He tapped my nose.

I thought about that for a moment. How would he keep me from besting him? Then, I remembered how Uncle Osirus kept Aunt Melina under control when she got too rowdy. It's a game for them, maybe it's a game for Valpar, too.

"So, to keep me from besting you, are you going to punish me?" I placed my hands on his chest. "Does this mean you are gonna spank me?"

Valpar's eyebrows rose high on his head, and my excitement soared. "Are you going to put me over your sturdy legs, and lift my dress and spank my bare bottom?"

Oh, I liked the sound of someone spanking me, and that someone being Valpar. He looked like he would follow through on his punishments.

Mom and Dad would never spank me when I did something wrong. In fact, they never punished me at all. They would scold me, then ignore me. Mom would just start blabbing, then go off and cook something, or tell Dad about it. He suggested taking something away from me like my coloring or writing journals. She said she could never do that. That I have been through enough.

Whatever that meant.

Hmm, maybe I was a bit of an attention seeker.

My butt tingled at the thought of Valpar spanking me. He wanted to take care of me, to make sure I was safe, and it was sweet. But playful spankings would be fun and sexy, too.

When I edged even closer, I tried to feel if his thing was there. I wiggled around and still didn't understand. Where was this thing? Before I could look down, he cupped my face and made me stare at his.

"Miresa, what are you doing to me?"

My eyes darted from side to side. I'm not sure what I was doing to him, I barely knew what I was doing half the time.

"I...don't know? I was just asking if spanking was a good enough punishment?"

Valpar groaned and scooted the chair back. "And is this supposed to be for punishment or pleasure, because your scent says pleasure?"

I trailed my tongue over my lips. "It can be both. One for keeping a mate safe and reminded of the rules, and one for playful smacks. At least, that is what Aunt Melina said."

Valpar studied me. "I think you would like both far too much. Being raised by fae has put funny things in your head. Did you spend a lot of time at the palace watching this sort of thing?"

I bit down on my cheek and nodded. "Well, I wasn't welcome to watch. They did it behind closed doors, but sometimes those doors were cracked."

I held up my thumb and pointer finger to show how wide the door would be. "I stopped watching when they started getting naked, though." I wrinkled my nose.

Valpar's mouth dropped open and his two big teeth looked even larger on the inside. "Wow, Mr. Orc, what big teeth you have!" I tapped them both with my fingers and he grabbed my wrists.

Valpar chuckled and held my hands in front of him. "We do need rules. You are silent and sneaky, and I need to protect you. No one will take my miresa, and you will not be sneaking and watching other mated couples during their—private moments." He wrinkled his face." Do you understand?"

"Yay, rules to break." I playfully shoved his shoulder, but he didn't laugh, instead he pulled me closer.

"How about I get a switch instead of my hand? How does that sound?" He raised an eyebrow in warning.

I covered my butt and shook my head. I wanted his hand to touch my butt, not a switch.

Nope, that didn't sound fun at all. It made my pussy dry, and even my lower lips sucked right up in my vagina.

Satisfied with himself, Valpar sat back in his chair. He wasn't wearing the dress pants he was last night. Today, it was a long loincloth that left little for the imagination. Well, actually it left a lot, because I still couldn't see the *little orc*. Which didn't look like a *little* orc because it was on the inside of his leg, covered by a loose leather cloth, and the outline was enormous and rather bumpy.

I hoped it wasn't sick.

Valpar caught me staring, cleared his throat and stood. "Tell me where this door is that Simon got through. We need to close it so your scent doesn't attract anyone."

Darn, those cloths must be magnetic to cover it because his thighs were on display, but his thing and his bootylicious butt and crack were covered just so.

So disappointing.

Once I led him to the door, he shut it, using the lights that covered the cave walls, as he took a large timber of wood to close it.

"What if you're pooping again, and Simon needs to go potty?" I asked. I didn't want to call him out for taking care of himself in the bathroom, yet. I think that was a little premature to do that.

Valpar froze and let out a breath. "I wasn't—ah, wait. Why does Simon need to use the bathroom?" He stared at Simon, who decided at that moment to walk into the bathroom. He kicked the door shut, and we heard little farts come from inside.

"To go potty, duh? He's potty trained. He's super smart. Me being his person, it's my job." I puffed out my chest.

The toilet flushed, and out came Simon, who let out a loud yell and walked past Valpar. Simon didn't take his eyes off my mate; he wasn't too trusting of anyone, and after Valpar said he was going to eat him, I didn't blame him.

Valpar on the other hand, looked utterly confused, and I wasn't sure why. Has he not seen a goat that could go to the bathroom? I've never been to the Monktona Wood before, but surely, they have some pretty cool animals where he's from.

"Do you have a pet?" I asked walking back toward the kitchen area. I pulled out some muffins and fruit, and began munching on them while I leaned on the table.

Valpar strode over, rubbing his temples with one hand. "I have a companion who I share a bond and understanding with."

"So, a pet," I said, between bites.

"No, he isn't a pet. He doesn't sleep in my bed, eat my food or use the *toi-let*."

I wagged my finger at him. "Simon isn't my pet. I am his person, his emotional support person. If he didn't have me, he would be falling over all the time. Now, he only does it some of the time."

Valpar didn't look convinced. Instead, he sighed, picked me away from the table and set me on his lap, taking away the muffin I was eating. "Hey! That's mi—"

He put it up to my lips and I took a bite.

"I will feed you from now on. Do you understand? This is rule one."

I frowned while I swallowed. "What if you aren't around and I'm starving? My stomach is eating itself alive. Can I eat on my own?"

Valpar frowned deeply. "No, because you will never be alone. You will always be with me."

"I don't see how that will be possible." I folded my arms to match his.

Valpar chuckled mischievously and, for the first time, gave me a big smile. "No, because you will be tied to me, with a long rope like a tiny orcling. You will never be out of my sight again."

Chapter Fifteen

Valpar

My miresa gasped. "You cannot tie me to you! I am not a child!" She squirmed, attempting to free herself from my lap, but I held her firmly, enclosing her in my embrace. I inhaled deeply, savoring the sweet scent of her hair as I pressed my nose against it.

"You are quiet and tricky like a fae, I will not have you running off on me again."

Calliope stilled and turned her head. "You think I'm like a fae?" She smiled widely. "Truly?"

I frowned and brushed her wild, pink hair from her face. "Why does being a fae mean that much to you? You are human, be proud of your species. You are soft and smell much better than those flying balls of glitter and light."

Calliope scoffed and shook her head. "I was raised by fae, so, I think it's only natural to want to be like my parents."

When I gazed over my mate, I saw she looked nothing like King Osirus, and I had not seen her parents, whom I now believe are fae. It made me wonder what her lineage was and how she was here.

"Where do you come from, little fairy? Why do you have the fae raising you?"

My miresa bit her lip, the sound of a soft whimper escaping her delicate lips. I gently used my claw to pry her plump lip from between her teeth, feeling the warmth of her skin against my touch. A powerful urge surged through me, compelling me to bring her lip into my mouth, to savor its taste and engage in this intimate mouth dance, that I had witnessed countless mated couples perform at the balls.

Thorn had always been oblivious to the mouth dance. He was always talking to the kings and queens about the security since the wall came down, letting the ogres roam their lands. But I had watched, and I very much wanted to mouth dance.

"Tell me, female." I urged her as she continued to stare at me.

"My dad isn't really my dad," she admitted. I took a minute to hunt inside my head for the term *dad* and tilted my head upwards. I believed it was a common term that humans, and even creatures around here, used. *Dad* had the same meaning as orgamo, which orcs used.

I nodded for her to continue.

"And my mom, well, she isn't really my mom. She is my mom's sister." *Mom is ogamie.*

I gently glided my hand, tracing a soothing path up and down her back, feeling the softness of her skin beneath my fingertips. As I did so, I noticed a subtle shift in her demeanor - my miresa appeared to be filled with a sense of shame. I remained perplexed as to why her ogamie's sister had taken on the responsibility of caring for my beloved miresa. However, I chose to be patient, allowing her the space and time to reveal the truth in her own way.

Drawing her closer to me, I could feel the warmth of her presence against my chest. A low, comforting rumble emanated from deep within me, as if offering solace to her burdened soul. In that moment, she surrendered, leaning into me.

Yes, I was being a good mate. I could do this.

"I don't remember my real mom. I remember little of Earth. Mom, that isn't really my mom, but I call her that because I don't remember my other mom—" My miresa continued to ramble and I smiled.

I don't think I have smiled as much, since the day I found out the wall would come down and I would find a miresa of my own.

"Mom said she took me from Earth, with Birch. That is Uncle Osirus' brother. He found Mom— her name is Theresa by the way," Calliope played with her fingers, "and they brought me here. That's what they said, anyway. The only memories I remember are waking up in Uncle Osirus' palace with everyone standing around me. Osirus, Melina, Mom, Birch and a sorceress named Tahlia."

I hummed and threaded my claws through her hair. I did not like where this was going. She had no memories of her past? Of Earth, where she was born, or her birth ogamie? "And how old were you then?" I tried not to sound upset, or pry. These were things I needed to know. I wanted to know everything about her and her connections with the royalty here and her parents.

Where were her parents?

"It was just after the war when I was brought here; fifteen?" Her finger traced over a large scar on my knee. "What happened here?"

I delicately weaved my fingers through her hair, gently untangling each knot. The lustrous texture of her flowing locks captivated me, shimmering like silk under my touch. The subtle fragrance wafting from her tresses enveloped me, calming the drums in my chest. "I didn't get it from the war, if that is what you are thinking. I was a foolish orcling and caught myself in a trap."

Her eyes widened. "It's a big scar."

Does she always skip to the next subject so quickly?

I chuckled. "My seeded orgamo, that is my father who planted his seed in my ogamie,- my *mom*, set a trap for an ogre. Have you heard of them?"

My miresa nodded quickly. "Yes, if I ever hear or smell one, because they stink something hideous, I am to hide, preferably in a field of flowers, so they can't smell me. They have bad noses."

My miresa was smart. "My good, fairy. You always do that. If for any reason I am not around, you continue to do this, but you will not have to worry about being alone anymore because I will protect you." I squeezed her hip, and her eyes widened. "You like it when I say you are my good fairy, don't you?" She nodded slowly.

Did her orgamo and ogamie not praise her enough? Did they not watch her enough? By the gods under the soil, why would they let her be alone.

Unless she was escaping all the time, she seemingly has a tendency to get into trouble.

"But, yes, my orgamo told me to stay home and tend to chores. I didn't listen, and the trap he set had serrated edges to snap onto the leg of an ogre. I decided to track my orgamo, and instead of looking at the footpath where a trap could have been set, I placed my foot in the middle, setting off the blade. I wasn't quick enough to escape. It grazed my leg, leaving a large gash. If I was a second later, I would have lost my leg."

My miresa placed her hand over it. "How old were you?"

"A young orcling, many, many moons ago. I healed quickly but my ogamie was furious with me. She made me stay in the cabin for weeks as punishment. Just as I will make you do if you disobey me."

Calliope crossed her arms. "How can I disobey you if I'm always tied to you?"

I barked out a laugh and rubbed my hand over her head. "Ah, that will keep you out of trouble and not hidden in our cabin, won't it?"

"No, it won't, I'll find other ways to annoy you." She stuck out her tongue.

My miresa was feisty and bratty. Her innocence and freedom were clear, and I couldn't determine if it was due to her upbringing by the fae or her memory loss. What in the Moon Fairy's name happened to her?

"Miresa, you are twenty-five now?"

She hummed in agreement. "Yesterday was my first time attending a ball, though. Uncle Osirus has been trying to get me to go since I was eighteen, but Mom is really protective of me. She doesn't let me do anything." She rolled her eyes. "I have to sneak out to have any fun and then I get caught. She just tells me not to do it again, so, of course I'm just gonna." She laughed and slapped her knee. "Silly Mom."

Hmm, yes. Silly.

My miresa should have been attending the ball for years, so that meant her brain was not that of a child. She was considered an adult in both body and mind. Then, why was she so playful?

But even the queen could lack common sense when she was playful with the king. Perhaps this was just a courting gesture?

I scratched my chin and watched her as she petted her companion. I dared not even think to call this goat a pet, because I believe she would scold me. She had an intuition about certain things. She did not fear me, and she seemed to trust me.

For now.

I had vows to keep, and Calliope is one who would be devastated if I do not keep them. I could tell just by her personality. If I said I would hang a star for her in the night sky, I best do it.

I placed another bite of muffin in her mouth. She said nothing as I fed her and continued to thank the Moon Fairy for this gift in my lap. It wasn't long until the peace was broken when I heard murmurs down the passageway, on the other side of the rock wall I replaced so no one could get inside.

"We know you are in there," I heard. My hearing wasn't as strong as a shifter, but I did know it was a male, muffled voice. *"Valpar, you need to come out. We must speak with you."*

I growled and held my miresa tightly in my lap. *Mine.*

"What's wrong, big guy, did you want a muffin to?" She took a muffin from the table and placed it next to my mouth. I took it in one bite and sucked on her fingers. She gasped as I licked each one, and the blacks of her eyes grew wide.

Bassza! I wanted her now! She tasted so good on my tongue, and it wasn't even her cunt I was tasting.

"My miresa, you need to stay here. There are visitors on the other side of the boulders."

Calliope's body perked up and she tried to get off my lap. "Oh, I wanna go meet them! Maybe it's Uncle Osirus and Aunt Melina!" She threw her hand out in front of her, reaching for the passageway.

I gently grasped her waist, lifting her effortlessly, and guided her towards the plush bed. As I reached down, I seized the smooth leather ropes strewn across the floor. The air was filled with a mix of anticipation and forbidden desire. She resisted, refusing to stay put, while I remained resolute in my decision to shield her from her family's gaze. No soul should lay eyes upon her until she was rightfully claimed and marked by the undeniable imprint of my brand; my cock.

"Hey! What's the big idea! Put me down!" Calliope yelped, when I set her on the bed and tied the leather on her ankle, and then to the bedpost.

"We don't know who is on the other side. You will stay here, tied to the bed until I return," I growled, tying her securely.

Her tiny drum beat as quickly as a hummingbird's when she tried to kick me. "You cannot tie me up! That's... You can't!" I grunted and stood as I gathered the other rope and tied her wrists. I will not be outdone by this female.

"What if I have to pee!?" she argued.

"Do you need to go now?" I raised an eyebrow.

Her jaw tightened. "Yes, I do. Now let me go." I took her wrist and felt her drum beating in her body, feeling for the lie.

"Do you need to go to the bathroom, my little fairy? Don't lie, if you lie you will be punished. If you tell me the truth, I will reward you."

My miresa's cheeks turned a beautiful pink. "W-what kind of reward?"

I smirked, leaned forward and whispered in her ear. "I shall taste between your legs again and stretch your body so you can take me. You are quite small for my shaft."

Calliope gasped, but along with it I smelled the hefty scent of musk that fluttered into the air.

Hmm, rewarding her will be much better than punishing her. The thought of her over my knee, though, her tiny ass in the air and reddened by my hand. Why does that seem so appealing?

She calmed.

"Good fairy. I will be back soon. Don't move." I turned my back and made my way down the passage.

"Ha, sure thing, Mr. Meanie," she snapped. I turned my hand and held up my finger. "That is one, if I get to three you will be punished for your sharp tongue!"

She licked her lips. "That a promise?"

This. Female.

My steps hastened, wanting to get back to my miresa. More and more, I want to take her into my mouth and explore her. My shaft was constantly restrained, rubbing against the leather. I groaned as I tried to get relief from the tightness of the bond to my leg, but there would be no relief. Not until she learned of my anatomy.

I stopped, regardless of the incessant yelling on the other side of the boulder.

Had she seen another male's appendage? The thought had come to me before, but now I was even more angered by it.

I would have to kill them.

I grunted, finding my strength and pushed the boulder to the side. A male voice told people to step away, and the dust settled to reveal King Osirus, his mate and my brother Sugha, on the other side.

Bassza! Why not bring the entire tribe?

I stood in front of everyone, my fists clenching, my breath still heaving from moving the heavy boulder. I would not let them inside.

"Did you think that we wouldn't find her?" Osirus gave an amused smirk. "Simon, obviously, doesn't trust you."

"You gave the goat the basket?" I jutted my chin toward the King.

Melina raised her hand and waved. "I did. He came right to the palace. I gave Simon the basket to make her think that he just went to the market. Calliope and Simon always go, it's their thing. One of the guards followed Simon back and told us where you were. And I would be careful how you speak about Simon. Simon and Calliope are besties."

I sighed heavily. "The goat doesn't like me."

"You threatened to eat it, didn't you?" Sugha snorted, trying to contain his laughter.

"I did not know the goat was her companion. Once you get a miresa, I cannot wait to watch how you handle her!" I stomped toward him to hit him in the face and match bruise on the other side of his face. He dodged and hopped on my back to pull my hair. "Get off, you worthless piece of fungus!" I pulled on his leg while he laughed, and I slung him onto the ground. He continued to laugh as I huffed.

Osirus pinched the bridge of his nose and sighed. "Valpar, we have something important to discuss. First, where is Calliope? Melina and Sugha can keep her company."

I cleared my throat and straightened my shoulders. "No one will see her. She's mine. I don't need my brother to try and take her from me." I glared at him. "And I don't need your miresa trying to talk her into leaving the cave without me. She's mine!" I roared, banging my chest.

Sugha covered his mouth, his eyes darting between me and the king. "Wow, I guess orcs get unstable with this whole miresa-mate thing, huh?"

The king nodded. "Noted. You orcs are possibly more possessive than the shifters. It's rather fascinating to me, but her parents won't be pleased."

Melina scoffed. "This should have happened years ago. Valpar should have taken her sooner; my girl needs to get laid. With that being said, I need to go talk to her. She snagged herself an orc and I need to tell my girl some moves." She pushed her hips forward and backward. "I'm super jealous. She will be one of the first humans to get some orc dick—"

"Darling!" The king snapped. The king's eyes lit up a bright gold, his eyes narrowing at his female. "Calliope will be quite fine. She's read enough of those books you kept sneaking into her room. Now behave."

The queen's smile turned mischievous. "You think so? You know how she can be sometimes. A bit oblivious, but she is quite resourceful. Where is she, Valpar?" Melina smiled sweetly, and I got an uneasy feeling in my stomach.

"She is tied to the bed where she will remain. What do you want? I will not give her back."

The queen's bright wings fluttered excitedly. "I bet she loves that," she whispered to Osirus.

These fae.

The king untied the top part of his tunic, letting the light sources beam down on him. "Come Valpar, it's best we talk about Calliope in private. I'm sure you will want to understand where she has come from and why she is the way she is."

"She's perfect," I roared as I stepped forward. "I wouldn't change a thing about her. I dislike how you speak of her that way."

Osirus gave a small smile, his eyes twinkling with warmth. "It's true you are best for her, no doubt about that, but even you must recognize she acts differently than most of the souls you've met in Bergarian thus far?"

My rigid stance softened, and I loosened my fists. It was true, she was different, but I hadn't spoken to any other human before. The only concerns I had were why she did not remember her past and why did she hold hardly any fear. The king would have the answers.

Whatever it was, Calliope was perfect for me.

"Fine," I heaved out a breath. "No one enters the cave." I crossed my arms.

"Fine." Melina crossed her arms in return. "We will wait until you and Osirus are done. Just hurry, I can't guarantee how long your bonds will keep Calliope in place." She brushed her nails over her dress.

"What?" I turned around as she stood guard by the cave entrance.

"I've taught her everything she knows when it comes to restraints. She can get out of any knot." She wiggles her eyebrows.

I chuckled deeply. "Well, if she wants to be rewarded, she won't leave the bed."

CHAPTER SIXTEEN

Valpar

I REFUSED TO VENTURE too far from the mouth of the cave. The queen was standing just at the edge, talking to my brother. They were highly engaged in conversation.

Too engaged.

Were they plotting something?

"I'm not going to sugarcoat about Calliope's past, Valpar. I don't think orcs appreciate fluff in conversation," Osirus said as he put his hands behind his back.

No, we didn't. We took what we wanted; we meant what we said. We don't like formalities with other species. They were pointless. The peace treaties we all signed with each kingdom were not straightforward. There were balls and handshaking, bowing, for-mal cloths and showing best behavior before we signed a piece of paper. I would rather poke out my own eyes with my sword and willfully let a vampire feed off my ass than do the extra fairy-glitter defecating nonsense these creatures wanted.

"Is it about my miresa not knowing her past?" I snapped. "I do not care where she comes from. She is mine and I won't give her up."

The king's eyes widened slightly, and he sighed. "Ah, at least she has told you that much. And that her parents aren't her blood?"

I nodded. I still haven't figured that out, and I knew my miresa didn't understand it either. She didn't care to know though.

"I have brothers," the king began. "Five of them, to be exact. They all left Bergarian many years ago for Earth to look for their destined ones and explore new lands. My brother Birch was one of the lucky ones, and he found Theresa. A human. She agreed to be mated, bonded and become like him, but before she did so, she worried for her niece. Theresa's sister, Hattie, was—troubled." Osirus' lip curled into a snarl and his wings turning a hint of black.

"Hattie was sick, both in mind and body. Theresa said it happened to humans when they consumed drugs that were meant to heal the body, but used them to make themselves feel good. They got a high or a rush. They didn't think straight, and they couldn't take care of themselves, let alone a child." Osirus stared out over the sea, a distant look in his eye.

Does this mean she couldn't take care of a child, of my Calliope?

"Hattie couldn't get enough of these human drugs. It started shortly after Calliope was born, when the father left. I'm guessing she was trying to numb her heart."

"Father—?"

"Her seeded orgamo. He left her and her ogamie." Osirus knew of our terms, thank the Moon Fairy. These creatures had many words with the same meaning. It was frustrating.

How could an orgamo leave his seeded? I have never heard of such a thing. An orcling was precious, cherished. How could one leave a female and their seeded? My drum beat furiously in my chest. And then her mother, she made herself sick. She wanted to forget the orgamo, but forgot her orcling. Why? Why would she forget such a beautiful person like Calliope?

Hattie could have given that love to her child instead of ignoring such a precious gift. I gritted my teeth, my brow furrowing in anger. I let out a low growl, my fist balled up and I banged on the tree that we stood under.

"I do not understand human thinking, Valpar. Each soul deals with pain differently, especially humans—"

"No excuse," I snapped. "What happened? How was Calliope raised? What happened since this human was tainted with these *drugs*?"

Osirus' jaw clenched, his wings' veins now fully black, filled with anger. I do not believe I have seen them this black since the war.

"Calliope was ignored most of her life. Neglected. She went to school, but received bare minimum attention. Several times, Theresa went to collect Calliope from Hattie, even called the proper authorities in the human realm, but like most things in the human realm, Calliope slipped through the cracks. Calliope was stuck with her mother."

A growl erupted from my chest as I heaved my breath in and out.

"With Birch's help, they stole Calliope in the night and took her away. It took them several weeks to get her strong enough to make the journey to the portal and arrive at the palace. She slept the whole way, slept for days, like she hadn't slept in years." He rubbed a hand down his face, pacing in front of me.

"I knew Calliope was going to be stunned when she woke. She was slowly waking up as Birch carried her up the steps to me. Melina and I greeted them, when Calliope finally opened her eyes." Osirus winced. "Calliope was weak, thin, tinier than she is now. She had raven black hair, gray skin, but those eyes, they were still as blue as the ocean. Still light in there, even after all she had been through." Osirus swallowed and turned to me. "She was a fighter. She hadn't given up. I was waiting for her to scream, to shout, something, because she still didn't know that Birch was a fae yet and here she was, at a palace with Melina's wings on full display and me in my garments." Osirus put his hand over his mouth as if he couldn't speak.

"She didn't, though, she didn't scream. Your mate looked straight up at me and asked me, 'Did I die? Am I in heaven, now?'"

I had never seen King Osirus shed water from his eyes, except for when Melina was stabbed during the war. He thought he was losing her; thank the Moon Fairy he didn't. Now, he looked as if he was going to shed water again.

For the second time in my life, I felt heat in my eyes as well. Water gathered there, and I wondered if I might let a stream run down my face. To imagine if my Calliope would have never arrived, to not have gotten well? I would have been a lost orc and truly alone. I would have never had her.

"Calliope spoke little. She wouldn't tell us everything that happened in that house. Theresa said the house was worn down. Men and women frequently came in and out of it, and Calliope slept in the cold basement. That's where they found her," Osirus sobered.

I growled. "This female better be dead, or I shall go and hunt her down."

Osirus' wings faded back to their opaqueness, his shoulders relaxing. "A year after Calliope's arrival, I ventured to Earth with Melina to do just that. She's gone. There is nothing to worry about there." He waved his hand and turned his back.

"The reason I tell you these things, Valpar, is that I had a powerful sorceress, Taliyah, rid Calliope of her nightmares and memories of her past. That was Calliope's one wish. To start a new life, here." The king turned to me, with his hands folded gently in front of him. "At first, I was against it, but the way she pleaded to forget her mother, what she went through, I couldn't say no. She was old enough, and been through so much I could not deny her such a request."

I swallowed heavily and gazed back at the cave. My brother was yelling inside, most likely talking to my miresa to keep her company. I didn't care. My insides were out of sorts. My miresa had suffered much before me, and she didn't even remember it.

"What sort of memories did she want to forget?" I rasped.

Osirus shook his head. "As I said before, she didn't want to talk about it. She wrote a letter, however, when she was trying to get through the pain on her own, the first couple months before we wiped her memory. She thought writing it down would help her get her emotions out. It never did." He pulled a parchment out of his coat. It was worn, like it had been folded and unfolded many times and held the king's seal.

"I'll always remember the scars on her arms, how skittish she was. Calliope feared for everything that moved. She trusted Theresa the most because she knew that Theresa always tried to get her away from that situation. It took longer for her to trust the rest of us, but soon we were a close-knit unit."

I licked my lips. My pain for my miresa was now my own, yet she did not feel it. How was I to keep this from her, to know that her life before Bergarian was troublesome, and now it was all sunshine to her.

I let out a frustrated grunt. "And why are you telling me this? I would have accepted her no matter what." *Even if some male had touched her. She was mine, and I would find out who had touched her, even if that meant going to the Earth Realm.*

Osirus smiled and his wings fluttered in excitement. "I knew you would, and I know you would never give up on her. I think that is why the Moon

Goddess chose you for her. You are strong, capable and possessive. You will protect her at all costs, especially now that you know what she's been through."

"I would protect her as fiercely as if I had never known of her past, King Osirus. She is my gem, the third light source of my life. There is no other." I vowed.

The king's smile widened, his fangs descending. "Of course. And with that, I have advice and a warning."

I did not need to be given a warning. If he thought I would hurt her he was mistaken, and I did not care if he was a royal; I would run my blade, my claw, my teeth through his tiny little neck if he thought I would do anything to hurt her.

"One," Osirus held up one finger. "The spell we cast, took away her memories of her past and her scars. She has no fear. She trusts everyone, like a child would. The fears she may have could be irrational, such as thunderstorms or a tiny bug." He smiled at that.

I grunted. Good, then I would appear even stronger to my miresa.

"Two, she needs boundaries set, even punishments." He raised an eyebrow. "Theresa and Birch have been too soft with her. She gets into trouble. Falling off of balconies and trees, not doing what she's told. She needs warnings and punishment. Theresa and Birch don't have the heart to do it, but it is necessary. She needs a good spanking, and not just the fun kind." He winked.

I rubbed my chin and smirked. "We have already talked about this. I will make sure she will not leave my sight."

"I figured as much. And three," Osirus rubbed the back of his neck. "The spell we cast; it erased the memory of the abuse. She is who she is; her personality, her love, the hope, is all who she is if the darkness did not befall upon her." Osirus' eyes softened and he crossed his arms. "When you mate her, bond her—"

"Brand," I said. "When I brand her."

"Yes, that," Osirus replied uncomfortably. "When you brand her, the spell, the block we have on her mind, it might break."

I stopped breathing. "W-what do you mean?"

"I mean, the spell might break. The memories she once had might come flooding back. Calliope may remember who she was. She could have nightmares again; she could become sad. Relive what she never got over." Osirus frowned and stepped forward, putting his hand on my arm. "I'm telling you this to warn you, Valpar. It may not happen at all. It was a powerful spell, but with you branding her, making her your own and your kind being immune to magic it—it's just a possibility. If it happens, we can't do the spell again."

The drum in my chest shook, beating several times before I thought it stopped completely. I did not want my miresa to feel any pain once I claimed her as mine. I didn't want her to think of her past. I did not want her to know what it was like before she came here. I want her to always be my happy little fairy.

If I claimed her, branded her—she would be sad.

"Valpar, do not overthink this. You must brand her. You have to make her yours." Osirus said firmly. "The Moon Goddess demands it. It will hurt both you and her if you don't."

"I do not want to hurt her," I whispered. "I don't want her sad. I never want to see her cry."

Only cry for pleasure, not pain.

Osirus patted my arm again. "The Moon Goddess takes care of all of her children. I know of a mated couple where the female went through many, many trials in her life. They have lost a child, they were kidnapped —"

My head darted to Osirus.

"— despite that, they love each other. The trial has made their bond stronger. They still look for her and have hope. You have forever together, only if you complete the bond, Valpar. You and Calliope will get through this. Do not wait because of your fears. Or hers."

That was easy for him to say. I just received my female, and now I feared I might ruin everything. She came to me so easily, unafraid and now I knew why. She feared no one, because of a spell.

The bond was still there, but now there was a pain in my chest. I rubbed where my chest felt heavy. I did not know if it was my pain I felt or my female's, my Calliope's.

"Don't." Osirus took the parchment from his pocket and put it into my hand. "Do not treat her differently now that you know. She hates it. She wants to be normal, and you see her as normal when no one else sees her as such. You are irrational, demanding, controlling, and she needs that. Be the orc you were before you came out of the cave."

I groaned and held the parchment in my hand. "What's this?"

"Calliope's letter to herself. Her past self to her future self. You have the choice to give it to her or not, she has no memories of writing it, but once she sees the handwriting she will know it's from her." King Osirus pointed to the parchment in my hand. "Her family wanted to keep it from her. Keep her in the dark and never put her through that pain again, but I am giving it to you. Let her read it and let her have the choice." I promised I would make sure her mate would receive this when the time came. That he would know when the right time would be to give it to her."

I did not like this. I did not want to be the one to give my mate pain. I did not want her to open this letter, either. How could I be the bearer of bad news to the other half of my soul.

I let out a painful grunt, casting my eyes down and away from him.

Osirus chuckled. "You know, Calliope didn't believe she would get a mate after all that she had been through. Let alone have someone to care for her. And here you are."

"And you knew?" I eyed him suspiciously.

Osirus eyed the parchment. He put his hands behind his back, walking back toward the cave where Queen Melina and my brother were nowhere to be found.

Bassza. Those fools.

"I'm a king, Valpar. I know everything."

CHAPTER SEVENTEEN

Calliope

VALPAR REALLY SUCKED AT tying rope.

It was a basic handcuff knot with rope twine. It was kinda funny because even Simon could bite through the stuff with a few minutes of nibbling.

The question was, did I sit there like a good girl, or get out of it and march right out of the cave and take a punishment?

Decisions, decisions.

On one hand, it made my tummy flutter with excitement to wait for Valpar to come back and see his mate sitting waiting for him. On the other, seeing him get all mad and gruffy and put me over his leg was exciting in itself. I wanted to see if he would follow through with a punishment.

I've never really had a good punishment. Spanking looked like fun, and with some of those books I read, it was more than the sexual part I craved.

It was the care that came with it. It was how the person delivering the punishment showed their love.

On the outside it sounded twisted and messed up, but I really wanted that. Mom and Dad just ignored my cries for attention, ignored the unacceptable behavior, when I was basically screaming for them to pay attention to me.

"Calliope!" I heard my name sung at the mouth of the cave. My ears perked up and my back straightened. It was Aunt Melina.

"Hi!" I waved both hands in the air, knowing dang well they couldn't see me.

I snorted and Simon let out a bleat of excitement.

Aunt Melina always gave him treats. He trotted closer to the passageway, and I still had that decision to make.

Do I make a break for it?

Valpar's head between my legs was pretty tempting.

Good girl or bad girl?

"How's it going? Is Valpar treating you right?" Her voice echoed, and I nodded my head.

Oh, right, she can't see.

"Yup, kinda caveman-like, but that's okay. The matching cave works great. He tied me up and everything."

There was laughter echoing down the passage, and soon footsteps followed. Why they were coming in the cave I wasn't sure. I didn't think Valpar would let them inside.

He didn't leave, did he?

Surely he wasn't tired of me already?

I pouted while I sat there waiting, and Aunt Melanie and Sugha appeared. Simon yelled and ran towards Sugha.

"It's my favorite goat, and human! Hi, Calliope!" Sugha lowered himself to pet Simon, and Simon rubbed his horns all over the orc. At least Simon got along with one of the big green men, if only Valpar hadn't threatened to eat him.

Was still out there?

Melina pranced over to the bed and landed at my side, as she studied the ropes. "This is a terrible knot," she said. "You should have been able to get out of these by now, why not?"

"I'm still deciding between the two P's."

"Two P's?" Sugha stood and sat on the chair in the kitchen area. He was leaner than Valpar, more of a slim athletic build, and had a short haircut, very different from the rest of the orcs at the ball. I guess you could say he was more—indoctrinated into the ways of Bergarian.

Melina nodded. "Yes, the two P's. Pleasure or punishment. Is she gonna be a good girl or a bad girl? She gets it from me." She puffed out her chest. "What are you feeling up to, Calliope? Have you figured out what you want?"

"I don't know, is Valpar still out there?" I nodded my head to the mouth of the cave.

Melina made a face. "Duh, he's talking to Osirus." She nudged me with her elbow. "Guy stuff."

Oh. My shoulders relaxed. Good, he hasn't tired of me *yet.*

"Well, what's your decision? The P's?" Melina prodded.

I shook my head. "No. I've only had a little bit of one of them so far, and I want more of that one."

Melina smiled and shoved my shoulder. "Atta girl. You got time to explore each. You picked the right place for that, too. That door over there—" She pointed to a large wooden one on the other side of the room with a large, heavy chair blocking it. "— has a bunch of toys inside. There is a chest full of dildos, and some straps, so if Valpar wants to take some in his ass, he can." Melina winked and my face grew red.

I started giggling uncontrollably when she did, too. I didn't think I could ever do that to Valpar. I would have to stand up while he was bent over.

Plus, Valpar is too dominant, I don't think he would want anything in his butt.

"They are all brand new," Melina blurted, "the dildos. Before we sealed the cave this was Odessa and Creed's rutting cave, slash, my parents' home away from home. But then, Creed and Odessa started having all those dragon babies, and they made a cave closer to the tribe so they could come home if they really needed to. And my parents, I force them to stay in the palace now, because I'm worth it." Melina fluttered her lashes and flipped her hair.

Sugha's eyes bounced between us. He looked very lost.

"What's a... *dil-do*?" Sugha tilted his head and scratched his cheek. "Does my future miresa need one? Do I need a collection?"

We both started laughing hysterically, flopping all over the bed.

"I don't know. Depends on your girl." Melina cackled. "If your height has anything to do with the size of your dick, I don't think that you will need them. Sometimes females and even males like to experiment, put things in places that might be *taboo*."

Sugha tapped his temple. "Do you have a book for me to study? I want to know all these things my miresa might like."

Melina rubbed her hands together. "Yes, I certainly do. I'll help you once we leave here. But right now, let's concentrate on you, Calliope. Do you have questions? I didn't get to speak with you before you were carried off by that barbarian. It was rather hot. It is the talk of the kingdom, you know."

I bit my lip and tried not to smile. "I liked it a lot. Last night, I felt like I was part of my own fairy tale."

Melina's smile was soft, but there was a sadness in her eyes that she sometimes got, like she was remembering something. I've never asked what it was, because I was afraid she would cry if I did. "That's wonderful. I'm so happy you are getting your fairy tale, Calliope." She held my hand and squeezed.

I beamed and gave her a big hug. Her wings fluttered, and I heard her sniffle before she pulled me up by my shoulders. "Do I need to give you a lesson about the birds and the bees?"

I gave her a bewildered look. "I've read enough romance stories. I know what happens." I looked away, my face turning red. Sugha was watching intently.

"I do have questions for Sugha, though!" I pushed my tied hands out to Sugha, and he pressed his hand to his bare chest.

"Me?" He squeaked. "What would you want to ask me?"

I got more comfortable on the bed, wiggling my butt into the furs. "Valpar wasn't honest with me in the beginning. I need to make sure what he has told me is the truth."

Sugha rolled his eyes. "I knew him being a grouchy piece of fungus would bite him in his rump one day. What do you need, little fairy? I'll tell you everything you want to know."

Sugha brought his chair closer to the bed, and Simon laid his head on his thigh.

"Well, what do orcs call their mates?"

"Miresa," he said simply. "We call them miresas. I plan on calling my miresa, 'mate', from the start. I have studied the book quite well, and I still study it every day."

"Book?" I asked. "What book?"

Melina put her hand on my arm, rubbing it gently. "Queen Clara made a book for the orcs, and it helped them understand the different female and male species of Bergarian. There is even a section on humans, since more have come into the Bergarian Realm. It talks about body parts, culture, certain words that we use. That's why we have the balls. The Moon Goddess promised them mates, but it has taken time to find them since—"

"We're different," Sugha interrupted. "Most of the realm shifts into animals or into humanoid bodies. We don't. We stay green, and we are monsters to much of Bergarian. Even our shafts are different." He looked away. "Some species are just curious what hides behind our cloth, but we have waited this long for our mates, and we will wait longer for them without exposing ourselves. Valpar became bitter that we hadn't found the females promised to us. He was always a bit of a grouch, though." Sugha winked at me.

"I like him grouchy, it's like a gift when he smiles," I said.

Sugha barked out a laugh. "What? Valpar smiled? Never, I don't believe it!"

I nodded, my face turning red again.

"Valpar is a good orc, Calliope. And I know he ran away at first. It was because he thought you were too good to be true, and he would rather believe you weren't real, at all, than to be disappointed. He is your mate." He wagged his finger at me. "I've known my brother a long, long time. I've never seen him this possessive and wanting. He almost crushed a fairy, on the way here, who threw herself at him."

I narrowed my eyes. *Some fairy tried to hit on my orc?* "What?"

Melina snorted and fell back on the bed. "Oh girl, you got it bad. You both are definitely mates."

I sat up straight, my anger fell away.

Sugha was his brother, and miresa meant I was his mate! So, it's all true, and I shouldn't have doubts about this. Should I throw myself all over him?

"And what about the tribe? Why won't he let me meet your tribe?"

Sugha scratched the back of his head and leaned back in the chair. "That, I'm not as certain about. I haven't been bitten by the mate bug yet. I can tell you that orcs are very alpha. We don't come together very often. The only time we normally get together is for trade, tribe meetings, and for this trek to the mating balls. We like our space, our own territory. Just finding a female that is destined to be yours, that could spark a whole new side I don't even know about. He must fear someone might take you away."

Sugha sighed dramatically and rubbed his large hands down his thighs. "I cannot wait for that day."

Melina and I blinked at him several times before turning away.

"Right, so, the dick is different. How different we talkin?" Melina asked. "Because, my girl here might have had a glimpse or two of a—a dick, but not a dick of orc caliber."

Sugha shifted in his seat uncomfortably. "Well—"

A throat cleared. "And why would my mate need to know what an orc dick looks like?" Osirus drawled.

"And what are you doing in my cave!?" Valpar shouted as he stomped inside.

My pussy fluttered when I saw him breathing hard, his eyes wild with anger.

Darn. Maybe I'll get a punishment and a reward. *Could I be that lucky?*

Melina and Sugha jumped out of their seats. Simon stilled, then fell over from the abrupt noise.

Oopsie, daisy.

"You told me to stay in the cave," I said innocently, as I held my hands up. "See, still tied!"

Valpar's face softened, and his eyes filled with warmth as he hurriedly approached me. Melina and Sugha stepped aside, making way for Valpar. Meanwhile, Osirus, nonchalant and relaxed, leaned against the cool wall, exuding an air of calm indifference.

"You did, little fairy. I'm so proud of you," Valpar crooned as he untied my hands. "That deserves a reward."

Goodie.

"The rest of you can leave," Valpar barked. "And stay out! Keep your female on a leash, Osirus."

Uncle Osirus's lip twitched.

"Don't be a meanie." I flicked Valpar's nose.

He turned to me and growled, sucking my finger into his mouth.

Oh, my!

"It's alright, Calliope. We will see you before you officially move to the Wood, if that is what you want?" Melina raised an eyebrow to Valpar.

"Please," I asked Valpar. "I talked to Sugha about everything. But I haven't talked to my parents yet. I think they would be worried if I just moved and didn't tell them goodbye." I forcefully pulled my finger out of his mouth. "Wouldn't it be fun to hang out here, get to know each other, just for a time?"

Valpar picked me up and made me wrap my legs around his massive trunk of a body, then he tied the leather around my ankle so it was long enough for me to move around the bed, slightly. He cupped my butt so no one else could see it. My bare pussy was right up against his hot skin, and it took everything I had not to make a whimper of pleasure.

"You talked to my brother? About?" he rasped.

"About the miresa thing, and you being grouchy and not claiming me at first. I get it, waiting for so long for a mate, and thinking I was just another fairy trying to trick you would make me double check things, too." Valpar's face softened even more.

"I do wanna go find that fairy that hit on you and rip her wings off." I let out a growling noise. Valpar smiled, his forehead touched mine, and his shoulders shook.

"Moon Fairy above! Valpar just laughed," Sugha muttered.

Valpar put his hand over the side of my head and cradled it into his chest. "Out!" he roared. "Get out of this cave and don't come back! I swear to the Moon Fairy, I will hunt you down, Sugha, and rip off your shaft and feed it to you!"

Sugha's eyes widened, and he bolted out of the cave. Melina and Osirus still stood there, laughing to themselves.

"That means you, too, you kinky-ass fae."

Osirus gave a small bow, something he didn't do often. Only to the people he really liked. It made me happy that he liked Valpar, because I cared a lot about what he thought. My aunt, uncle, mom, dad and, of course, Simon were my everything before Valpar.

"Please, come to the palace for dinner." Uncle Osirus turned for Aunt Melina to hook her arm around his. "Drop in anytime. You both are always welcome."

"Bye, Uncle Osirus, Aunt Melina!" I waved.

Valpar grunted, holding me tighter against his body. My pussy rubbed up against the heat of his skin, and a zing of arousal went through my body.

He better stop doing that.

"My miresa. You obeyed me, you stayed in the cave. What a good little fairy." Valpar cupped my cheek.

My breath caught and I leaned in further to his touch.

"Does that mean I get rewarded?" I whispered, almost too shy to ask.

Valpar's growl in his chest vibrated, tickling that spot between my legs.

"I don't know if the reward is for me or for you," he confessed. "I would really like to try mouth dancing."

Mouth dancing?

He stared at my lips and his head leaned closer, pausing halfway.

"Ohhh, you mean kissing!" I smiled and wrapped my arms around his neck. "Yes, I would very much like to kiss! I've never done that."

"Good, I will be the only one you kiss. First and last." Valpar held me tight and crawled onto the bed as I held onto his body. He lowered me on the soft furs and groaned, pushing his body into mine, just enough so I could feel the weight of him. "I will be the last to touch you, lick you and place my shaft inside you. You are mine, every part of you, miresa." His eyes turned from yellow to deep gold.

My fingers dug into his shoulders, as my body lit on fire.

Come on, give me the good stuff.

"Your body is small." He came closer and my heart sped up. "We will need to go slow."

I don't know if he was telling me or himself, but I was tired of all this talking.

"I don't want to hurt you—I don't want to make you cry—"

"You talk too much!" I snapped and grabbed both sides of his face as I pulled him toward my lips.

CHAPTER EIGHTEEN

Valpar

I WANTED TO TAKE things slow after speaking to Osirus, but that all changed faster than an anole, a feline-like creature back in the Wood that could change direction quickly mid-run.

My miresa had both hands on either side of my face and brought her lips to mine.

She delicately separated them, firmly placing them on various parts of my mouth. The edges, the center, and even against my sturdy tusks.

"Kiss back?" she breathed

This is kissing?

As she continued, my mind was in a whirlwind. This kind of affection was new to me, something I had never seen before between my orgamos and ogamie. In my culture, tusks would have gotten in the way and made *kissing* impossible. The closest thing we could do was rub noses or foreheads, and caress each other's faces with our hands.

But here I was, experiencing something *different.*

I did not dislike it.

Her lips were soft, like flower petals against my rough ones, my miresa was exploring every corner of my mouth. My body was responding in ways I never thought possible from just touching one's lips.

I couldn't tear my eyes away as she ran her tongue along the seam, the sound of her soft licking filling the air. The faint scent of sweetness wafted towards me, and I felt a mix of anticipation and curiosity building within me.

Moon Fairy above, help me! I thought to myself, as I struggled to process all these new sensations.

As her lips moved from mine to my tusks, I let out a low growl of pleasure. She seemed to understand and pressed her body harder against me. Our mouths danced together, their movements becoming more frantic as the kiss deepened.

I lost myself in the moment, letting go of all my reservations and just enjoyed the feeling of her lips on mine.

But then, suddenly, she pulled away, leaving me breathless and wanting more.

My drum raced with excitement as I looked at her beautiful face and realized that from now on, things would never be the same for me again.

I wanted her. I wanted more of this.

I pressed my lips harder to hers, my body surrounding her and pulling her close. I felt the snap of the leather around my leg holding my shaft tightly to my body and groaned, feeling its relief.

Calliope licked my lips again. This time, I parted them, and she slipped her tongue inside.

Bassza, what was this?

She licked the inside of my mouth, my tongue meeting hers as fire lit across my body. I ground my shaft into the furs and felt the wetness gathering beneath them.

My miresa moaned into the *kiss*, and her fingers tangled into my hair. I continued to push my shaft into the furs, gaining any sort of friction.

I was going to leak all of my seed on the bed, and I did not care! Her mouth tasted and felt so good. It made me wonder if this was what it would feel like when I stick my cock inside her body, how wet and warm it would be.

My miresa sucked on my tongue and I whimpered, feeling my heavy sack fill with more seed.

"Mmm, my little fairy," I whispered into her lips. "You are being naughty."

She giggled, and my hand wandered, roaming up her side stopping near her tits. I wanted to taste them too and put the small mounds into my mouth, but I was having too much fun with this *kissing*.

It should not be called *kissing*. It should be called *mouth mating* because I was rutting her mouth, and my shaft was about to explode.

I grunted, my hips flexing onto the bed. I couldn't let myself seek pleasure until she did. Could she come by just kissing?

She was enjoying herself, but not in the way I was.

My shaft continued to leak, my sack heavy and becoming far too painful. I rubbed my shaft harder onto the furs, this time feeling the soft touch of her leg. The hot skin of her body, even though it was just her leg, touched my shaft, and I parted from her lips to let out a large groan and sucked on her right shoulder.

Calliope gasped, her fingers running down my back. My seed continued to pour from my body, but I was now energized once more. "Miresa, I must taste more of you," I growled into her shoulder. "Down there. Now be a good little fairy and pull up your cloth."

My miresa's cheeks turned a beautiful pink as she pulled up her dress, revealing more of her soft skin. My drum beat wildly in my chest, and I shifted down the bed to take in her body. I may not see her tits yet, but I was far too hungry, and desired to make my mate feel the same pleasure as me.

"Mm, your scent is strong," I whispered, taking in deep breaths of her arousal. She was bare, with no cloth covering her cunt, because I'd torn it from her body the night before.

She gasped and squirmed under my gaze, her hands fidgeting with the hem of her long cloth. It was clear she was still nervous about showing herself to me, but her scent betrayed her true desires.

I leaned forward and brushed my lips over the small tuft of pink hair covering her mound, making my miresa whimper and clench her thighs together.

I hadn't noticed it much the night before, my tongue too busy tasting her, but in the light and being able to see her properly, I was quite fond of her having hair there.

"Relax, my little fairy," I murmured against the softness of her thighs as I spread them. "Let me taste you, as a good *mate* should."

She hesitated for a moment before nodding slowly and released her hold on the fabric. Her legs gave way easier, giving me access to the heat between them.

I couldn't resist running my tongue along her seam, taking in the droplets of her arousal. The sight of Calliope's glistening folds made my cock twitch eagerly.

I wasted no time burying my face between her thighs, lapping at the slick juices that flowed from within. My miresa cried out and grabbed onto my hair, pulling me closer.

Her taste, just as the night before, was like nothing I had ever experienced—sweet and tangy all at once. I delved deeper with my tongue, flicking over every sensitive spot I could find.

I wanted to know every place on her body that would bring her pleasure. I wanted to be the only one that knew how to please this female. Because she was mine, and mine alone.

When she bucked against my mouth, I knew she was close to release. I wanted to give her more, not just pleasure with my tongue but, to also give her the feeling of being full, to stretch her, so that I could—

I nearly paused when my mind took me elsewhere.

If I brand her, she may regain all her past hurtful memories.

I snarled and let my tongue curl up into her pussy. She was happy with my tongue, happy to feel its slickness against her clit and the feeling inside her. My miresa screamed as she came undone beneath me. Her walls clenched and fluttered around my tongue, as her body trembled with pleasure.

My cock spilled, making a mess all over the furs again. I groaned and reached below me to milk my shaft to empty my sack fully. I would need to empty it again, soon, if I was to be around my female.

But that thought, *those* horrible thoughts, that the king had put in my head still lingered.

"Valpar," my fairy panted and sat up on her elbows. "Goddess, that was... Wow!" Her hair was a mess, her cheeks flushed, and her lips swollen from the assault of my teeth nipping at them. "It's my turn now, right? I wanna take care of you."

Moon Fairy, Almighty!

She got onto her knees and crawled toward me. I pushed my loin cloth over my semi-hard shaft and sat up on my knees, exposing the mess on the bed.

Guardard snap!

Calliope stopped and tilted her head to the side. "Woah, did you come already?" She looked on in amazement and gave me a big smile.

"Come? I expressed my seed. Why would I not? My miresa was in front of me, and you allowed me to touch you and give you pleasure. Of course I would express it."

Calliope smiled brighter and clapped her hands. "Just by touching me and giving me pleasure?" She pointed to herself. "You came—I mean, expressed your seed? That's so hot," she whispered.

She lunged forward and wrapped her arms around my neck. "This makes me feel so pretty."

I pulled her away. "You are beautiful! *The* most beautiful female. Why would you not think you are?"

Calliope rolled her lips. "Well, I'm human. I don't look extra special, is all." She looked around the room at everything other than me. I grabbed her by the chin, to make her pay attention to me and to only me. "I'm rather plain compared to everyone else, even you."

I growled and cupped her backside. She let out a small squeak. "My drums beat for you, and my shaft only rises for you, female. To give you pleasure makes my body happy. You are not plain. You are my light source."

Her eyes widened, and her tiny fists curled onto my chest. She chewed on her bottom lip but she did not answer.

"Do you understand, little fairy? Next time you talk bad about yourself, I will put you over my knee and you will be punished, and you will not like it."

Her arousal flared again, and I groaned. "I mean my words, little fairy."

"Uh, huh, sure." She pressed her chest into mine. "I'll be waiting for the day."

I swapped out the furs for clean ones. I would need to use the furs in the forbidden closet, unfortunately. I did it quickly while my miresa cleaned herself in the bathroom, so she did not question why there was a chair by the door.

Already, I was making plans to change the cabin back in the Wood, and to make her a bathroom for herself. One with a tub, a shower and a toilet. The toilet here is far too small, and I will have to go outside myself.

I tried to think of everything, of what supplies I would need to gather before our departure at the end of the month. Unfortunately, the haunting memory of King Osirus still lingered.

I did not want my miresa to relive her memories or her nightmares. What would happen when I brand her, and all her pain and suffering return? Would the Moon Fairy be so harsh to let any magic given to her, to help her, be taken away?

I rubbed my chin and shook my head.

My miresa was very young and free-thinking. Perhaps she would not know, or understand, how an orc brands his mate. She was the first human. I could postpone the brand— the bond— as long as possible, so as not hurt her.

Perhaps avoid sticking my shaft into her altogether.

Simon bleated at me from the far end of the cave, as if he could hear my thoughts. The animal had probably watched me eat his emotional support person's cunt. The sick animal!

I don't think my little fairy will let me get away with not putting my shaft inside of her.

After she saw that I had released my seed, she was hoping she could see my shaft. She even tried to lift my cloth. Then I told her we needed to take things slow.

Ha.

There was no going slow with her, not in the slightest. My little fairy was starved for attention and touch. I wanted to give that to her. I wanted to have it as well, but I couldn't very well hurt her in the process.

I did not want to be the one to break her.

I let out a heavy sigh and took a large breath in. I could still smell her arousal around my mouth.

I did not want to think or feel. I just wanted to hold my female, claim her, protect her—how was I to do that when claiming her could hurt her?

I snarled, balling my hand into a fist. I needed to release my anger.

CHAPTER NINETEEN

Calliope

I OPENED THE DOOR to the bathroom; the steam came with me. Wrapped in just a big fluffy towel, I saw Simon at my side immediately. He rubbed his horns against my thigh, and I scratched behind his ears. "Hi Simon, sorry, I hope you turned around earlier." I winced, remembering that he'd been in the room.

Valpar stood before me, his back facing me and his hands firmly rested on his hips. As I observed, his broad back seemed to pulsate with tension, the muscles rippling beneath his skin. Even his long, ebony hair swayed in sync with his movements.

I couldn't help how tempting it was for me to imagine the sensation of running my fingers through its silkiness.

The other orcs had their hair braided or shaved on the sides, all with the exception of Sugha, who had the shorter cut. Valpar's hair was wild and unkempt, but I really liked how his silky strands lay halfway down his back. I wanted to brush it and play with it. I wondered if he would let me braid it for him.

"Something wrong?" I finally asked when he didn't give me his full attention after I'd come out of the bathroom. I didn't know why that irked me, but I wanted all of his attention.

Bad Calliope. Don't be selfish.

When he turned, his grumpy face was in full force, just as it was the night we met. It melted once he finally saw me, and it turned into a look I could not describe.

"Miresa, what are you wearing?" he rasped.

"A towel? I don't have any extra clothes." I pulled the overly large towel up to my nose to hide my heated face, and Valpar came close to me. Instead of pulling me to his body, he grabbed a spare blanket from the bed, a clean one, and dumped it over my head.

Um, what?

"Let me find you some cloth. Stay there," he said gruffly.

Simon let out a grunt and pulled on the blanket that covered me from head to toe. He pulled on it just enough, so it came off my head, and the blanket pooled onto the floor. When Valpar finished looking in his sack full of his supplies, he stood up and groaned as he took in my appearance.

"You don't know how to stay put, do you?" He gritted his teeth, came toward me and shoved a black dress tunic over my head, while I still held the towel over my body. "I must go outside. You will remain in the cave, and I will be outside watching. Do not leave, do you understand?"

He didn't look at me when he began to walk away.

Great, he was already tired of me.

"Valpar?" I whispered, so silently. I did it when Mom and Dad were upset with me and would just walk away. Even with their hearing, they never looked back.

It was the silent treatment, that's what they called it. They'd leave me for long periods of time so I could think of what I had done wrong. I knew I deserved it most of the time. Jumping out of trees, letting some of the livestock go free...

Only this time, I didn't know what I did to Valpar, to know what I had done wrong.

I pursed my lips together and pushed the towel down then threaded my arms through the holes of the dress. I crossed my arms, feeling cold and alone, but warmth engulfed me before I could think more dangerous thoughts.

"My sweet fairy, I am sorry." He petted my still damp hair and pressed his cheek to it. "I am a male with few words, and I have been blessed with a female who requires many," he said.

I sniffed and tried to wrap my arms around him.

"Please do not water your cheeks, I fear I might knock over every tree in this forest."

I shook my head into his chest. "I don't want you to hurt yourself by knocking stuff over."

Valpar picked me up, and I straddled his waist.

"I am insulted that you would think your puny, soft trees would hurt me. I can push them over with one hand!" He took one of his arms and showed me his muscles.

Hubba, hubba.

"Hmm, yes." I pinched his muscle. "It is very strong. You must test it for me." I smiled. "I have not seen such strength from an orc before."

Valpar's eyes lit up. "You haven't? Well, none better than your male. You shall come with me as I show you my strength."

Valpar carried me outside of the cave and I clung to him tightly, not wanting to let go. The sun was shining brightly, and I squinted as we stepped into the light. Valpar walked with a confident stride, and I felt a bit like a princess as he carried me everywhere.

"I didn't bring the leather lead to keep you tied to me. Are you going to stay where I put you?" He lifted an eyebrow in warning.

My pussy fluttered and I opened my mouth to say something smart back, but he put a hand over my mouth.

"Think before you speak, or I will march back into the cave and get it."

I shook my head, and he released his hand. "Nope, no sir, Mr. Big Bad Orc Sir. I will stay where you put me."

For like five minutes.

Pleased with himself, he nodded as he brought us onto the beach and took a sharp turn to the left into the forest. After a five-minute walk, with Simon trotting behind us, we entered a large clearing surrounded by trees and tall grass. In the center stood a tall, sturdy tree with thick branches reaching towards the sky. Valpar set me down gently on a large, flat rock nearby and grinned mischievously at me.

"Watch this, my sweet fairy, while your male shows you his strength." He flexed his muscles once more and cracked his neck. Then, he strutted over, placed both hands on the trunk of the tree and with a loud grunt, he pushed against it with all his might. The ground trembled beneath us as he put all his strength into it. Slowly but surely, the tree began to tilt and creak under his force. Pixies screamed, and I almost felt bad, but all of them could fly just fine.

Finally, the giant tree came crashing down with a thunderous boom.

Yup, he was definitely a lumber snack!

Pixies screamed again. The females were all swooning and fanning themselves while the males look a little ticked.

They got interrupted playing the hokey-pokey!

The tree Valpar picked wasn't a homing tree for pixies, it didn't have any ribbons in the low-lying branches as a warning. The male pixies were just mad because they were interrupted.

I giggled, watching the females flutter around Valpar. He waved his hand to push them away and looked at me.

I beamed at him. Both, that he would wave the pixies away, and that he had that much strength. I don't think I've ever seen a shifter push over a tree. I'd never asked Creed to do it, maybe I'll ask him next time I see him.

Valpar let out a roar, his muscles rippling under his skin as he went for another tree. His face had turned grumpy and determined, and my eyes lit up when he wrapped his arms around the trunk and squeezed.

Oh, his butt muscles are just so nice.

Just wanna bite them.

Chomp, chomp.

The wind blew, so I got a good look at his right cheek and my mouth dropped.

"What the hell is that orc doing!?" I heard Karma's voice come from my right, and I groaned. "He's gonna wreck the whole forest!"

Burgers and fries, it's my *nemisisis.*

Yes, *nemisisis.* He needs extra *is* because he is so evil.

I waved my hand like he was a fly. "Ugh, why are you here? Why don't you fly back down to the bowels of the Underworld and go buzz around one of Hades' trees? Maybe he'll set you on fire for me," I whispered.

Karma let out a strangled noise.

"Besides, isn't it your and the nymphs' jobs to fix broken trees when the elves aren't around? He's just giving you work to do, so you aren't lazy and eating people's cupcakes."

Simon let out a long bleat and tried to bite his wings. "I will tell the king about this, Calliope. He will be disappointed in you, in...that thing!" He pointed to Valpar, who was really amping up his movements, pounding into random trees.

It was...really hot!

I crossed my legs and made sure I tied the top of his dress tunic, so nothing showed. My hair was finally drying but between my legs was another story.

Karma's nose turned up. "Don't tell me you are becoming a whore, too, now, huh? You are really falling for that thing? For your babysitter?"

I snapped my head to Karma. "I'll have you know he is my mate. You are just a jealous flying glitter-turd, who is upset you aren't in the court helping with my uncle. You would think you would want to get on my good side, instead of terrorizing me, so I could help you with that, but you have to be a dingus."

Karma's wings fluttered agitatedly as he stared at me with a mix of annoyance and disbelief. "You can't be serious, Calliope. He's an orc! You can't possibly feel a bond, anyway, you are a *human*. Humans have no feelings or blessings from a goddess."

I narrowed my eyes at him and ignored the stab at me. "He may be an orc, but he is my orc. You are just jealous he won't be sticking his pinky up your tiny little asshole and pricking your shoulder to claim you."

Karma gasped as the other pixies giggled, while they mended the tree Valpar just broke.

Simon tried to take another bite out of Karma while he wasn't watching but he flew to the other side of my shoulder.

"Then, you two are made for each other." Karma snorted and put his hands on his hips. "Two barbaric creatures that have no right to be in this kingdom. I can't wait until he carts you off into the Wood and I don't have to see your face."

I rolled my eyes dramatically. "That makes two of us."

"Should have happened already. Real mates claim them the same night. Why hasn't he marked you." Karma looked over my shoulder for a bite. "I see nothing. Maybe he doesn't want you. You must have said or done something. Did he see your scrawny body and decide he didn't want it? Is that why you are covered up?"

I parted my lips and looked down. He did throw this tunic over me rather quickly.

But he came all over the bed when he was licking my lady parts.

He's done it twice now. Why would he go back for seconds?

"We—we are just taking things slow because—"

"Because you are probably too small. I bet he couldn't get one finger inside you. He's gonna reject you."

I gasped. Simon backed up and took a running jump leaping into the air, headbutting Karma until he fell into the mud. I heard him mumble and squish, and Simon bleating in laughter, but didn't revel in his misery.

Instead, I was watching Valpar destroy large boulders, tree trunks and punch the ground with his hands. He was sweating, with large beads of sweat dripping down his back, face and chest. I was in awe of him, how wonderful he looked and yes, he was very different from me, but I couldn't be more attracted to him.

I wondered if I was enough.

Karma always had a way of getting under my skin.

I took a deep breath and slowly approached Valpar, who was still destroying everything in his path. The other pixies flew away in fear, but I couldn't help but be drawn to him.

His sharp claws tore through the ground and his loud roars echoed through the forest. But I felt an inexplicable pull towards him, like a magnetic force that I couldn't resist.

As I got closer, he turned to face me with a wild look in his eyes. But, instead of feeling scared, I felt a surge of adrenaline rush through my body.

Without hesitation, I reached out and touched his arm. His skin was rough and hot against my fingertips, but it only made me want him more. He looked down at me with surprise and confusion, but then his expression softened into something else.

He leaned down and inhaled my scent deeply, before pulling me into a fierce embrace. His powerful arms wrapped around me as if he was trying to protect me from something.

I buried my face in his chest, taking in the musky smell of sweat and adrenaline that surrounded him. It was intoxicating and alluring at the same time.

For a moment, we just stood there holding each other. He needed this, to release a frustration, an anger. Our breaths mingled together and our hearts beat as one.

I just wished I knew what he was angry about.

But like he said, orcs are males of few words. How am I going to get him to talk?

But then, Valpar suddenly pulled away with a growl, breaking our connection. He turned back to destroying everything in sight, with even more intensity than before.

I watched him for a moment before stepping forward again and placing my hand on his back. This time, he didn't push me away or react at all.

He simply continued to destroy everything in front of him with renewed vigor.

Eventually, Valpar stopped and looked down at me with a mixture of exhaustion and pain.

Is it me?

Was Karma right? Why else would he be ripping up the forest? Am I too small for him?

He hasn't let me see his thing, yet.

But why would the Goddess pair two souls that were not compatible? It wasn't right—couldn't be right. He'd better not be afraid of breaking me.

"Wow, you're super strong," I joked, rocking back and forth on my feet. "Remind me not to make you too angry." I snorted at my joke and Valpar came toward me with a sad look on his face.

"Little fairy, I would never, ever, ever harm you. I would rather die than let anything happen to you." He put his hand on my lower back, pulling me toward him. His muscles bulged and his breath was ragged.

I hummed in agreement. Valpar wouldn't physically hurt me. It was Karma's words that were hurting me.

Stupid Karma. I hoped he gets the clap from fucking some wood sap from a woodpecker hole somewhere.

The sweat glistened on Valpar's body, and my heart raced in my chest. He really was a snack, and I was ready to just take a bite out of his giant man boob right in front of me. I smiled sweetly at him and took a lick at his chest.

He groaned and his free hand cupped between his legs. "This was why I was out here, trying to relieve stress and here you are riling me up again." I tried to take a quick peek, but he pulled my chin back up to look at him. "Not yet," he warned.

I took a playful lick again and then bit his nipple. He jumped and grabbed his chest, rubbing it, while still holding me to his body.

"What-what did you do that for female?" he growled at me.

"I licked it. I bit it. It's mine, now!" I smiled brightly.

CHAPTER TWENTY

Calliope

FOUR DAYS PASSED, AND he hadn't touched me in places I wanted to be touched.

He hadn't brushed my pink fairy bits with his tongue, and I was really missing it.

I was starting to believe that Karma's words are true, that Vapar didn't see me as his mate, anymore.

I'd become just a human companion or cuddle toy.

Valpar's words were strong. He claimed I was his mate and would hold me tight in the night, but he kept my body covered, and he has yet to show me his *mini orc*.

He hasn't ventured between my thighs again, and I longed for it. I've been so turned on by just the small things he does. How he bends over, how he changes the furs, the way he takes care of me in the smallest of ways that no one else had but, I was selfish and wanted more.

Isn't that what mates do? They do more, right?

And I needed more.

Each morning, Simon brought in the basket full of supplies. Inside it would be filled with food and clothing for me. The clothing Aunt Melina sent didn't leave much to the imagination. I loved it. It made me feel pretty, and I liked to spin around as I'd show it off to Valpar. He just looked at me, stared at me with the hunger in his eyes he had had the first night we met, but he'd never take action.

I've often attempted to seduce him, mirroring the women in the books which I devoured. I'd softly place my hand on his thigh as we have picnics outside. I even delicately traced my fingers across his chest as he held me in the darkness of the night. When he held so still, I would press my lips against his warm skin, but then he would swiftly maneuver me, positioning my back against his chest, leaving me powerless, unable to make any further advances.

And it hurt.

Karma's words buried deeper.

Aunt Melina had gotten bolder with each basket. One holding a black loin cloth for Valpar. I guessed it was supposed to be lingerie for an orc. He was utterly confused at first and I pushed him to the bathroom to put it on, but he refused, saying it was too short to wear.

Such a party pooper.

Maybe it is because the *mini-orc* is too long and I'd see it poking out.

I'll never know because I will never see it.

This morning Aunt Melina sent tea, a special drink for males. Each night he is to drink it to prevent pregnancy. When I told Valpar he needed to take it for when we bonded to each other, his dark-green face turned lime-green.

It was then I realized that there was something very, very wrong.

And that *something* was me.

My mood turned sour after that. I'd had enough trying to coax him into wanting me. I didn't care to look at him and didn't care to talk to him. He went on with his tasks the rest of the morning. Cleaning up the cave, making me food that I refused to eat, and that only made him more anxious.

"Female, you must eat," he growled when he picked me up from the bed and sat me on his lap. "Why won't you eat? You will become too thin."

Like it mattered. He wouldn't touch me, anyway.

"Why don't you go hit a tree or something? That might make you feel better," I muttered.

Valpar raised a brow and turned me so that I was straddling him. Fortunately, or unfortunately, Aunt Melina packed my underwear as well. It was a thong, but it still covered the part that really needed attention.

That. He. Won't. Touch.

"Eat," he growled again.

I opened my mouth, took the food he offered and chewed. Slowly.

It was like he was a step above my parents. He was attentive, affectionate but not overly so, he talked to me but that was where it ended. He was my mate that wouldn't go further with me because... I didn't know why.

Just like everyone else in the realm, I put him off.

Was it how I acted? The way I looked? Did I stink?

I discreetly sniffed my armpits while he took a bite of his own food.

Do my lady bits?

That would be more awkward to sniff but I was a super clean person. Maybe he wanted it shaved. It was neatly trimmed down there but maybe he was a clean pussy kinda orc.

Once the food on my plate was done, he sat me back on the bed and wrapped a blanket around me, and I watched him clean up.

He was annoyingly sexy, and I couldn't even get a bite out of that scrumptious butt he had.

It was like a large biscuit. Soft, yet firm.

I clicked my teeth together.

Valpar glanced back at me. His eyes narrowed when I let the blanket slip, and maybe the strap from my dress fell a little, too.

Yeah, you like that, my big green giant?

Valpar cleared his throat and came toward me. "I need to step out. Will you be alright if I go alone?"

I stared at him for a moment. Valpar had done this several times throughout the day. He would go out, maybe twenty minutes, and come back inside several times a day. He'd be slightly sweaty but took a towel to wipe himself off. He was never dirty, even after he punched the heck out of the trees outside.

He told me orcs had repellant skin, that they didn't have to bathe often, and didn't have odor either. Lucky them.

My guess, he was punching trees outside. Valpar said orcs were active creatures and need to expel a lot of energy. They do that by pounding, hitting and other *things*. Things he wouldn't explain.

I'd let him pound me if he would just...

"Sure," I shrugged my shoulders as I wrapped myself in the blanket and reached across the bed for one of the romance novels that Aunt Melina kept putting in the baskets. I huffed out a long sigh and didn't look back when Valpar let out a sigh of his own.

If he had any sort of brain in his head, he would know something was wrong. Which, I think he did, but he didn't have the communication skill to express it.

And I had never been in a relationship before, so I don't know how to bring it up, other than sitting on his face while he was sleeping and letting him suffocate on my little fairy parts.

I didn't know how many times I'd asked what was wrong. After the third day, I gave up.

Once his footsteps were gone, Simon hopped up on the bed, carrying a tiny compact mirror. When I looked into it, I didn't see my reflection, but Melina's.

"Hey, favorite, why the long face?" she asked sweetly.

Communication mirrors were common for royals to use. A witch had to cast a spell on a mirror in the royal palace and then smaller mirrors could pull magic from the main mirror to be used in them. To my knowledge, my aunt and uncle didn't like to do that unless it was necessary, so I was a little surprised that I could see Aunt Melina.

I shrugged my shoulders, my head lying on the pillow. "Why are you calling? Is something wrong? Are my parents okay?"

Melina shook her head. "Everyone else is fine, Calliope. It's you that I'm worried about. You know there are eyes all around the forest, and it sounds like Valpar is being too tender with you, isn't he? My little light isn't shining as bright." Aunt Melina tried to console me further.

I nodded, sadly. "He was fine the first day. He's great, very thoughtful and nice and...

"He isn't the barbarian you saw the first day, hmm?" Melina quirked her eyebrow.

I sniffed. "Maybe there is something wrong with me. You know, like always." It wasn't a secret people didn't like to hang out with me. Either because I was human, or I liked to play too much.

If my nemesisis wouldn't get in my head, I don't think I'd be so worried. How many isis should there be in there anyway?

Melina's face morphed into anger. "I think your uncle had something to do with that, and I'm sorry. You know how protective he is of you, how we are all protective of you, but you are stronger than all of us. I think it's time we bring out the big guns, love."

I quirked a brow. "The big guns?"

Melina waved a hand in front of her face. "It's a saying. Anyway, you know that big door with the chair in front of it?"

I glanced over to the other side of the cave. Valpar put that big chair in front of it. He only went in there to get fresh blankets, but closed it and placed the chair back before I could even look inside.

"Have Simon help you move it, and this is what you are going to do." Melina smiled and rubbed her hands together mischievously.

I giggled. Oh goodie.

The idea was so dirty I would have never thought of it myself. That is why everyone should have an Aunt Melina.

There was this chest, full of dicks. A chest-o-dicks. Literally, a chest of dicks. There were so many colors, sizes and... well, textures.

Which one do you freaking pick?

Melina told me to pick a plain one, one that resembled more of a humanoid penis. At least I knew what that looked like.

She said it would give Valpar a complex if I picked some big, funky colored one.

The one I picked was about the size of—well, I didn't have anything to compare it to. I'd never seen one close up. It wiggled when I held it and then when I walked it stared at me. It had a suction at the bottom of it.

Where the heck does that go? The floor? The wall?

I tilted my head and started bobbing it. *That would be cool.*

Peaches and cream. This was not normal. Do real ones feel like this too? Do they wobble like this?

Melina warned me that this was close to the real thing, but not quite. A real one feels better. They are warm, they get harder and she said I would have to figure it out for myself. She also said she'd never seen an orc dilly, so she didn't know what I was getting into.

I just had to perform, and hopefully, I would get some action from Valpar. This was just an appetizer.

I walked out of the closet, holding the vibrating dildo in front of me. *Cheesus.*

Simon let out a noise, trotted out of the cave and looked behind to check on me several times before disappearing.

"Right. Let's get to it, then."

I laid down on the bed, taking off every bit of my clothes. If I was going to do this, please myself, put myself out there for Valpar, I was going to do it the right way.

Right, what do I do first? My mind drew a blank until I switched my mind and tried to think, what would I want Valpar to do right now.

All the things. I wanted him to do all the things.

I closed my eyes first and then I started playing with my nipples. I didn't like how small they were, but I loved how sensitive the little parts of me were. I instantly reacted when his face flashed in my mind, thinking of him putting his mouth on me.

I moaned, wanting to prolong the feeling, but I was already needy. I was so hungry, so deprived for days. If Valpar walked in here and wouldn't give me what I wanted, I at least needed to have one blissful bit of pleasure to myself.

My other hand traveled lower, not a bit sorry that I was doing this alone, even though I had a mate outside. I was done waiting. Now that I'd had a taste of how my body could feel, I wanted more.

My finger became coated, and I jerked into my hand when I found pleasure rubbing the small bundle of nerves side to side.

My other fingers reached between my folds. I was already wet, the furs beneath me becoming damp.

I whimpered.

I wasn't going to need the lube Aunt Melina said would be beside the bedside table.

No, too far gone for that. I stuck in one finger, loving the feeling. I haven't had much else inside, and I wanted another. Two fingers, and then three. My fingers were slender. I knew three fingers weren't that much of a stretch. I'd just like to wish it was.

Just so Valpar could at least stick the tip of his cock inside me.

I moaned, wishing so much to feel him there. The heat of his body above me, for him to want me the way I wanted him.

But he wasn't here.

I felt a shiver run down my spine as I surrendered to the vividness of my imagination. His hands, strong and possessive, caressed every inch of my body, leaving a trail of electric sensations in their wake. I could almost feel the soft pressure of his lips as they traced a tantalizing path from the nape of my neck, down to the curve of my shoulders. His warm breath created a delicious contrast against my skin, igniting a fire deep within me. The intensity of the moment consumed me, as my heart raced and my senses heightened, lost in the intoxicating fantasy of his touch.

I thrust my fingers in and out of my pussy, trying to replicate the feeling of his cock inside me. I was wet and warm and ready for him.

But he still wasn't here.

The frustration built up inside me, and I took a risk, reaching for the dildo with a vibrator option beside me. My fingers shook as I turned it on and pressed it against my clit. My whole body jolted at the sensation, and I let out a loud moan. It was as if he was there with me, pleasuring me himself.

I closed my eyes, my back bowed, and I felt my release coming. "Valpar!" I cried and pushed my fingers deeper inside me while the vibrator tickled my clit. My fingers were coated in the heat of my arousal and I panted, but I wasn't tired, not in the least.

I wanted more. I slid the tip inside. It was smaller than the other *things* inside the chest, but this one was stretching me.

I winced, and then a roar came from across the room.

"FEMALE!"

I froze, my fingers still inside me, but I took the vibrating dildo away from my body. A low growl rumbled through the room, and I turned to see Valpar standing there, his eyes blazing with fury and desire.

His muscular chest heaving as he took in the scene before him. I could feel his eyes on me, drinking in every inch of my exposed body. But I couldn't move. I was frozen in shock.

Like, duh, you knew you were gonna get caught, Calliope, it shouldn't be a shock.

Valpar took a step towards me, his gaze never leaving mine. "What are you doing?" he demanded, his voice rough with emotion.

I couldn't form any words. My body was screaming for release and yet at the same time was paralyzed with fear of what Valpar was going to do.

He took another step closer, his eyes darkening with lust as he saw the tears forming in mine.

Valpar climbed onto the bed, his body hovering over mine. "I have... neglected you?" It came out in the form of a question rather than a statement.

I nodded. "You don't touch me anymore." I whispered. "Mates touch each other. Love each other."

Valpar hung his head.

"Bassza!"

CHAPTER TWENTY-ONE

Valpar

I'VE NEGLECTED MY MATE and that has been my fault. Now, she had taken matters into her own hands, by touching herself.

I am jealous of her fingers and of this thing she had near her cunt.

What in dark soil is that thing?

"I have another rule, you aren't to touch yourself," I rasped as I climbed up the bed, pinning my forearms against either side of her head.

My mate wrinkled her eyebrows, and a pout formed on her lips.

"You can't tell me what to do! You-you don't want to touch me!" she snapped, and trailed her fingers lower down her body.

I grabbed her wrist and pulled it in front of my face. Her fingers were wet, slick with the sweet arousal from her cunt. I took them into my mouth and licked them clean. Her eyes widened as she watched my tongue dive between the two fingers to get every drop.

Moon Fairy above, I had missed her taste. I'd missed touching her, hovering above her, watching her squirm beneath me. There was something animalistic seeing her as prey and I the predator. To take every innocent part of her and claim it as my own, like when we first met.

And then to learn of her past, bassza! I froze. I didn't want to hurt her...even when King Osirus said she does not want to be seen as fragile. How could I not, with a past like hers? I wanted to wrap her in the leaves of a dragon scale tree so she would never get a scrape or a scar or be hurt by the outside world.

A monster like me should not be mated to her. I could break her. Look how small she was.

Her hole was small. How would I stretch her without harm coming to her? I had second guessed everything I planned for her after knowing her past.

I groaned when her hand ran up my chest. My miresa's fingers grazing over my hardened nipples. I groaned at the sensation, my body betraying me despite my inner turmoil. Her touch ignited a fire within me, a primal need to claim her and make her mine.

How could I, a monster, be mated to someone as pure and innocent as her? I could break her with just one wrong move. How could she ever handle being with an orc like me?

She deserved much better, but I was a selfish monster.

I laid my body on top of her, but not so much that it suffocated her. My mind raced with doubts and fears. She watched me with concerned eyes, her hand still rubbing over my chest.

"What's wrong?" she asked softly. "Did I do something?"

"No," I replied gruffly. "It's just...you're so small."

She tilted her head in confusion. "What does that have to do with anything?"

"I will break you," I said, not able to meet her gaze.

Her hand moved from my chest to cup my cheek, forcing me to look at her. "You won't break me," she said firmly. "I am stronger than you think. Besides, I don't think the Goddess would have paired us if that were to happen?"

I wanted to believe her words, but a part of me knew the truth. Her hole was small. How would I stretch it enough for our mating? What if the spell broke? The thought made me feel sick to my stomach.

"I don't want to hurt you," I admitted, feeling vulnerable in front of her for the first time since we met. "I want to rut you into the bed, I worry I will have no control. I have been planning..."

It was partly true. How far could I go with my mate without having her break the spell placed on her head? I could give her all my brands but one, not completely branding her as mine. She would not know the difference. Orcs claimed differently than the rest of Bergarian.

The question was... could I hold my final brand back?

Her expression softened and she leaned in closer to me. "Tell me your plans," she said in a whisper that made my shaft twitch against her leg.

I took a deep breath, but that made my mouth water. Her arousal was thick and musty in the room, and I feared that the few minutes I was outside releasing my sack of seed was not enough.

"You need to be stretched, little fairy..."

Her breath hitched. "You know, I haven't even seen your stuff, yet. Is it bigger than this?" She reached for the small worm beside her and put it between us. It wiggled and then it vibrated.

I looked on in horror at the small, pink worm in her hand. I slapped it away and it flew to the floor, the vibration stopped. "What was that thing?

And why was it near your cunt? What were you doing with it?" My tender voice reverted to dripping jealousy and I hovered over her once again.

She didn't fear me, instead she laughed and covered her face. "It's a dildo. It's like a copy of a male's penis!" She laughed, again. "And it has a little button so it can vibrate, too. A real penis can't do that. I was going to use it to help stretch me."

I reared my head back and stared at the worm on the floor. My miresa needed no such thing. My shaft was much larger, anyway, and would feel better in her body.

"You will never pleasure yourself again, especially with that!" I pointed to the floor. "I will be the only one that touches your cunt, do you understand?" My voice was laced with anger. I feared it could have been too much, but she quieted and nodded.

"Okay, but you have to touch me." She scowled. "Because you haven't touched me in days. How else am I going to get my needs met? You give me a taste and then leave me hanging. I can't handle that." My miresa crossed her arms and her tits were pushed upward. They are tiny, pink and are begging for my mouth to be placed on them.

I groaned, my hand sliding up her body and cupping them.

"You will take what I give you, my little fairy. You are not in charge."

She whimpered when I squeezed her tiny tit and I licked it, savoring the taste of her and incensing my hunger for her. I couldn't help but feel a sickening thrill as I considered the size difference between us and wondered if I could truly give her what she desired.

Her body responded to my touch, her hips pushing against mine, seeking more contact and friction. Her eyes were filled with a mix of apprehension and desire, her lips parted slightly, gasping for air.

I felt a renewed sense of determination, an urge to show her just how much I could give her, despite the monstrous nature I carried within me.

A part of me wanted to prove that I could be gentle and tender, that I could be a good male to her, like I had tried the past few days.

I could still give us both pleasure, I just had to do it carefully.

As I continue to give attention to her tit, teasing it with my teeth and tongue, she shivered beneath me. My hand slid down her body, resting between her legs, feeling the dampness that has seeped between her soft skin. I knew she was ready, aching for my touch, and I was torn between the desire to claim her and the fear of hurting her.

"Please," she whispered, her voice barely audible. "Please, Valpar."

And there it was – the begging, her desperate need for me. It made me feel powerful, knowing that I held her desires in the palm of my hand.

I hesitated for a moment, then my fingers traced through the small curls, feeling the heat radiating from her body.

I was careful of my sharp claws as I continued to rub the outside of her cunt. I wanted to know every curve, every fold, every part of where the slick would soak.

The heat of my miresa's eyes were on me, as I stared at the lower part of her body in fascination. How dare she put that vile worm next to it.

"Was that worm real?" I snarled and gripped one of her legs, pushing it up near her shoulder.

She gasped and her face turned a pretty pink. "W-?"

"That worm next to your cunt? What was that again?"

"It's a dildo. They aren't real. It's for self-pleasure, when a male isn't around to—"

I lowered my head and snarled into her cunt, taking a tentative lick at the puckered hole just below it as well. She let out a scream and I snarled further, pushing the other leg to her shoulder, so I could take a look at her.

My miresa was displayed in front of me, her lower half completely exposed. Her face was red, she was panting and that made me feel taller than the trees outside.

"I am bigger than that worm. Did you know that?"

She shook her head.

"If you are going to take me, I'll need to stretch this pretty cunt much more than that." I took my finger, brought it to my mouth and licked the remnants of her arousal. Once I reached the tip, I broke off my black claw and spat it onto the floor. I ground it down with my tusk, smoothing down the edges.

My miresa watched me, as I did it to another finger and her legs slowly fell onto the bed.

"I didn't say you could let your legs rest. Hold them back to your shoulders," I commanded.

She squeaked and held herself open for me. My shaft, barely covered by my loin cloth wept, soaking the furs below us.

Once two of my claws were worn down enough, I placed kisses down her stomach, down the little patch of pink hair that I liked. My tongue flicked her clit, and she let out a throaty moan.

My eyes flicked to see her face. She bit her lower lip, her eyes locking onto mine once more. Good, she was watching, my brave little fairy.

And with that, my hands dipped lower, sliding beneath her waist, my fingers digging into her backside. She shivered beneath me, her breaths quickening as I slowly wrapped my lips around her clit and sucked.

As I stared at her, this delicate, small creature who had entrusted her body and soul to me, I felt a surge of protectiveness and desire. I wanted to claim her, to mark her as mine, but even I knew that I may never get that far.

With a deep breath, I forced my claws to stop trembling and focused on the task. I slid one finger into her wet entrance, feeling the tightness and heat that surrounded me.

Bassza! It would feel so good against my shaft.

"Mmm, you are so tight, little fairy. I have much work to do."

I pushed deeper, stretching her as much as I could. She winced, her walls pulsing around me but still, I felt the desire to give her more, to show her the full extent of what she was getting into.

Because this was nothing, nothing compared to what was to come.

Her body buckled slightly beneath me and her breaths became shallow as my finger moved inside her.

"Do you like me inside you?" I whispered, my voice low and husky.

She nodded, her eyes locked onto mine, a mixture of fear and anticipation playing in her gaze.

I pulled my finger out and thrusted it inside her several times. She whimpered softly. Inch by inch, I pushed deeper, my finger searching for the unimaginable depths within her. She let out a whimper, almost a cry, and I paused, ready to pull my finger away.

"No!" She grabbed my wrist and pulled me back inside her. "More, please more!"

"I hurt you," I growled. "What did I do?"

She shook her head, pulling my finger out and pushing it back in. "It feels good, please."

I slowly reinserted my finger, and she sighed.

As her body adjusted to the intrusion, she rose to meet my finger, her hips gyrating in synchronization with my movements.

I could feel her drum pounding against my chest as I decided to hover over her. I wanted her to feel like I truly was rutting her, even if it was from one of my fingers.

I thought of adding another finger, but with her cry of pain earlier, I thought the better of it.

A bit at a time, you fool. We have all the time in the world.

"More," she pleaded with me. My miresa wrapped her arms around my neck. "Please, more!"

I thrust my finger inside her, as my shaft continued to leak on the bed. There was no way I could get the friction I needed. I needed to release my seed, but first I would take care of her.

She screamed my name from her lips and my body shook with pride as I felt her cunt clamp onto my finger. I was too elated, too excited that one day her cunt would be mine and I could feel it around my shaft. Bassza, even just the head.

She panted, her arms letting go and fell to the bed. My shaft was hard, my sack heavy, and I pulled my finger from her body. As I quickly put it into my mouth, I tasted a tinge of metal on my tongue. When I looked down, I saw something I never wanted to see.

Red, tiny droplets of red surrounded the outside of her folds.

The drums in my heart beat wildly and I clutched my hand to my chest.

"Calliope?" I leaned down and got closer to her cunt to inspect it. I pulled back her folds and blood was smeared with her slick.

I wished there was a way to see inside her. I could not pry into her cunt with two fingers. One almost broke her in two.

Moon Fairy, my shaft will surely break her.

My miresa frowned. "You called me Calliope."

"It is your name! You are bleeding! Why is there blood? What have I done? I broke you!"

I jumped off the bed and ran to the cooking area. My shaft pointed outward and knocked over bottles and glasses from the table, while I searched for a towel and one of the baskets with a first aid kit.

As I rummaged through the now destroyed prepping area, I heard my mate calling my name, but I ignored her.

I hurt her!

A tiny hand slapped my backside. I stilled and turned, my shaft hitting her in the stomach.

"Oh my, that is quite large." Her eyes widened and her hand went out to touch it.

I pulled away and pushed it down the best I could. "Calliope, what are you doing? You are hurt. You should be in the furs. Here, let's go back. I will stop the bleeding. Come, please."

My miresa had a thin blanket wrapped around her, covering her breasts and slink down to her ankles. I could see the perfect outline of her body and my shaft did not get the message that I needed to take care of our female.

"You called me Calliope." She stuck out her lip. "You are supposed to call me your little fairy or miresa."

My shoulders slackened. *Is this why she is upset? Not the bleeding?*

"Miresa, you are bleeding." I pointed to her cunt.

She slapped my hand. "That's normal for a first time, you silly. You broke my hymen. Well, you stretched it. I'm pretty sure it was already broken because I've used tampons before, it's just that you got a big finger. And after seeing that big dilly you have, I'm pretty sure we have our work cut out for us." She tapped her chin. "You were great, by the way, ten outta ten!" She smiled up at me like I just handed her the moon.

"Little fairy." I knelt down in front of her and held her hands in front of me. "I made you bleed. I was too rough."

She shook her head again. "Did you not read that book? Have you not read about humans and their bodies?"

I looked away from her. "It has been a while."

"Then, can you trust me on this? You popped my cherry, you took my innocence, it's just a little barrier all women have. Some don't even have one." She patted my shoulder. "It just means you are doing your job, stretching me out. Don't be such a worrywart. If you want to go talk to Aunt Melina, you can. Just don't talk to Uncle Osirus." She leaned forward. "He's protective of me, and I don't think he wants to think of me as a woman yet."

I frowned and pulled her toward me, taking in her scent.

I did not like that she bled.

I did not like that I had hurt her.

I did like that I was the one that took this innocence that she talked about. I was the one that took it from her and would be the only one here after.

However...

"Miresa, what is a *tam-pon?*"

She backs away, her eyes wide. "Do...do you not remember that from the book, either?"

I shook my head.

"Do you remember the part where they talk about—" she leans forward again whispering into my ear, "periods?"

I shook my head. "That did not look very interesting."

My miresa groaned and slapped her forehead. "Cheese and crumbs."

Chapter Twenty-Two

Valpar

My MOUTH GAPED AFTER my little fairy told me what this *period* was.

Females bleed. Regularly. Once every twenty-eight moon rises, give or take.

I did not know if my ogamie did this. I never asked, and she never told.

My female cannot do this. I cannot have her bleeding. She will hurt, she will have cramps in her stomach. I cannot see my female hurt. She cannot cry unless she cries in pleasure.

"You can't!" I stood from the stool where I sat and pulled her off the table. She yelped when I threw her over my shoulder. "You will tell your body you are not allowed to do this."

"Valpar!" She groaned. "I can't just tell my body not to menstruate. It's normal. I won't be having a period for a while, I just finished before the ball.

You will get used to the idea." She patted my backside. "I have medicine I can use to take care of the pain, but it really isn't that bad. I don't bleed much, I'm small for an adult human, too."

A stab to my drums made me falter. It was because of her past. She did not grow to her full height. I shook that thought away.

I growled and set her on the bed. "And you bleed because you are not with an orcling?"

She nodded. "Yup. But don't get any ideas. I don't think we are ready to have any orclings, yet." She wagged her finger at me.

I growled again and wrapped my arms around her waist. "No, we are not. I want you to myself for as long as possible. I do not want to share your tits or your body until I have had my fill."

She giggled, placed both hands on my face and rubbed our noses together. "Goodie. Then show me the good stuff. Where is little orc?"

Little orc?

"You know, little orc that hides in your loin cloth? I'm ready to meet him. You pleasured me—" She counted on her fingers. "At least three times. Now it is your turn for me to get some." My miresa blinked several times from one of her eyes.

"Is there something in your eye?" I leaned closer to check.

"No, I'm winking. I'm letting you know I'm ready to play with your little monster."

I huffed. "There is nothing little about my little monster—er, big monster! Stop talking like it is another orc! It is a part of me!"

My fairy shrugged her shoulders. "Fine, suit yourself. Now let me see the big dilly properly."

I rubbed my hand down my face. "No, you are not ready. If you think that worm over there is what my shaft looks like, you are sorely mistaken."

She groaned. "Then give me a little peaky poo, and I won't have to try and guess what your serpent looks like," she cooed.

I groaned again. *This. Female.*

"Not yet," I grumbled. What if she was afraid by its appearance? It was mostly covered before when she saw it. It wasn't pink and it wasn't smooth. It was larger than any of the other *dil-dos* that were in the chest. Or even worse, what if she was excited by it?

I could not put it inside her—not yet. I did not have the strength to hold back the last brand.

"I've only seen two sausages before, and they were pretty similar. They didn't look like that pale pink one over there. They were kinda veiny looking, but I didn't get a great gander at them." She tilted her head back like she was trying to remember.

I snarled fiercely, the sound echoing in the tense air, as I firmly grasped her delicate chin with my thumb.

"What do you mean you have seen a sausage? I thought we were talking about shafts!"

My miresa tried to hold back her laughter. "I am. Just another word for a talley wacker. That worm on the floor over there. But it's attached to a body."

"A shaft? Are you talking about a cock?"

My little fairy blushed and giggled. "Yeah, I don't enjoy calling it that often, though." She leaned forward and whispered. "It sounds so dirty. I like coming up with different names. I can't wait to see yours and give it a proper one."

Moon Fairy help me, I cannot keep up.

I sighed heavily as I pushed my long hair away from my face. "What males have you seen? I need to know." Jealousy beat heavily through the life force of my body.

"My dad's..."

"What!" I roared and stood up. "How could—what!? Did he touch you?!" I stomped across the room and picked up one of the chairs and threw it across the cave. It shattered into pieces, splintering across the floor.

My miresa stared in awe.

"The muscles," she whispered.

"Miresa, why have you seen his—"

"He accidentally came out of the shower without a towel. And one time I walked in on Mom and Dad doing the—" She made a circle with one hand and stuck her finger through the hole. "— hokey pokey. You know, you put your dilly in, you put your dilly out?"

I stared at her with a blank expression.

"You saw your parents—"

"It was an accident!" she sighed. "They were being quiet for once and I saw them doing it. It was gross." She stuck out her tongue and shook her body.

"And the other male?" I gritted my teeth.

My fairy's shoulders went up to her ears. "I'd seen Aunt Melina get spanked when she does something naughty. It just fascinated me. There was one time I watched too long and Osirus' thingy kinda popped out."

I let out a low growl. "Do not lie to me, miresa."

She rolled her eyes. "Fiiiiine. I've seen it several times. But I don't watch them do the dirty. I leave before anything happens. They are my aunt and uncle, like yuck."

I rubbed my hand down my face again. My miresa needs a leash on her for sure. "You will not be watching the king and queen doing any of that from now on. Do you understand me? The only shaft you will look at is mine."

My little fairy raises a brow. "Can't promise that if you don't show me what you're packin'." She smirked and lifted a brow. "I'm pretty sure he wants to meet me. He's been pointing at me for the last twenty minutes."

I snarled and pounced on her, tickling her sides. She screamed and laughed, and the drums in my chest became lighter as her smile continued to widen.

Calliope

Valpar was on his back. He breathed heavily while he slept.

He said that orcs need little sleep, but since I've known him, he sleeps each night with me. On top of him, too. He kept both hands on my butt, my head on his chest and when he stirred in the night, he would take a whiff of my hair.

I don't find it weird, many souls in Bergarian do that. Especially the shifters. They are always sniffing their mates because they are part animal. Good thing they don't sniff each other's butts, or at least, I don't think they do. Whatever they do in private is their own business.

One of Valpar's hands fell away from my butt cheek and I lifted my head to see him still fast asleep. His face was relaxed, his brow wasn't creased or filled with worry. He'd done a lot of that lately since talking to Osirus, and I'm, actually, a little mad at my uncle for that.

Valpar was still holding back, I could feel it. Something else was bothering him. He was afraid of breaking me. Just like other people close to me.

I rubbed my lips together and felt something poking my butt. When I turned around, I saw it was his little-orc that was still covered by his loin cloth.

My eyes widened then narrowed. He was sleeping, he wouldn't mind if I took a look at it now, would he?

Nah, it would be fine.

Not like he would punish me, anyway. Or maybe he would?

I slipped off his body carefully and put a pillow on top of him. He still didn't move as I crawled to the lower part of the bed. He didn't need a blanket to cover him because he stayed so warm, but he had kept a blanket on me the whole time.

Such a thoughtful orc.

As I got to the loincloth I rubbed my hands together. I felt like it was Christmas morning and I was going to unwrap my present.

With the mushroom jar by the bedside table giving me enough light, I moved the loincloth to the side. What I saw before me was nothing I had ever seen before.

Valpar was large to say the least. He was long and girthy and his shaft was not smooth and veiny like I'd briefly seen before. Of course it was green, just like his skin, the head was purple and just under it were three distinct knots? That went down to the base. His balls were large and heavy. What made me lick my lips instinctively was how the tip of the head had a light blue, iridescent pearl of come. At least, I hoped it was come.

Why did I find that hot? When I got all needy I thought Valpar might not like it ,but he certainly did. I'm starting to see the appeal.

And for some reason, I really liked that he had a drip going.

I tilted my head and put my hand around it. When I gently squeezed it, a groan came from Valpar and more of the shining liquid seeped out.

Oh Goddess, his dilly reminded me of an eclair.

Mmm, I wonder if it tasted like frosting.

I bent down, taking a lick. It didn't taste like frosting, but it was still sweet, like a flavor of candy I could not describe. I wrapped my hand around the base of the head and slowly put it into my mouth.

Valpar groaned, his hips raising upwards.

I no longer cared if Valpar woke up, I was too busy savoring his taste. More leaked into my mouth and, as it did, I was able to take him deeper.

I hummed, his come coating my throat. It was relaxing the muscles, helping my throat take more of him, and I was both intrigued and horny at the idea of getting more of him inside me.

I cupped his heavy sack, kneading them. Valpar groaned and his hand reached for my head.

"Little fairy, what are you doing?" he rasped while trying to push me lower.

Mmm, more.

"Bassza, you are trouble," he growled louder. "You will be punished for this."

My body trembled and my heart raced at his dominance. The thought of being punished filled me with excitement, and I knew I would do anything to please him.

Best decision ever!

I let out a small whimper, my eyes locked on his and the heat that came from them made my clit pulse with desire. I longed to touch between my legs, and I slowly took my hand away from his balls and reached between my legs.

"No!" he barked.

I let go of him with a pop.

"You do not pleasure yourself. You are not allowed to touch yourself. Now suck."

I panted and placed my hand back on his balls. My pussy fluttered, wanting to be touched but I was too entranced by his command. No one has ever talked to me that way, and I really loved it.

I took more of him into my mouth, my lips skimming the veiny, bumpy shaft, my tongue stroking the underside, savoring every inch of his arousal. My hands gripped his thighs, pulling him closer, wanting more, needing more.

"You like that don't you, being told what to do." He gritted his teeth while I sucked.

Valpar's breaths were ragged, and his hands tightened in my hair, pushing me closer to him. I could sense his desire growing, his body trembling beneath me. The knowledge that I was causing him such pleasure only fueled my hunger.

"Female, look what you do to me." His words were a mix of anger and lust, his voice a deep, gravelly growl that sent shivers down my spine. "You've started something you have to finish, little fairy. You have to take me deep."

With renewed determination, I took him deeper. I don't know how I was taking him all. He was freaking huge. His length stretching my lips, my throat constricting around him. His groans turned to grunts. I wanted him, needed him, and nothing would stop me from having him.

"That's it, drink me in."

Valpar's hips bucked, thrusting harder into my mouth, his body tense. I gripped his thighs, pulling him further into me, my mouth moving in a frenzy, my lips slick with our combined desire.

More of his leaking come filled my mouth, it soothed the tightness in my throat to let him slide deeper. I dared not touch my neck, because if I did, I knew I would feel him at the base of it.

"Drink all of my seed, don't waste a drop," he said with a strained voice.

Valpar's body shook, and I could feel his release building as his sack contracted under my hands.

With a final, desperate effort, I took him to the base, my throat expanding to accommodate his size. I hummed when I felt his release, hot and thick, coating my throat.

His come soothed my throat aching from his large shaft. I panted when I pulled away and licked my lips. For a first blow job, I hope I did okay because I very much enjoyed it myself.

Ten out of ten I would do it again.

Then, with a soft growl, Valpar's hand went to the back of my neck, his lips brushing against my ear.

"What a naughty little fairy you are," he whispered, his voice filled with both warning and promise. "I think it's time to face your first punishment."

CHAPTER TWENTY-THREE

Valpar

MY MIRESA WAS SORELY mistaken about her punishment.

She would not receive the spanking that she very much desired, but a time-out facing a cave wall. I had never seen my tiny fairy so angry and red-faced.

I found it adorable. She looked like a field mouse defending her nest, trying to slash me with her small colorful nails as I lifted her and placed her by the blank rock wall.

She cursed my name and stomped her feet. She would look over her shoulder and glare at me. It took every ounce of me not to throw myself at her and forgive her for what she had done-touching me when I told her she wasn't allowed.

She needed this.

Boundaries.

I enjoyed everything she had done to me, and I would let her finish all over again, but she will learn that her actions will have consequences.

My little fairy stood and stared at the wall for the longest time. I did not leave her alone because my body would not let me venture far. My drums hurt too much to be away from her. It hurt me to see her like this than she it did her, I am sure of it.

Once I felt she had learned her lesson, I allowed her to turn, and she immediately fell into my arms and landed with a grunt.

Had I done the right thing? I still wasn't sure, but I knew I could not do this *spanking* she wanted me to do. How could I do such a thing when I knew she was abused in her previous life before she came here?

I swallowed heavily at that thought alone and held her closer. My little fairy thanked me for what I had done for her.

An outsider might be confused by this but, in a way I understood.

My fists tightened when I held her. If she had truly been wiped of her memories, then she lacked boundaries and her mother--aunt has done a poor job of teaching her. There were other ways to teach my little fairy the dangers of not listening and obeying.

Especially in a realm such as this.

This was beyond what I was expecting of having a miresa. I have never raised an orcling, I was far too young to pay attention to how my ogamie or my orgamos raised the rest of my brothers. I was going to need help.

Sadly, that meant I would need to leave the cave and go beyond the forest to ask for help from the Queen herself, who gets punished regularly.

Because she was an attention seeker, just like my miresa.

I did not like the prospect of taking my miresa to the palace, especially with so many unmated males there and the risk of another orc seeing my female.

But a trip was in order, and there was nothing in the book, that I recalled, on taking care of a female that did not understand about listening to their males.

When it came to my female, I would do what was needed to be done.

"I don't need to wear this." My little fairy grumbled as I held her close to my chest. As more precaution I had a leash around her waist in case she wiggled out of my grasp. "You are carrying me. It is not like I'm gonna jump off and run away. It's so embarrassing."

I grunted and shifted the leather strap that held a gigantic sword on my back. "But when I put you down, I don't want you to get too far from me."

My female rolled her eyes and laid her head back. Her long pink hair danced across the marbled floor. "I won't. Besides, there are few places to run to in the palace."

We took the long walk down the hallway leading to the throne room. No one was escorting us, not when Calliope was in my arms. She was rambling on, telling me stories about running up and down the halls and bothering the guards, finding hidden passageways when her family spent the last two summers here. Several guards looked at her fondly and gave her a wave when we passed by. Once she looked away I would send a deathly glare to let them know that they weren't allowed to look at my female again. They swallowed heavily and stood upright, and didn't dare to take a second look.

If they knew what was best for them they would ignore her entirely once we left the palace.

My little fairy laughed, giggling and pointing at how one of the younger guards was shaking. "Look how nervous he is. It must be his first day." She gave him a thumbs up, but I glared while her eyes were glued to him, and I swear he urinated in his cloths.

The drums in my chest beat faster as we got to the heart of the palace. There were noises coming from the other side of the throne room. The double doors were opened wide and a hoard of creatures outside of it.

"It must be Assisting Day," Calliope sat upright in my arms. "They might be busy. Why are you wanting to visit with Aunt Melina and Uncle Osirus, anyway?"

I kept my reasoning why I wanted to visit with her family to myself. I didn't need for her to get excited about the prospect of spanking her. For all she knew, her punishment would always be to stand in front of a wall until she understood what she had done was wrong.

"I need to ask them questions," I simply stated, as we entered the room.

Immediately, Queen Melina saw us and waved her hand for us to come forward. The people in the line stared at us as we came forward, but I paid them no mind, although, there was one creature that stood out in front of the rest. The fairy that I had told to leave me alone, when I first traveled to the Golden Light Kingdom hovered over the rest of the crowd to see the commotion.

I groaned internally and pretended not to see her.

"Guess he goes for the king's favorite, huh?" The fairy lifted her nose and elbowed her friend who was flying alongside her. "See that, picked a human over one of us. Guess he wants to show off his manhood by ripping her apart." The small fairy cackled, and my miresa wiggled in my arms and pushed away to land on her bare feet.

"He's my mate, you dumb bitch!" She tossed her hair over her shoulder and stared up at the two fairies.

My eyes widened at her tone and language, but a sense of pride swelled in my cloth.

Good thing I strapped it tight to my thigh before we left.

"I don't see any mark!" The fairy replied, before she used her magic and transformed into her larger body, hovering just above my miresa.

I stood beside Calliope, putting my arm in front of her. I would not have my female get hurt because I would not take this fairy's advances.

"Leave, Calliope is my miresa and you are not. You know the ways of bonds."

The attention was now on us. The room quieted down, and you could only hear the fluttering of wings from fairies and pixies that flew above to see the commotion.

The fairy sucked on her teeth and crossed her arms. "I see no proof. Not a mark on her, or you." She waved her hand in front of us. "Karma was right," she muttered, "king's favorite gets what she wants, that spoiled little human child—"

My miresa snarled and screamed for Simon. Simon belted out a loud scream and stopped in front of her. My female used Simon's back as a springboard to jump higher in the air and grabbed onto the fairy's leg. "I'm not a child, you stupid flying piece of glitter shit!"

The fairy screamed, pulling on her leg. She was unable to fly away because the leash I had around Calliope's waist was tied to my wrist.

I am a smart orc.

"You are certainly acting like a child." King Osirus sauntered up to us with Queen Melina, who was smiling brightly, leaning her head on his shoulder.

"She grew up so fast, didn't she, Osirus?" Melanie beamed up at Calliope. "Taught her everything I know."

The king sighed and waved his hand. The guards began leading everyone out of the throne room. Surprisingly, no one groaned as people walked away. That was when I saw the guards handing out parchments to the people. "They will get compensated for their time," Osirus said plainly.

"Miresa, let go," I growled. My female looked down, still holding onto the fairy's feet. The fairy still screamed, unable to fly any higher.

"Do I have to? I think I'm wearing her down." She wiggled and my shaft grew tighter against the leather.

A growl rose in my throat, and I pressed my hand against my thigh. My female was, again, wearing barely anything beneath the *dress* she wore, and I could see her cheeks perfectly.

What if someone else sees her?

"Female!" I barked. I raised my eyebrow, and she let go. She landed in my arms immediately, so I held her close and took in a deep breath of her scent. "Good little fairy." I hummed in her cheek. "You listened, so you will be rewarded."

She shivered in my arms and grabbed onto the strap that held my sword.

"A-a reward?" She breathed. "Right now?"

I chuckled darkly, shaking my head.

"Your Majesty!" The fairy landed and put her hands on her hips. "I know you are partial to Calliope, but honestly, you cannot condone this sort of behavior. Attacking one of your subjects like this?" The flustered fairy pointed to my mate, and I jutted my jaw forward, showing off my tusks and emitted a low growl.

King Osirus rolled his head making his neck crack. My teeth were grinding against themselves waiting to see what the king would do. Of course, since he was king, he had to be fair to all his subjects despite Calliope being his family. My female did attack physically first. What would the king do?

I'd protect her with my life and I would destroy this fairy if I had to.

King Osirus raised his hand. His gaze swept over Calliope and the fairy an unreadable expression.

The unruly fairy continued to speak, throwing her hand toward my miresa. I felt my anger growing, but my miresa sat in my arms with reverence as she waited for the king.

"Enough," King Osirus commanded in a voice that held the weight of authority. "Calliope, Simon, step forward."

Reluctantly, I put Calliope down. She patted my arm and stood in front of me, so I put my hand on her shoulder, ready to pull her away from the evil fairy. Queen Melina's eyes sparkled with a mixture of amusement and pride.

"Explain the encounter that sparked this remarkable display in my throne room," King Osirus commanded, his voice firm but not unkind. A smile tugged at his lips.

Calliope took a deep breath, her voice steady as she recounted the events that led to the confrontation with the fairy. She spoke of the taunts, the insults and, finally, the physical altercation that had ensued. She was unusually calm as she spoke, more than I would have been if I was forced to explain. I wanted to ring the little fairy's neck.

The fairy tried to interject, but a sharp look from the king silenced her.

When Calliope finished her tale, there was a moment of tense silence in the room. The king steepled his fingers thoughtfully before finally speaking.

"Violence is never the answer," he began, his gaze sweeping over to Calliope. "But in this case, it seems there was provocation. Ivy, you are aware that any two souls claiming to be mates is considered serious. Valpar claimed Calliope at the ball, and it was downright savage. You are lucky that Valpar, a decorated warrior from the war, has not asked me to punish you."

I wanted to smile at that, I didn't think that this would go in my favor. I kept my face plain of all emotion, but my miresa did not know how to hide her emotions.

"Ha!" Calliope pointed. "Told you we are mates. You can't lie about it! He's my big orcy-poo and you are just jealous you can't get his wiener schnitzel."

I groaned and wiped my hand down my face. "Miresa."

"Sorry, I mean his big club." My little fairy snickered.

"Miresa!"

"Okay fine, his lumpy third leg."

I covered my female's mouth and took a deep breath.

King Osirus ignored Calliope completely and turned his attention to the fairy with a look of disdain.

"You have overstepped your bounds, Ivy." King Osirus stated firmly. "You will apologize to Calliope and to Valpar for your blatant lack of disrespect and not following the laws this land has set for mate claiming. Mates can take their time and claim each other when they see fit, do you understand?"

The Ivy bristled but ultimately bowed her head in begrudging submission. "I am sorry for my behavior. Truly. It won't happen again, Your

Majesty." She turned to the both of us and apologized again. I did not feel she was sorry, but to move this along, I nodded.

King Osirus nodded in acceptance. "And you, Calliope? Do you have anything to say?"

Calliope twisted her lips. "Sorry for attacking you. I have powerful feelings toward my mate. I have this urge to claim him, but we have decided to take things slow. I can't help it, I just saw his giant dilly yesterday, and I'm ready for him to impale me with it, and the urge is just so strong. I'm just so lucky to have a big, strong, handsome orc to be my mate—"

"There is no way in the ever-loving Underworld that he is your mate! You're a human!" Ivy screamed back with a reddened face as she landed on the floor.

My miresa snickered. "I think someone is jealous I have a big, handsome orc, you know, for a **mate**." Calliope rubbed her hand all over my chest again, her hand drifting toward my shaft.

I leaned over and whispered in her ear. "You are being very, very naughty little fairy."

"Good naughty, or bad naughty?" She giggled.

My shaft twitched against my thigh.

"Good. I like it when you think so highly of me." And I did. My chest filled with pride that she was taunting this other female and staking claim on me that I was hers. Never in my wildest dreams would I have thought it would happen the other way around.

She pinched her thumb and finger together and ran them across her lips.

"Leave, Ivy, before I have Valpar choose your punishment." Osirus snapped.

Ivy faltered for a moment, she opened and closed her mouth wanting to say something. She lifted her finger and narrowed her eyes at Calliope to speak but before she could say another word, Simon lifted his leg and urinated on her.

CHAPTER TWENTY-FOUR

Calliope

THE FAIRY, KNOWN AS Ivy, was escorted out by the guards, while I was trying to hold in my laughter, but, failing. Aunt Melina was trying to hold in her laughter as well. As the queen, she should, but I'm no princess and my face is absolutely red from holding in my giddiness.

That fairy had what was coming to her. How dare she try and steal my orc when she had no claim on him whatsoever? She was jealous, and what made it worse was that Karma had gotten in her ear. How many other fairies and pixies has Karma talked to?

Is he spreading rumors about me?

I'm not one to get overly angry about things, but being with Valpar has struck new feelings within me. I'm very much in tune with my angry side now. It must be because of the bond we share and the possessiveness I have over him.

We haven't claimed each other in the traditional sense yet. There was no attempt to rail me. He treated me like I was a doll. I don't know if my little display earlier was enough to show him I was willing to scratch a bish to anyone who tried to question our bond. I was tough too! I just wanted him to throw me on the floor and take me right there.

No such luck.

I felt my temper rising once again until Simon bumped me in the thigh with his horns.

"Great job, bestie, gimmie noggin!" I leaned down and he tapped his horns on my head. I rubbed my hair and gave him a thumbs up, while I watched the guard clean up the puddle he left behind where he peed on Ivy.

Classic!

Uncle Osirus rubbed his hand up and down his face, while Melina threw out her fit of giggles after Ivy had left the room.

"What am I going to do with the three of you?" Osirus groaned.

I pointed to myself and to Valpar, but Osirus shook his head and pointed to Melina, Simon and me instead.

Melina gasped mockingly.

"I didn't do anything!" I let my hands go, slapping at my sides. "She started it, saying we weren't mated. I don't see how it's any of her business, anyway. Valpar told me she was trying to get up all in his junk before he arrived at the palace, so, I was staking my claim since he won't stake his on me." I narrowed my eyes at Valpar and crossed my arms.

I swore I saw a flash of guilt gloss over his face before his hard, stoic expression returned. "You are mine! I claimed you in front of the entire kingdom." His hand gripped the leather lead that tied me to him, and he pulled me toward him.

There wasn't a point in pulling away from him, he was far too strong. So I weakly went to him as he wrapped his arm around me and tilted my head up to him. "You are mine. It makes no difference in time when I bond us."

I hummed, because I would not fight in front of my aunt and uncle. Not in the palace, not with people around. I had enough of everyone watching me.

Valpar's arm tightened around me again and he squeezed, like he was trying to pull me into his body.

"Valpar, we need to speak with you in private," my uncle finally spoke.

I took a quick glance at Uncle Osirus and he sent me a smile. "Calliope, why don't you head to the kitchen? We've set your favorites out."

My excitement soared at that. Despite being brought a basket every day with sweets such as muffins and cupcakes, Valpar wouldn't let me eat them unless I ate the vegetables and meat he prepared.

He was a rather good cook, considering he was a male. Not that I should stereotype him at all for being a guy and being a good cook. Males can be good cooks, but he was an orc and I didn't think orcs really cooked. They just threw meat on the fire and bit into it and banged on their chest, from what I saw those first few nights when I looked over my balcony.

"Kay! See ya later, biscuits!" I slapped my mate's butt and pulled the leash that was tied to his wrist as I began walking away, until his arm wrapped around my waist and pulled me back to his side.

"No, she won't leave me." Valpar grunted, smashing me to his chest. "She's my charge, my miresa, and I will not have her running around the palace unattended."

Osirus took a confident stride, the hem of his long cape gracefully trailing behind him. The rich fabric whispered against the marble floor as he moved. Adorned in his fancy, embellished robes, he exuded that regal look, fit for Assisting Day. It was rare that Osirus would don such attire, only for special occasions such as today and mating balls.

"I assure you, Calliope will be just fine. If you prefer, I can have two of my most trusted guards take care of her. They are mated and know Calliope's personality, so she won't pull one over on them." Osirus' smirked and I rolled my eyes.

"I don't know what you are talking about, Uncle Osirus. I'm never naughty."

Valpar grunted and squeezed my ass in response.

"As long as you swear she will be protected." Valpar ran his strong jaw over my forehead.

I can tell he doesn't want to let me go, but I think we both needed this. A little time apart would be good. I don't know what he wanted to talk to Osirus and Melina about, but they obviously wanted to talk to him, too.

"I'll be okay, big boy. I've run this place for a while now."

Osirus chuckled, his deep laughter resonating in the air, as Valpar's grip on me weakened, before finally giving me a kiss that sent a surge of warmth through my body. A low, satisfied groan escaped his lips, as he pulled my waist closer to his. My feet swayed in the air, and I felt the sensation of weightlessness. When his nails dug into my hips, my nails pressed into his chest

Holy hot lumbersnack, what the heckers is happening?

Valpar growled into my lips and when he put me down, his eyes flickered up and down my body and he licked his lips. "Don't ever say I won't claim you. I will, my little fairy. Give me time."

And now, I'm wet!

A door flew open, slamming against the walls. "Hey, where is my favorite human!?"

I was breathless when Valpar let me down. He paused for a moment and stared at me. "Behave," he whispered, and I stood up on my toes to lick him on his cheek.

"Mine," I whispered back, and took off across the throne room before I could climb my orc like a tree.

"Calliope, I haven't seen you in weeks. Have you grown?" Finley and Everett, two fae that are both tall and more muscular than some shifters, hugged me tightly to their chest and made me a Calliope sandwich.

"Missed you guys!" I barely got out before Valpar roared and stomped across the room.

"Let go of her!" he shouted and the Red Fury Guard, because of their bright red hair as Aunt Melina had named them, dropped me with a thud and I rubbed my butt.

"You don't touch her, don't smell her!" Valpar picked me up and took a deep draw from my scent.

"Hey, big orc daddy, they are mated. They got their own females." I patted his shoulder as he stood up tall, puffing out his chest and making him tower over Finley and Everett.

"Don't care," he growled. "Don't. Touch. Her."

They both stood back and smirked at each other, holding their hands out in surrender. "Never again," Finely said. "Now, come along, we will get her to the kitchen. You can go have your talk with the majesties."

I reached up and licked Valpar on the cheek again. Valpar grumbled and I waved for the Red Fury to follow. Finally, more sweets for me.

"Maybe there is something wrong with his cock," Everett said as he swallowed a cupcake.

Finley slapped him in the chest. "You can't say that word in front of her."

"Sorry," Everett rubbed his chest. "What I meant to say was, maybe there is something wrong with his dick. Maybe he can't get it up."

I snorted and shook my head. "No, he can. He can just fine." I smiled, thinking how Valpar had to strap it to his leg. No one was the wiser when they looked at the strap on his leg. They might think of a hidden knife, but nope. It was his big club being pushed down so no one would see it.

"So, he just won't claim you, eh?" Finley said as he stuffed another cupcake in his mouth.

I shook my head, licking my fingers. "Not yet, anyway."

"He must have a good reason," Everett said. "Calliope is small, she is human. Osirus was the same with Melina. It took them some time to solidify their bond."

"That was because she wanted to wait. She was stubborn. Calliope is throwing herself at that orc out there and he hasn't done his thing." Finley, who talks with his hands, made a large gesture and the icing on the cupcake flew across the kitchen, landing on the sous chefs' forehead. "Sorry." He tilted his jaw to the sous chef, who removed the icing and put it into his mouth.

I shrugged my shoulders. "Valpar was so barbaric the first night. He slung me over his shoulder at the ball and looked like he was gonna take me that night. It was so hot." If I could make little twinkling stars above my head appear, I'd have made them appear then. "Then, I got tired." I shrugged my shoulders. "He wanted to take me away from everyone, even his tribe. It took him a while to find a place for us to hide."

Everett nodded. "Yeah, I saw you both running past the cottage. Sundew wanted me to go after ya, but I figured how he was holding you and you weren't screaming, he was your mate. You didn't look in distress and your arousal could be smelt a mile away."

I felt the heat return to my face, and I hunched over to cover my face.

"Ah, nothing to be ashamed of. I hadn't smelled that scent on a human before, but once I knew what it was, I let you both be. Surprised it was an orc. Just know he will claim you. Perhaps he is worried, since you are a human. You are small even for your kind and Calliope, Valpar he is—well, large." Everett pulled on his beard. "How big is he, by the way? I know you, have you at least sneaked a peek?"

I bit my lip and kicked my legs where I sat on the counter.

"Oi! She has!" Finley sat next to me. "How big we talking?"

"I shouldn't say." I covered my mouth. "But it doesn't look like—well, a normal one. It isn't smooth."

Everett and Finley edged closer, along with the sous chef.

"It's not?" Finely asked. "If the shaft isn't smooth, then what?"

I pinched my finger and my thumb together and pulled it across my lips. "I cannot tell. He is my mate, and I will not betray him."

Everyone in the kitchen groaned and I giggled.

"That's what's so good about you, Calliope. So trustworthy. Now, don't worry about him completing the bond, yet. Everyone is different. And you know Melina was human when Osirus her met. Everyone has their own time to bond. You are not a fairy or fae, they are expected to do it right away."

I put down the cupcake and set it on the plate beside me. "I know, but I've been raised by fae. My mom, well, Theresa, is the only mother figure I know. I can't help but want to follow those traditions."

"But your mother wasn't born a fae," Finley wagged his finger at me. "She was human, just like you."

I nodded solemnly. I didn't know mom before she was a fae, at least I didn't remember. I never really wanted to know. I was happy in the now, and that was enough for me. I'd had no worries. I enjoyed just living.

Where did all my time go? What was I like when I was younger? Before Theresa brought me here?

I fiddled with my fingers, trying to remember what it was like on Earth. A house, darkness.

I put my hand to my temple and fought back a sharp pain in my temple, until another thought came to me.

"Goddess," I whispered, and stared at Finley and Everett. "When Valpar and I bond, am I...am I going to turn into an orc!?" I squealed and slapped my hands over my face.

Simon jerked his head up. He hated that shrill of a squeal I made when I got upset. I saw his body freeze and he fell to the floor.

When humans bond to a shifter, a fae or a fairy, they become just like their bonded mate. If mates are mixed, such as a werewolf to a fairy, they have a mixture of genes to make sure they are compatible with one another. Such as a siren with a land dweller or a wolf with a vampire. Their children, however, take on only one of the parents' original genes in the womb, so the Bergarian Realm isn't overrun with a melting pot of mixed genetics.

Go gods for thinking ahead.

But what about me? I'm human, Valpar is an orc.

"Oh my gods, I'm going to be green!"

CHAPTER TWENTY-FIVE

Valpar

I LET OUT A low groan, my face contorting in discomfort as Osirus delved deeper into the concept of the spanking my miresa had mentioned. The mere thought of it made my body tense up, causing me to wince. My miresa's perception of the spanking was more of pleasure, not punishment.

The spanking was a game to the king and queen. They both play roles with their rutting encounters. It was one that I did not find very—arousing.

Fae were different, my rutting experiences were limited and I'm sure in time I would want to experience more with my female, but to have her call me 'Daddy' did not settle well.

The spanking, however, did have appeal.

There are two forms in which the king talked about; both awful to hear him speak and difficult for him to deliver. One was that of pain for consequences, which was what my miresa truly needed. The other—for fun!

"Theresa has coddled Calliope. If you had seen Calliope when she was at her lowest, you would understand why." Osirus wouldn't look at me as he spoke.

He didn't have to tell me about my miresa's pain because I already felt it. When I lie awake in the night and my miresa sleeps, I'd try and concentrate. I wanted to feel all of her, not just in body but in her soul. She was mine, she was part of me and I swore I could feel pain deep within her that she ignored. It was so deep, I barely felt it myself, but it was there.

She had suffered and I didn't want to bring it to the surface. I wanted her to be how she was now.

"But she needs boundaries, as you know. Calliope has been ignored and Theresa has turned a blind eye to her behavior. She can become bratty, just like someone else I know." King Osirus lifts his eyebrow at his female, who sat on his lap. She shrugged her shoulders as if she had no idea what he was talking about.

"Don't know where she got that from," she muttered under her breath.

"Just be sure to know how to distinguish between the two spankings, like we discussed. Follow through and don't let that pout get to you. I commend you for putting her in time-out, especially staying with her during her episode. She has a hard time staying alone with her thoughts."

I grunted in reply. The more and more the king talked about her parents, the more I disliked them. They thought they were taking care of my female, but they were causing more problems. Birch wasn't technically her orgamo so he felt he had no say. Theresa saw Calliope suffer for too long and just wanted to protect her, not punish her and give her what she needed.

If she was my orcling, maybe I would have done the same, but who is to know for sure? I wouldn't have left her alone to punish her, I wouldn't have let her out of my sight. I'd talk to her, even if it is not my strongest ability.

In my drums, I felt Calliope craved someone to care enough to put a stop to her. She acted out for someone to pull her back and put her in her place. To show her they cared enough for her.

I am that orc.

I denied her my physical touch for four days. I had not claimed her. I was as bad as Theresa and Birch.

My drums plummeted into my stomach at that thought alone. But I had so much more to worry about. Stretching her, her memories returning, I never thought having a female would require so much thinking.

"Valpar, are you alright?" King Osirus's voice entered my ears, and I jerked my chin up in acknowledgement.

"Sorry. Thinking." Thinking alone wasn't something I was used to. Not unless it required me to think of fighting, hitting or destroying something.

The Queen slid off the King's lap and approached me. She gave a small smile and looked up at me, while I hung my head.

"We know you are trying. I can't imagine what you are thinking and going through. Just follow your heart, your body, your emotions. The Moon Goddess wouldn't have paired you with her if she didn't think it was right."

I grunted again, crossing my arms.

I was a terrible male. I have done everything wrong with my female. Claiming was supposed to be easy. I was to take her, shelter, feed, clothe and make her happy. I had failed on all fronts, and most of all, I left her alone multiple times a day.

I couldn't help my body's urges. I had to relieve my sack. Being near her for just a few moments rendered my shaft to be too hard. Cock was such a better word; it felt more dirty and vile. I was glad there was such a vulgar word for a shaft in this land.

Even now, I cannot get her body out of my mind. Her smaller form, the tight hole she has. When I was out in the forest, the many times I left her, I would think of my face between her thighs, the tiny pink lips that would welcome my tongue.

Her tiny tits, her smooth body made my cock constantly hard, and when I rushed out of our cave, I immediately would loosen the strap that tied myself to my leg and let my seed coat the outside of my shaft.

Bassza, it felt good, having my shaft coated in my seed. It was enough to make it wet, to make me feel more like I was inside her. Buried deep in that wet cunt, taking all of me.

I closed my eyes, wishing I could be in the forest right now, releasing my heavy sack. Every stroke I thought of her, how it would feel on that small nub, that she liked to have licked so much.

At the time, I thought it was best to stay away, after the news was delivered to me. I had to rethink how to claim her, what was best for her.

Then, she had to say I was supposed to love her. I didn't know this word... love. Is it another word for rutting? Sex? What was it?

I could feel distant drums banging in my head.

She made me want to drink.

I gritted my teeth. I needed to leave this room, to relieve myself again of my seed.

It took me days to realize how she needed release as much as I did, and now I will have to do more for her. And I will. That was why I was here. She will get this spanking that she wanted, the pleasure that she needed until I find a way to claim her without having her past memories resurfacing.

"Valpar?" The Queen's troubled look startled me when I opened my eyes again. I shifted my cloth, making sure my cock was covered.

I cursed under my breath. I swear my cock would have fallen off before this meeting was through.

"I will take care of my female. Thank you for your...informational customs that will help our bonding." I winced as I tried to put the memories away, of King Osirus putting the Queen over his lap.

King Osirus stepped down from his throne and put his hand around the queen's waist. "Our pleasure, Valpar, truly, do not worry yourself. I believe you have gained extra wrinkles around your eyes. Would you like me to send the guards with you to help guard her?"

I growled, snapping my jaw toward him. "I can handle my female just fine!"

The king chuckled, placing a kiss on his female's head. "It's funny. Thorn is quite territorial, too, with his female. It isn't just you. It must be an orc trait."

"My-my brother has found a female?" I asked in disbelief.

"Yes, and he's got his dick strapped to his leg, just as you. I am rather curious now, too. What are you orcs hiding?"

Queen Melina silently clapped her hands. "Yes, we are."

I groaned. "When, where? Has Thorn claimed her, yet?" I'd like to ask him questions but of course the king shakes his head.

"I don't know. He basically chased me off. I have no idea what is going on, but I'm sure she's being taken care of. He's very possessive. Maybe even more so."

I huffed. The only reason I let Calliope out of my sight was because the guards were bonded to other females. These were guards I had fought with in the war. I knew of their loyalty to the king.

"I must find my miresa. It's been too long." I turned and heard footsteps behind me. They were muttering about Thorn while I tried to adjust the strap to my shaft. The leaking had stopped, but I knew I needed to relieve my sack, since I had thought too much about my little fairy's naked body.

She was always on my mind.

Perhaps we could find her room in the palace. I could—

I palmed my shaft, feeling my seed leak down my leg. Yes, we would both benefit. Try this spanking. I could palm her ass, as Osirus said. Melina said she would like that, feel the heat of her body—

As strange as it was, getting advice from the King, it was...useful.

Distant cheers from the outside caught my attention. It stopped me in my tracks when I heard familiar, deep voices. They sounded like my tribe, so I went toward the windows in the long hallway.

"Half of the tribe went back to the Wood, but the other half stayed. Sugha led them back so you could take your time," Kind Osirus said offhandedly. "A lot of the tribe was hopeful they could find their mates, since you found yours here..."

The king's words became a mere murmur as my attention shifted downwards. My gaze fell upon the bustling crowd gathered at the foot of a decorated chair mimicking a throne. The tribe's faces blurred into a sea of green, the male's voices merging into yells and laughter.

Among the commotion, an intense heat emanated from within me, starting from my chest and gradually spreading to my face. It was as if a dormant volcano had awakened, igniting a fiery energy that coursed through the branches of my forearms. The surge of life force within me seemed to boil, matching the intensity of my emotions. A primal rage simmered beneath the surface, causing my teeth to clench and grind together. The sound reverberated in my ears. My very being of calm, since meeting my miresa, was eroding away at the barriers that held me back.

I'm sure I could have broken my jaw myself with how hard I was clenching.

The queen came beside me. Her wings touched my shoulder, and I snarled, causing the king to pull her away. "Valpar, what's wrong?" she gasped when she looked outside.

Down below, the tribe, or what was left of it, was cheering. A bonfire sat in the middle and there was a small platform in front of it with a chair, decorated in vines, flowers and gifts at the foot of it.

Food was being placed on the large table, showcasing a delectable spread of appetizers, entrees and desserts. Mouthwatering meats, such as succulent roasted chicken and tender beef, arranged alongside an assortment of artisanal cheeses and freshly baked breads.

This looked like a miresa claiming ceremony. Long ago, when females were scarce, a female would pick her males. Females picked as many as up to five males to complete their clan, so every male was blessed time with a female. The males lived separately from each other; they had their own homes, and the female would come to them, care for them all equally. It was hard for the males, my ogamie was a beautiful female that cared for all of her males and my seeded orgamo came to be friends with all the other orgamos.

That was in the past. The Moon Fairy promised it would not happen again unless souls were open to it, and I knew my soul was not.

Calliope was mine.

I watched as the guards, the males I'd trusted with my miresa, walked out with her on their shoulders and sat her down on the cushioned throne that my tribe had created. My miresa was smiling, laughing as another orc brought her a plate of food.

Someone brought her food.

Someone brought my female food.

I was in charge of feeding my female.

I gripped my hand into fists, feeling my claws prick my palms. This was, indeed, a claiming ceremony. They were setting up the games, the sparring. The tribe was going behind my back.

With my little fairy's delicate, slender hand, she plucked the plump grape from the iron plate made by one of the tribe members. Its vibrant purple hue contrasted against the iron. The succulent fruit disappeared into her dainty mouth, her lips parting ever so slightly in satisfaction.

But, as I witnessed this seemingly innocent act, a surge of fury consumed me, threatening to burst through my veins. My clenched fist, filled with mounting rage, collided with the unyielding surface of the immense glass window. A thunderous crash followed, and the transparent barrier shattered into a thousand glittering fragments.

The air filled with the clinking of breaking glass, the sharp shards raining down upon me like a torrential downpour. The tinkling symphony of shattered glass harmonized with my tumultuous emotions, each falling piece reflecting the shattered remnants of my composure.

As I stood there, a silent witness to the destruction I had unleashed, shards of glass settled in my disheveled hair, embedding themselves into my trembling shoulders. The weight of my unleashed anger, mingled with the icy touch of shattered glass, settled upon me, a chilling reminder of the chaos I had wrought.

Once it had all fallen and the tribe down below stilled, I let out the loudest roar I could and jumped onto the windowsill. "Get away from my female!"

CHAPTER TWENTY-SIX

Calliope

"CALM DOWN THERE, LASS. I think you are going a little overboard."
Finley put his hand on my arm and rubbed it up and down.

"Nope, she's right, she's gonna be green. Hell, she might have those big
tusks too." Everett took another bite of cupcake, and my mouth dropped
open.

I was going to be an orc.

I was having a hard enough time being a human, and now this? Mom
was human, then she turned into a full-blooded fae and she was gorgeous.
She said she didn't change much, just the ears, looked a little younger and
sprouted wings.

I loved Valpar and how he looked, don't get me wrong, but me? I was going to turn green, have teeth and what about my hair? I loved my pink hair that Osirus had given me.

My breaths came in quickly as I started hyperventilating. Finley swore under his breath and searched in the kitchen drawers for a paper bag. Once he found one, he shoved it in my face and patted my back as I tried to calm myself, while I breathed into it.

This. Can't. Be. Happening.

"Shit, come on, you can't pass out. Valpar will cut off our balls."

Everett winced, cupping himself, and I closed my eyes, trying to take slower breaths. This could not be happening. Would I really change who I was completely? Be an orc? I was trying to be a fairy or fae to fit in with my surroundings. I was just now settling with being a human and now... I had to change myself again?

Cheese and crumbs.

"Listen," Everett sighed, and petted his beard. "I'm going to give a hypothesis here—"

Finley laughed, "Ha! That was a big word, try not to choke!"

Everett glared at Finley and continued. "I highly doubt you would become like Valpar. Orcs aren't like any other species in Bergarian, they were segregated long ago for a reason with that wall. They were different in appearance. They don't shift like the rest of us. Their body is completely different and, apparently, so are their appendages."

I pulled away the paper bag and sniffed. "You think so? I'm attracted to Valpar but I don't know if I, myself want to be green. I still want to look like me, just like how everyone else still looks like themselves when they turn into their mate's species."

Everett chuckled and leaned on the counter. "I'm not into the genetics of it all, but in here," he pounded his chest with his fist, "the Goddess wouldn't let a pretty little human like you change green if she really didn't want to. Especially, if it was going to upset you so much."

I gave him a small smile, but still kept the idea in my head. As long as Valpar cared for me, for me, I think I would still be happy. It would just be—really different.

The door slammed opened and humming filled the room. A large orc with leather straps criss-crossing over his body, walked past us, opened the meat locker and headed inside. He didn't pay attention to us, while we all watched and listened as he sang to himself.

I put the paper back on my lap and when he came out, he was carrying a large, cold sack of meat over his shoulder. It wasn't until then that he glanced over at us and raised a brow.

"Greetings. I am Olur, I was just retrieving this evening's dinner." He looked us over and then his eyes widened. "You are Valpar's female!" He smiled, but it quickly faded. "Where is he? Why are you alone? Did he abandon you?" His tone grew darker, and he stepped forward.

Finley and Everett stood in front of me, their arms crossing. "No, he didn't." Everett spoke. "He had to speak to the King in private. She's none of your business."

Olur huffed and readjusted the meat on his shoulder. "Well, she is part of the tribe now. I want to make sure she is happy with Valpar. If not, I would be happy to hit him for you. I have the biggest hands of the tribe."

And he did. There were scars all over them and his fingers were as big as zucchinis.

Good luck to his future mate.

"No, no need to beat him up. He's fine," I said.

"Then, why do you look distressed? Your face looks whiter than normal." He assessed me again, and I shrunk back.

Finley wrapped his arm around my shoulder, lending me some of his confidence. "She's fine. She's just got a lot on her mind: The first human and orc pairing, is all. It's a lot to take in."

Olur pushed the meat back on his shoulder. "Well, if it was my female, I would not let her out of my sight. Especially, after my shaft had been lodged into her cunt."

Cheesus.

Heat rose to my cheeks. Not just at the words he used, but—at the idea that he thought I was claimed. I was wearing a sleeved dress today, so he wouldn't see a mark on my shoulder. I swallowed heavily and couldn't look him in the eye.

"I—uh, is it something I said?" Olur stepped forward with drooping shoulders.

I sat up straight and put a smile on my face, because it wasn't his fault he brought up a sore spot. I mean, everyone around here expects us to be mated already, especially his tribe.

"We aren't mated, yet. We are—"

"What?" Olur snapped. "You have not been branded? This is—this is terrible! Why would he not brand you, yet? This—this is unacceptable!" Olur huffed and paced around the room, running his free hand through his hair.

I giggled, watching this male hold a large hunk of meat over his shoulder while he mumbled under his breath. The Red Fury looked equally amused, their stances relaxed and even smiling.

"We must remedy this. We shall have to persuade him to hurry this branding along! I have an idea, and I do not have many, but this will be entertaining."

There was a gleam in his eye and a friendly smile on his face. He looked like a troublemaker, and I was here for all of it.

"Wait here. I will inform the others!" He dashed from the room, while Everett and Finley stood by my side waiting for our surprise.

"Braxton would be so into this," Everett said as he hoisted me up on his shoulder.

Olur had managed, in such a short amount of time, to recruit the few of the tribe who had stayed behind to look for their mates, to help. They don't normally stay as long as this, but since Valpar found me, they didn't want to miss any chances.

Olur was determined to make Valpar angry, feral even, to have him claim me. I didn't ask for this. I even argued a bit with Olur, telling him I didn't want to make my mate mad at me, but Olur shook his head and held up his hand in warning. "Valpar has always been the solemn, cranky one. This is payback."

The tribe got to work and quickly constructed a platform with a chair decorated with flowers, a cushion, and gifts at the base. They said they used to do this long ago when the last of the females were alive and had to take multiple males as mates.

Apparently, females had harems of males.

Which sounded kind of neat, but I don't think I could ever handle more than one of Valpar.

He was more than enough.

The females would sit on this fancy chair, and the males would compete for her affections. They would bring gifts, feed her food, spar, play games and do foot rubs. The party could last for days until she picked as many males as she wanted.

But, I only wanted one.

The longer I stood and watched as the males constructed the small platform, more guilt weighed heavily on me. I didn't like this, I didn't think it was a smart idea. I wanted Valpar, and if he wanted to take his time, there had to be a reason, right?

"Don't worry," Olur spoke when he approached me. "We are not claiming you, we are only doing this to hurry Valpar along, to make him sweat. You will pick him in the end. We want our own females."

I snorted and shook my head. "You guys are bad. What if Valpar goes crazy? What if he hurts you?"

Olur scoffed. "So what? We like this. We are males. We like to rough each other up. Now let's have fun with this." Olur stepped away, his big back filled with scars, another sign that they did like to play rough.

Finley scooted me over, so I was resting my other leg on his shoulder as well. "Where is Braxton?" I asked, trying to steady myself on my two guards.

"His mate is becoming of age. He's stalking her a bit."

Everett rolled his eyes. "He's had trouble staying away from her. I can't say that I blame him. Now that's she almost of age, he'll claim her soon."

Everett and Finley carried me out from the covered patio, and when he did, I saw all the orcs I had seen at the ball. They were all cheering, and there was a gorgeous spread of food laid out on a table, with all my favorite desserts and the infamous chair that Olur told me about.

"So pretty!" I squealed.

I didn't want to hurt any of the tribe's feelings either with how hard they worked. They thought they were helping me, but I quickly realized this was going to be a big deal.

Valpar was going to be so mad.

Finley and Everett put me in the chair, and Simon raised his head high as he sat next to me on his own cushion, and was given a plate of food.

That is so dang cute!

"Aww! You all get brownie points for taking care of Simon!" Simon lifted his head from engorging himself with a plate of grapes and let out a large burp, causing the crowd to laugh.

A plate with grapes and cheeses on it was brought in for me by an orc with a scar across his cheek and he gave me a smirk. "Food for the female?"

I smiled shyly back at him, took one and popped it into my mouth. As the juice burst onto my tongue the shattering of glass caught all of our attention, and we looked up where the noise had come from.

The huge palace window above us broke into a million pieces. They fell out of the windowsill and onto a dark figure. A loud roar, one that I had heard once before at the mating ball before I was claimed, came from the darkness and Valpar stood where the window once was.

"Get away from my female!" Valpar's voice laid like a heavy blanket through the courtyard and even I felt the harshness of his words.

The muscles.

He jumped from the second-story window and landed with a thud. The surrounding bushes shook, as he took heavy steps toward us. The rest of the tribe moved about, almost unnerved now that Valpar was approaching, but Valpar's gaze did not leave the males that were walking around me.

Olur stood in front of me, the bonfire had to be hot on his skin as he stood so close to it. "Valpar, great of you to finally join the claiming ceremony. We are going to be starting soon."

Valpar's eyes widened and narrowed again, and his head whipped in my direction. His loose hair was wildly tangled, and he was not put together like he had been the past few days with me.

"What?" he said deathly quiet. "Calliope is my miresa. There is no need for this ceremony. These ceremonies are no longer needed."

Valpar was showing a cool exterior, but I could see his fingers flexing against his palm, his muscles rippling underneath his skin and his jaw ticking.

I shuffled in my seat; my panties were damp and it was only getting worse.

Valpar's nose flared, and he pushed Olur to the side, causing him to trip.

"Female," Valpar snarled and took heavy steps toward me. "Let's go."

"Nah, ah!" The orc that handed me the plate of grapes appeared. "She accepted my grapes. She has chosen me to compete." His smile widened. "She has chosen Olur as well because he said he wanted to throw her a party." Valpar turned and scowled at Olur.

"And her companion has accepted my pillow for his ass!" Another orc stepped forward, petting Simon. "Ass is another word for backside, I have learned. I like this word! I want another!" He raised his ale, slammed it on the food table and the orc toppled over.

I bit my lip. "I think he is disqualified... he just passed out." I pointed to him.

"Agreed!" The rest of the tribe yelled, and I covered my ears from their shouts.

Valpar turned back to me, snarling. "What do you think you are doing, little fairy?" His shadow blocked out the sun and I slithered down further in my seat. He was so angry his veins were bulging in his neck, and he was huffing.

I didn't want to make him this mad. It was supposed to be a joke. I was not afraid of him, but I was afraid of hurting him.

"Valpar?" I felt the heat behind my eyes, my eyes filling with tears. Valpar instantly softened and knelt before me.

"Did my tribe put you up to this?" he whispered, so no one could hear. Finley and Everett sighed beside me, looking guilty themselves.

I chewed on my bottom lip. I didn't want to get his tribe in trouble, either.

"Truth, little fairy. I won't be angry at the truth." He kept his voice low enough so no one else could listen to our conversation.

I nodded my head slightly. "I didn't want to hurt your feelings, and I didn't know how to tell them no, either." I hung my head. "They said they were doing it as a joke. For not claiming me yet." You could hear everyone laughing in the background and the clanging of clubs and swords.

I felt so stupid. I couldn't even tell Olur 'No'. What kind of strong female was I for Valpar? I didn't deserve to have males fighting over me when I couldn't even tell them not to do these sorts of things.

"I'm sorr—"

Valpar growled and tilted up my hanging chin. "I'm proud of you."

My eyes widened. He was proud of me?

"I'm proud of you for telling me the truth and being my good girl. You knew it would upset me, but you are so sweet as honey you did not want to hurt the tribe."

My mouth dropped and I shook my head. "No, I was a push over. I let them walk all over me. I should have—"

Valpar leaned in and pressed a sweet kiss to my lips. It was a far cry from the usual ravenous mouth he had on me.

"You are the light source not only to me but to the others in the tribe. You give them hope. You have made them get along." He glanced over his shoulder, and my gaze followed. The other males were laughing and slapping each other. Though it was a bit rough it was also very family like.

"Orcs do not get along. We do not spend time together. Only for traveling to mating balls. We do not laugh and speak to one another like any other species. But you have given them hope again. My little light source has made everyone happy, even this grumpy orc."

My lip wobbled and I pulled on the leather strap that crossed his chest.

Valpar rubbed his chin. "We shall play this game they want to play. I cannot promise I will not show my jealousy as others try to win your affection. I'm going to win for your hand."

I tilted my head in confusion.

Valpar stood up and rolled back his shoulders. "I will show you how strong and attentive I am. Then, once I win, I will pleasure you until you beg me to stop."

I slapped my legs together.

I'm going to need me some new knickers.

"Do not fear me while I fight for you, my little fairy, because I will kill an orc or two if I have to." Valpar winked and walked away, showing off his glorious butt.

"You don't think he's serious about the killing part, do you?" I leaned over to Finley.

Finley shrugged. "No, pretty sure he was serious. Orcs are weird."

CHAPTER TWENTY-SEVEN

Calliope

THE ATMOSPHERE WAS ELECTRIC as the entire ceremony transformed into an extravagant celebration. It surpassed any previous formal or tea festival organized by Uncle Osirus or Aunt Melina. Mesmerizing fairies and playful pixies observed from their vantage point in the sky. Fae and shifters arranged rows of chairs for the spectators, filling the air with anticipation. The servants and guards, caught up in the excitement, enthusiastically cheered for their favorite orc participants in each thrilling event. The scene was alive with vibrant sights and joyful cheers.

There were so many events, I couldn't keep up. More than half I didn't even realize were events. Such as picking which napkin to use—who knew that some orcs could sew? Another event I didn't realize was who had the best loin cloth? I was handed several spares they had made and when I held up one that was not Valpar's he threw a fit so large he put a hole right through the palace wall with his fist.

The muscles!

Osirus chuckled and waved like it was nothing at all, too intrigued by Valpar's temper.

The orc who won the event, Taghig, screamed with triumph, flipping his loincloth over his back to give Valpar a perfect view of his butt.

Taunting was a thing, and boy, I was here for it!

In another event, I was presented a large tray with a variety of food on different plates made by each of the males. One plate had nothing but desserts, another with desserts, fruits and bread, and another was filled with steaming green beans, a hearty helping of meat, potatoes, a piece of fruit and a small treat on the side.

As I scanned the array of plates in front of me, my eyes landed on one that instantly reminded me of Valpar. It was filled with colorful fruits and vegetables, a stark contrast to the rich, indulgent treats that I usually enjoyed.

Over the past few days, Valpar had preached about maintaining a healthy diet, and it seemed like his words had finally sunk in. Without hesitation, I reached for the third plate and held it up triumphantly. In response, Valpar let out a deafening roar that reverberated through the crowded arena. He pounded his chest and stomped his feet, drawing cheers and applause from the audience gathered around us.

My cheeks flushed with a mixture of embarrassment and awe, as I watched him bound around our makeshift ring, surrounded by amazed onlookers.

Uncle Osirus and Aunt Melina had eagerly joined me on the sidelines at the beginning of the events. Melina's eyes sparkled with delight as she commented on the powerful muscles of the orcs, and playfully declared that my orc was undoubtedly the most handsome of them all.

I couldn't help but feel like a princess, surrounded by these strong and attentive orcs who were competing for my favor. Their grunts and roars echoed in the courtyard, creating an exciting atmosphere that made me feel like I was at the center of a fierce battle for my favor.

I felt so utterly special.

Uncle Osirus leaned back in his plain chair. The servants tried to switch out the chair to a more comfortable one, but my uncle opted out to sit in the simple one. *He* didn't want to be *the* center of attention. He said it was my day to shine.

I didn't know if I really liked that. All eyes were on me, and some of them weren't exactly happy.

"Ignore them, Calliope." Osirus leaned closer to me. "If you don't, I'll have their wings plucked and they will be grounded the rest of their lives."

Aunt Melina snorted. "Ha! That was good." She pointed. "Do you get it, Calliope, grounded?"

I chuckled nervously and played with my fingers. The orcs that weren't competing were clearing the area for the next event. We'd gone through so many challenges in a short amount of time, and I had lost count of who won what, but in my mind Valpar had already won.

"Why do they hate me?" I turned to ask Aunt Melina.

She frowned and shook her head. "What? Hate you?"

I nodded. "Yeah, no one has ever really liked me, but those creatures over there..." I nodded in the direction where Ivy, most likely with Karma, was hovering. "I usually play with the children. They are more fun anyway but the grown fae and pixies find me—I don't know." I shrugged my shoulders.

Osirus made to stand, but I grabbed his wrist and pulled him back down. I watched as a particular group of fae and pixies saw and gasped that I had pulled the king back to his seat. "Don't," I whispered, "it will just make it worse."

"Does it make it worse?" Osirus pursed his lips. "Is that why you keep things from me, Calliope?"

I frowned. "What do you mean?"

"I know you don't tell me everything. You try to keep your battles to yourself, little one. But I have my own spies in the forests. I may not see everything that happens, but I see most." He chuckled to himself as Valpar looked our way. "But I see enough. Karma still bothers you, and now you have Ivy. I intervene when I have to, but you can always come to us."

I shook my head. "I can handle stuff on my own." I crossed my arms in a huff.

"And I've let you." Osirus nudged me. "But when it comes to your safety, I want to know about it. If things become threatening, I want to know."

I settled back in my seat as Simon rested his head in my lap and let out a long snore. He has a long braid going down his back, and flowers and little beads of gold and silver were intertwined within the braid. He looked like a little Viking goat. The orcs had officially adopted him as one of their own.

Before I met Valpar I let things roll off my back. I knew people could be mean, so I'd skip to the next person to talk to and hang out with Simon. I didn't really care why they didn't like me, but now, for some reason, I cared.

I wanted to know why they hated me so much. Why they were upset I was so close to Osirus and Melina. Did they want his power? Did they not like me because I was human? I wanted to get along with everyone. I wanted everyone to smile and laugh and be happy.

"Your aura is worrisome, Calliope." Uncle Osirus petted my head. "It isn't your usual glowing, bright, beautiful sunshine. Do you want to talk about it?"

I pouted and played with Simon's hair, pulling one of the flowers out of it and sticking it in my ear.

"I just want everyone to be happy," I whispered. "I don't want them to be mad. Or hate me."

Osirus leaned closer and whispered in my ear. "No matter what you do, little one, there will always be someone who is never happy, no matter the circumstance. They will be jealous of who you are simply because they cannot be you. They will be angry because they think the world is against them. It is all in their head. They want someone to hate, they want someone to blame. They have decided to take their anger of the realm out on you, and there is nothing anyone can do about it. It will eat them alive until the day their bodies meet the soil." Osirus' usually opaque wings turned an ominous black.

My lip trembled. "That's terrible."

Uncle Osirus sighed heavily, his wings losing their blackness as he pushed back a tendril of my hair. "What's terrible is that I can do nothing about those stupid souls, right now. But, if they ever touch a single hair on your head again, Calliope, you let me know." My eyes grew wide when I heard the threat in his voice.

I blinked several times until it wasn't my uncle I saw but that of a woman. She had dark hair and looked similar to mom, Theresa, but it wasn't her. She had sunken eyes, thin hair and yellow-colored teeth. I could smell smoke and alcohol on her breath as her face came closer and closer to me.

I felt my throat squeeze when she came closer, and words that came out of her mouth were so horrible I thought my heart would stop at once. "I hate you," she hissed. When I blinked again, it was Osirus who was in front of me.

I gasped, my hand on my chest.

"Osirus!" Melina shouted and turned me around. "Calliope, are you okay?" She shook me again, and I nodded shakily. I went to grab onto her arms, but Valpar was there in an instant, holding me to his chest.

"What's wrong?" he growled at Osirus and Melina. "Why is she shaking?"

My hands threaded through Valpar's hair and my breaths came in more evenly. I don't know where that picture in my head came from, but it felt so—real. Like I had seen this woman before, but I didn't know where.

"I'm okay," I squeaked as Valpar squeezed me tighter. "I just had a bad daydream and panicked a little."

"Daydream?" he muttered.

I buried my face into Valpar's hair, grateful that his hair was down and I didn't have to see anyone looking at us. When I finally looked up, no one was. Everyone was watching two of the orcs throwing enormous boulders across the courtyard trying to see who could throw the farthest.

So embarrassing.

"Nothing to be embarrassed about," Valpar mumbled into my neck, placing a gentle kiss there. "I am taking care of my female. Are you alright?"

I nodded and pulled away from him. The angry scowl he had given everyone since he walked on the courtyard was now just a beautiful look of concern. For me.

This made my panties wet all over again, thank you.

"We will talk more about this later. Are you sure you are okay? Do I need to take you away?" He wiggled his eyebrows and I started giggling.

"No, I want to see more of what you can do, male."

Valpar growled playfully and set me back down on my throne with my posse.

"Just a few more events before I claim my female." He sent me a wink, and I swooned all over again.

And just like that, I decide to put that horrifying picture of that woman to the deepest part of my mind and concentrate on my mate competing for me.

CHAPTER TWENTY-EIGHT

Valpar

DAYDREAMS? WHAT IN THE good Wood does that mean?

When I held my miresa in my arms, I tried to see if the king could give any hints of what this could mean. He was too busy talking to his queen, so I was unable decide if what this daydream was and if it was good or bad.

I didn't have time to question. I wanted my mate happy, so I did my best to hide the dread building inside me and find out what the *fuck* was wrong, so put on a smiling face.

And yes, I liked these Bergarian words... fuck was a good one as Olur had said previously.

I stole another quick glance at the woman before me. She appeared delicate, perched on the imposing throne adorned with a profusion of vibrant flowers, though, none as beautiful as her. The air was filled with sparks of anticipation as I took in the grandeur of the claiming ceremony.

Memories of my orgamo's tales flooded in my mind, recounting his own pursuit for my ogamie's affection. This is just how I imagined it. Only now, it was my female sitting there and I knew I would be the only winner.

Olur and Taghig, their chests heaving, bumped together with a resounding thud after hurling their massive boulders. As I walked by, I playfully nudged Taghig's shoulder, prompting both of them to give me a smug once-over. The air was filled with the scent of food roasting over the fire, mingling with the sound of grunts and cheers echoing through the crowd. "Beat that Valpar. I've been practicing my throws." Taghig snorted and spat out a large wad of phlegm.

My miresa let out a long *ewww* sound in the background.

He would not win points for that, at all.

Not that it mattered. My miresa would choose me anyway.

"Doubtful. My core is stronger, I'll send this past the courtyard, you shall see."

They both shook their heads and snickered when I picked up the boulder.

"I guess you can lift it. Especially, since your shaft is not hard and in the way," Olur said. "Can you not get hard in front of your female?"

Gritting my teeth, I couldn't help but fight the urge to snap back, as the male's words about another male's shaft would make any orc snap. The taste of frustration lingered on my tongue as I released the heavy boulder, its thud echoing through the surroundings. Determinedly, I stomped towards Olur, his wide grin mocking me. He was taller than I, but I was stronger. I refuse to be deterred. With each step, the ground trembled beneath my feet, matching the strength that surged through my veins.

"What are you saying, Olur?" I bit out.

The crowd fell silent, and not even a bird in the sky could be heard. My sweet miresa gripped the seat, in my peripheral vison, and her head cocked to the side in wonder.

Olur leaned forward, his arms crossed. The light sources that were slowly beginning to descend cast a glow on the side of his face. He tipped up his lip and Taghig slapped his friend's arm in warning.

"Don't do this, this is too far," Taghig said.

I growled. "No, he has said it. Let him finish what he has started."

Olur tutted and leaned back again. "I am saying your shaft has not lifted since you have been around your miresa. I think you might have a problem pleasing her and that is why you have not claimed her."

The creatures in the crowd snickered and laughed. When my eyes set on them they all quieted, but it was Olur that I wanted to wreak my wrath upon.

I leaned forward to whisper to my fellow tribesman. I did not want attention brought to my female. "I hold my shaft back with this leather belt." I pointed to my leg. "To not scare my mate at my constant desire," I muttered under my breath. "Her body is small, and I will not hurt what is mine. I will take my time to stretch her until I claim her, so I do not ruin her tiny hole," I snarled and Olur's mischievous face fell.

"What? She is too small?" Olur asked as we both turned to my mate, but she stood up in the chair, both hands on her hips.

"Valpar's thingy is not small! It's freaking huge! How dare you talk about his junk in front of other people like that!" She pointed to Olur.

Taghig held back his laughter, and I nudged him to shut his enormous mouth.

I pushed out my chest in pride, as my mate defended me, and crossed my arms.

An unknown shout came from the crowd. "What about a dick showing contest?!"

The crowd went wild in agreement and my miresa's face paled, along with the rest of the orcs. Our shafts were sacred and meant only for our miresas, to be presented to them when it was time to claim them.

All eyes were on my little fairy, who was standing on the chair. I knew my miresa wanted everyone to like her, to love her. She craved friendship, but as soon as everyone chanted her name she raised her hand as the king would and shook her head.

"No, we will not be having that sort of contest. I will not have my mate, nor any other orc tribe member, show off his private parts. They have a different culture than the rest of Bergarian. They don't show off their bodies like that and that needs to be respected."

Groans came from the audience. It was not the answer they wanted, but even with those groans and complaints my mate smiled and gave me a thumbs up.

"Throw that boulder, big orc daddy!" She waved again before falling onto her backside on the cushion.

This. Female.

"Orc daddy?" Taghig asks. "What is an orc daddy? Does one want to be an orc daddy?"

I walked away from both of my opponents, not wanting to speak to them about the topic. I was still getting the *ick,* as my miresa called it from talking to King Osirus about rutting.

Whispering under my breath, I muttered, "I'm going to need some ale after this," as I felt the rough texture of the boulder against my calloused hands. With a firm grip, I pivoted on my heels and hurled it skyward. The air filled with a tense silence as the massive rock soared through the atmosphere, passing the two other boulders. It crashed outside the courtyard, shattering the tranquility of the marble tiles near the meandering pathways leading to the palace's grand entrance. A twinge of guilt washed over me, and I winced, fully aware that I had once again marred a piece of the magnificent palace's construction.

The crowd cheered anyway, and my mate stood and pranced toward me, trying to wrap her arms around my waist. "You did great! Is it over now? I've been sitting in that chair all day. The light sources are melting and I can't stand sitting there another minute."

"The light sources? Melting?"

My female nodded excitedly. "Yeah, doesn't that sound so much better than setting? They look like they are melting into the trees."

Her face was bright, and she was smiling. Her blunt teeth, which could not help her in a battle, were white as the cleanest of pearls, and her eyes sparkled with mischief. She was sweet and innocent, and all I could think about was ruining her with my cock.

Being selfish with her.

But she wanted it, too.

I huffed and pressed my forehead to hers. "Yes, I do like your word better."

I felt the bodies of my tribe come around us. They were blocking out the light sources and the darkness made me hold on to my miresa tighter. She grabbed the strap that hung over my chest, watching the males gather in a semi-circle around us and bend their knees, then laid their hands on their thighs.

"You have officially claimed me, little fairy. I am your male." I puffed out my chest.

My little fairy tugged on my leather strap. "Like with your parents?"

I nodded, my eyes warming. "Yes, but none of us have ever seen a claiming ceremony. We were all brought to life after. I suppose they wanted to relive it at least once. Now that we do not have to fight for females and breeding rights, we don't have to do it any longer.

My miresa blushed and shrugged her shoulders. "I don't know, I think it should still be done, at least every once in a while. It's a history, it shouldn't be forgotten."

"I think it is because she liked all of our muscles." Taghig ran his hand up and down his torso and I let out a growl.

Olur patted Taghig on the shoulder. "We wanted to perform the Icha since we didn't get a chance. We all knew that Calliope would have chosen you, anyway, but we wanted to at least try."

My female leaned her head on my shoulder. "I think they might have been doing this as a joke, but really, it was for all of them. Continuing a tradition."

I squeezed her arm tighter and grunted in agreement. The Icha would be loud. Once the females had chosen their males, the tribe would harbor no hard feelings— at least while the female was around. The orcs would gather, bang their chest, yell and scream, show their tongues and scream a battle cry. This send-off was more to let off steam for an orc who did not gain a female.

And I was the only male, I would not have to wait my turn to be with her.

I growled, happily, my hand raking down her back and cupping her backside. She squeaked, and I pulled her up into the crook of my arm so she could sit up higher, so she could see what my tribe was going to gift us both.

Their blessing, their surrender.

The surrender was the best part. They will never try to take her from me, never try these foolish games ever again.

My female's smile was wide, and I felt jealousy flow through me, but the way she held onto my neck and did not give the other males affection through the games kept me grounded.

Olur's mighty roar echoed through the clearing, his heavy footfall causing the ground to tremble. The gathering appeared disorganized, their movements reminiscent of the teachings from their elders. In a synchronized effort, they aligned themselves behind Olur, emulating his actions. The thudding sound of chests being struck and feet stomping reverberated through the air. The onlooking crowd remained hushed, their anticipation palpable as the tribe unleashed a cacophony of unintelligible roars, soaring into the sky.

The light sources continued to set as they continued for over ten minutes, slamming their hands into one another's chests and backs. They jutted their jaws forward to make frightening faces like when they went into battle. My chests puffed up as I watched. This is what my orgamos, and my seeded orgamo must have felt like when they claimed my ogamie.

Once the orcs finish pounding the dirt, their heavy feet creating a resonating thud, they let out one last roar that echoed through the arena. The crowd, filled with anticipation, remained still, their breath held in suspense, until the deafening silence of the orcs engulfed the air for a fleeting moment. Then, a thunderous cheer erupted, reverberating off the palace walls, as the spectators released their pent-up excitement. Amidst the uproar, the young ones, eyes wide with wonder, attempted to mimic tribe's fierce dances, their tiny feet tapping against the ground in playful imitation.

Olur and Taghig approached, giving us a nod. My female held onto me tighter and placed her head under my neck.

"The ceremonial bedding is being brought." Taghig wiggles his eyebrows. "We know that you are waiting to... uh," Taghig scratched his cheek and looked away. "But this is part of the ceremony."

My miresa climbed higher up on my shoulder, her short dress coming up too high for my liking, and I shielded her backside with my hand. "Why are there so many blankets and pillows? What's it for?"

I groaned and wiped my hand down my face.

"No," I groaned and faced the tribe. "Not this. I will not give you this."

"It's tradition! They want to uphold some of what we lost. What better way to celebrate than with your miresa?" Olur said.

It was a tradition to have a large claiming ceremony, then a celebration. However, the tribe found that this was a celebration enough. After being at the ball and the claiming, they want us both to be bonded, in the open.

They had not witnessed a female body. They wanted to know what to do. I would not let them figure it out from me.

Did they not understand that I could not? My female was not ready and my possessiveness over my female was far too great to let everyone in the kingdom see her naked before me.

"I cannot do it!" I hissed at him. "You know this! I will not—do that to her. I will not do that to us. As long as my drums beat, I will not expose her body to any other male. Only I can see her in her flesh!"

The orcs around me tilted their heads in confusion. It would be confusion because past matings had taken place out in the open. The tribe was to witness it. We were all possessive, and I did not like, nor did past orgamos like our females subject to others watching but it was true. We did not have markings to mark our females like the Bergarians did. No permeant bites. Witnessing was our only way it--was tradition.

Things were different now. I had my female. Soon they would get theirs. I did not want to share anything of my female.

King Osirus strode up to us, seeming to have heard our conversation. His face was not strained with anger, nor was he showing any signs of being upset. "You have a dilemma, I see?" His voice was calm.

We all stood our ground. We had never been afraid of the king, but we had never been comfortable to share our traditions.

"I know we have different traditions, but I'm sure Calliope would not appreciate what you have in mind." The king looked back at the blankets and pillows set up on the grasses. "Especially with this sort of crowd."

Orcs, fae, pixies, shifters and even a few sirens dusted the crowd. No, even I didn't like it.

My female squirmed in my arms until she leaned over my shoulder. I cupped her backside so others couldn't see her ass. "Where are all the children going?" She tilted her head as the parents led the children away, but most of the adults stayed. "What's going on?"

"No, we will not do this," I hissed. "Tradition or not, I will not share my female."

The other orcs groaned in disappointment. "We just want to be a part of something our orgamos and ogamies had. We want to celebrate too—" one orc said from the back. My shoulders slumped, but I still shook my head.

No, my female came first.

Before I could turn away, the king put his hand on my forearm. "I have something that will satisfy everyone's needs and keep Valpar and Calliope's mating on their own timeline."

The king snapped his fingers and whispered to his servants who stood by him. They hurried off and my miresa was whispering to Melina. She was giggling and playing with my hair while watching the rest of the crowd that refused to leave.

Assholes.

I like this word, too.

Soon, King Osirus erected a tent and filled it with hanging lanterns that cast a bright light, spilling out of the tent. As my miresa would say, the light sources have melted into the trees and now darkness has descended upon the land.

When one of the servants went inside to place a tray a food, I was shocked. I could see the silhouette of their body. You could see the outline of everything, even their wings. I now knew what the king was doing. The light would cast shadows of our bodies, so the tribe and the king's people could see that we had solidified our rutting—mating.

This was more than just the tribe being here, knowing how precious it was. It felt like half the kingdom were here, and the king and queen no less. How would my miresa feel about this? And I would not bond with her, not now, not in front of these people.

Taghig nudged me with his elbow as the orcs continued to set up the large tent. Pillows and blankets were being brought from the palace, and I could hear the queen's joyous cackles coming from beside my mate's throne.

"Just make it look believable. This is the best outcome." He shrugged his shoulders. "You do not have to mate her. Obviously, you care for her, but she is not physically ready."

I jutted out my jaw. "I'm not doing this unless she wants to." I stepped up to Taghig. "You both started this." I pointed to both Taghig and Olur. "You thought you would meddle, and now you have started things you do not understand." I took my free hand and balled it into a fist. "She is human. She listened to our culture, saved all of your cocks from exposure and you expected her to show off her body and let people hear her cries of pleasure. I won't have it." I snarled.

I couldn't let my miresa do this. Even if the king was trying to help keep peace with both of the Wood and his niece. How could I subject my mate to something as this?

"Only the Orc tribe shall remain." King Osirus' voice echoed through the arena.

My mate turned around and slid down my body, so she sat in the crook of my arm. Her hand cupped my face to have her face to face with me.

"Hey, are we gonna go do the dirty in there?" She nodded to the tent. "While everyone is outside of the tent?"

"Do the dirty?" I asked.

"You know, the nasty. The good stuff. Like what we do when we are naked." She wiggled her eyebrows.

I didn't speak, too stunned at what she was saying. *What was she saying, exactly?*

"This is gonna be like a rated X puppet show," she whispered.

"Female, I don't know what you are saying!" I growled at her.

My miresa sighed and patted me on the chest. "It's okay, to get performance anxiety. I bet I will get that too, once we are in there. Just know, I'm here for you. All of me, right here." She rubbed her hand down her neck and to her chest. Her tits hardened under her touch and the strap on my shaft grew too tight for me to bear.

Sweet Moon Fairy.

"Well? Are you ready," she whispered, "because I cannot wait for Ivy to get super jealous when I choke on your dick."

CHAPTER TWENTY-NINE

Calliope

I HAD VALPAR'S ATTENTION on me, which is what I wanted. My heart was racing, and I was trying my best to keep his nervousness away, by not thinking about the crowd that surrounded the courtyard.

Valpar's tribe would remain, obviously. The Golden Light Kingdom's subjects were thinning out, mostly taking their children away. At least some did not care to witness this tent ceremony, but there were still quite a few that were still here. Freshly mated and single souls that were used to the debauchery of a kingdom that was freer with their sexuality.

Valpar and his kind were not—at least, this generation from what I could tell. His tribe wanted to experience this because their parents did, and I wasn't sure if they knew what they were getting into.

I had to be strong for my mate, because the tribe did a lot for me as well as the kingdom. We got a peek at what it was like to be an orc, and the males also took their time to sniff around and check for females.

It was a win-win for both, right?

As Vapar and I settled into the tent, a wave of nausea twisted my stomach into tight knots. The interior was adorned with a plush padding, giving the impression of being enveloped in softness. Blankets and pillows were scattered in every corner, creating a cozy and inviting atmosphere. The air was filled with the comforting scent of freshly laundered fabric. In one corner, a delightful assortment of snack foods awaited, their aromas tempting.

We weren't here for food, though, were we?

Valpar's hand sought mine, his touch grounding me amid my rising anxiety. I could sense his own apprehension, his grip a little tighter than usual when he lifted me up and set me in his lap.

"I don't like this," he whispered.

I knew he didn't. He said it the entire time we walked over. His glare was to the crowd, mostly those not of the tribe. Some of Osirus' subjects left, not really feeling the orc tradition, thank the goddess.

Even Ivy, who stood with her arms crossed and shot daggers toward us, didn't stay, and she was the only person I wanted to.

I wanted her to know that Valpar was mine.

I straddled over Valpar's waist. He sat up straight in surprise and I cupped his face. "Let's just pretend they are not out there," I whispered.

The tent was situated toward the center of the courtyard, while Uncle Osirus ordered the crowd to be pushed far back to not disturb us. The orcs were complaining they wouldn't get a better view or be able to listen very well, but Valpar argued that we should have time alone.

"How can you be alright with his?" my mate grumbled, his forehead kissing mine. He took his calloused hand and pressed it between my breasts. "You are scared."

He pulled away but kept his hand on my chest. "I can feel you." Valpar tilted his head. "You are worried, excited and aroused." His lip tilted up, and he took a tentative lick of his tusk. "I thought you wanted this. I thought you were going to devour me?"

I swallowed heavily, my hand running up his chest. "I do. You keep forgetting I was raised around these crazy fae that do the nasty. Besides, am I not allowed to have other feelings?"

"You have many. All at once." Valpar pulled me closer, my pussy feeling the warmth of his abdomen. "Does it not hurt your head?"

I snorted. "No? Women can have many emotions at once. Can you not?"

Valpar scratched his face with one of his claws. "It makes my head hurt. It makes me want to hit things, to push all feelings out."

"Is that why you go outside so often when we were in the cave? To let out all your emotions?"

Valpar hummed. "Yes. Amongst other things. I have many thoughts. I am used to one at a time, one problem to fix. With you, I have many."

I frowned and played with the strap on his thigh. I could see the knot where he had it tied tight. Melina said that Valpar had kept his dick tied up so I wouldn't be afraid of him and his constant desire for me. I don't know why he was so concerned about that. Not once have I ever been afraid.

I fiddled with the knot, trying to undo it while he spoke.

"I don't want to hurt you, and I want to be a suitable mate." He swallowed. "I want to give you these spankings you desperately want, but not hurt you."

I blushed and leaned my head on his chest. "Sorry, I speak my mind. I think that is why people don't like me so much. I should not have overwhelmed you, it's just... I like the idea of you being rough with me. Flipping me over, slapping my butt, digging your claws into my hips..."

Valpar's eyes widened, his breath heavy with want. "W-why? Why do you want me to be rough? Is this why you defy me? To get yourself in trouble?" he growled.

I grinned and patted his chest. "With you, yes. I enjoy pressing your buttons. With Mom and Dad, it was more to get attention. When you stuck me in that corner, and stayed with me, that was the first time I didn't feel alone. You were there. I know it only happened one time, but for the first time I felt like someone would stay and call me out, then still care about me after."

Valpar's chest rumbled. "Of course, I will always be there. You will never be alone again."

My face heated. "With my parents, I just wanted them to notice me. They protected me, sure, but too much. They stuck me in my room and left me alone, because it was like they didn't know what to do with me. And I don't blame them, they were newly-mated when they got me, I guess." I wrinkled my nose in thought.

Valpar's jaw flexed and the muscles in his neck tightened. "I felt like I was doing poorly, so I sought the king and queen's advice today. More about these spankings—"

I gasped, trying to hold in my laughter. "That's what you wanted to talk to them about?"

Valpar's cheeks turned a deeper shade of green. "Yes, I didn't want to hit too hard. I didn't understand this game they play."

I giggled and wrapped my arm around Valpar's neck. The strap knotted around his leg came undone and his dick stood up to attention.

"Fuck! What in the gods' names?" He tried to push down his junk, but I shook my head.

"And no more hiding yourself. I'm not scared of anything from you. We need to talk more—communicate." I tapped his nose like he often does to me. "Let's do that, okay? That way, you don't have all those *feelings* stuffed up in you like some hard tummy dumplings and have to go bang on a tree."

Valpar groaned, fell into the bedding and rolled me on top of him.

"Now, is there anything else bothering you? Any feelings you want to get rid of? Any way I can help you?" I tilted my head and let my hair cascade around us.

I felt my mate's dick beneath me. I couldn't get how thick he was. The bulges of his shaft rubbed up against my pussy and I let out a breathy, involuntary moan.

I needed this. He needed this.

"Female, the only feeling I want is to have your slit rubbing against my cock."

I can do that.

He pulled me closer, the soft breeze caressing our faces as his warm breath tickled my lips. His strong hand gently found its place at the back of my head, tangling in my hair, and he pulled me tightly against him. I suppressed my whimpers, the faint sounds of distant chatter reminding me of the presence of others.

Valpar's hips swayed, causing a tantalizing friction between my clothed core and his body. The tips of my blunted nails pressed into his chest, eliciting a soft gasp from both of us. As the fabric of my dress inched upwards, I could feel the anticipation building.

Gods, I wanted him to touch me.

Valpar was not patient. Instead, his claws raked down the side of my body. I gasped when I felt it nick part of my skin. The ripping of the clothing sent shutters down my body, and he growled into my neck reaching for my underwear.

"No cloth between us," he snarled. "Nothing."

His razor-sharp claws ensnared the delicate thong I wore, causing it to snap with a swift motion. The sudden release exposed my bare buttocks to the cool air, igniting a shiver down my spine. In a reflexive gesture, his hand landed on my backside with a slap, promptly shielding my exposed flesh.

"Is this what you wanted?" He growled and pushed me lower, the head of his dick so close to my pussy, and I whined when it missed it entirely and slid past. His shaft was slick, and it wasn't from me. His cock was leaking. It was all over his stomach and now my pussy had gathered it and was using it as lubricant.

The tent quivered with each swift motion, casting dancing shadows around us. The flickering light abruptly plummeted, its brilliance now nestled in a distant corner, enveloping us in the shadows.

Groans from the outside were the last thing I thought about.

"Valpar?" I whispered, my nipples scraping against his happy trail.

"I want you to rub your cunt all over me. I want your scent on my body, female." Valpar leaned forward pulling my pussy over his bumpy shaft. I whimpered when my nipples dragged over his stomach.

Valpar groaned, his hair cascading in front of him as he helped me rub against his cock. But damn, it felt so good. His thick bulges rubbing against my clit, the constant leaking of his come was coating the both of us.

He chuckled deeply, the sound sending a shiver down my spine. "You are so wet, so aroused. I can feel it, dripping down my shaft, a slick present for me to enter you with one day."

Hummed loudly, my body trembling under his touch. He silenced me when he took his clawless finger and stuck it inside my mouth. "Suck, I don't want anyone to hear you," he rasped.

As I sucked his finger, the bulges in his dick grew. I could feel them beneath me growing the more I rubbed myself on his body. We started off slowly, but Valpar was becoming erratic as he tried to rub me faster along his length.

I tilted my hips to another angle, rubbing my clit just right. I felt our arousal mixing together. I moaned as the sensation enveloped me, the friction of his swollen cock rubbing against my clit driving me wild.

"So greedy." Valpar's chest rumbled, his eyes hooded as he watched me riding him. "You're such a sinful temptress, female. So wet and needy. You're driving me insane with your desire for me."

I sucked his finger harder when I felt myself tip over the edge.

"That's right, female. Rub yourself against me," he ordered, his voice rough with desire. "Show me how much you want me."

I groaned, arching my back and speeding up my movements. The sounds of our skin slipping and sliding together filled the tent, along with our heavy breathing and whimpers. I felt his come completely coating my entrance when he stopped me.

My head dropped to his chest as I listened to his rapid heartbeat. "Valpar, I want you inside me," I gasped, my voice barely more than a whisper. "Please, fuck me. I need to feel you."

He groaned, his cock pulsing between my legs. He dug his claws into my backside and let his hot come shoot between my legs and drip down my slit.

"Please...fuck me," I begged, my body trembling with anticipation. "You are so close you are right there." The thick head of his cock nudged me, and I swear if I moved just a little lower I could have had the head inside.

And he was still hard, despite him getting his release. I knew he could go again. I just knew it.

Valpar emitted a low, menacing growl as he forcefully flipped me onto my back. His eyes roamed appreciatively over my form, his hand, adorned with neatly trimmed claws, gliding smoothly across my skin, leaving a faint tingling sensation in its wake. "Your cunt is swollen, just rubbing my cock, my little fairy. Do you really think you can take me now?"

I licked my lips and nodded.

Valpar chuckled deeply. "I will not brand you here. Not when we are being quiet so no one else can hear, but I will stretch you further."

His hand traced down my stomach, his fingers rubbing against my clit.

"Valpar, please," I whimpered.

He smirked and leaned down, his mouth capturing mine in a deep kiss. His tongue sliding against mine, tasting me and begging for more.

Slowly, he lifted his body, hovering over mine. I felt his thick finger rub over my stomach, gathering his come and placed it at my entrance. I moaned into his mouth, my body trembling with anticipation.

Valpar pulled away from the kiss, his nose trailing down my neck. "You like any part of me inside you, don't you, little fairy? Any way to fill up this greedy little cunt?" he said as his eyes narrowed.

I nodded, concentrating on his thick finger slowly sliding easily inside. It was much easier this time, it didn't sting, and I felt my insides contract around him.

Valpar hummed, pulling his finger out of my body. "I like filling you with my come, even if I can't stick my cock inside you yet. I will do this more often, so you smell of me."

He gathered more on the outside of my leg and pushed it inside, my body shuddered.

"Valpar." I squirmed, and he moved the rest of his body on top of me.

"Do you fear me?" He paused the thrust of his finger, and my pussy contracted around it.

I shook my head.

"Speak, I need your words, little fairy. Do I frighten you?"

"No," I whispered. "I-I just. I don't want to have a baby—not right—"

Valpar leaned in and kissed me gently on the lips. "I've taken care of that. You will not carry an orcling until we decide. This is just the primal part of me wanting to paint your womb with my seed."

My throat bobbed, and another finger probed my entrance. "Be my good little female and take another one of my fingers. I want you stretched for you to receive me."

His face went to my neck, his tusk grazing my collar bone until his lips attached to my shoulder. He nibbled as he pushed the second finger inside. It didn't burn. I felt myself stretch and felt the sweet fullness my body was being given.

Cheese and crackers!

With a low growl, he thrust the full length of two fingers inside with one powerful movement. My eyes widened in surprise and my breath caught in my throat as I was stuffed.

I gasped as he withdrew and then thrust again, a little deeper this time. My hips bucked slightly, adjusting to his size. He continued to fill me, his chest heaving with each thrust.

"Calliope," he rasped. "My miresa, my mate. You have taken two of my fingers." He said as I watched the rise and fall of his back, his muscular shoulders heaving. "How?"

I wrapped my arms around his head, keeping him in place. The room was filled with the sounds of our bodies moving together as I felt his dick rub up against my leg. Valpar's took his free hand, cupping my butt and steadying me as he continued to pound into me.

I wrapped my legs around his waist, pulling him deeper into me with each thrust. My nails dug into his back and my hips matched the rhythm of his hand.

"I can't wait to put my cock into you. Feel your warm cunt around me, milk me of my seed and coat you on the inside," he snarled and sucked harder on my shoulder. "I want all of you, Calliope, my little fairy. I want to tuck you away and let no one gaze at you, let no one touch or harm you ever again."

My fingers threaded through his hair, and I threw my head back in a silent cry. Valpar didn't stop he continued to pump his fingers inside me.

Valpar lowered himself, his lips enclosing around a sensitive nipple while penetrating me. A deep moan escaped my lips, my trembling body succumbing to waves of intense pleasure. "Please, I want the real thing." I begged, my voice a thick whisper.

Valpar's tongue swirled around my nipple, his thrusts slowing. He looked through his messy, tangled hair, his eyes wild with lust and I knew I looked just the same.

"Female, do not tempt me." He pulled his fingers from my weeping core and slid them into his mouth, not caring if his own come was on his fingers.

"Please, a little. Just the tip?"

Valpar snarled, pulling me lower into the blankets and spreading my legs wide. "Fuck, you are making this difficult."

My hair and arms were fanned out above me, my body completely bare and exposed to him. "Just the tip," I begged again.

He groaned, his eyes rolling to the back of his head, and he hovered over me. "You know that won't happen. You know I will want to fully sheath myself into you."

Yes, that was the idea.

While he stared into my eyes, he took the broad head of his angry cock, which still dripped with his seed and played with my clit. I squirmed as he played with me until he parted my folds and nuzzled it inside.

"I will not last." He huffed as my body took him inch by inch. I felt the head and then the first and second bulge until he stopped, and pulled it from my body and inched back in. "You feel far too good squeezing the life from me."

Instead of complaining he had not put it all in, I sunk my nails into his back. "Then, my male must come inside me."

Valpar let out a noise between a grunt and a roar. One hand cupped my back side so he could angle my hips just right and the other dug into the blankets. I heard them rip and tear beneath his palm while he held in every last restraint.

In one swift, powerful thrust, Valpar entered me. The sensation was exquisite, a mix of pain and pleasure that sent me over the edge. I cried out, his mouth slamming against me to hide the noise. My body convulsed as wave after wave of ecstasy washed over me.

Valpar groaned, his hips pumping rhythmically, yet shallow.

"Mmm, you coat my cock so well, female." He said against my cheek. "I... ah, fuck."

He filled me completely, his body tensing with pleasure as warm streams of him coated every inch of my insides. The weight of his body pressed against mine, his powerful arms trembling from the effort. Eventually, he shifted to the side, allowing his semi-hard cock to slip out of me. But his desire was still clear as he skillfully plunged his fingers back into my quivering body, intensifying the sensations that consumed me.

I squeaked when he rolled me, so my back was to his front. His fingers securely inside me, not letting any of come escape. "Sleep," he commanded. "Do not tempt me more with your cunt or tits, or I will brand you here."

I smirked, grabbing a pillow and holding it to my front. "And that is supposed to be a threat?" I whispered back.

"Female. I will know if you leave, my fingers will become cold. It is for your safety you remain. I will brand you in a more romantic setting."

My smirk turned into a smile, and I buried my face in the pillow. "You know about romance? But you are an orc. And you want to be all romantic with me?"

After you rutted me in the tent with a crowd outside?

Which, actually, I didn't hear them anymore...

He sighed heavily. "Yes, the queen said it was important. I will make it special. For my miresa I will do anything."

"Crowd of kinky people outside or not, this is special," I muttered. "It's special because all of it is with you.

CHAPTER THIRTY

Valpar

MY MATE WAS TROUBLE. I knew that from the very beginning, but she continued to surprise me. She could distract me and help forget the people outside, with her delicious body and her arousing scent, but apparently it was nothing to worry about, anyway.

When I stepped out of the tent the next morning, leaving my exhausted female to rest, there was no sign of any of the king's subjects. Just the tribe on the far side of the courtyard, sick from their drinking of ale and overstuffing themselves with meat and sweets. If they continued to act in such a manner, they would have a rounded belly such as myself.

Once they woke, Olur informed me that there was nothing to be seen nor heard from the tent the night before. The lantern that hung had fallen and our bodies could not be seen. The king's subjects soon left afterwards, groaning in disappointment and sought their entertainment elsewhere.

My body felt lighter after that fact. No one saw the outline of my female's body. No one knows how our bodies moved.

As for any sound, that sound that came from my female, the tribe could not hear it. They were upset they could see or hear nothing, so drunk amongst themselves.

The tribe dared to question if anything happened at all, but it was quickly dismissed with the gentle breeze and my stepping forward. Being coated with your miresa's arousal was certainly an impressive achievement.

Pride washed over me. I had satisfied my female, and they were indeed jealous.

Their joyful laughter and rambunctious attitudes from yesterday were long gone. They were forlorn and a hint of jealousy was in their gazes. They spoke little, but congratulated me once more before they packed their things and all decided to take the long trek home.

They'd been away from their homes for a long while. They also had been together in the presence of many other males. Most of us were lonely creatures who only wanted a female at our side, not another male, to fight for land and possessions. Yet, they stayed to find a female, like I did.

Most males had gardens, animals and traps that needed tending. They had their own duties to their homes and baskets, plus, leather and food to trade when we gathered once a month. They needed to get away from here, away from the brightness and light of the light sources. It would only make them more irritable as time went on. Even I was tired of being in the open and not shaded by the trees.

Part of me was jealous of them. I longed to take my female back to my home, even if it was not ready like it was once was.

I had abandoned, half made furniture, such as a sofa for comfortable sitting, a half-completed bathroom and trunks of cloth for me to make her clothing.

I groaned. *Will I be able to make her pretty things?*

There were many things I needed to accomplish, but the only thing my body wanted, what I wanted, was to be with my female.

My cock would not allow for anything else.

She was devilish, a temptress, and I could not withhold myself from her body.

This communication she wanted was important, that much I knew. How could I tell her in the tent, with her half-naked body on top of mine and her arousing scent surrounding me, that her past was what was holding me back?

I would always have her, keep her. She was mine and I would never let her go. To have her suffer every day and it be my fault, that I would never allow. Luckily, I could hold myself from branding her. My brand was far too large to force that inside her. I would have to put in more effort for our bond to take place. For how long I would be able to withhold myself, I wasn't sure. The want to plant my cock completely inside her, so her bones lined up with mine, sent shivers down my body I couldn't ignore.

I wanted it, to claim her fully, but I would not put my miresa's happiness at risk. Ultimately, it would need to be her decision if she wanted her memories back.

I swallowed heavily. Yes, her decision. No more letting others decide for her, even me, when I was trying to protect her.

The tribe left my horse at the palace stables. When it was time for my female and I to return to the Wood we would take him with us. I knew Ulam would be unhappy with me not spending time with him, but being a horse, they were not the smartest of creatures, anyway. As long as he were fed, cleaned and had the accompaniment of other horses in the fields, he would be happy.

When my female emerged from the tent, her hair was tangled, her eyes swollen and my smile emerged so wide, my lips hurt from my tusks tugging at the skin. She wore a silk blanket covering her body. I narrowed my eyes and took another look around the courtyard to make sure there were no wandering eyes to behold her body, then, softening again once I approached her.

My miresa gives me a lazy smile, leaning her head far back, as the sun cast a warm golden glow on her face. I could hear the soft rustle of her hair as a gentle breeze brushed against it. "Hi," she whispered, her voice as delicate as a feather, and her cheeks flush a lovely shade of pink, mirroring the vibrant hue of her hair.

I took my claws and ran them through her hair, taking out some knots that gathered there. A rumble of pride erupted from my chest. "Female, you look thoroughly sated this morning."

She playfully bit her bottom lip and shyly buried her blushing face in the soft fabric on my chest. I couldn't help but chuckle, taking over the role of the amused.

I wrapped her in the blankets, covering her from head to toe. She grumbled about being too hot, but my grip on her tightened and I shook my head at her request to take some of the clothing away.

If it were ever possible, my possessiveness with her had doubled overnight. I did not know if it was because my cock had met her cunt or, simply, because I had to take her within the sight of my tribe the night before. Nevertheless, I would keep her covered until we reached the cave, where I could pamper her.

"Does your cunt hurt?" I whispered, as we entered the forest.

She lifted the blanket and covered her face. "You can't just say things out loud like that!" She squealed and shook her head. I smiled and I leisurely I took our time through the forest, waiting for the sound of rolling waves to fill my ears.

I felt calm, even though I had nudging in the back of my mind that I needed to speak to my mate about her past. This communication she wanted would be done. Now that I was of somewhat sound mind, I intended to give her what she wanted.

Before I opened my mouth to speak, she leaned her head on my chest and blurted, "Tell me more about your family." I stopped in surprise and gazed down at the bundle in my arms. This was sudden, but by the bright smile she gave me, I knew I could not deny her.

I continued walking. "You already know Sugha. He is my brother, a half-brother, as your kind would say. Another male seeded him to my ogamie—mother." I tried to remember the words from the book bestowed upon the orcs. "I also have another brother, Thorn. He is the eldest brother of the clan."

My miresa's lips parted. "You lost me."

For the rest of our pleasant walk, I explained about the purpose of a clan. How the females were so few among the orcs and that females would choose their males through a ceremony similar to what my female had endured. Each male had their own cabin, each had their own time with their female. They were very much like a mated couple, as the Bergarians would say, but she had many males that took care of her. This was a clan—a family.

"Like a reverse harem," my miresa whispered.

I did not know about this reverse harem she spoke of, but as I continued to speak about how my ogamie got sicker and sicker over the years after each orcling was born, her face grew somber.

"She was cared for. So very much," I told my miresa as we came to the cave.

The mighty waves crashed forcefully onto the sandy shoreline, their frothy white crests reaching towards the heavens. Above, a symphony of bird cries echoed over the vast expanse of the sea, their calls blending with the gentle whistling of the wind. As I stood there, I could sense the approaching storm, carried by the salty breeze that brushed against my skin. A shiver traveled through my entire being, like the creaking of timbers on a weathered ship.

I made my little fairy stand as I took the boulders and locked us inside, leaving the smallest of gaps so her companion could slip away if we rutted again.

Which we would.

"That's so sad, and I'm guessing there weren't any girls born, either?"

I shook my head. "Never, at least to my knowledge. My seeded orgamo doesn't even remember his father. As far as we know, my brothers and I may be the first generation."

My miresa gaped in surprise.

"Or, they are just so old, they do not remember. We live for a long time. I do not believe the moss in our head can hold that much memory." She laughed when I picked her up, her legs kicking when I brought her deeper into the cavern until we reached the opening of our living area.

The torches flickered alive, their warm glow guiding us towards home. The air carried a hint of fae, a cloyingly sweet fragrance that lingered. A fresh basket rested on the table, while delicate flower petals led a trail into the bathroom. I shook my head in disbelief and gently carried my precious miresa to her intended destination, for a soothing bath.

I know the king was trying to help our joining, but I did not like him to meddle in my affairs. I was perfectly capable taking care of my female. Once we got back to the Wood, I would show my little fairy how good of a male I could be.

"So, you have three dads. That's so lucky. What are their names? What are they like?"

I set her down on the edge of the massive tub, which looked like it was carved right into the stone, and when I twisted the knobs, water came pouring out. I found glass bottles on the shelves. I took a tentative sniff of each one and poured them in the bath.

"Thorn's father is Zarfu. He was the first chosen of my ogamie's clan. I guess you could say he was the more level-headed one. Thorn takes after him. Sugha's father is Eman, and he is— different—just like Sugha. They always joke, get into trouble and like to cook and make sweets far too much." I rubbed my stomach. "They are very good sweets."

My little fairy laughed and nodded. "I like Sugha. He was fun to talk to, and what about your dad?"

"His name is Azuk, the best of all the males my ogamie picked." My miresa smiled as I dragged the blankets from around her body. I took my time unwrapping her, like a beautiful present just for me.

I continued to tell her how orcs were very possessive, how the males could not spend a lot of time with one another while they knew they were with the same female. They each cared for her, wanted her for themselves but they never fought in front of her, knowing it would upset her.

Eventually, all the males cared for one another over the years. It took time, but still they did not sleep under the same roof. They understand one another from a distance.

After I pulled the blankets away, I inspected my miresa's body. She wouldn't look at me and crossed her arms to hide. My gaze on her was not for lust, though I knew my body reacted as such, but I wanted to check the marks I'd left on her body, to make sure I had not hurt her.

A dark bruise marked her shoulder and neck where I sucked on her there. It was like a marking spot, but more pronounced, like most the creatures had on this side of the wall. They bite and rut, which was how they claimed. For orcs, it was much different.

I pushed my miresa's legs apart while she sat on the edge of the tub, and she snapped them back together. I raised my eyebrow and shook my head, placing my hand on her knee. "Let me see if I have hurt you, my mate."

Her cheeks turned a darker shade of pink, and she bit on her fingernail, slowly letting me part her legs.

"Mmm, good girl for listening so well." She put her hands on my shoulders to keep her balance, and I decided to continue to speak about my orgamo to keep her nervousness away.

"My father was head-strong and was not the most pleasant to be around."

"Oh, like you?" she quipped.

Her eyes widened as I parted her legs further, giving me the perfect view of her back-end's hole. I leaned in closer to inspect her lower lips. I could see fine before, but if she was going to *sass* me, I was going to make her more uncomfortable.

"Valpar!" she squeaked and tried to close her legs again.

Her efforts were useless, and my tongue licked at her swollen folds. She took in a shallow breath and held onto the side of the tub to keep her steady.

"Orc spit is known to help for cuts and sores. This will soothe your pussy."

I took a longer, tentative lick to the top part of her cunt, making her back arch and her hand land in my hair.

"Please?"

I laid my tongue flat against it, taking a long lick and stared up at her. "I do not know. You said I was not pleasant to be around."

"To other people, maybe! Not to me!" she argued, while trying to pull my head back to her pussy.

"You are a greedy female. So greedy your body accepted my cock fully." My shaft pressed against the side of the cool stone tub and my body shivered. "Now you are going to get into the tub, and I will treat you more afterwards."

She sighed deeply and nodded, and I carefully slipped her inside the warm waters.

"Good girl, now lean back and let me wash your hair." She turned toward me and cocked her head.

"You are...going to wash me?"

I grabbed the oils from the shelf and smelled each one to find the right one to put in her hair. "Of course, it's what a good male would do for his mate."

She sensuously licked her lips, and I gently ran my sharp claws through the tangle of her vibrant pink hair. The room filled with a faint scent of floral shampoo, as I massaged her scalp. Her eyelids fluttered shut, surrendering to the pleasurable sensation.

I should have done this from the beginning.

"Tell me more," she muttered under her breath as I poured water down her hair. "About your dads."

I hummed and watched the water droplets run down her arm. I don't know why I felt compelled to share with her, but the thoughts of my orgamos and their health flashed into my mind. "All the orgamos are sick," I spoke without really thinking. "I mean, they look weak. They have aged since the war. Their black hair is turning white and grey, and their strength is leaving. They also look tired."

My miresa licked her lips as the water ran down her cheek. "They are growing old," my miresa said without looking at me. "Like a human. Humans don't live long; their hair turns grey, and they get wrinkles on their faces." She patted her hands on her cheeks. "If a Bergarian saw a human— an older human— for the first time, they would think they were sick, too. Maybe your dads are getting old, like humans."

I raked my claws through her hair, which was now free of the tangles. "What happens after they get *too old?*" I asked, while I got a cloth from the table to wash her with.

My little fairy shuffled uncomfortably, so I took my claw and pulled her chin toward me. "Speak, what happens?"

Her lip wobbled. "They, go to sleep, but they don't wake back up. It will be like your mother and they will meet her in the stars."

The drumming in my chest slowed. This had come across my mind many times. All three had become sick, and Zarfu told my seeded orgamo that his time was short. Ogamie visited him in a dream and told him so.

My seeded orgamo had said nothing about Ogamie visiting him, so, I believed he would have more time, but I was not for certain. Nothing was for certain.

Perhaps it was my orgamo's time to meet Ogamie. He had been sad for many moons and, when I visited him, he talked of her often. It would not surprise me if Zarfu passed into the stars, that my seeded orgamo would follow him shortly after.

I did not know how to feel about this. I was a selfish orc and wanted him to stay, but I also wanted him to be free of pain and be near the female he cared for.

I let out a sigh, took the cloth and rubbed my miresa's back, cleaning her arms and her body. She watched me quietly. It was the quietest I had ever seen her and it worried me.

"What are you thinking?" I took the cloth and parted her legs. She gasped when I cleaned between her folds and her hands grabbed the tub.

Good, she knew not to push me away. Maybe time in the corner did do her good.

"What was it like?" She didn't look at me, but gazed off into the distance. "What was it like, when you were younger? With your brothers and growing up?" I paused my cleaning of her body and she turned to me. "What was it like, to be young?"

CHAPTER THIRTY-ONE

Calliope

As I SETTLED ONTO the soft bed, feeling the smooth sheets against my skin, I admired my hair, meticulously brushed and intricately braided into stunning designs. The room filled with laughter, echoing off the walls, as Valpar, a master storyteller, weaved his tales. My sides ached from the sheer hilarity, and I couldn't recall a moment in my life when I had laughed so hard.

Thorn, Valpar and Sugha were troublemakers as children. Their age differences were large, and Thorn became the leader of their brood. Thorn told Valpar what to do until he was old enough to understand. Each respective seeded father took care of that child, ultimately, but all the fathers took care of each orcling. They worked as a team because apparently orclings have a lot of energy, and his mother had to spend time with each male.

I couldn't imagine going to another cabin to spend time with another male and leave your baby behind, but Valpar said when the babies were young his mother took the babies with them. Once they were no longer *feeding from the tit* as Valpar said, the seeded father would take over while his mother spent time with another male.

No male felt jealousy toward any orcling when she had to take care of it. They all loved the little babies that came into their home. When they got older, though, once they went through their change to become adult males, there was a shift. They had to fight, earn their keep and move out of the cabins, but that was much later after their mother had passed on.

Thorn and Valpar were older, had spent a lot of time together and knew their mother very well. How she smelled, her likes and dislikes, they remembered the foods she would cook and the desserts she would make.

Valpar remembered that his mother would often sleep when he was a child, while Thorn said she didn't sleep as much when he was young. Then, when Sugha was born, it was like it was too much for her body to handle. She wanted that baby so much for Eman, though. He wanted an orcling for him as much as she wanted Sugha for herself.

Once she was done feeding Sugha from her body, she got worse until she went to sleep and never woke again. It had me in tears to hear the story, as he finished my bath, but he didn't once cry. He told me it was how the gods wanted it, that she was one of the stars looking down at all of them and helping the Moon Fairy find mates for her children.

I did my best not to cry after that, especially after he said he was the one in charge of taking care of Sugha's hair.

Valpar was apparently good at braiding hair. He proved it just fine after doing mine. It wasn't too tight, and he even made it so it would stay without the help of any bands or cuffs. My hair was in its own wrappings.

All he used was some oil in his bag and a comb and brush to make me feel like an orc princess.

I guessed if I turned green, the braiding part wouldn't be so bad.

Valpar loved to braid, which I found a complete surprise. He would do Sugha's hair every day. Sugha got so sick of it that one day he chopped it all off and shaved the sides. Valpar was so upset, he said that was when he started to get really grumpy.

I bit my lips and tried so hard not to laugh, as he told me the story about how mad he was at Sugha. It was an intimate thing to braid someone's hair. A mother or a father would do it to an orcling. To help him get over the grief of losing his mother, his fathers had let him do theirs, but when it was over he was just devastated because he had no one else's hair to braid. To demonstrate how angry he was, he never braided his own hair.

Talk about a grumpy orc.

I asked if he ever would braid his hair again and he grunted in reply, crossing his arms.

Which he doesn't. He learned how to do it on others, but not himself.

"What if I braided your hair?" I asked him.

He narrowed his eyes at me and looked away.

"Maybe."

I touched my hair again, feeling how soft the ends were.

Valpar braided *my* hair.

The rest of the afternoon I asked him to tell me more about his life as a child. I became obsessed with it. I wanted to know, not just about the life of an orc in the Wood but, what it was like to have a family at a young age.

Because I didn't know mine.

Why didn't I know it?

I've never thought about it before. I didn't care to, didn't want to know because part of me felt like it hurt.

From time to time, as he told me the tales of when his fathers took them on hunting trips, giving them life lessons on how not to get your foot chopped off or not to get sick by eating the wrong fruits or roots in the forest, a pang of hurt would hit my chest.

I—don't think I knew my real father.

There was no image that came to my head, there wasn't a warm feeling that flooded my chest. There was emptiness when I tried to search inside myself, and the more I looked the more disappointed I grew.

I listened, though, I listened whole-heartedly because I liked the stories he told. He was different when he was small. he would smile when he talked about his mother and how soft she was and different from his fathers, and I tried to remember what my mother was like.

Theresa said that my real mom was not a very good one. I trusted Theresa, because she had always taken care of me. She fed and clothed me and, overall, tried to keep me safe. I'd known nothing else.

But that was it. I know nothing else.

Valpar's hand cupped my cheek. I felt his warm hand pull me closer and sighed when he pulled me into his body. "Where did you go, little fairy?"

I blinked several times before I stared up at him. "I'm sorry. I was thinking about my mom."

Valpar hummed and played with one of my braids. "Yes, I must meet her and your father."

I shook my head. "No, my real one. The one that gave birth to me."

He stopped playing with my hair and dropped the braid. "What about her?" His voice grew hard, his body stiff.

"I was thinking what she was like. Why don't I remember her? Why I don't remember when I was little." I rubbed my finger across my lip. "I remember nothing of when I was little."

Thunder rumbled outside, as it'd been doing it all day. This time it was closer, louder and I swore it shook the cave. As I closed my eyes and scooted into Valpar's side a little closer, another vision of that woman I saw yesterday came to mind She wasn't yelling at me. Her dark hair covered her face, and she had a stick in her mouth that lit up at the end. Smoke came pouring out of her mouth, and when my eyes opened again, the vision was gone.

She looked so sad. Not as scary as before, but if she was a connection to my mother, I wasn't sure I wanted to know.

Call me a scared little chicken for it, but I just found my happy place with Valpar, and I wasn't ready to see it, yet.

I let out a shuddering breath and listened to the thunder roll away from the cave.

"Little mate, do you want to know who your mother is?" Valpar's hand touched the top of my head where a loose braid sat on top

I shook my head. "No, no, not yet. I just—I guess I was just wondering why I didn't know."

Valpar cleared his throat. "I know why you do not know. I have the answers you seek and if you want—I can give them to you."

I pulled away from him. "You know why I don't remember my past? How?" I lifted my brow in question and made to move away. He didn't like this and wrapped his arms around me to pull me back.

I grunted in response, but he growled and pulled me into his lap.

"Why do you know?" I demanded.

Valpar buried his nose into my shoulder and took a long whiff of my scent. "Your uncle told me. He told me the day after I brought you to the cave."

"He knows too? How many more people know?"

Does everyone know why I don't remember everything? How could everyone just not tell me?

Because you never wanted to know, you dumb butt. You never asked.

My mouth hung open as Valpar told me Mom and Dad knew, too. That seemed to be all, just five people. *I guess that is not so bad.*

I wrapped my arms around his neck. "And how is it I don't remember?" I whispered in his ear.

"The king and a sorceress put a spell on you to forget your past."

I squeezed my eyes shut and that woman appeared again. She was angry and yelling at me. This time, she was waving her arms at me, shooing me away until a door slammed in my face and it all went dark.

My eyes popped open.

"Do you want to know why—"

"No." I snapped. "I don't want to know." I shook my head violently. "Not yet."

Valpar held me in his arms and rocked me. "If you ever want to know, I will tell you." His thumb rubbed under my cheek. "I will help you and always be here. You know this, don't you female?"

I nodded my head, not verbally answering.

Happy thoughts, cheerful things, that's all I want to have. No more thoughts of bad things.

Simon leaped onto the plush bed, causing a gentle creaking sound to resonate through the room. Valpar released a deep sigh, his voice carrying a low growl as he expressed his frustration. "Off, animal."

Simon tilted his head, and his mischievous gaze fixed on me. With a sudden burst of energy, he shot out his tongue and blew a series of playful raspberries. The air filled with the sound of his silly antics, making me burst into laughter. I couldn't help but feel a warm sense of joy as I extended my arm, inviting Simon to come join us.

Simon turned his butt around and planted his rear end right into Valpar's lap.

Valpar grunted. "What is he doing?" He went to shove off Simon, but he let out a loud bleat.

I smiled and scratched Simon behind his ears. "He's trying to be friends with you. Even if you tried to eat him. He knows he's going to be coming back to the Monktona Wood with us, so he's trying to make amends. Which is weird because he doesn't forgive people very easily."

Simon yelled again and licked me on the cheek.

Valpar's eyes widened and his jaw went slack. "You mean he's coming with us? To live with us?"

I tilted my head. "Yes, why wouldn't he? I'm his support companion. He'll start fainting all the time if I'm not around."

"Bassza, this cannot be happening." Valpar fell back onto the bed, letting Simon and I stay on his lap. "He cannot sleep in the furs. He will sleep in his own space."

Simon and I both groaned, and I scratched his ears again. "Sorry, buddy. It was a good try." Simon lifted his butt off Valpar's lap and he let out a little toot.

I waved my hand in front of me and stifled a giggle. "No more dairy for you. Your tummy is getting upset." I turned to Valpar. "He's lactose intolerant. You don't have a lot of cows over in the Monktona Wood do you?"

"Female, you make me want to drink." He laid his arm over his eyes, but I see the big grin on his face stretch over his big teeth.

I just needed to remember life can be like a wiener... it can get hard, but it can't stay hard forever. I just hoped my life from now on wouldn't be super hard like Valpar's wiener because his seemed to stay hard all the time now.

CHAPTER THIRTY-TWO

Valpar

I HAD HER POSITIONED on all fours, her rear nestled in the firm grasp of my hands. Despite her small body, the undeniable satisfaction flooded over me as I witnessed myself being pulled into her tight cunt.

With each thrust, I delved deeper, drawing closer and closer until I reached my brand. It was the largest, the throbbing knot-like bulge that would bind us forever. Once I forced it inside her, my essence would be imprinted upon her skin and her soul, forever marking her as mine. From that moment on, there would be no doubt or questioning of her ownership, as her scent alone would serve as a reminder to everyone of our bond.

I pressed my brand against her entrance, and felt my breath shudder. Her back arched, a silent plea for more. Her warmth engulfed me, her desire obvious. I emitted a low growl. My primal instincts took over as I firmly gripped her hips and my claws sank into her flesh.

My head leaned back, and I tried my hardest not to push it inside. I needed her like I needed air, the fish water and the bees nectar. I wanted, with every fiber of my being, to be connected to her. My soul needed her.

"Valpar," her quivering voice caught me off guard and my attention snapped to her as my last bulge sat waiting to enter her.

"Not yet, I'm not ready yet."

My eyes snapped open, the darkness that surrounded the room a reminder that it was all just a dream. My cock was unbearably hard. I wrapped my hand around it and took in deep labored breaths.

It'd been days since we were stuck in the cave. My miresa said that there must be a tropical storm outside. It happened every so often, when a storm came from the sea causing wind, rain and thunder. During those days we played some *board games*, fucked, and she has shown me how to draw.

I even let her play with my hair.

She was not good at braiding but getting better. I had fun showing her and it brought me great joy that she would want to learn.

Would she want to braid our future orclings' hair?

My throat grew tight at the thought.

My little fairy had not brought up the subject again, about knowing of her past. Not that I would want her to. Knowing that her past was erased was enough for her to be upset, I would not push the idea for her to know.

It was enough of my burden being lifted that she came to terms with it herself. She knew I would be here for all her answers.

I did worry when she started to push the issue of our bonding. I could not bond her without her knowing the full truth, and I don't want her to feel like I am forcing her to know.

Why did having a female have to be difficult?

I shifted and rolled to my side, searching for my female and her comfort. I didn't want to leave her in the cave alone and beat a tree out of the soil or rub my shaft until expressed my seed. I wouldn't leave her in the cave by herself anymore. I would bear the stiffness until she woke in the morning, so that she was properly rested.

Then, I would relieve myself inside her body.

She had been in deep thought the past few days, and I believed she was having trouble coming to terms with losing her memory. I didn't believe she had thought about it before, or even wanted to think about it. Now that I have talked about my family, she was more curious.

She knew about my past, my time as an orcling, and so she wanted to know hers as well. Something was holding her back. It had something to do with those daydreams.

I reached over the bed to find her. Normally, she slept on top of my body and I found it strange she was not there. "Little fairy?" My voice was raspy when I sat up and I didn't find her there. The furs were cold and my eyes darted around the cave to see if she had gone to get something to eat.

"Miresa?" I sat up completely and saw Simon in the corner. He yawned, stood and seemed to look for her, too.

The drums in my chest beat rapidly and I jumped from the bed and went to the bathroom. The light was on, but there was no sign of my miresa.

"Calliope?" I roared and there was still no sound or sign of my mate. With a snarl, I took in deep breaths, trying to find her scent, but the trail was old, stale and panic ensued.

She was not here, and it had been hours.

Had she left me? Did someone take her?

No strange smells other than the stale scent was in the cave, but I would not take any chances.

I pulled on the leather bindings around my forearms, placed my weapons around my hips and my sword on my back. I swore to the Moon Fairy I would find her and drag her ass back here before the night was through.

Simon was already trotting down the hall, letting off noises of worry, and I stomped after him.

Calliope wouldn't just leave her companion, surely there was something wrong.

Once we got to the mouth of the cave, I saw the boulders were still in place. My miresa must have squeezed through or someone had come to retrieve her and put them back. Simon didn't wait for me, he squeezed through the small opening that I had left him. I pushed the boulders with little effort, my anger and panic increasing by the minute.

Why did she not make any noise?

Once the boulders were pushed away, a clear night sky greeted us, but it did nothing to ease my nerves. The waves continued to pound into the sand, the surrounding scents pure from the freshly fallen rain.

This would help, all scents washed away and the soil was soft, good for tracking.

Perhaps the gods were on my side.

I quickly found tiny footprints, just one set, and I realized they were just hers. Perhaps she was following a flying creature, why would she do that.

I worried that she could be persuaded easily, because of her good nature and believing the good in all.

I pulled my sword from my back and took off into the darkness of the forest.

I wanted to scream her name, demand that she come back to me, but doing so would be foolish. It would alert others she was missing. Others, meaning ogres. They still roamed the land since the wall came down, and though there were not many I would not take that risk.

I would not put her in any more danger than she might already be in.

One of those things being my twitchy palm.

I grunted as I picked up the pace. I traveled past the palace, where I nearly lost her footprints. Her scent became stronger once we reached the other side, to another forest but then I lost her footprints entirely. I scouted the area and pulled at my messy strands. I was panting, frustrated and wanting to push over the trees in the area.

These trees, however, were filled with low-lying lights and ribbons, meaning they were homes to someone. I could not take my anger on these trees, I could not pull them from the soil, let out my frustration and wake up the rest of the forest.

Fuck!

I let out a growl and a panting Simon came up behind me. He pulled on my cloth and fell to the ground, whining.

"I don't know where she is!" I hissed. "Where is my miresa?!"

I should have put my fingers into her cunt while she slept. I would do this more often. Better yet, I would tie her to me at all times. It was a mistake not to do this, I would do this always.

I picked up the goat and he sighed in relief as I carried him with me. I could not believe my miresa would have traveled this far, but she was an energetic female. She did not sleep long. She craved me as much as I craved her, and I would find myself waking up with her mouth around my shaft.

Simon groaned and lifted his head, nodding his horns to the right. I watched him as he continued to nod, his groan long with exhaustion, and I turned to where he wanted to go. Her footsteps were long gone, but I still smelled her scent. It grew stronger and light was building near the middle of a clearing. A stream of water curled around a tree where I stood.

I laid Simon near the water, where he greedily lapped it up, and I gripped hold of the hilt of my sword when I heard water splashing.

Blue lights swirled in the distance. I closed my eyes and groaned and immediately knew it was a whisp. I tried not to let them distract me when one comes into view. Those annoying lights that had a mind of their own flew above the foliage where humming was coming to my ears.

It spiraled upward, showing off a rope. Another whisp flew up parallel to the other, and I gritted my teeth as I watched them disappear into the trees. The ropes tightened and it was like I could hear the whisps tenfold. They swayed underneath the branches and a hum came from the other side, with splashing sounds echoing through the darkness again.

The blue lights fell back down from the trees, landing on the other side of the brush. I took tentative steps toward the sounds, my miresa's smell becoming stronger, and I knew she must be on the other side. I didn't smell anyone else or hear anything that could be a danger, but I could not be certain. Not with these whisps playing with her.

The whisps are legends, here long before any of the souls that had lived in Bergarian, but I worried what they were up to. They liked to frolic with the females, liked to cause trouble, but others said they were the ones that ultimately led to your destiny.

I had found my destiny already, so why would these whisps be here?

My steps became frantic. I rushed forward, unable to take the anticipation any longer. I pushed through the bushes and found my miresa sitting on a board, swaying with the ropes bound on either side of it. She was swaying over the stream, her feet dangling over the waters and she kicked, making water splash over the embankment on the other side, dousing the blue wisp.

"Female!" I roared, and the whisps squealed and shot up into the trees.

As she turned, the delicate crunch of the purple moss beneath my feet released a burst of golden light, illuminating her face. The radiant glow momentarily distracted me, causing my anger towards her to fade into the background.

"What are you fucking doing?" I sheathed my sword and stormed over to her, my feet leaving footprints in the soft soil, and stomping into the stream.

The seat had slowed, and she was no longer waving about over the water. I picked her up by her hips and carried her back over the shoreline.

"Swinging?" she said innocently, when I dropped her onto the grass and her toes weaved into the blades.

I pinched between my eyes. "*Swing-ing*? Is that what you were doing? In the middle of the night?" I growled and paced in front of her. "You left me in the cave," my voice rose. "You left me in the furs, alone, and you left Simon. You walked out, into the wilderness by yourself and you didn't think to wake me? You are MINE! I am supposed to take care of you. How am I to do that when you wander away from me?"

Her bottom lip curled, and her hands went behind her back.

"Why? Why are you out here, Calliope?"

She gasped. "You called me by my name!"

I jutted out my jaw. "Of course I did!" I roared. "You ran into the wilderness and who knows what creatures could have taken you from me. Another orc? An ogre? A dragon? I would burn down the whole kingdom to get you back!"

Instead of looking guilty, she smiled. "Aw, you'd do that for me?"

Moon Fairy above, please help me.

"Why, my sweet human, would you put me through this? You will give me hair grey as my orgamo's."

My miresa stood up on her toes and pulled on my hair to inspect it. "Nope, still black. I still got a little more time."

I groaned and stepped away from her, pulling at my strands.

"The reason I was out here," she began, "was because I had to think."

Think? She had to think?

"About what?" I hissed. "What did you have to think about out here alone, that you could not do in the cave safe and within my arms?"

She winced and my little fairy made circles in the grass with her toes. "Um, well, I wasn't alone when I came out here. I was perfectly safe."

My head ticked to the side, my eyes narrowing. "Who was with you?"

She giggled and cupped her hand to her mouth, whispering, "I can't tell you yet. They made me promise."

She stopped digging her toe into the grass, winked at me once and then took off on swift feet and ran through the bushes.

She did not just—

Simon groaned and fell over onto his side, after he had just gotten up, letting out a cry of defeat.

I snarled and threw my weapons to the ground, puffed out my chest and felt my body shake with anger. "Stay, Simon. I will catch my female."

A primal force surged from within me, as if a hidden chest had been unlocked. It unleashed a ferocity so intense that I knew, it would ceaselessly pursue its target until I had this woman within my grasp. She had stirred something deep within me, transforming me into a predator, while she became my helpless prey.

I was the monster, and she was the helpless human.

How dare she run from me.

Her laughter echoed into the wood. "Come find me, Valpar!"

I snarled and took off into the forest where she had disappeared. I would find her, and I would rut her in the forest, and I didn't care if the fae or the pixies watched.

CHAPTER THIRTY-THREE

HOURS EARLIER

Calliope

As an itch began to tickle my nose, I instinctively wiggled it back and forth. The itch persisted, so, I gave in and gently scratched it with my fingertips. Suddenly, a dazzling brightness emerged from behind my closed eyelids, causing me to hastily blink them open. Before me, a radiant, blue light illuminated the surroundings, casting an ethereal glow. The light playfully danced, twirled, and even executed a graceful backflip, captivating my wide-eyed gaze. Mesmerized, I watched as the ball of brilliant blue gradually retreated, revealing a mysterious face hovering within the shadows.

Her vibrant purple locks cascaded down her back, impossible to ignore. The corset top she wore hugged her figure, exuding a fierce, rebellious aura.

Paired with her ripped black jeans, the ensemble emitted a strikingly edgy vibe giving her bad-assy look.

Instantly, I knew who she was.

"Fairy God—!"

Her arm bolts out and covers my mouth. "Don't be so loud, you will wake malicious, mean and scary."

I tilt my head in confusion. "Who?"

"Your orc monster boy-toy. Now, come here," she whispers and motions me to come off the bed.

I took a quick look at him, and he was out cold.

He should have been out cold. We did the dirty, like four times, before we both passed out.

"Quit thinking about the dirty things you just did, and hurry," my fairy godmother said and put her hands on her hips. "And do it carefully, that's right. Put a pillow on top of him, that way he won't notice you're gone yet."

I did as she said, took his hard grip off my butt and slid a pillow in its place. He had a thing for holding my butt at night. Not that I complained, it kept me firmly planted to his chest. Sometimes he would start rubbing my lady parts up and down his shaft and we would both get off in our sleep.

He was kinkier than he realized, the little stinker.

Once I got off the bed, my Fairy Godmother looked me up and down and waved me toward the hallway. The little blue light, which I recognized as a whisp, danced around my hair and kissed my cheek.

"What's going on? Where are we going?" If she was taking me out of the cave, I knew Valpar would not be happy. He liked me close to him and, if I left, I would be breaking one of the rules.

Standing in the corner again did not sound fun.

My fairy godmother snorted. "Ah, it will be fine. You need to live a little. Come on." She stepped through the boulders like a ghost, and my eyes widened. I touched the boulders with my fingertip to see if I could follow her way out, but the whisp gestured me to follow him through the small hole that Valpar left behind for Simon.

Go through the hole it was, then.

Why did I feel like my role was reversed here?

Oh, I knew why. Because I'd been the one getting my holes filled, not filling holes.

Duh.

I had to wiggle through. It was a tight fit but once I get on the other side, I see my Fairy Godmother tapping her foot and her hand on her hip. "Alright then, let's go."

"Wait just a minute! Are you a ghost too? I didn't think a fairy could walk through a rock!" I ran to keep up with her fast pace.

She shrugged her shoulders. "Technically, I'm not here." The whisp following us sat on her shoulder. "You are sleepwalking and I am just guiding you where you need to go." She pointed toward the forest, and I just mindlessly followed.

"Sleepwalking? I don't sleepwalk!"

My Fairy Godmother raised a brow and wrapped her arm through mine. "Not normally, but I'm short on time. I swear, I'm not getting paid enough for this." She ran her hand down her face. "Two humans at once are just about to kill me. At least I didn't have to explain much to you since you already lived here. But ow, we need to work on your thinking department." She tapped her finger in the middle of my forehead.

I grabbed her finger and pushed it away. "Hey, I can think, just fine! And, what do you mean two humans?"

"Don't worry about that." She waved her hand. "Anyway, I know you can think just fine," she chastised," but you are refusing to. You are wasting precious time and getting on my nerves with your nonsense, by being afraid of the past you no longer control. The time is now, darling, embrace the future like you always wanted, but in order to do that you must understand the past."

I groaned and slapped my forehead. "I don't wanna. I like how things are now."

My Fairy Godmother let out a disdainful snort, her grip firm as she pulled me along. Her words were few, but her presence guided me through the dense forest, where the moonlight filtered through the rich green leaves above. As we emerged from the trees, we entered the deserted courtyard of the Golden Light Palace, and the silence was deafening.

The air carried a faint scent of flowers, mingling with the earthy aroma of the surrounding forest. With each step, I could feel the coolness of the ground beneath my feet, leading us back towards the familiar path that led to my parents' home.

"Are you taking me back to the tree house?"

She shook her head. "No. Do you happen to remember how you came to the tree house, Calliope?"

I twisted my lips, my eyebrows forming into a scowl. "Mom and Dad brought me, having spent a day in the palace after waking up. I was sick and still tired, but they said I would do better at home."

She nodded and continued to pull me. "Anything else that stands out? Who was there when you woke up?"

"Uncle Osirus and Melina, of course. And there was another woman, a sorceress. She was really nice. I haven't seen her in a long time."

"Taliyah. Yes, she is very nice," my Fairy Godmother said. "She's very powerful and can cast spells so strong she is almost equivalent to one of the greatest sorceresses, Serene."

My lips parted. Serene was so powerful she helped close the portal to the Underworld during the war, capturing all the demons and rogues and sealing them inside.

"Taliyah was the one that helped hide your memories." She squeezed my arm.

That means her power was strong enough to keep my memories away. Then, why was I seeing that woman flash in my mind? Was it just a nightmare, something my head was coming up with on its own?

My Fairy Godmother tugged on my arm. "Come on, what are you thinking?"

I shook my head, my loose braids hitting her on the arm. "I don't wanna."

She hummed, not bothered in the slightest. "Is it because you are having flashes of memories, perhaps? Or at least you think they are memories because you have no idea why things are popping up in your head."

I gasped. "Can you read minds?"

As we trod on a patch of vibrant purple moss, she threw her head back, laughter filling the air. In response, bursts of brilliant yellow lights soared out, illuminating the surroundings with a mesmerizing glow. The explosion of colors created a breathtaking spectacle, enveloping us in a warm and enchanting light.

"No," she calmed. "But I know it is something that could happen. Even the most powerful sorceresses, such as Taliyah's magic, are no match for a bond."

I rubbed my lips together. A bond was more powerful than any magic?

"We haven't mated, yet though. He hasn't bitten me. He wanted to make it special, romantic." My face heated, and I rubbed the area on my neck. It was sore, black and blue, even where he liked to suck and nibble. He had seen other creatures in Bergarian with bites. It seemed the norm for people to bite their mates, but they had fangs. Orcs had big teeth with their under bite and it would be difficult to leave a mark that way.

And it looked like it would hurt like the dickens.

"No, he hasn't," my Fairy Godmother hummed in thought. "But he doesn't have to claim you for a bond to break a spell or a curse, Calliope. Once you both met, the bond wove you both together, tighter and tighter like a giant hug." She squeezed my arm, and the whisp jumped off my godmother's shoulder and tickled my nose.

"We have been inseparable. He's all over me."

She nodded. "And I'm sure he's having trouble not claiming you, too, hasn't he?"

I nodded and kept my eyes on the path. We passed the treehouse and continued through the trees.

"Yeah, but he hasn't said anything, especially, after I told him I didn't want to know about my past."

My godmother breathed a long dramatic sigh and put her hand to her forehead. "Who knew the grumpy, irritable orc, of the three, would have such a sweet spot and keep his selfishness to himself?"

Huh?

"Sweetheart, your uncle told him that once he claimed you there was a chance your memories would come back. Valpar has held off, because he wants you to make the choice on your own about knowing your past."

I didn't know what to say to that. If he told me he couldn't claim me until I knew of my past, that would have been an ultimatum. It would have made me angry that I had to choose and force myself to remember my memories. It would have made me angry because he had a power over me.

On the other hand, I was a little miffed he didn't tell me...but why should I be? He was trying to protect me. I didn't think there was any right decision in this; I didn't think there was a right answer, because I didn't think I would have been able to make the decision if the roles were reversed.

No wonder he was so grumpy in the beginning, hitting trees and being so distant for those few days.

And there I was, teasing him by playing with my lady parts on the bed.

I slapped my forehead. *Wow, what a mate I was.*

He had been going against everything he was for my sake. He wasn't being the rough orc that I was demanding because he didn't want to hurt me, not just physically but mentally. He didn't want to see me break. Whatever my past was, it must be... life-altering.

I'd been so busy with these flashbacks; I hadn't thought of him. I was being a terrible mate to him, not thinking about his feelings, too. He must be so sad that I hadn't asked him to claim me, yet, as well.

Fairy Godmother stopped in her tracks and pulled her arm away from me. She settled her hands on my shoulders and looked me square in the eye. "You stop that right now, little fairy." My eyes widened. "You stop overthinking. Valpar is taking care of you. He understands how big this is. He knows your past, he knows where you come from and he would wait years to claim you, until you said it was alright."

My lungs filled with air and I let it out slowly.

She dropped her hands and let them lie at her side. "The reason I am here is to do an intervention. I'm here to help the orcs along with their bondings and the claiming of their mates."

"And I'm messing everything up?" My lip quivered, and I held my hands together. The whisp who had been traveling with us waved in front of my face and kissed my cheek.

"Gods, no, sweet thing. No, not at all. I am here for another reason entirely. This visit is about you. My intervention is about you."

"But I'm not on drugs. I don't drink that fae wine." I sniffed and wiped away a lone tear.

"Stay with me, Calliope. We are almost there." She patted my head. "No, I'm here to say you have a choice. One, you can let these memories creep up on you. You will continue to get these flashbacks because the bond is slowly breaking the spell."

I nodded for her to continue.

"Two; you can bond with Valpar, and your memories will return."

I rubbed an arm under my nose. "Right after? All at once?"

Fairy Godmother huffed and sighed. "Yes, right after. Bonds are powerful and are quick to break spells."

Two options which sucked. Let the memories slowly come back, so Valpar and I have to suffer not bonding with each other, while letting my mind slowly regain the memories, or I bond with Valpar and he gets to deal with a crying mess afterward.

Obviously, I wanted to forget my past for a reason, that is the only explanation why I would want to forget.

I swallowed and Fairy Godmother's hand wrapped around mine. It wasn't but a few steps later that she sat me down on a boarded swing sitting over a stream. She stood behind me and pushed.

"This is your thinking swing, a little present," she muttered as she pushed me. "I know what I told you is hard to hear, Calliope, but I wanted you to know all will work out in the end. You will always be the same

Calliope after you find out what happened to you. The sweet, innocent little fairy who is curious about the world around her."

"You are just making me have to think more, not less."

She laughed, pushing me harder.

More delicate whisps gracefully floated down from the towering trees, their ethereal forms twirling and swirling in a mesmerizing dance around the babbling stream. With a gentle touch, they plucked droplets of water from the surface and playfully tossed them, creating a sparkling spectacle that shimmered in the partly clouded moonlight. The cool mist lightly caressed my legs, and I laughed when they began to twirl my braids and spin around my hair.

I gazed back at her as she continued to push. "Am I gonna turn green?"

Godmother's hands landed on her knees, her laughter filling the air around us and I tilted my head to see if she would fall over. She stood, her purple hair falling back around her shoulder.

"Gods, no. You won't turn green. You will stay human."

I kept my hands tight on the ropes. "And how do you know for certain?"

Godmother smirked and pushed me again, this time higher. "I know these sorts of things."

I squealed when my feet grazed across the water, and the whisps followed me with each push.

"Loved your performance, by the way, with the tent ceremony. I have to say, it was almost as entertaining as a hole in the wall performance I saw recently."

"Hole in the wall—?"

Godmother snickered. "Yes, Valpar's brother Thorn chased his female right through their wood and he fucked her through a wall."

I smiled wildly. "Really? Tell me more! Did they like it? This chasing thing?"

Godmother's eyes glittered with mischief. I think she was trying to set me up to do something naughty. I didn't really care. It sounded fun.

"If I tell you, will you promise to make a decision about what you want to do?"

I nodded quickly. "Yeah, I'm going to talk to Valpar. I want us to make a decision, together."

She smiled back, halting the swing and gave my shoulders a gentle squeeze. "Good girl, now about this chase thing—"

Chapter Thirty-Four

Calliope

I KNEW THIS FOREST like the back of my hand. The emerald green leaves danced in the gentle breeze, casting dappled partly-clouded moonlight upon the moss-covered ground. I leaped through the rustling bushes, their branches brushing against my skin, as the chirping of crickets filled the air.

The soothing sound of water trickling echoed through the forest, oblivious to what was coming. The earthy scent of damp soil and the fragrance of wildflowers filled my lungs, lightening my mood further. With each step, my heart raced, and a surge of adrenaline coursed through my veins, propelling me further into the depths of the enchanting wood.

The whisps followed me as I slung my head back in laughter.

Valpar was going to be so mad.

After my Fairy Godmother told me how Valpar has held back for my sake, how he's taken care of me, to protect me from my past, I knew right there I had to break him. I felt this was for her own entertainment, though. She was an entity helping the Moon Goddess with this job she had to do, to give the orcs their mates. She needed the entertainment.

And heckers, I kinda liked the idea of poking the orc.

Overall, the Moon Goddess was helping me, a human, and a monster of a creature come together to be one.

A bond is a bond and with that power to bring two souls together, it didn't mean that we would fall in love. It most defiantly meant one day we could—should fall in love after being with one another for so long. And I was so utterly and irrevocably in love with him.

Valpar didn't know what love means, my Godmother told me, and it was a word I'd be happy to tell him once this chase was over with.

Another fun fact my Godmother elaborated on was that orcs loved to chase, just like any other animal in the Bergarian Realm. Now that I knew Valpar had really, really been holding back, I could unleash *the Calliope*.

It was the only way he could let out his frustration. He couldn't hit trees forever and we couldn't be doing the horizontal limbo every ten minutes. We could start a fire down there. He just needed a good roughing up, as Godmother said.

Somehow, I don't think a one-time chase will calm him down.

As my feet sank into the cool, rushing stream, the water splashed around me, creating a symphony of tiny droplets onto the rocks. In the distance, his mighty roar reached my ears sending shivers down my spine.

Despite Valpar's colossal size, there were no thunderous footsteps echoing through the dense forest. He moved with grace, like a silent predator. I couldn't help but feel a mixture of awe and fear. This towering figure was not only massive, but also possessed the cunning of a seasoned hunter and warrior. I knew fully that he would outwit me before I even realized it, leaving me with no chance for escape.

And then, my panties were damp.

I darted to the right, trying to find a tree I could climb. He couldn't be that great at climbing. There's no way. I found the first one with a low enough branch and took my first step. The whisps helped me and I felt the wind blow up my dress.

I climbed higher and higher until I felt a warm hand grasp my ankle.

Aw, bummer, that wasn't a long chase.

"How did you find—" I turned around and look down to see Miss Sprinkle Tits pulling at my leg. "Ugh, what do you want, Ivy?" I scowled. "I'm busy."

"Did you chase off your orc friend with your nasty human puss? Looks like he didn't even mark you!"

Trees in the distance shook and I ground my teeth. I didn't want Valpar to win so easily, I wanted him to hunt a little more.

"No, I like to play hard to get. Something you wouldn't know about," I snapped.

The whisps fell below me, gathered around Ivy and pulled at her hair. They bonked her on the head and she turned back into her smaller form. They dragged her off, wailing and screaming. I grunted in annoyance because, now she'd given away my location.

Valpar jumped from the bushes, his chest heaving and his eyes wild. His hair was a mess and his body looked like it was vibrating with pent-up energy. I could see the smooshed flower petals on his arms and the smears of dirt on his face, evidence of his long angry run through the forest. His gaze locked onto mine, a mixture of determination and something else I couldn't quite decipher.

I could see the frustration in his eyes, the desire to finally catch me after I had eluded him. But there was something else there too, a glint of amusement, a spark of challenge that mirrored my own.

Valpar was not just a mindless beast; he was a warrior with a keen intellect and a playful spirit that matched my own. Even if he didn't want me to see it.

"Calliope," he growled, his voice low and guttural. "You thought you could evade me forever, little one?

I clung to the branch, trying to maintain a composed facade even though my heart raced at the sight of him. Valpar was a formidable orc, tall and powerful, with an air of primal strength.

As he stood below me, his muscular frame and intense gaze, I couldn't help but feel a thrill of excitement run through me. This chase had been fun, but this party was about to get real.

"You are quick on your feet, Calliope," Valpar rumbled, his voice deep and gravelly. "But this time, there will be no escape for you."

"I was just testing your hunting skills," I retorted, my voice wavering slightly despite my best efforts to sound defiant. "Can't let you get rusty now, can we?"

He let out a rumbling laugh that echoed through the forest, causing the birds to take flight in a flurry of feathers. His eyes gleamed with a fierce light as he put his foot on the large root of the tree.

"You may be quick, little one," he said, as I felt his warm breath near my leg, "but I am quicker."

With a smirk playing on his lips, Valpar crouched down and then leaped up with a surprising agility for someone of his size. His hand closed around my ankle before I could move higher into the tree, and he pulled me easily, catching me before I fell.

I twisted and turned in his grasp, and he fell backward. I used all my agility to slip out of his hold. I landed gracefully on the forest floor on top of him. I could see the determination in Valpar's eyes intensify. He was enjoying this game as much as I was.

"I got you," he snarled as he sat up his nose landing into my neck.

"Not yet!" I sang and wiggled from his hold.

Unlike an orc, I had become sweaty, a slight sheen coating my skin. I wiggled down his stomach because his come was already coating between his thighs. He grunted and tried to grab me, but I slipped free and rolled on the ground next to him.

"Female," he growled, pounced and pinned me to the forest floor. The softness of the grass tickled my back and I panted, almost in defeat. I wiggled against him, his dick rubbing up against my leg. I felt the warmth of his come coating my legs.

I wanted to fight a little more, get him really wound up, but I was getting far too turned on and the rage in his eyes was dissipating. It was now turning into desire.

"Little fairy, you don't know what you have done."

I lifted my leg, running it up his shaft and let out a breathy moan. "I like it when you are rough with me, showing me how powerful you are."

As my fingers brushed against Valpar's skin, his eyes widened, reflecting the flickering light of the moon. The conflicting emotions danced across his face, accompanied by a subtle mix of scents - the faint aroma of burning wood and the underlying hint of desire. I could sense a fire within him, an intense longing to dominate. Like, really dominate me.

"You don't know what you unleashed, little fairy," he breathed, his voice low and husky.

I didn't back down, instead, I ran my hands over his skin, tracing the lines of his muscles and feeling the heat emanating from his powerful body.

"I know," I whispered, my voice barely above a whisper, "and I want it—all of it."

His lips crashed down on mine, and I could taste the wildness of the chase in his kiss. It was as if every moment of pursuit and evasion had built up to this moment, and I reveled in the raw passion that consumed us both.

I wrapped my legs around his waist, pulling him closer to me. I knew this was where we belonged – in each other's arms, lost in the heat of the moment.

With each thrust of his dick rubbing against my core I could feel his muscles flexing beneath my touch, and his growls of pleasure fill my ears.

"Mm, what I good male I have. Showing me how strong he is."

Valpar whined.

He damn whined.

And, yes, I used a bad word, but that was just all I could say.

My pussy gushed. It was downright dripping, mixing with his dick that was a constant drippy faucet any way.

"Be my big strong orc and make me come. I want to come hard. Can you make me come? Be rough with me."

Valpar lifted his right hand away and laid a hard smack on the side of my hip. I cried out feeling the surprise of the sting.

He spanked me, oh sweet baby Zeus, he spanked me.

"More, just like that. That felt so good. Give me more." I dug my nails into his broad, sinewy shoulders, feeling the tension of my body intensify. With a sudden burst of strength, he effortlessly flipped me over, the rush of adrenaline heightening my senses. I eagerly bent my knees, showcasing my backside, and in a swift motion, he ripped my lacy underwear away, the fabric tearing with a satisfying sound. As he firmly slapped my buttocks, the sharp smack reverberated through the surrounding trees. Every sensation, from the sting on my skin to the pulsating heat between my thighs, consumed me, leaving me craving more.

It stung more than I thought it would, but the sting was welcomed when he palmed it.

"Damn, it's becoming a deep shade of crimson," Valpar' whispered, gently cradling it in his palm as if it were a precious jewel, until his hand collided with it once more. A soft, involuntary moan escaped my lips.

He wore a sly smirk as his hand connected with my other cheek, eliciting a mix of pleasure and pain that escaped my lips in a cry. His movements shifted, positioning himself behind me, and the sound of his hand stroking himself was evident, clearly with his come sliding up and down his shaft. I could feel the weight of his throbbing desire pressing against my drenched folds, and I was ready to accept him.

"I'm taking you hard. You fucking ran off on me. I shouldn't let you come," he growled.

I plunged my fingers into the coarse, gritty dirt, feeling its rough texture against my skin. With every ounce of strength, I pushed my knees and arms forward, desperately trying to break free from his grasp. The sound of his menacing snarl echoed in my ears, shooting pleasure between my legs.

His razor-sharp claws sliced through the fabric of my clothing, creating loud tearing sounds. My body got caught in the grass, and with the recent rain I felt my limbs getting covered in the mud.

Valpar grabbed my ankles and pulled me back toward him. I heard his cock slap across his thigh. "And where do you think you're going, female? I'm not nearly finished," his voice had changed. It was deeper, guttural, more animal.

So hot!

My stomach fluttered and I think my pussy clamped down onto nothing.

Is that really a thing?

I giggled as I pretended to fight with him. It stirred him on. He manhandled me, trying to get a better grip, but the mud and dew on my legs made me slippery. It didn't help I had a heavy coat of lotion on either.

Valpar's growls grew louder and more desperate as he tried to maneuver me into the right position for the primal mating ritual he had going on. I wriggled and squirmed, feigning resistance, but deep down I craved the intensity of his dominance. He clenched his teeth, his eyes flashing with a wild hunger that caused my heart to race even more.

Finally, he managed to get a firm grip on me, his claws digging into my flesh as he yanked me onto his lap, impaling me with his throbbing erection. I cried out in both pain and pleasure and my body trembled uncontrollably. The sensation of him inside me was overwhelming, and I knew in that moment that I belonged to him completely.

"Take it, little fairy," he grunted, his voice low and dark. "This is what it means to be claimed."

I arched my back, my nails digging into the soil as he thrust into me with an animalistic fury. The ground beneath us was muddy and uneven, making our movements uneasy and slippery. The wet, earthy smell surrounded us as we clung to each other, our bodies slick with sweat and tangled in the grass.

"Yes, Valpar," I moaned, my voice a breathy plea for more. "Fuck me harder, my good male."

With that, he thrust into me, his cock sinking deep inside me with a wet sound. I gasped, arching my back as he began to fuck me with a frenzied intensity. Each stroke sent pleasure coursing through me, igniting a fire deep within my core.

"Yes," my head lulled back.

Valpar continued to slam into me with reckless abandon. He changed our positions, all without taking his dick from my body so that I was on all fours again.

"My female," he growled into my ear.

The wind rustled through the trees above us as he pounded me from behind, and I cried out his name with each thrust. My orgasm was building, an intense rush of pleasure that I knew I couldn't control.

"Come around my shaft!" he commanded. "I want that tight pussy to milk me of my seed."

He grunted and thrust deeper, driving me closer to the precipice. Then, just as my orgasm crested, he brought his two dulled fingers and flicked at my clit.

My voice cracked as I came. Valpar didn't hide my noise but let me make all the cries I wanted.

"Mmm, I pleased my female."

I nodded as he continued to push his throbbing cock inside me. I felt like it was growing with no end in sight.

He chuckled low, his voice rumbling through me. "You're such a temptress, my sweet. Such a perfect mate." His fingers found my clit again, teasing me as he continued to thrust into me. "You're so tight, so warm. I could stay inside you forever."

He picked up the pace, his hips slapping against my ass with each powerful thrust. Our wet bodies smacking together. I'm sure we had awakened the entire forest by now.

"Fuck, yes," he gasped, his body trembled.

With a roar, he plunged into me, his cock hitting my sweet spot. The pressure built, the intensity of our coupling reaching a fever pitch.

"You come again," he growled, his voice echoing through the night. "You're going to feel my seed inside you."

The thought of him filling me sent a jolt of pleasure through my body. I arched my back the same time he pulled my hair and pushed almost everything inside me.

"H-here, n-now," I barely muster to say.

With a final thrust, he buried himself inside me, releasing his seed deep within my core. I felt it spill, hot and powerful, filling me in a way I'd never known.

"Mine," he growled, his voice thick with possession. "You're mine, little one."

And soon, too, it will be officially forever.

CHAPTER THIRTY-FIVE

Valpar

SHE HAD VEXED ME and my primal urges gave in.

I wouldn't say I regretted it, because she had the biggest smile on her face and I had one to match.

We were bare, our bodies exposed to the world. The cloth that once adorned me was gone, leaving me feeling the cool breeze against my skin. I had ripped her dress like a savage beast, mercilessly shredded it into pieces. All cloth was now laid in tattered, unusable pieces on the ground.

We were both sated, exhausted, and my seed leaked out of her body, so much so, that I wondered if I would die because I had no life left in me.

I scooped her up, after the fifth time of expelling my seed. I only stopped because she said she couldn't take it anymore. I gave her ass a slap, she moaned like my good female and leaned into my body seeking comfort. If she ever ran again, I'd take her twice as hard.

She was stronger than she looked and I could move the little fairy in such interesting ways.

I cleared my throat and tried to start the inevitable conversation while we walked back to get my weapons. I didn't know why I was dreading the response that she was about to give me. I needed to know who accompanied her to her *thinking swing*. Was it a male? Was it her uncle? If it was anyone she was related to, they should have known I would have been insanely worried and covered with fury.

"Little fairy, what happened? Why, in all the rich soil in which we step, did you go to the swing and then why did you run?"

Her naked body, plastered to mine while I carry her, was already giving rise to my shaft. The cool night air blew on the tip of the angry head and more seed gathered.

I guess I do have more seed to give.

"My fairy godmother led me out. Apparently, I was sleepwalking, anyway."

I blinked several times. *There was a lot to unload in that statement.*

"I need more information, before I rip the trees from the soil and start rutting you, again."

My female slapped my chest and laughed. "Oh, my fairy godmother. You probably don't know the fictional stories, but she is a special fairy in—fairy tales? Wow, this might get complicated. Let me see." She tapped her finger to her lips. "Fairy Godmothers are fairies, they are legends, that have magical powers and act like your mentor or someone to look up to and guide you to where you need to go. She helped me find you!" My miresa beamed. "She isn't really a fairy godmother though, she's actually a witch—that's what she keeps telling me. She's pretty bad-assy. Starla has purple hair and wears dark clothes. She's got this awesome corset and these giant melons—"

"Female, that's enough." I shook my head as I watched my little fairy make pretend big tits on her body. My miresa's tits were perfect the way they were, and I could not imagine having them any bigger. "And why was she here, why did she lead you out?"

My little fairy twisted her fingers together and winced. "Technically, she wasn't really here. She was in my dream. It takes a lot of power for her to transport herself from the Earth Realm back to Bergarian. She came to me in my dream and had me walk out here."

A deep growl resonated in my throat. "You were alone, then."

"Not in spirit, though," my miresa corrected.

"You will spend time staring at the wall when we get back, which I do not think we will make it before daylight. The light sources will rise soon." I stopped us in front of my sword, just as Simon walked around from the bushes. His eyes widened when he looked between my legs, let out a long yell, tipped over and fell onto his side. "Bassza, what did I do? I was just standing here!"

Calliope wrapped her arms around my neck as I gathered my supplies. "He saw your dong. It would scare me, too, if I was a poor, defenseless creature. He probably thought you were going to hit him. You might have to carry him. Want me to walk?"

I grunted and heaved the goat up under my arm. He was frozen solid, not just fainted. His legs were stiff, his head moved in an odd position. *Strange.*

"We can go to my parent's tree house. It's over yonder." My miresa pointed to the left, and I carried them both in my arms.

My shaft was not that scary, and I did not see how a goat would faint over something as simple as a naked orc.

By the time we reached the tree, my miresa was yawning and rubbing her cheek against me. The dirt and grime was falling off my skin, but human bodies were not resistant to the outdoors and their bodies were prone to sickness. I had to get her clean and warm, and hopefully this treehouse would have a way for me to do that.

I wanted to wash her in the stream we traveled through, but she refused, saying she would rather have a warm *show-er*. I was not looking forward to holding two bodies against me while I climbed, but when we reached the tree, my miresa pointed to a small hidden *lev-er* and a mysterious *ele-vator* came from the thick branches of the tree.

She motioned for me to step onto the platform, with its wooden surface cool beneath my feet. With hesitation, I tested its sturdiness, feeling the weight of my body press against it. Satisfied, I tightened my grip on my precious cargo, feeling its weight in my arms. Her laughter did not bring confidence even as she assured me that the platform could bear more than just my weight. It was a claim that seemed unbelievable. As we ascended, sounds of creaking branches and rustling leaves surrounded us, and my tension did not ease until I jumped off the platform.

As we came into the main living area, my eyes widened. It was not a simple treehouse as I had imagined, but a grand house woven into the very fabric of the trees, a strange fusion of nature and cabin.

The spacious living area was created with comfortable sofas and chairs, while vibrant cloths dangled from branches, making the room a rainbow of colors. The sight of the colorful fabrics brightened the space, while the gentle rustling sound they made added a soothing nature.

I did not have these colors back at our cabin, and I would need to make sure that we would bring many colors back to decorate our home together.

"The shower is back there," my miresa pointed. "You can set down poor Simon over here, that's his bed."

Simon was still stiff. When I set him down, he toppled over and let out a long whine.

"When he gets over-tired, sometimes his body won't unlock for a bit. He'll be okay." She patted my shoulder, and I shook my head.

This goat was going to be trouble when we took him back to the Wood. There were creatures twice his size that would eat him alive. Not only would I have to keep my miresa tied to me, but a goat as well.

I would be a laughingstock.

My miresa showed me where their bathroom was. There wasn't a tub, but a shower. It was large, a place for sitting and even a lounger where someone could lie. There were many shower heads that all came pouring from the walls and I looked in awe at how many knobs there were.

"Mom always wanted a fancy shower, so Dad built it for her. I don't like it so much; I'd rather take a bath."

"But there is no tub." I looked around more as she turned on the knobs. Steam rolled out of the shower and the water on my muscles instantly relaxed me.

"Nope, I usually go bathe in a hot spring."

I felt a sudden surge of tension, as my muscles contracted and swelled, creating a taut, rigid sensation in my back muscles.

"Naked?" I growled and watched her as she squirted oil onto the towel.

"Well, one tends to get naked when they bathe." She snorted and continued with her bathing. I watched as the water droplets dripped down her breasts, her nipples hardening.

"You will not be naked, not without me. Do you understand?" I stood next to her and my shaft rubbed up against her leg.

She squeaked and stared up at me. "Never? Without you? So, are we always bathing together, then?"

"Yes."

She stuck out her lips into a pout and shrugged her shoulders. "Okie dokie."

I blinked several times, waiting for her to brat back at me, but it never came. Satisfied with her answer, I washed the rest of me and helped her with her hair, combing it with my claws and fixing it into a large braid so she could sleep.

When she showed me her room, I knew my stature was far too large. I had to squeeze inside the doorway and when I finally did, I could see the variety of color she had created on the walls. Pinks, yellows, and purples swirled together in patterns of flowers, streams, mountains and forests. I wanted to wait until the light sources came above the horizon, so I could see what she had done to create such beauty.

Could she paint our cabin this way? Make it bright and beautiful? Perhaps I didn't decorate my cabin because my miresa would make our house into a home.

My miresa yawned again, and I shook that thought away, wrapping my arm around her waist.

"Come, we sleep." I grabbed a ribbon from a shelf and tied it around her wrist and then to my ankle. She eyed me for a moment, but again, she did not argue.

"I'm gonna put some pajamas on." She rubbed her eyes. I shook my head and took the towel that she used to dry her body.

"No, your body goes against mine. Consider it your punishment for leaving me alone in the bed of furs."

My miresa muttered under her breath, "But is it really punishment?"

I chuckled, and she fell into her bed, which was far too small for my body. She curled up next to me, her cheek resting next to my chest.

"We still have stuff to talk about." She yawned and closed her eyes. "Lots of important stuff."

I hummed, stroking the little piece of hair around her face. "We will, in the morning, sweet female. Sleep long, we have all the time."

Her nose scrunched up, and she blew out a breath.

If she wasn't so tired, I was sure there would be an argument there.

"Oh, don't pet the fart squirrels, if they come by at light sources rise," she added.

My eyes darted open.

"Fart squirrels?"

"Yeah, they are black and white, and sometimes hang outside my window and I give them treats. Don't go near and pet them. They throw stink at you if you scare 'em."

I tried to contain my laughter, but my body shook. "My little fairy, that is a skunk."

She grunted. "No, it's a fart squirrel."

I rolled my eyes and let her be. Soon after, I fell into a light sleep, because I would not have her running off without me again.

Chapter Thirty-Six

Calliope

VALPAR SNARLED AND HURLED his body on top of me. "Stay down!"

A scream pierced the air, causing me to shout in surprise. Valpar growled and tightened his body around me. The screaming behind him didn't stop the shrill, high-pitched scream.

I screamed, too, because I recognized that scream. Panic rose to my throat because my mother had just walked in on Valpar and me... completely naked!

"What the fuck!" I heard my dad's voice come through it all. "Whose ass is that!?"

What? This juicy biscuit? "It's my mate's! Don't kill him!" I shouted.

Huh, I did not see this coming.

Probably should have, since this is my parents' house, and I didn't really believe they would stay a whole month away from me.

Valpar forcefully twisted my body, positioning me right in front of him. As I moved, the soft fabric of the blanket trailed along my body, providing a thin shield to protect my nakedness.

The sound of Valpar's heavy panting trailed down my neck, his breaths coming out in ragged gasps. His grip tightened around one of his menacingly large daggers, the cold steel gently touching my arm reminding me he was in protection mode.

So hot.

"No one will kill me or touch my female!" Valpar hissed.

My mom was restrained by my dad, his face wearing a smirk reminiscent of my uncles. I could see the amusement in his eyes. Meanwhile, my mom's face reflected sheer terror. Her complexion had turned pale, and her mouth agape wide enough to let a pixie sit inside.

"What in Hera's name is going on? Birch, get that thing away from Calliope!" She struggled in his hold, her body trembling with anger as she tried to get free.

Birch held onto her tighter. "I don't think there is a problem here, Theresa."

Mom screamed, again. She jumped and squirmed in his arms. "What do you mean, there is no problem? He's got her tied to him!"

Birch looked at the ribbon, which wasn't a strong material anyway and frowned. He let go of Theresa and put his hand to his hip, which held a sheathed knife.

Uh oh.

"Wait, wait!" I held out my hands, but Valpar grabbed them back.

He gripped me by my waist and lifted me, his dick was hard, despite the circumstances, and I groaned when Mom screeched again, her hands slapping her face.

"Cut it off!"

Nope, can't do that.

"Mom! He's my mate! I swear to you!" I held onto Valpar's forearms to steady me.

Birch eyed Valpar up and down with a slightly skeptical look. "Osirus did say that Calliope had found her mate. Let's hear them out."

Theresa shook her head. "Not to an orc, there is no way she is mated to this green monstrosity!"

I gasped. "Mom, are you racist? I can't believe it!"

Mom took a step back. "No, no, that is not what I am saying! It's just...you are both completely different, this is... no, this is a mistake. You are so... and he is just..."

"Just what?" Valpar snapped

I snickered. "Aw, you talking about his junk being too big? Don't worry, it fits!" I pointed at the club between his legs.

As Mom gasped for air, her eyes fluttered and rolled back into her head. The room filled with a tense silence, broken only by the sound of Dad's knife slipping from his grip. He swiftly reached out, catching Mom just in time to prevent her from collapsing onto the cold, hard floor.

Birch sighed and shook his head, putting an arm under her legs and one behind her back. "Why don't you both get dressed? Meet us in the living room." Birch eyed us one more time and swallowed. "And please, take the restraints off of Calliope. I can only do so much with Theresa, and having you tied to her is going to throw her into a fit."

Valpar grunted and jerked his jaw toward Dad in understanding. At least, I think it was understanding. Or maybe it was just an 'Okay, I'll appease you for now, but I'll tie up my mate later,' sort of deal.

We dressed quickly, although. we didn't have a leather loincloth to cover Valpar's jewels, so we had to make do with some silk wrappings that hung around the walls. I picked the manliest color, a dark blue, but he had to use a bright pink to tie his pecker to his leg!

Please Mom, don't ask why he has a tie around his leg.

By the time we walked into the living room, with Valpar's hand tightly around my shoulder. Mom was coming to. She was still pale, lying on the ornate deep purple couch that Osirus gifted Birch for a mating present.

"It wasn't a dream?" Mom groaned, and I fisted my hands into the extra fabric of Valpar's cloth. A little of me was disappointed that Mom wasn't happy for me, but the other part knew why.

She knew what was going to happen to me. *She knew I was going to get my memories back.*

"Don't talk to my miresa that way," Valpar growled, and the branches shook in the tree.

Birch didn't turn around, just swiped a cloth over Mom's head.

"The Moon Fairy gave her to me, and I will protect her—"

Mom sat up from the couch. "Ha!" She interrupted. "You, protect her? You think you can protect her from what's coming? You do not know what you have done, what you have subjected her to. Now, she will be heartbroken because this—" she pointed between the two of us, "This cannot be a completed bond. Not on my watch."

Before Valpar could growl or snarl, I did it on my own. I ripped myself from Valpar's hold. Mom leaned back onto the couch and her eyes widened as she saw me approach her. I leaned forward, my lip curled.

"You will not separate us. You will not break us apart. You think you know everything when you don't. I've grown up a lot since you have been gone. I should have grown-up years ago."

Mom's eyes softened. "Calliope—"

I shook my head. "No. I... I know you were trying to protect me. Whatever it is, I was trying to protect myself, too, and maybe I needed that break for a while. I know what's going to happen if we mate." I felt my throat closing up around me, then, I felt Valpar at my back. His warmth enveloped me when his arms wrapped around my waist and his jaw touched the top of my head. "But now, I need to make some decisions, and now that I have a mate—" I stared up at him, his face was void of any emotion and I knew it was because he didn't care for Mom very much at the moment. "—I can get through it."

Mom leaned her head back on the couch, her arms limp in defeat. "I just love you." She sniffed. "I just remember seeing you—holding you when—" I jumped into her lap and she let out an oomph, wrapping her arms around me.

"I'll be okay." I nuzzled her neck. "It will be fine."

Valpar's throat let out a rumble, and I stood up and felt him pull me back to his body.

Birch stood and held out his hand, ready to grasp Valpar's forearm. "We haven't been properly introduced. I'm Birch. Calliope's adoptive father. This is Theresa, Calliope's adoptive mother." He nodded to Mom.

For the next couple of hours, Dad took the lead in the conversation. Valpar was mostly quiet and answered questions in a gruff tone. I was able to explain how we met, how I deliberately disobeyed her, followed my Fairy Godmother's advice and went to the mating ball, anyway.

Mom said nothing, but Dad had to hold Mom's bouncing thigh still with his hand. He whispered to her, *"It was the Goddess' will for her to be there."*

Mom went to the kitchen and prepared us food. I offered to help but she waved me off and said she needed time to process. It hurt, but I understood. She was trying to protect me, but it was time for me to stand on my own.

Mom brought back the snacks and food, but Valpar ate little, his hand was on my thigh, my butt on his lap. On occasion, my Mom would let out a sad sigh, but dad would just pat her back in reassurance.

Mom was really upset. I wasn't sure if it was because I was going to be leaving the treehouse for good, or what was yet to come for me.

After I explained to both Valpar and my parents about Starla's visit in my dream last night, about what was going to happen, Mom started crying and Birch consoled her. Valpar, again, showed no emotion on his face but I felt his body tense. His arms tightened around me, his hand on my chest. He was reading me, just like in the tent, and after a while his eyebrows furrowed. I knew he wanted to take me away from my parents and have us be alone in our own little world, to discuss things on our own.

"Have you decided what you are going to do, honey?" My mom wiped away a tear. "With the whole, take it all at once or a little at a time? You know, about the memories?"

I felt Valpar's gaze on me, and I squeezed his arm. "That's something Valpar and I will talk about. I think we need to do that alone."

Mom nodded.

I knew she had to feel some sort of jealousy, maybe hurt. I could see it in her body language as she curled up on the couch and her head leaning on Dad's shoulder. She'd done everything for me since I came here. It was her time, though, her time with Birch to start her own family.

There wasn't anything I could do to make it better for her. I couldn't rely on them anymore. My past was mine and I knew Theresa and Birch were in it. They saved me but they didn't have to keep saving me anymore.

Valpar was my future.

"Please don't worry," I whispered. "This was meant to happen."

Why else would my fairy godmother be pushing this, especially right now? Unless it was her own agenda, which I didn't believe.

Mom hummed. "You really fell out over the banister, did you?"

I buried my face into Valpar's chest.

Mom rolled her eyes and smacked her head. "Calliope, I swear you are the most accident prone, little thing I have ever seen. I remember when we first brought you to the tree house, you almost fell out of the tree ten times, in ten minutes. We had to have a witch put an invisible ward up the first year."

I giggled, but Valpar stiffened around me.

Birch huffed. "Valpar, you will do fine with Calliope. She is a lively one, but it seems you have calmed her. She appears to have slept-in this day. She is usually awake before the light sources rise, and playing with the woodland creatures on her balcony or climbing down the tree wreaking havoc through the forest before we can stop her."

Valpar's large hand squeezed my thigh.

"That's because he thoroughly wore me out last night," I chirped. "He did me dirty on the forest floor because I made him chase after me."

Mom was halfway drinking her tea when it all came spitting out of her mouth.

Birch leaned his head back on the couch. "I see she has not gained an ounce of restraint on that mouth, yet."

Valpar chuckled, squeezing me tight against his chest. "No, but I enjoy her this way."

We talked for longer, and the longer we did, the more I felt myself grow anxious. I wasn't used to sitting this long, but I was doing it for Mom's sake. She would look at me occasionally and smile, but I could see the worry and, maybe, sadness.

I quickly realized our time was short and I would have to travel back to the Wood with Valpar.

They eventually told us of their travels. Which comprised of visiting Creed and Odessa, the dragon shifters who were relatively quiet and private, raising their two daughters. They were now pregnant again with their third, maybe fourth child. They were excited, but could only visit for a day with them, since Creed was very territorial over Odessa and their children. Birch said he felt sorry for his daughters that they may never find their mates.

Word traveled up to the mountains that an orc found a mate at the ball and that it was a fairy. The last part being it was, in fact, not a fairy but a human that dressed like them gave them pause, and they flew their butts right back down the mountains. Because there are no humans that dress like a fae, but me.

They just had horrible timing.

Birch and Valpar, then, got started on the war stories. Birch wanted to know what Valpar's position was during the war and how he helped solidify the win. I stood up because I needed to stretch my legs. Valpar's eyes didn't leave my body. I felt the heat of his stare the entire time as I walked around the room, I fiddled with all the trinkets in the room to commit it to memory.

In the pit of my stomach, I felt like I wouldn't be returning to the treehouse for a long time. This was going to be my last time staying—well, living here. I wasn't a single lady anymore. I was going to be mated soon.

There were a lot of fond memories here and I wanted to remember each one.

Birthdays, holidays, accidentally walking in on my parents in compromising positions. I giggled to myself when I reached Simon's bed. It was empty, and I tilted my head when I saw that one of the flowers that was braided into his hair had fallen out.

The flowers the orcs used could last weeks without water and they had done a great job weaving it into his hair. There was no way it could come out, with how tight they wove it.

The room grew quiet, and I felt Valpar's warm body behind me. It was so weird how I could feel him, know where he was.

"What's wrong, my miresa?" His hand touched my shoulder.

"Where is Simon?" I continued to stare down at his empty bed.

Valpar shrugged his shoulders. "Perhaps he is roaming outside. You said his stomach was upset. Grass would settle it."

I shook my head. "If I am in the treehouse, and Mom and Dad are home, he stays with us. No matter what."

Birch and Mom came up beside us looking at the bed as well. It wasn't much, but Simon was pretty simple. We tried getting him a miniature bed like Mom and Dad's, but he would just chew on the knobs, eat the blankets and throw the pillows off it. It was just a mattress on the floor with bits of hay on top of it. Except now, there was no Simon.

Valpar kneeled down and touched the bedding. "It is cool. He has been gone for a while. Perhaps he left when he heard your mother's screams. She has a loud voice that would terrify an ogre."

Birch hid his laughter beneath his palm.

"Hey, careful Dad, you can get loud, too." I joked.

Mom let out a bark of laughter. "Yes, he does, during the hokey pokey. Am I right?" She nudged him. Valpar chuckled, watching my parents and I saw his shoulders ease as he witnessed them relaxing more around him.

I knew Valpar had reservations about them, especially about how they treated me. Perhaps once I knew the full extent of my past, I'd understand why they treated me the way they did.

"I'll tell you what," Mom said, clasping her hands together. "Let me make us an early dinner. We can tell you about our adventures up in the mountains and you can tell us more about yours. We can leave out the, uh... private stuff." She cringed. "Creed was very interested in hearing about one orc finally getting their mate. Just didn't realize it was my Calliope."

Valpar's back straightened. "Creed, the black dragon. Yes, I remember him."

Mom nodded. "Yes, the one that you fought with in the war. He spoke highly of you."

"He is a fit male. I would very much like to see him again, one day."

"Perhaps he can make an appearance before you go? I can send word you would like to meet with him." Mom gave him a tentative smile.

She's trying.

With an agreement, Dad then pulled Valpar to one side. It was the most engaged I've seen him with anyone besides Mom, Uncle Osirus or me. He pulled out a few of his weapons from his bag, showing them to Valpar. Valpar went and grabbed his weapons as well and join in with the guy thing, looking over each other's stuff.

It was like bro-bonding.

Mom's arm wrapped around my shoulder and hugged me. "It's going to work out," she said, more to herself than me. "And Simon will come back. Perhaps I scared him. After dinner Birch and I will go look for him while you and Valpar talk."

I bit my lip, because we both knew that Simon not being here was out of the norm. Simon was always here when the family were, especially when it was getting close to dinner.

He wasn't upset that we were leaving, was he? Did he think I was going to leave him behind? Or did he not want to go? I didn't give him a choice, really. Or was he mad at me that I left in the night without him?

I bit my cheek. I needed to talk to him and Valpar.

CHAPTER THIRTY-SEVEN

Valpar

LATER THAT NIGHT, ONCE the door closed to my female's room, I grabbed her by the waist and pulled her toward me gently.

"I need you," I breathed before I pressed my lips against hers. It wasn't rushed or forced. This wasn't a primal need, thinking with my shaft like I would normally take her. It was slow, soft and it was thoughtful. I needed her in a different way, not physically, it was a way I could not describe.

My mind canceled out all sound. All I saw was her and the room bathed in a soft, golden glow from the dimmed lights, casting soft shadows of our bodies along the colorful walls as my body surrounded her.

I leaned in, the sound of our hushed breaths mixing together while our foreheads touched, creating our own music. The touch of her lips against mine was equally tender. It was a delicate connection that sent a shiver down my spine, a moment of pure vulnerability, where time seemed to stand still.

I concentrated on every movement of my lips with hers. She didn't fight it, her arms immediately went to my arms to steady herself as I encased her into my body. I wanted to pull her into me, like so many times before when I kissed her, to hide her within my grasp, so no pain would ever come from her.

But I couldn't protect her. My body, my strength and warrior qualities could do nothing. I was a failure.

I was consumed by *fucking* anger. The intensity of my emotions was so far gone, knocking down a tree, banging rocks or the soil, even fucking her—wouldn't help. There was a raging storm that had taken hold of my being. All I yearned for was to ease her pain, to shield her from the burdens she carried. I longed for my female to radiate pure happiness, to be carefree like the day she fell into my lap.

Why did such a pure soul have to deal with a horrible past? Are the gods that cruel?

Our kiss deepened, and I cupped her ass, grinding myself to her. I needed to be inside her. I wanted her as close as possible to me.

"I need you," I murmured, kissing her cheek. "I need you closer, right now."

My miresa dug her fingers into my loose hair, pulling me back. "I can't get any closer, you silly male." She laughed and bit my lip with her teeth.

"Inside you," I whined. "I need to be inside you."

I gently guided her back onto the soft padding of her bed, carefully positioning myself on top of her. The taste of anticipation lingered as my lips and tongue caressed her skin, exploring every inch. Her body responded, arching with a graceful curve, causing her breasts to rise and meet my touch. Swiftly, I moved towards her chest, my mouth latching onto the fabric that encased her breasts, drawing them in with my teeth.

She hissed. "Then, get inside me." I felt a tug in my hair pulling me back up to her mouth, but I shook my head.

"I must prepare you to take my shaft." I kissed down her body to lick between her folds.

My female grunted. "We both know I'm already wet enough."

I growled softly, my voice vibrating with desire, as I watched my hair spill like a waterfall around her head. The scent of her hair mingled with the air, intoxicating me. With gentle urgency, I pressed sweet kisses to her lips, feeling their softness against mine. "This," I whispered, my words filled with longing, "is how I want to claim you. Sweet and soft, just like you."

She whimpered when I tickled the broad head of my cock at her entrance.

"Such a good, sweet mate of mine, letting me be so close to you when I need it. Fuck, I need you so bad."

After hearing what she said about the choice she will have to make—and then wanting to talk to me before she made it almost made my chest burst. I truly didn't deserve her.

I let the head of my shaft coat her clit and drip down her cunt. As I did, I felt her muscles relax around her opening and I pushed the broad head of my cock inside her. *Fuck, she felt good.* Every damn time she felt better than the last. I let the first knot inside. Her cunt squeezed me, and she gasped.

I used to crave speed, but damn, savoring her slowly is equally satisfying. Perhaps I was too impatient, too eager during our previous encounters.

She whimpered, again.

I could feel the sweat on my brow, from trying to hold back. It took incredible strength to go slowly. A cruel torture that I was bestowing on myself, but that I needed. I needed to feel some sort of pain.

"Valpar," she whispered into my ear while I buried my face in her neck.

Her cunt tightened, sucking me inside. "Little fairy, only you have the power to break me," I grunted, and pushed forward until my brand was the only part of me outside her.

I longed for the day to claim her. It would be soon, I don't know how I knew that, but even she wouldn't be able to deny it. Each day we tortured each other.

I slipped my hand between her breasts. I felt her —*heart,* she liked to call it.

She ached.

Sadness, excitement, worry and this other emotion I did not have a word for. It was caring; it was joy, it was...so many happy things all wrapped up into one.

Warmth enveloped me while I slowly drove in and out of her.

"Give me all of you," she whispered. "I can take it," her voice choked, eyes glassy.

I felt my throat constrict, and I shook my head. I knew what she was asking for and I couldn't, not yet.

"If I give you the rest of my cock, my brand, I will fully claim you." I gritted my teeth and pressed my brand to her pussy without entering her.

She softly hummed, her smooth leg entwining around my waist. The movement tilted her hips, allowing me better access to passionately stroke and press my body against her throbbing pleasure. A gasp escaped her lips, but I silenced her with a tender, lingering kiss.

"Soon, I'll make you mine, but not when we have so much to talk about. Just enjoy this."

She nodded, her hips moving along with mine. I took her as deeply as I could, holding my seed back so she could find more pleasure.

Once she cried out for a third time, my body shook, unable to hold back anymore.

"I love you," she blurted, her hand pushing to my chest. "I love you."

I pressed my hand to her chest again, not stopping my movements as I felt the tingling at the back of my spine.

"This feeling?"

She nodded weakly. "Yes, it means *I love you*. With all the good feeling in me."

I let out a grunt, as warmth spread through my heart.

Her body trembled against mine, sending shivers down my spine. I couldn't resist the overwhelming pleasure as my hips surged forward, plunging into her with an intensity that bordered on ecstasy. Every inch of me yearned to explore the depths of her, careful not to cause any pain. With a grunt, I poured my seed into the depths of her womb. A soft whimper escaped her lips, blending with her satisfied sighs. Her delicate nails etched into my back, holding onto me tightly, as if her life depended on it.

I collapsed onto her, with my body supported by my forearms. Tremors coursed through me, a mix of physical exertion and intense emotion. My heart pounded in my chest, echoing the lingering sensation of that inde-scribable feeling she spoke of... love. The room spun around us, filled with the scent of sweat and the sound of heavy breathing.

We stayed like that for a while, the sweat of our bodies mingling as we caught our breath.

Her delicate fingers gently traced the strands of my hair, sending a tingling sensation down my spine. I couldn't help but shiver, feeling the subtle reverberations that followed. Never before had I experienced such an intense release.

"Valpar," she whispered softly, her lips brushing against my ear. "For the first time, I feel accepted. Feel like I belong. It's what I always wanted but never thought I would have."

Her words filled me, and I could feel a lump forming in my throat. It was a strange sensation, to be *loved* so deeply by someone so special. She was so small but had feelings so large.

I pulled back to look at her face. Her gaze was soft and angelic, not a hint of fear.

"I want to give you everything, my little fairy," I said, my voice barely above a whisper. "It kills me to know that you will face demons of your past. I don't want you to remember pain."

She took a deep breath, her eyes never leaving mine. "But I have to. Our past shapes our future. I know that now."

I took her hand and pressed it to my chest, my heart thundering against her touch. "Can you feel me?"

She frowned and shook her head. "Your heart beating, but that is all."

Perhaps when I claim her, she will feel it.

"I want you to know, I love you too." I reassured her. "And everything I do, I will do for you. I will fight your nightmares. Find another witch even after we have bonded powerful enough to fight the memories again, if you wished. Even if it means I have to win you over again."

My miresa's face paled and shook her head. "Valpar, no!"

I leaned on my elbows, refusing to pull my cock from her body and grabbed her hands. "I swear to you, my little fairy, I will do anything to take your pain away."

"Y-you can't do that. We will be bonded. Magic won't work on me if we are together. Orcs are immune. When people bond, genetics mix, you get the good qualities of both species. I'll live longer just like you, be immune to sickness." She smiled. "And immune to magic."

I growled. "Then, I will find someone who can. Perhaps Starla—"

She cupped my face and kissed me. "No. I don't want to forget the journey of how we got here. Don't make me forget falling into your big bulky arms. That's the most romantic thing ever. I want to tell our future babies."

My cock twitched inside her and she giggled.

She laid back down and I pressed my head to the crook of her neck. We lay there for a while, while she played with my hair once again.

"Before you decide what you want to do," I muttered, "I have a letter. You wrote it before you forgot your memories. A letter to you, from you. Your uncle gave it to me. Told me to give it to you when it was time."

Her fingers stilled.

"I believe it was to help you decide if you wanted to know your past, or help you come to terms with remembering your past."

She bit her lip. "Do you think I should read it?"

I rubbed my hand up and down her body, watching goosebumps rise on her skin. I could not tell her what to do. This was her decision to make. It was her pain to come to terms with. As much as I wanted to claim her.

"It is your decision. Perhaps it would be good to know how we both can prepare." Her fingers dove back into my hair, scratching my scalp.

I groaned when she used her nails, and she laughed when I kicked my leg how good it feels.

"What a good little orc you are." She snorted and continued to scratch the delightful spot behind my ear.

"I am not little, female! Fuck... don't stop." My eyes rolled in the back of my head and nuzzled further into her neck. "Female, you will be the death of me."

"You also deserve all the good things, Valpar." Her nose went into my hair and took in a deep breath.

Chapter Thirty-Eight

Calliope

EVEN THOUGH MOM, DAD and Valpar were getting along better than I had hoped, the next morning at breakfast, I was still uneasy. Simon was still missing and my parents stayed up late looking for him. I tossed and turned the night before, too worried about where he could be.

It didn't help that I had the same ominous dream of a rundown house, with missing shingles, dark laughter, and the smell of heavy smoke. I still wasn't sure if I was ready to face it all head on or get the missing puzzle pieces one by one.

"We will check the palace today," Mom said and placed a blueberry muffin on my plate.

Blueberry muffins were just naked cupcakes. I try to get past their naked-ness and eat the darn things, but it was so hard when it didn't have icing. It was too dry and not enough sugar for my taste.

My mom raised a brow, knowing I was trying to skip breakfast. "Perhaps Osirus and Melina have seen them. What do you think, Birch?"

Birch had his arms crossed, chewing on a piece of dry jerky. "I don't know where Simon could have gone. Maybe he found himself a female. Now that Calliope has found her own male, perhaps he got the idea he needed to go find him a companion of his own species."

My lip trembled. This only made me feel worse. I didn't even get to tell him goodbye. Wouldn't he want to tell me goodbye? I thought he would want to go with me and Valpar. He sounded like he was into moving with us.

Valpar's rubbed his hand up my back in comfort. "We will find him. We will go to the cave today, gather our supplies and return here by sunset. Don't worry yet, little fairy."

I let out a defeated sigh and pushed my muffin around on my plate. I wasn't hungry. I worried for Simon and the letter we would bring back. I decided I would read it, but only if Simon was with me. He'd been with me from the beginning, it was only fair he was there too. My entire support system should be.

Dad wiped his mouth. His wings fluttered behind him when he pushed away from the table. "Right, let's get going. I'll see if Osirus would have the guards be on the lookout, as well. That goat has given them all sorts of entertainment over the years."

That was true. Their favorite part was when Simon climbed up to the highest part of the palace and started screaming for help. His voice echoed for miles, and they had to make sure not to scare him or he would have fainted and fallen to his death.

Silly Simon.

"Thank you," I said when Mom finally stood up from the table.

She clapped her hands together and her eyes softened. She opened her mouth several times but before anything could be said, Dad pulled her arm and nodded his head toward the door.

Valpar had me on top of his shoulders as we walked our way back through the forest to the cave. I continued to look around for any signs of Simon. I called out to him with no answer back. My shoulders slumped further, and I knew the longer it was that we didn't find it...the least likely we would find him.

It was like in those mystery books from Earth. If you don't find them within the first forty-eight hours, you are less likely to find the missing person.

What if he fainted into a puddle and he drowned? What if he got his head stuck in a bush somewhere? What if he really did meet a lady goat and didn't know what to do? I didn't teach him about the birds and the bees yet! He's just a baby!

Valpar's hand wrapped around my leg and tugged on the leash he had tied around my waist. "Female, if you squeeze your legs any tighter around my head, I will think you want me to stop for a snack."

I released my legs that were, in fact, squeezing his head like a giant melon and let go. "Whoopsie, sorry."

"We will find him. I know it. I will begin tracking him once we grab our supplies."

"Do you have a good nose, like wolf shifters? Do you get on your hands and knees and sniff around?"

Valpar scoffs. "No, I do not sniff around like a dog. Unlike shifters, I use both scent and tracking abilities. I check for breaks in branches, drops of fur, foot—or in Simon's case, hoof prints."

"You know a shifter would take offence if you called them a dog," I said playfully.

Valpar sneered. "Isn't that what they are? Just humans that shift into wolves. I can wrestle ten at a time without getting a scratch." He pulled up his arm and flexes.

"What big muscles you have," I giggled and squeezed the rock on his arm. "And what big teeth and big–"

Valpar growled playfully and slapped my back side causing me to rub my crotch against his neck. He hummed and rubbed up and down my thighs. "That's it, female, rub your cunt all over my neck so I can smell you all day."

I hunched over, my face turning red. "You are shameful, don't say things so loud!"

As we got closer, I saw the boulder was carelessly rolled away. Probably from hastily running out of the cave to come find me. I probably should not worry about him so much, but then that wouldn't be as fun.

I had to keep this male on his toes. He kept telling me he was going to get some gray hair, but I was yet to see it.

He pulled me off his shoulders and carried me inside. The furs were thrown off the bed and Simon's bed of pillows was still fairly neat.

"Can you untie me?" I tugged on the leash.

Valpar's eyes narrowed, their piercing gaze on me and the open passageway outside. The air was heavy with tension as he firmly uttered a resolute, "no". The rustling sound of his movements filled the space as he turned his body, his muscles tensing to meticulously removed items from his bag so he could repack everything.

What a dingle berry.

He said he didn't have much to pack. He kept most of his weapons on his back, thigh and calf but he had to wrap his tent up tightly and even a few furs for easier travel. Valpar said he put the letter in his bag and that was what he wanted to look for first.

Valpar rearranged items out onto the table. A few of his tools fell with a plunk and the blankets fell to the floor. I went to reach for them and he slapped my hand.

"I will take care of it, female. Go sit on the bed and rest." He slapped my butt, and I yipped in surprise as he led me over, tying the rope to a metal ring, bolted into the bed frame.

Wow, what kind of bondage did Aunt Melina and Uncle Osirus get into? It looked kinda fun.

"Sit," he ordered and raised a brow.

"You're kinda bossy." I crossed my arms.

Valpar huffed. "You like me bossy, and I like to know where you are. Now stay."

"I'm not a pet." I retorted. I bit my lip, enjoying this little game I knew he was playing.

Valpar leaned in, his nose grazing up my neck. My body shivered, my nipples tightening underneath my dress. "Ah, but you are my pet. My little human pet that I like to fuck into the furs. You like it too, don't you, my little fairy? Using your hole for my pleasure."

Good gravy.

My mouth dropped and Valpar pulled away. The smirk on his face let me know he was satisfied with my reaction.

I plopped my butt on the bed and when his back turned, I stuck my tongue out at him.

Poop on him.

He was pretty smart to tie me here, because I would have definitely done something to get back at him for turning me on. Not sure what, but something.

I could grab one of the dildo's out and smacked his butt with it. He'd have a fit over that.

But we needed to hurry, we needed to go find Simon.

I let out a sigh, and he ruffled through the bag. When I leaned back into the bed, waiting for him to finish, I felt something touch my hand.

It felt like a bug, so I shook my hand and laid it back down on the bed, but it happened again. I groaned and looked over to see that it was Karma.

Oh, so it is a bug.

My nemisisis...

"What do you want?" I hissed. Karma flew up and slapped his hand over my mouth and shook his head. He held up a small piece of paper and stuck it right in my face.

"If you want to see Simon alive—lose the orc."

I'm gonna kill that son of a bi—

He slapped my nose and held the paper up again. I nodded angrily and grabbed the rope at my waist. I watched as Karma zipped down the cave passage and I knew I had to follow him.

Great, sneaking past an orc that had just bragged about his tracking skills was going to be dang near impossible.

Valpar was humming, though. He was happy and somewhat content right now because I was supposedly listening to him by sitting on the bed. Only problem was I was going to disobey him and really have some corner time later, and maybe a spanking not of the high-pleasure proportions I love so much.

I inwardly groaned and undid the poorly done knot he'd made. Thankful that I never told him what a terrible knot-maker he was, I slipped it off of my waist. I grabbed several pillows and tightened the rope around them, so he would have some resistance when he moved, thinking it me following behind him. It would give me a little more time to get out of there.

My butt tingled as I tip-toed closer to the passageway.

Goddess, he's gonna pop me good, later.

Valpar was still humming, though looked rather disgruntled as he rummaged through his supplies on the table.

"Where is it?" he grumbled to himself. "I put it in here. It should be right there!"

I swallowed and turned, taking off down the passageway, making sure my feet didn't slap the stone floor and welcomed the sun outside.

"Took you long enough," Karma hissed and pulled a small braid of my hair. I tugged back and his body flew past me.

"Get off me, you shiny turd, and tell me where Simon is!"

A rope dropped in front of my face, and I saw Ivy hovering above me. "Grab the rope and hold on." Her eyes narrowed and checked out the cave before looking at me again. "And be quick about it, or you will never see the annoying goat again."

I didn't think that Karma and Ivy could be so mean or that evil to do something. Karma picked on me because—he was just mean, and Ivy was just jealous I had a mate. Why go to this extent? Kidnapping a goat.

I snorted. *Kid-napping. Goat-napping a goat. That was just ludicrous.*

"What is your problem? Both of you? Why can't you just leave me alone? Leave my friends and mate alone?"

As if on cue, they both rolled their eyes.

"Get on the rope," Ivy barked. "Before the fat orc comes out here, or Simon will be fed to an ogre."

I ground my teeth together and made a bowline knot at the bottom of the rope, so I could stick my feet inside and wouldn't have to use my arms to hold me up constantly.

And my mate wasn't fat, there was more to love, and he was so damn comfortable to sleep on, more padding when he punches his hips when he sticks his dick into me, but I wasn't gonna tell her that. She would just want him more.

Right now, there was nothing else I could do. I had to find Simon. He was the first friend that I could remember when I came here. I trusted him and loved him. I couldn't wait for Valpar to come out of the cave and beat these two up. I didn't know if Simon was being held by someone else, and if they were told to hurt him if we arrived late.

I had to do this for Simon.

I tightly gripped the rough, coarse rope with my trembling hands as Ivy, with no warning, effortlessly hoisted me into the air. The wind rushed past my face, carrying with it the scent of fresh pine and the distant aroma of the palace gardens. Above the towering trees, the view extended beyond the height of the palace, revealing a breathtaking view. Despite the intense desire to shut my eyes tightly, I resisted the urge, determined not to show my fear. I had to remain composed, to absorb every detail of where we were going, so I could find our way home.

Because, obviously, Valpar was not going to be able to track us.

"Gods, you need to lay off the cupcakes," Ivy announced as we started flying south.

I leered up at the large form she took to carry me and scoffed. "And you wanted an orc in your bed. If you can't handle a small human to carry, what makes you think you can handle a heavy orc dick?"

Her fangs pulled back in a hiss and she stopped flying. She let us freefall for a few seconds, and I held onto a rope, for dear life, that I knew would never save me from my death.

She caught it, and pulled me back up, grunted before keeping our original flight direction.

"I could let you die right here. Not even worry about you any longer."

I pursed my lips and kept quiet. She was right. She could end me right here. Why was she carrying me so far away and not killing me now?

She probably did kidnap Simon and wasn't going to kill me but do something more sinister. Like killing Simon in front of me and giving me a deep-rooted pain that would forever gut me. I didn't think animals were within the laws of Bergarian to be considered murder if one was killed.

Cheese and crackers—how can souls be so evil?

CHAPTER THIRTY-NINE

Calliope

I NEVER ENJOYED THE idea of flying. Sure, I loved wings of the fae and the fairies, but the idea of flying super high off the ground, with your feet just dangling and not touching the ground, scared the dumplings out of me.

I was doing it for Simon, and I pushed that fear deeper inside me, the more I thought of him and the hot butt I was going to have later.

We flew for what seemed like forever, covering a lot of ground. If we had gone on foot it would have taken us days. That worried me for Valpar. For one, he wouldn't find me because there was nothing to track and two, I was too far away for him to get to me in time for whatever Ivy and Karma had planned.

As we approached Valpar's territory, our path took a slight detour to the east, bringing us nearer to the mysterious Vermillion Kingdom. The dense forests in this region exuded a darker look, with their ebony tree bark and foliage adorned in richer, deeper shades of color. I'd never had the desire to visit this kingdom. It was dark and gloomy, and from stories I read about anything being dark, it meant evil resided there.

It was terrible of me to think that. There were a lot of vampires that were super nice, such as the current king and queen. It was just the darker scene just wasn't for me. Plus, there were giant spiders.

And spiders were icky.

My calloused feet sank into the rough, scratchy rope, causing an incessant itch. The friction had left my hands blistered and tender, aching from the strain of gripping tightly. As I hung there, suspended in mid-air, a sigh escaped my lips, a mix of exhaustion and anxiety. I let out a tremendous sigh, but I dared not complain. I didn't want to freefall to my death; I wanted Simon and to make sure he was okay.

Ivy slowed down, and Karma wasn't far behind us. For a small thing, he was pretty fast, and he dove in a spiral waiting for Ivy to lower us to the ground.

As we made our way downward, the skeletal branches of the trees loomed overhead, devoid of leaves. I could feel their rough, jagged edges graze against my bare legs, causing a prickling sensation. Desperately, I tried to maneuver my body to avoid their grasp, but they seemed relentless. They tugged at my hair, my hips, and my arms, as if seeking to ensnare me. The branches left tiny, stinging cuts on my skin, eliciting a sharp intake of breath. Suddenly, one of them became entangled in my hair, causing the brittle branch to snap and tumble down with me.

Once we were five feet off the ground, Ivy dropped me without a care. I landed on my backside and yelped in surprise. She fluttered down, with a smirk on her face and I glared at her.

If only I could make her burst into flames.

She'd already died like six times in my head already. All being slow and torturous deaths.

Wow, now I am becoming the meanie.

I slapped my hand. "Bad Calliope."

Ivy glanced over at me and rolled her eyes. "Weirdo."

"Where's Simon? I came like you asked." I kicked off the rope around my ankles and dusted off my dress. "Come on, where is he?"

A faint, muffled rustling emanated from beyond a bush painted in deep, navy hues. As I strained my eyes, I caught a fleeting glimpse of a white tail protruding from the other side of the bush. With a sudden jolt, I lunged towards the source of the sound, my heart pounding against my chest. However, before I could fully react, Ivy swiftly extended her hand, clutching my arm and forcefully pulling me back. The unexpected motion caused me to lose my balance, sending me tumbling onto the ground, landing unceremoniously on my butt.

"Not so fast." Ivy waved her hand, sauntered over and unwrapped a rope that had Simon's neck tied to the bush.

Simon didn't do well if he didn't eat every ten minutes while he was awake. He had to be cranky.

He nodded his head, trying to buck at Ivy to get away. Unfortunately, he had a pillow wrapped around his head to pad his horns, so he could not hurt her. Poor Simon looked utterly defeated, yet unharmed.

I stood up and balled my fists at my side. "Let him go, you got me here!"

Karma snorted, his little booty shorts squeezing his junk a little too tight. *Does he like goat bondage or something? Is he into animal torture? What is his problem?*

I hoped someone would sit on him and he'd get squished like the bug he is.

"Not so fast. We've got some things to discuss." Ivy polished her nails with her dress and blew on it.

"Yeah, and what is there to discuss other than you being a sore loser?" I crossed my arms. "The only reason you have me here is because you're sad you don't have an orc."

Ivy growled and stomped her foot. "It isn't fair that a human gets a mate while the rest of Bergarians are still waiting for their mates. Why?" she yelled. "I'm fifty years old. I've been patient!"

I huffed in annoyance. "There are other Bergarians that have waited longer for their mates. Uncle Osirus waited eight hundred years! King Kane waited over a hundred. What makes you special?"

Ivy huffed through her nose. "And what makes you special? You are twenty-five! And human! Humans shouldn't get such luxury! The gods chose us to be their favorites. Humans ruin everything. Your realm is slowly dying because you can't take care of it." Her face turned red, and her voice grew louder.

Like that was my fault. I didn't even remember Earth.

Karma flew toward me and crossed his arms. "And why do you have to have the king so close to you? Why not someone else in the realm that is of his people? Why a human?"

I rolled my eyes. "You guys are racists to humans. I don't understand why. I don't have any power over any of you. I'm not the prettiest. I hold no powers. King Osirus gave pity on me because of my past that I—"

"—don't know," Ivy interrupted. "Yes, we are aware you don't know of your past. We've done our digging. You've been tainted with magic to forget who you are so you can be the ignorant, happy, little human. The little sunshine to the king and queen's eyes, who they can spoil. They only keep you around for your innocence, you know, because they can't have children of their own."

The harshness of her words pierced my chest.

It was well known that Uncle Osirus and Aunt Melina may never have children. Melina was stabbed in her womb during the war, with a sword imbued with deep, dark magic. She may never have children, but they don't let that come between them. They love each other. They wouldn't spoil me because I act like a child. I wasn't a child. They said so themselves.

I didn't believe her.

"I—"

"They are getting bored." Karma interrupted. "They need someone else to baby and to spoil. Like a real child. Birch and Theresa are pregnant now, you know. Once they get rid of you, the king and queen can spend some time with a real baby. Not an adult that acts like one."

My eyes widened and I clutched my hand to my chest. "W-what?" Why didn't they tell me?

"That's the whole reason they left for the mountains, isn't it? To become pregnant?" Karma cooed, flying around my head. "They are starting their own family now. Think about it, Calliope. They were trying to get you to that ball all along. Valpar hasn't claimed you yet, because you aren't really his."

"Liar!" I screamed and reached to grab him.

Karma darted away and flew to a height where I couldn't reach.

"That's enough," Ivy said, waving her hand. "Here is what's going to happen, Calliope. Listen real good, now, because I'm explaining this once and if your little head can't get it, then I guess it's over for the both of you."

She pulled out a piece of a worn envelope. It looked like it had been folded multiple times. It was discolored and even had drops of some sort of liquid dried on it.

I instantly knew what it was before she explained.

"This is the letter to you wrote to yourself." Ivy waved it in front of her. "Such a sad story where you came from. Tragic... almost made me feel sorry for you. No wonder you wanted to forget."

She read it. That bitch read it!

Rage surged through my veins, a fiery torrent. I felt like Valpar and his emotional turmoil to uproot a tree. The desire to extract her very life from her body, to squeeze her insides so they were on the forest floor, consumed me.

Dang, I got dark real quick.

Simon turned his body to kick her, but Ivy was on alert and jumped in the air to float above him. She tsked, shaking her head. "We've planned this too well to let it all go. Not for a stupid goat to mess it up. Karma, do you have it?"

Karma came fluttering down from the tree, carrying a bottle the size of him. He was stronger than he looked and held it, leaning it up against his body while Ivy took the time to tie Simon to the base of another tree.

"Stay there, Calliope, or I'll slit Simon's throat and let the rogue vamps come find the both of you." Ivy glared, daring me to step away from my spot.

It was useless. I stood there and watched as she tied Simon's neck to the tree, his legs kicked into the dirt, his grunts ripping my heart out.

"Hang on, Simon, I'm gonna make it better." I pleaded with him. He stilled and his went body stiff. He was tied so tightly to the tree I didn't know if he had fainted or not, because he couldn't move.

Goddess, we're utterly screwed.

But I was determined to get us both out of here. He helped me when I needed it all those years. Really, he was my companion not the other way around.

Ivy dusted her hands off and took the bottle from Karma. "Now for the show." She took the bottle and swirled it in her hand. It was corked at the top, but with the bottle being translucent, you could still see the liquid inside sloshing about.

"This is a magic-breaking potion. It has some fancy name." Ivy waved her hand carelessly. "All I know is it will break whatever spell that is on you, and you will remember every damn thing you've been through. Down to the last detail."

I threaded my fingers together and looked away from her.

"Drink this, or we kill your pet." She put her free hand on her hip. "You'll become the depressed little loser you really are, and not want to even go back to your happy, insignificant life with your adoptive family. Put everyone out of their misery, trying to push you off on some orc and give the rest of the fairies a chance."

If they had been spying on me, then they should know that the curse would be broken soon, since he was my mate. Did she really not think I was his?

"Why break it now?" I asked. "I'll have to remember my past soon."

Ivy strolled up to me with the bottle in her hand. She leaned forward, her nose close to mine. "Like I said, you aren't really his mate. Besides, once you take this and realize what sort of past you had, trust me, you won't want to live anyway. You won't want to go back."

Simon cried and huffed with the rope wrapped around his body and snout. He tried to shake his head, kicking the dirt beneath him.

Was my life that terrible before?

I tentatively took the bottle in my hand, and Ivy and Karma smiled in triumph. She backed away and grabbed a small flame from Karma that I had not seen before, putting it under the letter.

"Wait no!" I reached out, but she held it away from me, an enormous grin on her face.

I watched as the fire slowly consumed the letter and the pieces dropped to the ground.

Once I take this potion, I won't have my words to bring myself through the trauma of my past. What ever I had said to help me get through—they were gone.

Why did they have to be so cruel?

"We won't face murder charges," Karma said happily, "because technically, we didn't kill you. Supposedly, you were to remember your memories anyway. We just sped it along. We didn't kidnap you; you willingly came with us. We've broken no laws." He leaned his body back while he fluttered in the air, placing both of his hands behind his head.

They coerced me, but I couldn't argue anymore. I had to get Simon free. "Release Simon and I'll take it." I said with as much courage as I could.

"You aren't the one with the knife." Ivy said as she pulled it from a sleeve on her thigh under her dress. "I suggest you get going. Just drop it on your skin, that's all you need." She placed the knife under Simon's neck, and he stilled, his nose flaring.

I held on to the bottle tighter and placed my hand on top, feeling the cork. I knew nothing about magic, but just holding the bottle and knowing I would regain my memories just from the liquid inside, I knew that my life would change forever.

I wouldn't have Valpar or my family here with me. That was what Ivy and Karma were hoping for.

I couldn't believe they would go this far—how can people be so cruel.

I would do it though—for Simon. My first best friend.

Before I popped off the top, footsteps came from the right. The thicket, where branches barely holding dark navy leaves and dead flowers, moved.

The branches were so thick, I could hardly see the other side. Once it became louder, I backed away, moving toward Simon. Ivy didn't stop me, both her and Karma were stunned to see someone come out of the brush.

A tall woman, with snow white skin and hair that fell to her hips, approached us. Her features were delicate and ethereal, with high cheekbones and a slender nose. The woman's lips were adorned with a soft, gentle smile, contrasting with the mysterious aura that emanated from her captivating eyes. The pale blue irises seemed to hold secrets. Secrets I didn't really want to know. Her face was friendly, but the light blue eyes were unsettling. She wore a sage green dress with a matching cape that went over her head.

I clutched the bottle because I had nothing to hold on to, and partly, because it was my only way to free Simon.

Ivy walked around me with her eyebrows raised. "Esmeray? What are you doing here?"

The woman, Esmeray, smiled and lifted her hand. "I've come to see Calliope." Her eyes lingered on me and a chill ran down my body. "Here is your coin. I will take her, and you no longer need to worry about the human."

Karma and Ivy looked at one another, and Ivy shook her head. "No," Ivy stepped in front of me. "She's ours, we are—"

With a flick of Esmeray's finger, Ivy's body exploded into a burst of white petals. I jumped, falling backwards, holding onto the potion. Karma screamed and held onto the tree limb Simon was tied to, as if for dear life.

"I trust that the little pixie won't be interrupting me, will he?" she crooned.

Karma shook his head while I stared at her wide-eyed.

What in Hades was going on?

Esmeray giggled and offered her hand. I looked between her and her hand several times before I reluctantly took it, and she pulled me up to stand.

"Where is Ivy?" My voice shook as I watched the white petals fall to the ground.

Esmeray's shoulders rose, then fell. "With the soil now. She deserved it, she questioned me."

Snickerdoodle, we are in bigger trouble.

"Walk with me, Calliope." She held out her arm for me to thread into. I turned to see Karma shaking, and he waved his hand for me to follow her. I didn't have a choice. She could turn me into flower petals too, so reluctantly I went with her.

She hummed while she walked and led me past the thick bushes and slowly down a hill embankment. As she walked, small flowers flowed behind her despite the dead area around us. How can something so pretty do something so evil as to kill someone?

We stopped as we came to an old abandoned or fort more like. Stones lay overturned, debris scattered everywhere. It looked like it was once a grand fortress, maybe even a mansion back during its time.

"My mother used to run a coven here," Esmeray began. "Some of the strongest witches and warlocks trained in this area. They had a vision, one that would reshape how Bergarian would be today—if she and the rest of the coven and not been killed."

My body was stiff, but as she told me she'd lost her mother I relaxed. Perhaps she needed a friend to talk to. "I'm sorry," I said. "I can't imagine losing a mother. Especially one you deeply cared about."

Esmeray frowned and turned to me. "Indeed."

"What happened?" I tried to show sympathy toward her. Ivy wasn't a great person, but maybe this woman needed someone to talk to, someone to let out her feelings with. Perhaps she was going to rescue me?

Her frown deepened. "There was a golden dragon named Horus, led by Queen Melina, who stormed into the threshold and set fire to all the coven. Eventually swallowing my mother's entire body."

Uh oh! Nope, not a friend, not a friend.

Red flags, big, big red flags.

I slowly stepped away from her.

I've heard this story before. Aunt Melina told me about the coven that tried to overthrow the Golden Light Kingdom's court from the inside, before the war. The Sorceress Prinna was powerful and tried to pry apart Uncle Osirus' kingdom.

"Ah, so your mother was the Sorceress Prinna, the great Sorceress Prinna. Ah yes, she was, ah, very wonderful." I continued to back away and Esmeray watched me curiously.

"She was. She was a vision. My father, at the time, kept me in a cabin in Vermillion territory to keep me safe, since I was too young to fight. When I found out about her death, I swore I would get revenge one day. Lo and behold, just a few days ago, a vengeful little fairy and pixie searched for a witch who wanted to ruin the life of the king and queen of the Golden Light Kingdom's favorite human."

I continue to back away from her, my legs being scratched by the briars.

"I-I'm not the favorite. I think they find me just funny and interesting. Like a court jester." I held the bottle tight to my chest.

As I retreated, Esmeray took slow strides toward me, her presence palpable. Vines slithered in her wake, entangling the trees, constricting them, dragging them down with a resounding crash. The thud reverberated, igniting a tremor in my chest, as a surge of fear coursed through me.

"I don't believe that to be so," she said smoothly. "I've watched on my own. They do care for you. I just cannot get too close to the kingdom. You see, I am not as powerful as my mother—yet."

I felt the blood rushing to my ears, the pounding in my chest grew louder. When I turned to run a vine slipped around my ankle. It only gave me so much slack until it pulled me back for her to taunt me.

"You see, I'm still far too young to be a sorceress. I can't get near the palace because Osirus is too strong. So, I had to wait until the fairy and the pixie brought you here. Your orc won't find you either, and by the time the king finds out where you are, you will be long dead. It will pierce him through the heart and make him weak with sorrow," she crooned.

I panicked when the vines wrapped around my legs. I tried to push them down, kick them away, but she just giggled and held her hands out like she was some messiah to all of Bergarian.

"I'll put this realm back where it was supposed to be, under dark magic, and take over the Earth realm where humans will be enslaved." She cackled and put a hand over her mouth. "Baby steps, I'm getting a head of myself."

"Help!" I screamed out when the vines wrapped around my torso and my arms, pinning them down.

Her eyebrows turned downward, and a wicked smile crossed her face. "Slow, crushing, painful deaths have always been my favorite." The vines grew tighter, and I screamed, just as two deafening roars came from overhead.

Chapter Forty

Valpar

It wasn't here. The parchment was nowhere to be found, and I didn't know how to tell my miresa. What will she say? She was going to read it, prepare herself for what was yet to come, and I had lost it!

I wiped my sweaty hand across my clammy face, feeling the dampness on my skin. My brows furrowed, creating deep lines of worry on my forehead, as the drums pounded harder in my chest; the rhythmic thumping echoed in my ears. The weight of my failure settled heavily upon me, suffocating any ounce of confidence I had at being a good male for her. I had always prided myself on my strength, on being a shield to protect her from the harsh world outside. But now, I found myself utterly powerless, losing the one thing that could prepare her.

All I could do was hold her when the time came for her to remember. I still didn't know what she would decide: To know it after I had claimed her or know it little by little, but whatever she did, I would support her. She was mine, branding her or not.

Even if it killed us both.

I balled my hands into fists and leaned on the table. I waited for my miresa to say something. She would have by now, she was not normally this quiet.

Bassza.

I whipped my head to the bed to find the leash that I had her tied to still wrapped around the bedpost, but instead of her waist being tied, it was a bundle of pillows.

What?

I yanked the pillows off the bed, desperately searching for any sign of her. The sharp edges of my claws tore through the fabric, sending a flurry of feathers swirling through the air, filling the room with a cloud of downy chaos. As I tore through the layers, a surge of heat welled up in my chest.

"Calliope!" I roared and it echoed throughout the cave. "Come out, now!"

There was no answer, so I darted into the bathroom, the closet, and even checked the back of the cave to see if she went to the heavy door.

She wasn't here!

I turned my back for a moment, not even long enough for the dust to settle and my female had evaded me!

"Calliope!" I roared again and gathered my weapons. I strapped my sword to my back while I ran down the passage. I didn't care if I was making noise. I wanted all the fucking kingdom to know that I was coming, and I was going to retrieve my female.

I stepped out into the light sources and covered my eyes. I took a large breath, searching for her scent. She couldn't have gone far. I did not have my back turned for long, but when I took in the air around me, I could only find remnants of her calming aroma.

I tilted my head back, seeing if she had climbed the boulder behind, trying to toy with me, but when I gazed upward I saw something far in the sky. I squinted, covering my eyes from the glare of the light sources and what I saw, I could hardly believe.

A fairy—or a fae holding onto a rope and a person hanging below it.

I didn't think I'd ever seen that before.

My eyes widened.

She wouldn't.

She would.

If it was to find her companion she would do anything. Even if it meant putting her life in danger.

Fuck!

"Calliope!" I screamed, but she didn't turn her head, I cannot even tell if she was able to turn her head or not. They were so far away, and each second was a waste of time.

With a burst of adrenaline, I sprinted recklessly through the dense forest, disregarding any notion of stealth. My sole focus was on speed, determined to prevent her escape, refusing to let her slip from my sight. My pace quickened, propelling me towards the Golden Light Palace. As I crested a hill, a breathtaking sight unfolded before me: a vast pasture dotted with horses, leisurely grazing. The sight of these magnificent creatures filled me with a surge of exhilaration, spurring me onward.

I pursed my lips and let out a sharp whistle, the sound slicing through the air. Squinting my eyes, I scanned the scene filled with the horses, hoping to catch a glimpse of my horse, Ulam. Suddenly, a deafening rumble reverberated through the air, growing louder with each passing second. My heart leapt with anticipation as I turned around and my eyes widened at the sight of Ulam galloping towards me. As I soared over the last barrier of the courtyard, a rush of wind hit my face, accompanied by the unmistakable warmth of Ulam's breath on my neck.

He raced alongside me once he caught up. I grabbed his mane and jumped, pulling myself onto his back. I was grateful that Osirus gave us the largest breed of horses because I would need his strength to get us to my mate.

The guards near the palace gates must have heard the commotion, because they left their posts to see me coming around the side of the palace.

"Tell the king, Calliope has been taken!" They all looked at each other like idiots but I didn't have time to stop. I had to continue.

Sensing my urgency, Ulam quickened his pace, his hooves thundering against the soil, leaving deep indentations in the soil. As we raced through the forest, the overhanging trees seemed to taunt me, their branches reaching out like gnarled fingers, obstructing my view. I strained my eyes, but I was losing sight of her amidst the dense foliage.

"Fuck, fuck, fuck!" I tapped Ulam's sides with my heels. His breath was heavy, but I felt the excitement running through him.

He sped up even more, the wind whipping past us as we raced through the dense forest. Branches snapped and leaves swirled around us in a frenzy as Ulam charged forward with determination. My heart pounded in my chest, the adrenaline coursing through the branches on my arms as I pushed him faster, desperate to catch up.

As we burst out of the trees into a clearing, I could no longer see the floating fae with my helpless mate, dangling from a rope.

"Calliope!" I shouted, again, my voice raw with emotion. Ulam snorted beneath me, his powerful muscles rippling with each stride.

Ulam galloped faster, his powerful muscles rippling beneath me as we raced through the dense forest. I could hear branches snapping and leaves rustling around us, but my focus was solely on finding Calliope. The image of her being taken by that fae flashed in my mind, igniting a fierce determination within me.

Where the hell did she go?

I let out a roar, continuing our journey in the same direction. Who the hell was that, and why did she leave? Why the fuck would she leave the cave and not speak to me?

I jutted out my jaw, feeling my tusks tense against my lips. I wasn't about to give up. I would run my horse ragged and then continue my journey on foot, until I found her.

We burst into another clearing and as I was about to tap Ulam's sides again, a gigantic shadow came overhead. It circled and followed us until I jerked my head above me to see what it could be. The light sources cast a shadow, so I couldn't see the color of its underbelly, but there was no mistaking that a dragon was hovering above us.

I slowed my horse with a quick tug of his mane. He came to a stop but pranced when the large black dragon landed before us with a thud.

Creed!

My horse yelled in surprise. He cried out, jerking his head back and forth until he reared his front legs up. I jumped off, pushed Ulam away from me and slapped his backside to move away from the black dragon.

It'd been years since I saw the Black Dragon. He was a good male, but I didn't trust his dragon form not to eat my companion.

"You smell of Calliope." Creed's deep, dragon voice rolled like thunder. Unlike most of the shifters of Bergarian, dragons were the only ones who could speak in their animal form. Creed jutted his nose in the air, black smoke rolling out of his nose. "Are you mates?"

"Yes," I puffed out my chest and I put my arm over it. "She is mine, but she's—"

"Been taken," Creed finished for me. "I saw from the mountain. They were flying high enough to see, an impressive height. It's dangerous for a human."

I wiped my hand down my face. "Did you see where they went? What the fuck took her? I need to get her back. I will fucking rip that fairy shit to shreds!"

Creed shook his body, his wings unfurled, and his tail lashed around the ground. "I'll take you to her. If the wind is right, perhaps I can catch her scent."

Instead of feeling the weight of humiliation from my shortcomings in finding my mate, I choose to seek aid from the Black Dragon. Determinedly, I sprinted towards him, while my horse galloped back to the palace. Creed's powerful wings unfurled, and he soared into the sky. His sinewy talons firmly grasping my shoulders, sending a surge of adrenaline through me. I could hear the rush of wind in my ears as we ascended higher, the sound growing louder with each passing moment. The dragon's scaly talons brush against my skin. As we rose, I reached behind me, swiftly drawing my sword.

"Easy, it will take time. They are far ahead of us. Fairies are fast and you are heavy."

Did he just call me fat?

I growled beneath my breath, but soon we were in the air. I didn't have time to be frightened. I had flown in the air before by the fae one upon a time using a rope swing system. It didn't mean I liked it, but my mind was still stirring with my miresa.

Moon Fairy, who took her?

"A pixie was following the fairy—do you know," Creed began, but I growled and gripped my sword.

"That stupid pixie and fairy who have bothered my mate. I should have taken care of them. I never thought they would amount to something so brash! I'll kill them both!"

Creed's chest rumbled and he held onto me as we caught a headwind.

"I have failed her in so many ways. I have done it again," I whispered to myself.

Creed huffs. "That little human is resilient, strong even. When she visits during the change of seasons she watches my parents' hatchings. No easy feat for a female of her size."

I groaned.

Creed snorted. "When the Goddess is involved, she will bring the right souls together at the correct time and place. You being paired together is no accident, do not question if you are not good for her. It will only make you truly unworthy."

I turned my neck to see the underside of his jaw. "Since when did you paint pretty pictures with words?" The last time I saw him, he was a male of few words and thought the world might end at any moment.

His scarred, scaled lips curved into a smile. "Having hatchlings of my own gives me a new perspective."

The male differed from when I first met him years ago, before the war. It was good that he had calmed himself. I would smile more once my female was found.

He took us higher into the air. With two sets of eyes searching, I knew we would find her soon. The further south-east we traveled, the more worried I became. We were closer to the Vermillion Kingdom's territory and though not all vampires were evil, the ones I dealt with in the war were not pleasant.

"I smell her, she's in the thicket," Creed snarled, and puffs of smoke left his nostrils. "She isn't alone, the smell of a witch is near."

I took a firm grip on the hilt of my sword and my jaw jutted out. I had no problems facing a witch, her power would have no effect on me.

Creed took us down, bolting through the wind at top speed. I felt the wind beating at my face. As we got closer, I saw my miresa tied up with vines, a witch with white flowing hair and her arms reaching out. Fire burned in my belly, rage consumed me, and Creed and I let out deafening roars as he dropped me in front of the witch, where I landed with a ground-shattering thud.

The witch was taken aback, although her vines did not loosen around my female. I stomped forward, waving my sword and cutting the vines that connected to my female. My miresa shook them off and I felt Creed landing behind me, breaking the trees to make room for his massive body.

"Prepare to die, witch."

CHAPTER FORTY-ONE

Valpar

I GRIPPED MY SWORD tightly, feeling the cool metal against my palm. With a swift motion, I brought it down, slicing through the tangled vines. The sound of metal meeting vegetation echoed through the air, accompanied by the faint rustling of the retreating vines. The scent of damp earth and decaying leaves filled my nostrils as I continued my relentless assault. The witch's hiss pierced the noise of breaking of vines, branches and rustling of leaves, as she gestured to command the lifeless roots of the forest to encircle her.

I was immune to magic. She wouldn't dare throw a bolt of lightning, fire or whatever this nature witch could conjure. She could use items around her, and she was using sticks.

She obviously wasn't aware of my strength.

I kept my back turned to my female, feeling the weight of her presence around me. I could almost hear the soft sound of her breath reaching my ears. It caused a mix of emotions to stir within me. Her calming scent was tainted, soured from rotting vines and magic.

If I were to look at her, I know I would crumble. The burning rage inside me would consume every fiber of my being, clouding my judgment. I was a warrior, her protector and her male. Seeing her sadness, any cuts or bruises on her body would fuel my desire for more vengeance and wrath. I could not think with anger, I must strategically win this battle quickly so I may have my female in my arms once again.

"Valpar!" My miresa cried, and I balled my free hand into a fist

Creed's smoke had surrounded us, giving me the upper hand. We'd fought in the war—he knew how we orcs liked to fight.

Witches may have magic, but their eyesight is worthless unless they conjure something to deflect their enemies. Not that it would work on an orc.

"Stay female, you already have a hot ass coming to you later."

She gasped, and I heard her tiny little foot stomp. "I had to save Simon. He needed me!"

Didn't she know I needed her?

A root came behind me. I felt it before it struck and heard my female scream in panic. I smirked and dropped my sword, pulling on the root that tried to grip me by my waist. I ripped it from the soil, the tree pulling under the dirt. The witch was using all her strength to bend the tree, but her face contorting into anger and frustration made me huff out a laugh.

"No one touches what is mine," I snarled at the witch and took a step forward, pulling the tree with me. The dirt crumbled and the roots left trenches behind me. More and more limbs from above tried to pull me back.

I glanced over at my miresa. "And I don't care, Calliope, you are mine to protect. I would have saved him myself!"

Summoning every ounce of strength within me, I exerted an immense force, feeling the sinewy muscles in my arms and back strain. With a resounding crack, the tree wrenched from the earth as its roots violently tore apart. The sound of splintering wood echoed through the air, mingling with the gasp that escaped the witch's lips. In that moment, her widened eyes to reveal the realization that her control was slipping away, like sand through her fingertips.

"Orcs own the trees. You really thought that these twigs could hold me?"

With a thunderous roar, I gripped the towering tree, feeling the rough bark scrape against my calloused palms. The musky dirt scented forest filled my nostrils as I swung the massive trunk around and its weight propelled me forward. The air whistled past my ears, and more snapping vines and cracking branches continued. The impact reverberated through my bones as the defiant vegetation crumbled under the force of tree in my hands.

The witch stumbled backward, her power waning as she struggled to regain control over the chaotic nature around her. But was too late. I was unstoppable, fueled by the fury of protecting what was mine.

The witch had one hand in the air and the other in front of her. I grabbed the knife at my ankle ready to throw it straight at her forehead.

My miresa screamed and I darted my head round to see roots shoot out from the ground and pull her to her knees. The witch cackled as I turned and raced toward my female.

Creed crouched low on all fours, his sleek scales glistening under the light sources. With a swift movement, his muscular tail arced through the air, creating a whooshing sound as it cut through vines above her and toward the witch. The witch, surprised, lost her concentration dodging his attack.

My female struggled as I pulled her out of the roots that tried to pull her into the dirt. Seeing the red lines on her body brought new fire to my belly. "Don't move and stay with Creed."

Her eyes were glassy, her nose sniffled as I gave her ass I swat and pressed my lips to hers. "Now watch your male kill your enemy." She yipped in surprise and a smile pulled at her lips.

Creed settled his body above her, his tail wrapping around to keep my female protected. With a quick nod of thanks, I turned to see the witch recovering.

Creed could easily stomp over this witch, eat her whole but he knew the importance of showing strength to a mate. With a newfound determination, I channeled all of my power and yanked the tree out of the ground, roots tearing apart as it broke free. The witch's eyes widened in fear as she realized her control slipping away again. With a mighty roar, I swung the tree around like a weapon, knocking down the surrounding vines and branches that dared to challenge me.

The witch, desperate and enraged, gathers all her remaining power and unleashed a final, devastating bolt of magic. It streaked through the air, and for the briefest moment, the atmosphere trembled as the force of her wrath was unleashed. She was not strong, not like I had faced in years past, but it was many moons since I had faced any sort of magic like this.

My hand gripped the branch in my hand, ready to pierce it through the witch's heart. She stumbled, falling back on the very roots that tried to take me down, and stared at me wide-eyed.

"Wait, please hear me out!" She held up her hand in surrender, but I did not fall for the trick. The innocent look, the wide eyes; she was a witch and just like many before her, I would not hesitate for the kill.

I lifted the branch, taking the pointed end and drove it forward. Before I could drive it into her chest, her other hand came up, and the wood exploded. Thousands of splinters flew up into the air in the explosion. My vision obscured and I felt vines wrap around my legs and rip me from my feet.

"Valpar!" My female screamed.

I roared in protest. "Stay back!"

I heard the pattering of feet and instead of feeling panic for myself, because I knew I could take this witch, I worried about my female.

"Female—!"

A loud animalistic scream that did not sound of my miresa echoed in the air. Something jumped on my stomach and a white blur flew into the air. As my vision cleared, I saw Simon lowering his head and landing right on top of the witch, hitting her in the head.

The vines hovering over me and the roots that had grabbed me by the ankles all let go and fell into the dirt. The witch was knocked out cold, a large bump forming on her head. Simon let out a long yell and then tipped over, completely paralyzed and frozen.

"Simon!" Calliope screamed.

Creed had his tail wrapped around my female and I waved at him to let her go; I was ready to have her in my arms.

She ran toward me. I caught her as she was about to run past me. I growled and held her tightly to my body as I took her toward Simon and set her down in front of him. He was panting as his eye stared back at us.

"You saved me, Simon!"

I grunted and rolled my eyes. "Excuse me?"

Calliope turned to me and fluttered her lashes. "Yes, you did, too." She rubbed my leg. "Simon helped too, though."

I pinched the bridge of my nose. "I had her within my grasp. Can I not play with the enemy to show off my strength?"

Calliope turned her head. "Uh, huh, sure." She petted Simon as he woke.

This. Female.

I grabbed her shoulders to turn her to me while Simon stood up.

"Calliope, why did you leave the cave? What in the stars were you thinking? You could have been killed? You would have left me, and I have barely had you!" My voice became ragged and harsh as I spoke to her. I still couldn't believe she left me, and that she didn't trust I would have saved Simon. Did she not know I would do everything for her?

My female swallowed and grabbed my hand. Her thumb ran over the scrapes of my knuckles. "I'm so sorry, but... Karma said I wouldn't see Simon again if you came with me. I couldn't let that happen. I couldn't risk it."

I would never understand her relationship with this goat, but she needed to try. "If I lost you, my little fairy, do you know what it would have done to me?" I pleaded with her. "I would have left this world to be with you. I cannot breathe without you. You are everything to me. My heart beats for you alone."

I could feel my female trembling as I held her. She was still struggling to understand my love for her. With a deep breath, I cupped her face between my hands and gazed into her eyes, trying to convey the intensity of these feelings.

"Calliope, listen to me. I would do anything, risk everything, for you. You are my everything, my reason for living. Next time—tell me what's happening. We figure things out *together*. You are not alone. I promised you I would find Simon and I meant it. I would have beaten, tortured, killed those two until they told me where Simon was to make you happy."

She bit on her bottom lip. "I didn't think about that."

I sighed heavily and pulled her to my chest. "Please don't go willingly, ever again. You fight, you scream. I will always rescue you, and Simon. Nothing will ever happen to my family."

Simon bleated and nudged my side.

"And Simon will save you." Calliope gazed up at me and beamed.

I rolled my eyes again. "I was fine, female. He just helped."

She hummed, unconvinced and petted Simon between the ears. "Who is a good baby goat, huh? Who is my good baby goat?"

Simon groaned and stretched out his neck. My little fairy continued to scratch, so I narrowed my eyes and pulled her hand away from him to put it in on my head. "I deserve scratches too," I told her.

She grinned and used both of her hands to give us equal head scratches.

I'm not jealous of a goat, I'm not.

Fuck, I am.

I wrapped my arm around her waist and held her close, then made her explain in detail what happened to her. From Ivy flying her here, to the bottle she had in her lap and the witch.

I was disappointed I wouldn't be killing the fairy, but I still had Karma I got to destroy. How both idiots came up with the idea of contacting a witch took far more effort I thought they would ever go to. Their brains were the size of peas, and they hated the sweetness of my mate so much they wanted to ruin her life?

I kept forgetting that some souls are just more evil than others. They just want to see others suffer for their own enjoyment. I'd never seen it until I knew the world of Bergarian. Perhaps that is why orcs stayed to themselves. The world was too messy to get involved with others—all we needed was our females.

I could not wait to get hold of Karma.

I could pluck out his wings and have him fermented in some orc ale. I'd drink the dissolved, glittery piece of shit he was straight down. I scrunched my nose up at that thought. He might make the ale too sweet.

A groan came from behind us, and I paused my little fairy's scratching. I stood, ready to finish the witch, but Creed's silent footsteps, despite his size, marked him already dragging the witch deeper into the wood. She groaned again. Creed's nose let out a billow of smoke and when he retreated further into the brush, I knew exactly what he was going to do.

"Valpar?" My sweet female began as I pulled her to standing.

I shook my head and pulled her into my arms so that I may carry her away. I did not need her to hear the witch's screams if she awoke while Creed finished her. Dragons love to eat witches. They absorb their power, even if that one was still young and not as powerful as the ones we had fought in the war.

I carried my miresa through the wood, and she pointed to where Ivy and Karma first took her, and I could see the white petals where Ivy was destroyed. I huffed in annoyance.

Ivy was dead and I was angry I did not get to torture her.

So far, I had killed none of her enemies.

Annoying.

Wings buzzed overhead and we both looked up into the branches. My little fairy's parents had arrived, as well as King Osirus, his mate and soldiers.

Her mother screamed and cried, peppering kisses over Calliope's face while she was still in my arms. It took Birch several minutes to pull her away.

I debriefed them about what happened. My little fairy stayed silent while I told them the story, keeping her face plastered to my chest. King Osirus' wings instantly darkened and his eyes glowed golden with fury. He began to give orders to go in search of the witch, but I held out my hand to stop them.

"I didn't even know Prinna had a daughter." King Osirus said. "As a child, I'm glad she survived the war, but am sad she still had the same beliefs as her mother, however."

She had a choice. This witch could have chosen a different path—but she didn't. She chose the darkness and tried to take a life. The witch deserved to die, even if it wasn't by my hand.

When do I get to kill again?

I placed a kiss on top of my little fairy's head and squeezed her tightly. She would never leave my side again. She shifted in my arms and gripped the potion in her hands. Her thick lashes fluttered, and she gazed over at her parents. She looked her mother up and down until her eyes settled on her stomach.

"Um, Mom, can I ask you a question?"

CHAPTER FORTY-TWO

Calliope

I'D REMAINED SILENT AS everyone talked around me. For once in my life I didn't feel like talking, but listening and taking in the worried glances, and the anger my dad and uncle were radiating. They all really cared, and I really fudged up.

It was a split-second decision and, at the time, I knew I just had to save Simon. I didn't think of anything else. I didn't think it would all blow up in my face this badly. I just jumped at the opportunity of saving my bestie, without thinking of others.

Simon would have done the same, heckers, he *did* the same.

Simon beamed up at me, chewing on the rope he had somehow chewed off from the tree, to free himself. He was one smart kid.

Ha—kid, because he was a goat baby!

I leaned my head on Valpar's chest while he explained what happened. I couldn't bear to tell the story again, so I was glad he took over. The one thing I didn't tell him was that Karma said my mother was pregnant. I glanced over at her and Dad has his hand on Mom's hip. I noticed how his thumb grazed over to the soft part of her stomach.

For humans, it would be impossible to know this early if she was with child yet, but supernaturals knew. They probably knew right when sperm meets egg, but I didn't know the details.

Ew, I didn't need to know how they knew.

"Um, Mom, can I ask you a question?" I blurted before I realized what I had said.

Everyone paused and stared at me and Mom stepped forward out of Dad's grasp. Her eyes were soft and red-rimmed from crying, and I knew she cared about me. The doubt that seeped into me earlier had already washed away.

Wow, I was stupid to even doubt her care for me.

Ugh, Karma was such a bug.

"Are you—are you going to have a baby?" I smiled brightly to lift the mood because I didn't want to see her sad any-more. She should be happy, and should celebrate the moment, not worry about me anymore. She had worried about me for as long as I could remember.

"Calliope, sweetheart." She came closer to cup my face and Valpar stiffened. His hold on me grew tight, like my mom was going to take me away.

He let her near, and she rubbed her nose against mine. "I wanted to tell you sooner, but I was so upset about finding an orc in your bed." She laughed loudly. "Then, I had to come to terms with the fact you won't be living with us anymore. I didn't get to wake up to you and your bright smile, causing mischief with the skunks." She pressed a kiss to my cheek.

"You mean the fart squirrels," I corrected.

She snickered and sighed. "Right, the fart squirrels. Then, with Simon gone missing, I forgot to tell you about the baby. I'm so sorry. Are you angry with me?"

I shook my head. "No. I could never be mad. Things have been really exciting the past few days. And you will always be my Mom. We will come to visit lots and you can come visit us, too!

Valpar grunted.

"Besides, you shouldn't worry about me. I have Valpar, remember? It's his job to worry about me now." I tugged on his hair, and he let out a deep sigh.

"It is my honor to worry about my female. She's mine to protect and I will hold her to keep her in place," he growled.

I giggled, slapping his chest. "You are so funny, can't hold on to me forever. I need to walk sometimes. What if I have to go pee?"

Valpar huffed in annoyance. "No, even on a leash, you evade me. You will no longer be out of my grasp. You can relieve yourself in my arms."

Aunt Melina dry heaved in the background. "That's so sweet."

Mom pushed back some hair behind my ear, taking out some of the dead leaves. "And even though Valpar is your mate and he will protect you, I will, to some degree, worry about you. You will always be my first daughter, my first child. Even if you didn't come out of my body, you live in my heart."

My lip wobbled, and I dropped the potion in my lap to lean forward to give her a hug. When I wrapped my arms around her, she asked, "How *did* you know I was pregnant? I won't be showing for at least a few more weeks."

I went to open my mouth and I felt the bottle lifting from my lap and the loud pop of a cork. My body must have obscured Valpar's vision because all of a sudden, I felt liquid dropping onto my skin. I gasped at the cold liquid and Simon bleated in terror.

My eyes grew heavy and Valpar screamed in rage, pulling me away and covering my body with his.

"Calliope don't go to sleep! Don't! Simon! What's wrong with him?"

Uncle Osirus's booming voice hit my ears, demanding the area to be cleared. The urgency in his tone created tension. I could feel it in how Valpar held me and the sounds of scuffling feet.

I could hear Simon whimper as everyone scrambled around me. They sounded like they were underwater. My body felt heavy and when I tried to speak, no words came out.

Where was Simon?

Valpar cried out. "Fuck! Calliope, stay with me!" His panicked face was the last thing I saw as my eyes became too heavy and they finally closed.

The gentle flickering of light danced behind my closed eyelids, resembling a torch playfully waving before my face, and coaxing me awake.

My mind reeled as I struggled to piece together what happened. Was I really on a mountain, surrounded by fierce dragons spewing their fire? It took a moment for my consciousness to fully return, and my eyelids were heavy as if weighed down by a heavy fog. Memories flooded back to the first time I woke up in Uncle Osirus and Aunt Melina's grand palace, feeling groggy, disoriented, and weighed down by a sense of confusion.

As I sat up and vigorously rubbed my tired eyes. Slowly, my eyelids fluttered open, revealing a solitary lightbulb suspended from the ceiling in the dimly lit basement. It swung back and forth, its feeble glow casting eerie shadows against the cold cement walls. Faint echoes of thumping bass from the music playing upstairs reverberated through the air, creating a pulsating rhythm that seemed to echo in the space. The unmistakable scent of dampness and mustiness clung to the air and intermingled with the metallic tang of exposed pipes. In the far corner, a washer and dryer stood, silently waiting to serve their purpose.

I...remembered this place. It was a distant memory, more so a dream than real life, but I was remembering. This was who I was before—before I was saved.

I put my hand over my mouth and my eyes widened in shock.

I'm on Earth with her. My real mother.

No, she isn't my mother. Theresa, my aunt, is my real mother. She was the one that knew how to be more a mother than this woman. The woman upstairs is just the person who gave birth to me, nothing more.

Goddess, please, I didn't come back to live here, did I? Valpar wasn't a dream, was he? My breathing came in heavy pants and my head dizzy with panicking thoughts.

I couldn't stay in this basement. I couldn't live down here another minute.

I made to rise from my cot but a hand stopped me and pulled me back down. I screamed and that hand covered my mouth.

"Shh, I got you."

I instantly recognized her voice, but my heart still raced, and my breath still heaved.

I was going to pass out.

"None of this is real. It's just a memory." My fairy godmother patted my long, dark hair until she had me lean on her.

My fingers dug into the cot. I could feel the cold metal beneath it.

"Fairy Godmother," I whispered, trying to calm down as her familiar scent washed over me, filling me with a sense of safety.

She stroked my hair softly, her touch soothing the racing of my heart. "You're safe, Calliope. You're not back there, you're here with me," she reassured me with her gentle voice. "It was just a memory, a flashback. You are in your mate's arms, surrounded by those who care for you. Who will always be there for you."

"My Valpar?"

Fairy Godmother chuckled and squeezed my shoulder. "Yup, he's having a hissy fit, you being asleep and all. He doesn't want you remembering this alone. He's beating himself up that Karma snuck past him while he was holding you."

I gave her a sad smile. Yes, he would be upset. He didn't get to kill the witch, or Ivy. I hope he gets some revenge on Karma for blind-siding the both of us. But—the way I'm dealing with this sudden remembrance of my past, it may be for the best.

I won't remember these memories right after our mating and I won't have to draw out my memories. Perhaps the potion spilling on to me was for the better.

"You should comfort Valpar, not me. I don't want him to be upset."

Fairy Godmother blew a raspberry. "Are you kidding? The dufus is fine. He wouldn't like me, anyway. He would want me to be here with you.

You are such a selfless little thing, aren't you?" She hummed and placed her cheek on top of my head.

I didn't reply—all I could feel was the deep, heaviness of depression overtaking me.

I disliked this place, and I now remembered why I wanted to have my memories erased.

You're such a waste of space.

He wouldn't have left if you didn't come along.

No one will ever love you.

Such a klutz, can't you do anything right?

This place, this hellhole I used to call home, was my torture chamber for years. Words hurt more than my stomach shrinking, the sleepless nights and the nightmares that came. I was scared of everything, with no one to hold me in the night and no one to tell me everything was okay.

School was my only reprieve. I got a free lunch for those who needed it, but the cruel children who saw me as nothing more than poor trash still tormented me. All I wanted to do was make friends and enjoy the sunshine. Instead, from a young age I was dubbed the 'weird one,' when I was so fascinated with dandelions, watching the birds, making flowered crowns and lying in the grass.

She's so weird.

I heard her mom never wanted her.

Do you see the way she dresses?

That girl tries to fit in, it's just pathetic.

I always wore tattered and oversized clothes. They were nothing like what the other kids wore, even though Theresa did her best to sneak me clothes in the basement window. The woman upstairs would take them for herself when she saw me wear them.

When summer arrived, I found myself trapped in the stifling basement. I couldn't escape unless I took the risk of slipping out through a small window, while my mother was comatose from drugs or drowning in her own hangover.

Survival was a constant struggle in this suffocating prison.

I was a depressed, lonely outsider that just craved human contact.

I never fully understood why my mother didn't love me. She loved her drugs more, and spent every bit of money of those welfare checks on it. That woman wouldn't let me go, either. I remembered her sister, my aunt, try to take me away so many times, to save me.

Theresa was the only one that saw me, tried to save me, but that woman who birthed me wanted that check for her minute of a high.

Not to protect her daughter.

I worked to the bone some nights, cleaning, doing her laundry, cooking. That woman would even make me come upstairs for her parties and make food for the people she would bring over.

I closed my eyes, and felt the tears run down my cheeks when I remembered one night the people started throwing bottles on the floor. Someone ordered me to clean up the shattered glass and as I was doing so, I somehow fell forward, and glass buried deep into my skin.

I didn't have any way to keep the infection out, no way to clean it. It healed horribly and left nasty scars.

I pulled up the black t-shirt I was wearing and looked down. The tiny scars were there, in the dream. Now that I was awake from the magic that Uncle Osirus and the sorceress put on me, would they be there when I woke up?

What would Valpar think of me now? Would he still think of me as his little fairy? All those haunting memories were here now. The darkness was here to stay. I didn't have one ounce of happiness in my childhood. I could feel the fog surrounding me, suffocating me.

You're worthless.

My Fairy Godmother's touch calmed my racing heart. It was her magic. I could feel it flowing through my body. I could feel the rush come in like a giant wave off the shores of the Golden Light Kingdom. The warm waters made it up my ankles and to my knees until it reached up my neck.

"Shh," she cooed. "Shh," she whispered, "You are loved now." Her fingers threaded through my dark hair. "Think of the wonderful memories you have made in your new life, what has become of you in Bergarian."

I hummed, my hands balling into fists. I concentrated on warm waters, the light sources wrapping around me.

"You will never have to return to that life, Calliope," Fairy Godmother said firmly, her eyes full of unwavering determination. "I want you to close your eyes and concentrate on your new memories. The ones when you first woke up in Bergarian for the first time."

I bit my lip, not wanting to listen.

She nudged me and tickled my cheek with my hair. "Go on, or you'll get spanked later."

I let out a giggle and closed them.

"Remember your family. Theresa and Birch, they are your parents. Your real family. Osirus and Melina too, hmm?"

I nodded and thought of them. They were my family. They alone already outweighed a lot of my darkness, my torment of the past. My heart did not feel heavy or empty. It was becoming full and light again.

"Oh yes, don't forget Simon," she added, playfully.

"Never, I would never forget Simon." I shook my head.

She tsked. "And someone else. Who else is important to you?"

My heart felt so full it almost exploded. Valpar. For the first time in my life, I knew what love was when I was with him. Romantic love, the love where you feel so deep you know that when you are with a person, no matter the past, they are your future.

Valpar found me half-way across Bergarian and fought a witch for me. He put up with me running away and claimed me over and over again.

Valpar was my new home. He was my light.

I opened my eyes and Fairy Godmother nodded with a smile as I recounted the memories of my new life in Bergarian. She watched me intently, her eyes reflecting pride and reassurance.

"You have come so far, Calliope," she said softly, her voice filled with warmth. "You have found love and family, in a world far away from the darkness of your past. Hold on to those memories. Let them guide you."

Valpar was my anchor to this new world, where magic existed and love wasn't a foreign concept. He saw me, truly saw me, and loved me despite my past scars and the darkness that threatened to consume me before I even remembered it. His love was a beacon of hope in the shadows of my past, guiding me towards a future filled with light and happiness.

As I focused on the new memories that I had experienced since coming to Bergarian the memories of my past didn't seem so dark. Looking forward, I only focused on happy times with my extensive family, and a mate waiting for me for when I wake.

CHAPTER FORTY-THREE

Valpar

I WATCHED AS PINK color faded from my miresa's hair from root to tip. I tried to grasp it–like holding it would stop its change from pink to black. It was like the darkness was settling inside her. Once it reached the ends of her hair, my heart became slow rhythmic beats. Not that I was calm, no.

It is the opposite.

If anyone thought they had seen me angry before, they were sorely mistaken.

I knew I could save my female from a witch, from a fairy and a pixie, but there was one thing I could not save her from and that was the memories of her past. I knew there would be a day when I would have to watch while she suffered alone. The only thing I could do was to stay by her side and give her the support she needed.

And my little fairy needed me. She needed to know I would be there for her no matter what she had chosen, no matter what she remembered. I was her male, and I would stand by her thick and thin.

I did not get the chance to soothe her fears. I prayed to the Moon Fairy above that my miresa knew this, that I would be with her always.

The area that surrounded me went quiet. No one made a sound, no one moved, not even the fluttering of the wings of the fae or the sounds of the dark birds that caw in the dark forest.

"Where. Is. He?"

I turned my head slowly to the king. He knew what I sought: the male who had given my miresa her memories before she was ready. Before I could comfort her or let her know what she may see.

Osirus' gaze landed on my miresa and back up to me. He stepped back, along with Melina, who had her lips pursed into a thin line. A soldier held the pixie by his wings. He was flailing about, his mouth moving, but only the sound of bells escaped his lips.

"What is he saying?" I stepped forward, my body thrumming with an indescribable need to end the pathetic soul's life.

Osirus glared at the pixie, with his fists at his side. "To let him go, that the human deserved it."

I snarled, careful not to jostle my miresa in my arms.

The pixie hated her because she was human, hated her because she was different and got the attention that he thought he deserved.

The pixie had put me in a position where my miresa may not want me to touch her when she woke. She may fear me, think of me as a monster because the darkness of her memories will bring back her fear of life. She may fear all.

That part hurt the most, and it felt like my own sword had stabbed me in the chest.

"Your time is short, you flying piece of glittery shit."

The pixie's eyes widened, and he stopped struggling.

"I hope you know I will kill one of your own, Osirus. I don't care if we are in your territory and I don't care if he is your subject."

Osirus' lip curls into a wicked smile. "I didn't see or hear anything. Guards? Did you?" All of them shook their heads and pitifully gazed upon my female.

I shuffled her face away from their gazes and toward my chest.

Mine.

No one could pity her. She was strong.

I thrust out my hand to the guard, who shaking in fear himself. "Give me the pixie."

The guard didn't even glance towards his king. Instead, he extended his hand, offering me the pixie's wings he had tightly pinched between his fingers. As I reached out to take the delicate wings, tiny flecks of gold shimmered and fell from his body, causing a wave of disgust to wash over me. The sound of bells resonated from his lips, piercing my ears with their sharpness.

I was ready to end him.

"W-would you like me to hold Calliope while you take care of him?" Theresa asked. Her hands were covering her mouth with her wings drooping behind her.

I tightened my hold on my miresa and shook my head. "I need her."

I needed my mate in my arms where I could feel her, where I could touch her. It was the only way to make me feel better knowing the storm was raging inside her head.

Birch nodded for me to continue. I did not need two hands. It was embarrassing that I was fighting off her last enemy, a pixie. A tiny thing that I will squash with my fingers, but I will do it with her sleeping in my arms.

I flicked my wrist once, the force strong enough for the wings to stay between my fingers, and the pixie to fall to the ground with a thud. I rubbed the wings between my fingers, crumbling them into tiny pieces of dust and sprinkled it above his head.

"That is the worst punishment you could give any flying creature, clipping their wings." King Osirus muttered to his female, who was still learning the ways of their people.

I lowered myself to the ground, my knees popping as I stared down at the blasted creature. A tiny nuisance that had destroyed my female's life.

I picked up the pixie once more, my hand so large it covered his entire body when I fisted it around him. His head was the only thing that poked out, from the top of my hand, and I brought it to my face.

With a sickening grin, I squeezed. His wails were music to my ears as I felt his bones snap like twigs between my fingers. My grip tightened, fueled by an insatiable desire for destruction, until I heard the satisfying crack of his back, breaking under my fist. As the darkness in my eyes deepened, I watched with sadistic pleasure as the light began to fade from the pixie's eyes.

But I was not finished.

I continued to tighten my grip, relishing the feeling of power coursing through me as I slowly crushed the life out of him. Pixies are strong, despite them being small. Then, I dropped him to the ground with a thud that barely registered in my ears. Ignoring his high-pitched shrieks, I lifted my foot and slowly brought it down, letting my big toe feel the gratifying crunch of his skull shattering beneath it.

I closed my eyes, running my hand up and down my female's leg. It was over. Her enemies were gone.

It was far too quick. I could have made him suffer more but my miresa's health was far more important.

"Put his body into a bag. I'll drink his essence in my ale."

Before I could celebrate the small milestone, Queen Melina shrieks.

"Oh gods! Simon!"

I whipped my head to look behind me and saw my miresa's companion in the dirt. He was lying on the ground, and I walked over while others ran to him. However, he wasn't small anymore, he was growing.

"What's happening? What's going on?" I asked.

Osirus' eyes widened when he knelt, his hands touching the lower part of Simon's legs. "I-I don't know. Did Simon have that potion fall onto him?"

Theresa nodded. "Yes, he was trying to get Karma away from her. The rest of the bottle fell into his fur. Is there something wrong with the potion? Is this a reaction to it?"

Osirus petted the animal on its back to comfort him, and then a large clump of fur fell off of his body.

"Stay back!" Osirus had all of us rise and we backed away. He held onto Melina and kept her close. "It seems that Simon wasn't a goat at all, but another creature."

"What?" I snapped. "Did you know about this?" I turned my body to Theresa and Birch and they both shook their heads.

"No!" Birch snapped. "He was a goat gifted by the Toboki tribe to my brother. When Calliope was allowed to walk the grounds of the palace, she saw him and they immediately connected with each other. We said she could keep him as a pet!"

We all watched, stunned, as the fur fell off the enlarged goat. The head no longer looking animal like, but more like a human. A face with a nose similar to the goat's and two pouty lips. The braided mane on its neck was now atop its head, filled with flowers. The bottom part of his body stayed the same, along with his tail and hooves.

"He's a faun," Theresa whispered. "It's a faun, like in the Greek Mythology on Earth."

Osirus blinked several times and grinned. "Is it now? That's interesting."

"What the fuck is going on?" I held my female closer. "And has this thing seen my female naked!?" It was male–human like. It must think, talk and act like one of us it wasn't an animal at all.

Then again, it wasn't a shifter, Simon had never shifted in front of us before. I had never heard of a goat shifter, even in the book I was given to study.

They all stared at me in disbelief as Simon's nose and limbs twitched as his body moved to stretch. We were all going to get our answers, and hopefully soon.

We maintained a good distance, ensuring he had ample space. As his eyelids gradually fluttered apart, we were met with the familiar sight of his goat-like eyes.

"Simon?" Theresa steps forward. "Is that you?"

Simon's hind legs wobbled as he attempted to rise but lost his balance, crashing down with his face hitting the ground. He gazed intently at his hands, then back at his longer hind legs and hooves, before turning his head towards us, wearing a confused expression.

We were all confused.

"Simon?" I asked, adjusting my miresa.

His head turned to see me and then my female. He frowned and his body fell over into the dirt.

"Simon, she is alright." I did not know why I felt the need to comfort the goat—faun, but he looked after her when I could not. He looked just as confused as the rest of us. "You kept her safe. I will keep her safe now, too."

Simon shook his head and got on two hooves. He didn't stand tall but acted like a newborn kid and wobbled on his two hooved legs. He used his hands to steady himself on the ground.

"Can you speak, Simon?" Osirus came closer. "Do you know who you are? What you are?"

Simon shied away and before any of us realized what was happening, he was galloping away on his powerful hooves while gracefully using his hands for balance. The sight was strange, and I stood there like moss growing on the side of tree. I was worthless and of no use as I let him get away.

Theresa tried to move out of Birch's arms. "Wait!" she screamed but we all stayed still, unwilling to leave our spot.

Osirus sighed. "Simon will be fine—he knows the land and knows Calliope's scent. He won't venture far."

Worried glances shot between all of us, at what we just witnessed, and I held my female tighter in my arms. I placed my nose in the crook of her neck. It was the only thing that calmed me. She was the only thing keeping me tethered to the soil.

I stood in silence, my hand caressing my miresa's face as Theresa explains what a faun was. The creatures came from a lore that humans used to tell about the Greek Gods of their realm. Really, it was just the gods we knew of this realm, but humans just referred to them differently.

Fauns were half goat and half human. Depending on what lore you believed, fauns were merry creatures often carrying a flute and would bring joy to all those around them. These fauns also had a great sense of direction. There were many stories that fauns would help lead lost men to the right path so they could find their way home.

I suppose, in a way, Simon led my miresa to me.

I placed my hand over her heart. I could not tell if she was in destress, I only felt her heart beating slowly. I pressed my forehead to hers and let out a slow calming breath.

"Come," Osirus approached me. "We will take her back to the palace. Make her comfortable until she wakes. Humans take time to have magic recede from their bodies."

I listened to everyone shuffling around me, the guards and her parents. All these people cared about her, and I had done what my miresa had asked over the weeks, but I could not take it any longer. I had stayed away from my—our home for a long time. I had shown patience, more patience than any other orc would have.

"No," I gritted my teeth. "No, we will not be returning to your palace." I raised my head, and they all stared at me in shock.

"My miresa, my mate, is under my protection. I will no longer entertain anyone else's desires for my female. Ever since I arrived here, I have obeyed my mate's every wish. She made me promise that she could see her parents before I took her to our home. I have fulfilled my promise. She needs rest, she needs me, and I will give her peace within our home."

Theresa's mouth opened and closed.

I turned before anyone could say a word. My back was straight and there was determination in my step. I was done dealing with everyone else's desires, the only one that matters was my female. It was my turn to take care of her.

They may be her family, but I was her forever. Her male, her future, her protector.

I nuzzled my face into her long, raven-dark hair again. She was beautiful even with her dark locks. They matched my own and I hoped she would not be too sad when she woke to find them not the swirling bright pink she used to love so much.

All I knew was that I would hold her until she woke. I would be by her side and face any fears she may have. Even if it killed me that she might be afraid of me, afraid of our new home that I had whisked her away to, without her consent first.

Chapter Forty-Four

Valpar

I STARED DOWN AT the crate of supplies on the border of my territory. It had been four days since I arrived home, and this was the third crate left at the boundary. My nose scrunched in distaste as I stared at it. It was filled with fruit, fabric, dresses, pillows and other brightly colored items my miresa would like.

I ground my teeth.

I took care of my female now. I did not need any of their help. I did not need any of them to take care of her. I wanted her to myself.

However, there was a voice in the back of my head telling me that I must accept it. Each day I had denied these crates, but today I felt I should accept it. I was making the cabin a home for my female and each day was one day closer to when she would wake and, perhaps, I should have some things she might find...pretty.

I rummaged around the crate and found a small box of tea that prevented orclings. Instead of boiling and drinking it I took a small packet and ate it.

Orcs don't drink tea.

My miresa had squirmed in the sash I created to carry her with me. Her tiny moans had gone straight to my shaft, and it was all I could do to hold in my excitement for when she woke.

She had been in an unbreakable slumber for four long days. I tended to her every need, bathing her delicate body and coaxing water past her parched lips, all in the hopes that she would awaken soon.

She was close, I could feel it.

"Fine," I muttered. I knew they were out there, hidden amongst the trees. They wouldn't leave their daughter or their niece alone unless they knew she was awake.

She was mine; they couldn't have her.

They had given me space to process and to calm myself when I was in a foul mood. I was an orc. This was on my territory and if they crossed the line, I would not hesitate to beat them, her family or not. I had been far too forgiving since meeting my miresa.

No more.

I picked up the crate and made sure not to jostle the precious cargo that was strapped around my body. She nuzzled into my chest and her hand gripped my hair tightly.

I prayed to the Goddess that today was the day. It had to be.

With the crate in hand, I turned on my heel and headed back to the cabin.

The air was thick with the scent of damp earth and the sweet fragrance of the forest. Sunlight filtered through the dense canopy, casting the sprinkling of shade on the forest floor. The gentle rustle of leaves and the chirping of birds created nature's own soothing music. The cool breeze brushed against my skin, providing relief as I navigated through the forest, carrying the extra weight.

I'd cleared out a larger area around the cabin, so my miresa had a place to lie in the sun and I had even extended the garden, so she could plant the flowers she liked so much from the Golden Light Kingdom.

My nose would regret it, but as long as it made her smile.

My horse, Ulam, was grazing just on the north side of the cabin, which had the sweetest grasses. He raised his head in greeting, but I did not let him see my female today. His gaze followed me as I reached the cabin, which I had constructed around the base of a tree that had stopped growing.

There was a tree, called a sorrow pine, that expelled a cool energy from its bark. It was keeping the cabin cooler on the inside, and I enjoyed wrapping up in the furs at night when the tree pushed out the cooler temperatures, once the light sources set.

I hoped my miresa liked it, too. Since my cabin was built around a tree, it might remind her of the home she once lived in with her parents.

As the brisk wind whistled through the air, I cautiously walked past the delicate wind chimes and entered the rustic cabin. The weathered boards beneath my feet emitted a gentle creak as I firmly shut the door, enveloping me in a calming atmosphere. Relief washed over me, knowing that we had found solace away from prying eyes, observing us from beyond the cabin walls.

I carefully placed the heavy crate, filled to the brim with items, onto the weathered wooden table. The table creaked in protest, but I trusted its sturdiness. With the weight supported, I used my hands to caress the curve of my partner's backside, feeling her squirm within the sling.

I remembered my ogamie carrying Sugha around when he was an orcling. I found it funny how my little miresa could fit inside, just as easily. As I cleaned up our home over the past few days and made it more livable for my female, I kept her by my body because I could not part with her even for a moment.

This male was too afraid to let her out of his sight again, and for good reason. It wasn't just an enemy trying to take her from me, but her tiny feet would lead her into some sort of strange predicament.

I also did it because I hoped my voice and my touch would somehow let her know I was there.

Goddess, I hoped she knew I was here waiting for her. That I would always be here.

I took her to the only bedroom in the cabin. Thick furs filled the bed. Only the best and the softest. I sat on the bed, then gently removed her from the carrier and her eyes fluttered.

"Little fairy?" My drums beat excitedly. "Please tell me you are waking up?" I tried to keep my voice soft so as not to scare her. I tried to keep my anger and frustration hidden so she would not feel it.

Peace, Moon Fairy, I wanted her to have peace.

Her dark eyelashes fluttered again, and I held my breath. I dared not breathe on her skin, too afraid I would scare her. When she opened her eyes, her bright blue ones meet my yellow ones and her smile was wide.

"Valpar!" Her arms pushed away the rest of the carrier and threw them around my neck.

I embraced her tightly, feeling a surge of relief flood through me. She was awake! Finally, after days of tending to her while she slept, she was finally awake. Her laughter was like music to my ears as she nuzzled into the crook of my neck. I held her close, breathing in the scent of her hair.

"Little fairy," I whispered, my voice filled with emotion. "You're awake."

Her backside rubbed against my shaft. I tried my best not to groan, but she continued to rub, and I grunted, moving her to my thigh.

"I missed you," she whispered and kissed my neck.

Moon Fairy, help me!

"Miresa, I have missed you, too." I threaded my fingers through her hair and kept her at my neck. "Are—you alright?"

I let her pull away, reluctantly, waiting to see her droop with sadness, but I saw nothing. I saw nothing but her bright smile and the twinkling of her eyes.

"No, I'm fine. I'm here with you and—" She gazed around the cabin and raised a brow. "Where are we?"

I cleared my throat and pulled her against my chest again. "Our home, in the Monktona Wood. I couldn't take you back to the palace, your parents' home. I needed you here, it was—"

"Too much," she finished for me, her hand cupping my cheek.

I swallowed and let my head rest in her hand.

"You have been gone awhile. Orcs don't stay away from their homes long, do they?"

I shook my head and pressed a kiss to her forehead. I couldn't understand how she was not crying, shaking in fear or angry with me that I had taken her away from her home and family.

"It's so cozy here. I love it." She moved to stand, but I pulled her back down on my lap.

"You've been sleeping for days, you are weak. You will eat and I will carry you where you need to go," I grunted, then lifted her into the air and took her to the kitchen. She wiggled in my arms and I swatted her backside.

"Hey!" She rubbed her cheek. "What was that for?"

"Not listening, and there will be more where that came from. It is part of your punishment."

She bit her bottom lip, and her face heated to a beautiful shade of red. "Is that a promise?"

The scent of her arousal filled the room, and I stopped before we even entered the kitchen. Her hand rubbed up my chest and stopped on my tit.

"You know, I had some crazy dreams while I was asleep." She pinched it and I groaned.

I swallowed heavily, trying to ignore my hardening shaft. It had been stiff for days and I could not take it in hand to relieve myself. Not when my female was sleeping, not when she was suffering.

"Little fairy, what happened? Do you remember?" My brow pinched together as I tried to not think about my throbbing cock and heavy sack, filling with seed.

Her eyes softened, and her hand ran up my neck and scratched behind my ear. "I do remember," she whispered. "I remember everything that happened to me."

My eyes burned. "Miresa." I had never cried—not for anyone, but for her I would.

She shook her head. "When I first came to Bergarian I wanted to forget because the time in that house was all I knew. I didn't have a future to look forward to and I thought no one could love me. All my life I was told no one would."

A deep growl resonated in my chest.

She giggled and wrapped both arms around my neck. "Now that I have spent time here, with Mom, Dad, Uncle Osirus, Aunt Melina and especially you, I know that isn't true."

"Of course it's not true. Your family loves you. I love you the most. They cannot love you more. I am your male, and no one can match my love for you."

She threw her head back and laughed. Her hands cupped my face, and she pressed a kiss on my lips. "And the new memories we make will eventually erase all the bad ones. They will keep disappearing as time goes on, because of you."

I pressed my lips to hers again, kissing her more fiercely than before. I claimed her, kissing her deeply and hungrily as my hands roamed her body. I wanted to erase all of her bad memories, quickly.

Her hands gripped my shoulders tightly, pulling me closer to her, her hips moving softly against me. My cock throbbed even more, aching for release, and I knew I could hold out no longer.

I did not tie my cock to my leg while she slept, I let it hang freely. It was a constant reminder of my failure to keep her safe, a failure of what I was. It leaked everywhere. Fuck, it was annoying.

I carried her back to the bedroom and climbed on top of her where she fell into the furs. She licked her lips and stared between my legs, where my shaft was no longer covered by my cloth which I'd ripped away.

"Valpar," she gasped. "Your balls are huge."

I groaned and cupped them in my hand. "I have had no release."

My miresa pouted, and her hand moved down my body. My shaft twitched and I groaned, trying to hold back the need to release my seed. It would be embarrassing how much seed I could release and I felt sorry for my miresa's cunt.

"Let me help first." My miresa gently pushed me to the side. My shaft bounced against my stomach as she crawled down my body and stared at my sack. I groaned as she took her two hands to cup them.

"Valpar, it looks so painful." She massaged them and I let out a pitiful whine.

She leaned forward and took a long, tentative lick, her hot breath washing over my sack. My hips bucked involuntarily, my shaft jerking up and smacking against my stomach again. She giggled, her eyes sparkling with mischief as she continued to explore my sensitive sack with her tongue.

Moon Fairy, save me.

My female then took one ball into her mouth, sucking gently while her other hand toyed with my erect shaft. The sensation felt fucking good, a mix of pleasure and pain that sent a jolt straight to my cock. She switched, sucking the other ball into her mouth and the sensation was too much to bear.

My breath hitched and I gritted my teeth. "Are you ready, now? Will you let me release?"

Why I was asking her I did not know. Somehow, she'd become the dominate one over me.

She chuckled and winked at me. "I'm not finished yet. I enjoy staring at my big, beautiful, green cock. Don't you think you have a beautiful cock, Valpar?"

I swore under my breath. "It is not beautiful, it is massive. Like a battering ram."

She laughed and licked the swollen, angry tip that refused to stay dry. Seed leaked down my shaft, coating me, ready to slip inside her.

Fuck!

"You taste so good. Like my favorite candy. I'm going to lick you like a giant sucker." She licked the swollen head, her tongue circling and swept downward. My balls were so heavy, they could not even move to twitch.

My female had never been so attentive to my shaft and sack. It was like she was worshipping it. Moaning, petting, pressing her tits into my thighs.

I balled my hands into fists so I did not touch her. If I did, I would flip her over and rut her into the furs.

My miresa pulled away and her eyes were filled with desire. Her hands gripped my shaft, stroking it firmly as she dragged her mouth away from my sack. I growled softly and my body arched at her touch. My hands gripped the fur beneath me and my body was trembling as she continued to stroke me.

"Let me ease your seed, Valpar. Let it fill my mouth and make it a memory we'll never forget." She winked, her voice soft and sultry.

What realm have I fallen into? What has happened to my miresa?

She tugged at the tunic I put her in this morning and lifted it over her head. She had no undergarments covering her cunt and I could see the moisture gathered between her legs.

This female!

"Let me taste you, Valpar."

Before I could protest her mouth settled over my shaft and she sucked me into her.

She took me in, engulfing me with a fervor I'd never witnessed in her. Her mouth moved up and down my length, creating a tantalizing rhythm. I felt the warmth and wetness enveloping me, sending waves of pleasure coursing through my body. The flick of her tongue against the sensitive underside of my shaft intensified the sensations, causing tremors to ripple through me. I tightened my grip on the soft fur beneath me, desperately clinging to the remnants of my self-control.

I groaned, arching my back as she continued to pleasure me. My seed, waiting to be released, threatened to spill over, but she pulled away, her eyes gleaming with desire.

"Do you think you could share your seed with me now, Valpar?" she asked, playfully "Push my head down the way you like it."

Goddess above.

I ran my fingers through her hair to push her lower. I bucked, feeling my cock hit the back of her throat. She took it eagerly and hummed.

"That's it," I growled. "Take all of me. Suck me down, take what I have to give you."

There was a tickle at the back of my spine, and I arched my back. "Calliope!" I roared her name, and my seed was released. She swallowed, but it kept coming until she choked and had to back away.

My cock throbbed with more seed dripping down, landing on my sack. She licked her lips, her tongue savoring each drop. My erection refused to subside, as my primal instincts took over.

In that moment, I realized what I must do. The urge to claim her as my mate overwhelmed me. My brand burned fiercely with the intensity to be buried deep within her cunt.

There was nothing to stop us now, no reason to hold back any longer. I snarled and sat up on the bed. The face I gave her would scare any person or animal, but she just smiled at me and thrust out her chest like it were a meal ready to be devoured.

It was time to brand her, and I didn't care if she liked it or not.

Chapter Forty-Five

Calliope

HE WAS LOOKING AT me funny.

He had a vein that was pulsing on his forehead, sweat dripped from his brow and he was panting as though he was about to pounce on me.

Valpar jutted out his jaw and crawled towards me. I knew he was trying to look like a savage beast, a wild animal ready to pounce on his prey.

But I couldn't help it.

I let out a giggle, because he looked so hot. I was so in love with him, and I knew he wouldn't lay a finger on me.

"Why are you laughing?" His voice was deep, and my clit fluttered to the beat of my heart.

Oh, my lady parts were dripping. They were soaking the bed just like the big monster between his legs. Goddess, we were gonna have our own waterbed in a second.

He growled deeply, taking that slow crawl over my body. I could still taste the remnants of his come on my lips, which was sweet. I licked over my lips again and he groaned, then pressed his finger over my lips.

"Suck." He pried my mouth open with his thick finger and I greedily sucked on his massive digit.

His breath was ragged, and my hips moved on their own while I lay on my back, pinned under him. I'd gotten both legs straddled around his thigh, and I could feel the heat radiating off his body, with my clit so close to touching it. If I could get just a little closer I was sure I'd see stars.

"Your cunt is greedy." He mused and stuck his finger deeper into my throat. I gagged and he pulls back. "My cock is longer than my finger and now you gag?" He pulled his finger out of my mouth.

I coughed and shook my head. "It's because you don't have your come on it. It has magic."

He stared at me.

Guess his brain needs to reboot.

I took his finger, rubbed it up and down his shaft, coating it with his seed and put it back into my mouth. I mumbled behind his finger. "Naw, du it."

Valpar shook his head and pulled his finger away. "I'm claiming you." he said bluntly. "Right now, you are going to take my brand and will officially be mine."

I perked up and clapped my hands together. "Goodie! Let me get ready!" I laid back, put my hands over my head and spread my legs. "I'm ready, let's go! When you bite me, do it hard and fast. I don't want you to gnaw on me, okay? I'm not a chew toy." I shimmied my body with happiness, but Valpar still didn't move.

Valpar chuckled and swiped his finger down my cheek. "Orcs do not bite, we brand. Do you know what branding is, my sweet little fairy?" He placed kisses down my cheek and my body relaxed. My arms wrapped around his neck and my body was flush with his.

"Instead of biting, I shove the last bulge of my cock inside you. I will stretch your cunt and fill you up. Branding it as mine. You will smell of me always. Your cunt will only want me and only take me. Do you understand?"

That branding thing was big looking. I glanced down at it and back up at him.

It was going to be painfully hot and exciting.

I let out a whine, wrapped my legs around one of his powerful thighs and let my pussy coat him.

"Fuck, my sweet fairy, are you ready?"

"Mmhmm," I sucked on his earlobe. "Will you still suck on my shoulder and leave a nice bruise?" I still wanted other people to see that I was his. In Bergarian a bite was a sign of ownership, and part of me still wanted that.

Having love bruises was freaking hot.

He chuckled, his hands reaching under my but and squeezing. "I plan to leave plenty of marks all over your body. I want even the humans to know I take you long and often."

Pretty sure my vagina just convulsed around nothing, because I couldn't wait!

Valpar's body left me in an instant. The air in the cabin was so much cooler than outside, that my nipples hardened and goose bumps rose on my skin. A deep, dark laugh left his lips when he flipped me over and I landed on my stomach with a squeak.

"First, I will punish you for running from me."

Wait, what?

His massive hand connected with a resounding smack against my backside, sending shockwaves of pain and surprise through my body. The sound of my twisted moans and screams echoed in the room. With each subsequent strike, my once cool skin blazed with an intense, searing heat, as if flames were dancing across my flesh. The stinging sensation reverberated deep within me, igniting a desire for more punishment. My clit pulsed, aching to be touched, to feel the weight of his hand against it. The beating fueled an insatiable and desperate arousal, leaving me already teetering on the edge of pleasure and pain.

Fairy Godmother called me a little pain slut before I woke up. I wasn't sure what that was, but I think I knew now.

I wondered if he would swat at my tits?

"I want to take you badly, but first, you need to learn not to run from me." his words were rough, similar to the spanks he was raining down on my bottom. I writhed under his hand, panting and whimpering.

"No more running," I panted. My nipples rubbed against the furs of the bed, my body shook from the sting of his hand and the softness of the fur.

After peppering my butt with the blows, he caressed it. I hissed, feeling how he massaged the sting further into my skin. "You do like this spanking, don't you?" His finger trailed down the crack of my butt and through my folds. "You dripping, little fairy? Perhaps spankings are not punishment, only pleasure?"

I let out a whine and my hips pushed back. He slipped two fingers inside my pussy and my mouth dropped open as he began to thrust them inside me. "I have not tasted you, let me drink. Stay on all fours or I will make you wait longer before you receive me."

My body was shaking from the blows. I didn't know if I could hold on for long. He was quick though, and I felt him lay down and pull my pussy over his face.

"What a vision, sweet nectar for me, hmm?" He pulled my pussy to his face and licked.

I released a passionate cry, unable to restrain the intense climax that had been brewing. As his tongue delved deeper into me, I sensed the tantalizing brush of his tusks against my quivering thighs. The room filled with his licking, sucking and slurping.

"A good fairy takes what's she's given. Give me more of your cries, let me hear you."

I shook my head, my arms feeling unsteady. "I-I can't. I'm sensitive."

He hummed, vibrating against my pussy. "Be a good fairy, be my fairy. One more."

His praise made me arch my back and I came with a cry. He drew out the pleasure and I swear I had peed myself by the time he left me. I collapsed on the bed. Completely spent. I was panting but thankfully not sweating, because I felt the room becoming colder.

He rolled me onto my back. I saw my arousal around his face. He licked it eagerly, the desire swimming in his eyes. "What perfect tits you have." He leaned forward, sucking on one while he slapped the other. "Only mine now."

Goddess almighty, my dreams have come true.

I was panting heavily, my disheveled hair cascaded in wild strands, brushing against the soft fur around me. I watched as he firmly grasped his impressive length, giving it a few satisfying strokes. The scent of our combined desire hung in the air as his warm release trickled down onto the trimmed, dark hair between my legs.

"You're beautiful," he blurted his come still dripping down my opening. "Pink, blue, orange or black hair, you will always be beautiful to me."

I gave him a small smile and my hand parted my folds. "Please don't make me wait."

The wooden cabin creaked, and a refreshing gust of air wafted in through the wide-open window. Valpar's lips met mine, and I savored the lingering taste of myself on his mouth.

"You're mine now."

Valpar thrusted inside me in one swift, powerful motion. I cried out, a mix of pain and pleasure as he filled me completely. My body shook, a wave of ecstasy washing over me. It wasn't as I had imagined, but it was better. This wasn't a gentle coupling, it was raw and animalistic, a claim being made.

"I cannot go slow, not when I am branding you. I'm sorry." he grunted, each thrust getting closer and closer to the brand that was swelling at the base of his cock.

I tried to wrap my legs around his waist wanting to pull him in deeper.

Valpar's mischievous grin widened, and I couldn't help but notice the hunger in his eyes. I felt his strong fingers gripping my hips, their pressure intensifying as he thrust with even more force. With each deep penetration, an electrifying sensation coursed through my body, sending pleasurable shivers down my spine. Our bodies moved together in perfect harmony. In that moment, he possessed me completely, claiming me as his own.

"Your cunt is so tight," he panted, his breath hot against my neck. "And wet. So fucking wet! Fuck!"

Valpar paused, his eyes darkening as he looked down at me. He didn't speak, but the way he gripped my hips told me everything I needed to know.

Oh Goddess, here it comes.

As he forced himself inside, a sharp pain shot through me. When the larger knot was forced inside, a blinding burst of stars crossed my vision. My fingers dug into his biceps, feeling the strength beneath my touch. A primal roar escaped his lips as he continued to rhythmically push in and out of me. The limited range of movement intensified the pleasure as he tried to slip his knot back out.

"Goddess above, you are so small!" He pulled his brand out of me with a pop and forced it back in.

I screamed and my back arched. The pain wasn't there anymore, just a delightful stretching as my body was being molded to his.

"More," I was barely able to speak.

His hips convulsed abruptly, pressing against mine, and his face buried itself in the crook of my shoulder. I could sense the warmth of his breath against my skin as he hungrily attached his lips and applied intense suction. The overwhelming sensation sent me hurtling towards another climax, all while the slapping sound of our bodies filled the air.

"You're perfect," he growled, pushing deeper into me.

I cried out his name, my body shuddering in blissful release. He pulled out, leaving my pussy throbbing and vacant.

"And mine," he grunted, back pumping into me again and again. The sensation of his cock sliding in and out of me and the force of his thrusts was all too much. I felt myself building towards another climax.

"Fuck! Yes!" he roared, his cock pulsating deep inside me, lodging his brand deep. With that final thrust, he filled me with his seed spilling inside me. Instead of it falling out of me, I could feel it swell inside my stomach.

So full!

My walls convulsed around him, milking him dry as I felt his hot seed continue to flow into me.

He collapsed on top of me, his weight pinning me to the bed. I could feel his heart pounding on my chest, his breath warm on my bruised neck.

"Good little fairy," he whispered, his voice thick with satisfaction. "My good little fairy, my miresa, my mate."

He left his cock inside and rolled to the side so he wouldn't suffocate me. He was so large, every time he moved I could feel the knot rub across my clit and a shudder of pleasure ran through me again. My nipples tightened and I buried my face into his chest, letting my leg stay over his hip to be comfortable.

Was it weird that I didn't want him to pull out...ever?

Valpar brushed my hair away with one of his claws. His neck had to be at a weird angle because how we were connected he had to curl down to lean his cheek against the top of my head.

"Are you okay?" he muttered.

His voice was sweet, especially considering how feral he acted just seconds ago.

"So good." I let my cheek rub up against his chest. "I'm really full."

He chuckled and we felt the vibrations through our connection.

"That was the idea. And I plan on doing it again once it releases."

My eyes widened. Cheesus, again?

I closed my eyes and felt a burst of energy inside me. It was—indescribable. It wasn't an emotion that was mine, it felt like an extension of myself. As the burst of energy surged through me, I could feel my entire body tingling, as if electrical currents were coursing through my veins. It was as though every cell in my body had suddenly come alive, vibrating with an intensity I had never experienced before. The sheer power of this indescribable sensation was overwhelming, leaving me breathless and in awe.

As I slowly opened my eyes and the tears that had welled up now streamed down my face, a testament to the sheer magnitude of what I was feeling. It was growing, it was overwhelming, and it was coming from Valpar.

A sob escaped me as I rubbed my cheek against his chest. It felt his body move as he tried to pull me up closer to his face. I screamed for him to stop and wrapped my arm around him.

The warmth, the unexplainable joy and love radiated from him, but there was also fear, confusion.

Was I really feeling him?

"Miresa, what is wrong?" His arms were gripping me tightly and his claws buried into my skin.

"I think I feel you," I whispered, my hand roaming up his chest. My eyes warmed, and I felt a trickle of a tear run down my cheek. "You really love me, a lot." The emotions were coming at me like a tidal wave, coming at me so quickly it was becoming too much.

Valpar let out a shuttering breath and groaned, then I felt him adjust himself and tilted my head to look at him.

"My sweet mate, our souls are becoming one. Just as the Moon Fairy said. We have combined not just in body, but in spirit as well. You are mine and I am yours." His thumb brushed away my tears.

My eyes grew heavy once again, but this time I did not feel the fear of the darkness.

"Sleep. An orc's emotions are strong and it will take time to adjust." He pressed a kiss to my forehead. "My miresa, please sleep, do not fight it. I will be here when you wake. I will always be here."

I felt his love overflowing, along with his cock, which was shoved so far up my vagina; I swear I was going to be tasting his come again soon.

"Promise me something," I whispered, and I closed my eyes.

Valpar rubbed his cheek against my forehead.

"I'll need ice later."

"Ice?"

"Yes, to shove up the gaping hole you made for the giant log you just speared me with."

CHAPTER FORTY-SIX

Calliope

MY STOMACH GROWLED. "YOU know what I'm craving? A big ol' yellow tree dick."

Valpar paused while he was carrying me in his arms to the kitchen table. He slowly looked down at me, but I wiggled for him to put me down.

"Wow, and I see some on the table! Do they grow here? Oh, and you've got muffins, too?"

Valpar let me down, reluctantly, and he stood there with his half-hard shaft wobbling against his leg.

"Yellow tree dick?" He drawled and I pulled a big banana out of the crate on the table. "Yeah! Don't they look like dicks? I chuckled, peeled it and took a massive bite. I moaned and rubbed my bare stomach.

I was starving, and, apparently, I slept for four whole days while I was reliving memories and had my brains fudged into oblivion. My lady parts were still tingly and sore, so, I walked a little funny. I really needed some ice cubes, or maybe a frozen dildo, I could shove up my lady bits, but I doubted Valpar had any of those things in the cabin.

I peeled the rest of the banana and stuck it into my mouth. I moaned as I chewed, and Valpar huffed and shook his head. He went to the oversized chair at the table and slapped his leg for me to go sit with him.

"That is not a dick. It's a banana. Where do you come up with these weird names?"

I hopped onto his lap and swallowed the gigantic piece, and before I could speak Valpar already had a cup of cool water to my lips. "It's the shock factor, and let's face it, you looked pretty shocked."

Valpar pinched his nose and smiled. "You will run circles around me."

"That's the plan." I took another bite, and let out a long, erotic moan as I put as much banana in my mouth as I could.

Valpar watched, and his hand tightened around my thigh.

"You are enjoying that banana far too much," he growled in my ear.

Hmm, indeed I was. He was gripping the cup too tightly and watching me with eyes like he was going to pounce again.

This was fun.

"Mmm, it is so good though. And you know what, I think yellow might be my favorite color now."

Valpar slammed the cup on the counter, sloshing water on the table. "What?"

"Yeah, yellow. Such a bright happy color. Don't you think?"

Valpar pulled the banana away from me. "Green should be your favorite color and the only thing you should have in your mouth is my green shaft." He whispered dangerously in my ear.

"Where's Simon?" I asked, changing the subject and ignoring his constipated face. "He's probably not used to this place, and I want to make sure he's okay." I reached over the table to grab another banana, giving my mate a perfect view of my naked butt. I could feel Valpar's vibrations from his chest run down my legs while he palmed my butt.

"Little fairy, I have some news about Simon."

My brows furrowed when I heard his voice go serious.

"Is he okay? He didn't get hurt when that potion spilled on him, did he? He didn't die?" Panic rose in my throat and Valpar placed his hand on my chest.

"No, Simon is fine. It's just—he isn't the same Simon you remember."

I tilted my head and stared out the window at the front of the cabin. How could Simon not be the same Simon?

"When the potion fell on your skin, Simon panicked and jumped after Karma. The potion got into his fur. Normally, this should not have affected him, but Simon was under a spell that no one knew about."

I thought for a moment, running my fingers through Valpar's hair. If he isn't the same fainting Simon, maybe...

"Does he not faint anymore? That's... that's wonderful!"

Valpar winced. "No, that isn't what happened."

I tilted my head in confusion.

"He—changed. He isn't a goat. He's human on the top part of his body and goat on the other half. Your mother said he was called— a faun." Valpar scratched his head.

He continued to speak but my smile grew so wide I could hardly contain myself. "Where is he! I want to see! He sounds amazing!" I tried to jump off Valpar's lap, but he held me in place.

"He isn't here. He ran off." He grunted.

I frowned, still holding the banana in my one hand. "But why? Why would he run?"

Valpar shook his head. "I don't know. Maybe because he was embarrassed? Afraid? His scent didn't change, and I think I' smelled him around the cabin."

I tapped my lips with my finger. This was good. Simon wasn't far. He was still hanging around. He was just waiting for me to wake up. I will coax him to come out and talk to me.

Having a conversation with my best friend was going to be great; it wouldn't be one-sided anymore, and I could still be with him if he fainted. Yes, this is going to be flippin' awesome. I couldn't wait to see him and ask him so many questions. What was his life before me? What was it like to have two legs? To talk? Is he really always hungry?

Valpar grabbed my chin and pulled it toward his face. "What are you thinking so hard for?"

I bit my lip. "Just thinking about Simon. He's going to be talking now. It's gonna be great, we can all live as a family. Do you have an extra bedroom? He's gonna have to sleep in a bed now."

Valpar's eyes widened and he took a sharp intake of breath. "Let's not get ahead of ourselves. He didn't want to have anything to do with us after he changed."

"But I'm his best friend. He will come to me." I placed my hand over his chest. "I'm his human support companion. You'll see."

Valpar nodded and patted my thighs. "Whatever my miresa wants, she gets. Now eat more besides your yellow tree dicks. In fact, I'm banning them. No more of those things in the cabin." He narrowed his eyes. "You need meat."

I nodded my head. "Yes, I need some meat. Like yours?" I winked at him and looked between his legs. He was already hard, but let's face it, he was always hard.

He growled at me, put my naked back to his chest and pulled more food out of the crate. "You will eat, and then I will take you on every surface in this cabin, but not before. You are small and I do not need you to waste away."

I leaned my head back and stared up at him. "Ooo, is that a promise?"

He snorted and cupped my tiny breast. "My words are law, little fairy."

As we ate, Valpar grumbled how he would feed me food he prepared from now on. I ignored him and ate happily. I didn't care if the food was prepared by him. I just liked that he fed me. Right now, I had an enormous appetite and was eating triple what I normally would.

He said my parents were around the wood somewhere. They were waiting for me to wake up and refused to listen to his telling them to leave. Valpar complained more, and I had to take my thumb and iron out the wrinkle between his eyes, so it didn't get stuck that way. I smiled at him and urged him to eat, himself, but he just continued to call them ridiculous. I know my parents trusted him, it was just—they loved me, too. They wanted to see me happy.

Because they were my family.

My parents and aunt and uncle trusted Valpar, but they were my family and Valpar didn't understand they weren't going anywhere for a while. My heart warmed at that.

Karma and Ivy were so wrong.

I was disappointed to learn that my orc didn't sit and squish Karma with his magnificent butt. To be nearly squeezed to death and then squashed by his big toe will have to do.

Too bad I missed it.

Valpar cleared his throat several times and with my back leaning up against his chest I could feel the concern in his body. It was weird, also still overwhelming. I could feel all his emotions inside him, and it was upsetting not to know what it was. I finally had to pinch his nipple and ask what the heck was wrong with him, that I could feel his worry.

"I want to know what happened to you, but I do not want to cause you distress."

My sweet orc shone love through this bond we had. It had covered me in a giant blanket. He was angry at what I went through, and his concern was to know what happened, so he did nothing to trigger me and cause me issues later.

That would never happen. Not with Valpar.

I gently explained my story. I didn't provide him with gritty details, but I softly explained my story of being kept in a basement with limited food, facing numerous mental challenges of feeling unloved, and constantly seeking friendships that I never felt deserving of. My pain was more mental

I felt. Had I not lived with that woman for so many years, I think my personality would be just the same as it is now.

Osirus and the sorceress didn't change me at all. They just wiped the terrible memories away, so I could thrive like I should have from the beginning. I became who I was always meant to be. Happy. A little bit quirky.

I liked me. I liked me more when I was with Valpar, though.

Valpar's arms wrapped around me, and he rocked me—his favorite position to have me in. He made me feel like a giant baby and I couldn't lie—I really liked it. I liked how big he was, how over-protective he could be, because when I grew up I didn't have that.

I liked how he fussed over me, how he bathed me and how he never let me out of his sight. It was going to be worse now, and I couldn't wait to be a sassy little brat about it!

I beamed up at him, and using his claw, he brushed the dark locks away from my face. "And how did you get away?" Valpar murmured. "You said it was hard to sneak out."

I played with Valpar's hair that cascaded around us and started to braid it. "Birch came to the rescue." I chuckled. "Birch burst through the front door; I heard it. There was a party upstairs and everyone was screaming. I heard glass break, people running out, the woman who kept me was screaming Theresa's name and telling her she was going to call the cops."

Valpar's grip tightened.

"Cops are people who are supposed to help you. The cops in the town I lived in were—bad. Anyway, Mom—Theresa —held her down and Birch burst through the basement. It was at the end of summer, and I was weak because I couldn't get food as much as I could during the school year. Mom did her best to sneak it through the window in the basement, but somehow the woman upstairs always knew.

"But Birch came in like a knight. He had his ears showing and I remember he had this cool outfit on. It felt like a dream. His sword was strapped to his side. I thought I was getting sucked into a fairy tale. He carried me upstairs and Theresa was there, and she held my hand while that woman just screamed. I worried about Theresa, but she told me not to worry that I would never see that woman ever again."

Valpar growled low and buried his face into my neck. "She's gone. That female. She's dead."

My eyebrows shot up in surprise. "Dead? Like dead-dead?"

Valpar huffed and kissed my bruised shoulder. "Your uncle went to finish her. When he got to her home, she was dead. From those drugs she used."

Sick satisfaction flooded me. *Good.*

I tried to see the good in people, give them the benefit of the doubt that maybe they were having a bad day, or an awful life. That was no excuse to make other people suffer. I'd never understand why people could be so cruel and want to see other people unhappy.

Kindness is free. Just a smile at someone from a distance can make that person's day a little brighter. It isn't hard.

Being angry, plotting, scheming, putting other people down, just to be mean, it seems like so much effort.

Valpar leaned over me, placing his hand over my chest. "Does my female need a happy memory to erase the sadness she is feeling?"

I squeezed my thighs together and I swear I felt my lady parts trying to suck up his thigh.

My pussy is turning into a vacuum and I'm gonna leave a hickey on his leg.

Valpar groaned when I rubbed my pussy against his thick muscle. "Female, I don't want to take you if you are sore."

He turned me around and my chest lined up against his. The cool air in the cabin cooled my back while my breasts were warmed by the heat of his body. A shiver ran down my spine at the different temperatures.

"Rub that wet cunt on my leg. I can feel your wet pussy coating me already."

I whimpered, holding onto his arms. My body felt different down there, like I was seeking his cock. It was the weirdest feeling. My breathing grew heavy, and I moved my pussy against his leg.

"That's it, my greedy little fairy. I'm going to let you ride me until you come. Only when you get off on my leg, will I give you my cock."

Oh, Dommy Valpar is a hot Valpar.

CHAPTER FORTY-SEVEN

Valpar

"I SAID TO RUB that cunt on my leg." I snarled into her mouth and kissed her deeply.

I could hear her heart pounding in her chest. Her core was alight with fire against my leg. I felt bumps rising on her skin, partially from the tree, putting off cooler air in the cabin and my body heating hers at the same time. Mostly, I had hoped it was from my strict command.

Her eyes were heavily lidded, locked onto mine as I claimed her lips. My miresa had her legs enticingly parted as she slid her slick heat against my thigh. The strategic decision to keep us both undressed was a good decision. It gave me unrestricted access to her cunt. To my desires to keep her filled with my seed. I could have her anyway I wanted. Whenever I wanted.

This should be a rule. Yes, a rule. That way, I can have her at all times in our home.

I could feel that her clit was swollen, and it was indeed swollen. I remember checking it before she woke. It was red and irritated and my seed had coated the outside of her pussy. When I tried to shove my seed inside her, she woke. It was foolish of me to want to keep my seed inside her when we were preventing an orcling, but my animalistic side would not allow me to let it go to waste.

My hands cupped her behind. I helped her rub her needy clit against me. Her tits tickled my chest, and her fingers dug into my shoulders. They were sharper than I remembered, and I knew I would have claw marks by the time she came, and a sick satisfaction fell over me.

I hope they scarred. I wanted her to mar my skin with those tiny claws.

I let out a low, frustrated groan, feeling the friction of my hard shaft against her smooth leg as she sensually pressed herself against me. The scent of our arousal filled the cabin, heightening the intensity of the moment. My orcish desire consumed me, urging me to forcefully plunge inside her, but I couldn't betray my word.

She must come first.

My fingers tightened around her hips, feeling the warmth of her skin beneath my touch. I guided her in a deliberate, unhurried rhythm against my leg, the friction between us igniting a primal desire. The air was thick with the scent of her pleasure, intoxicating and heady. Her moans mingled with the sound of her slick coating me, creating pain in my shaft that I could not deny much longer.

The anticipation built for both of us. Torturous for me but her release coming quickly. Her breath was erratic, and she whimpered against my mouth. I reveled in the knowledge that she was about to release on my leg of all places.

"That's it, little fairy. Get me dirty. Put your scent all over me so no other female would dare come close to me."

She let out a snarl, and my lips curled into a smile. My little fairy could be jealous, and I liked how feisty the little snarl was.

"You don't like it if some female looks at me, do you?" I cooed.

My miresa's fingers dug deeper into my skin.

Bassza.

I leaned forward and tugged at her ear with my teeth, my tusk rubbing against her jaw. "Then mark me, coat me in your slick."

My miresa shattered around me, I felt warmth on my leg and groaned until she rode out her pleasure. I didn't wait a second more and lifted her so her cunt was just hovering over my shaft. "More," I rasped, and she widened her legs, gripped hold of me and guided me into her warmth.

Her eyelids gently closed, blocking out the world as she reveled in the comforting touch of my essence saturating her depths. I clenched my jaw, delighting in the exquisite sensation of her enveloping tightness, as she sensually molded herself to my shaft.

Pulling her closer, I bit down on her shoulder, her skin tasting salty and sweet, the pain making her back arch and releasing a heated moan. I ground my hips against her, reaching deeper, seeking the sweet spot that would send us both careening over the edge.

I was ready to give her the ride she has never had before until I realized her cunt was tightening around me tighter than I ever thought possible.

"Female!" I gritted my teeth and stood.

She wrapped her legs around my waist. My little fairy was panting heavily, and she was moving her cunt up and down my shaft. I had no control. She was using me instead of the other way around.

I pushed the crate forcefully, causing it to topple off the table with a loud crash. Bottles shattered, their contents spilling and mingling with the scent of shattered glass. The fruits from within the crate scattered, rolling across the floor, filling the room with a chaotic mix of sounds as they collided with various objects. Amid the commotion, she moaned heavily, her chest pressing against mine, creating a tingling sensation. Overwhelmed by the moment, I feared I may release my seed prematurely, struggling to comprehend the intensity of the situation.

"Miresa!" I called out to her. I had her back on the table. Her hips were moving slightly, but her cunt was sucking me in further. It was like she was eating me alive.

My fairy moved her legs above my shoulders. I was folding her like a furred blanket.

I did not know if I should be frightened or enjoy the ride. It may be my last time rutting her the way her cunt was suckling me.

I ripped my little fairy's arms from around my head and laid them above hers. My hips thrust almost involuntarily into her body.

Somehow, her strength was tenfold. She pushed my hands away and her fingers wrapped around my arms. She clawed at my forearms as I drove myself into her. I was lost in this passionate frenzy, her cunt pulling me in deeper with each thrust. My animalistic instincts took over, and I couldn't help but feel a primal satisfaction as I rode her to the edge and followed her cunt's commands.

"Come for me, my little fairy." I growled, my voice rough. "Show me just how much you want me."

Her pussy sucked in my brand and I choked when her cunt clamped down on it. She was a strong female.

Her hips bucked, her inner walls tightened around my shaft, and I felt the familiar sensation of her orgasm tugging me closer to my release. I thrusted harder, my hips moving in a frenzied dance, our bodies pounding together.

Her cries filled the room, punctuating the sound of flesh slapping against flesh. I wanted to hear her scream my name, and to know I'd given her the most intense pleasure she'd ever experienced, or maybe it was the other way around.

It was her cunt controlling my shaft. I only liked to think I was in charge.

Her cunt was milking my brand and had me locked me into a place where I couldn't move.

With a roar, I buried deep inside her, my seed flowing into her as I emptied myself into her. She shuddered beneath me, her body trembling in the wake of her release, her cunt massaging, petting me like everything was going to be alright.

Bassza, I thought I'd gone cross-eyed how hard I came.

I rested my head gently next to hers, my large tusks grazing her delicate jawline. She tenderly traced her fingers along the spot I adore, eliciting a sensation that sent shivers down my spine.

I let out a low, guttural groan, sensing another release from her as I poured myself deeper into her. She exhaled softly, a contented sigh escaping her lips, while her abdomen gracefully expands, creating a gentle swell.

"I don't know what just happened." She said in a whisper. "But I'm really tired now."

Her pussy did all the work. I could see exactly how she would be tired.

I planted soft kisses along her jawline, trailing down to her delicate neck. As my eyes fixated on the massive bruise marring her shoulder and creeping up her neck, a wave of dread washed over me. On sight alone it appeared as though I had violently harmed her. It was far from it, however. I had a sick satisfaction of leaving the love bruises on her body.

Her family were going to think I abused her.

Then, I felt the trail of blood running down my shoulders and smirked.

We both liked that hint of pain.

"Sleep, my miresa." I took a large whiff of her hair. She gave off nothing but that same calm and soothing scent I craved. It drove me wild and again my cock shot a burst of seed inside her.

"I will watch over you."

She was asleep before I finished speaking, completely passed out. I didn't know if it was normal for her to sleep so long, because she had never slept this much since I've known her.

My cock twitched inside her, but she lay still, like a sleeping little fairy that she is. I didn't want to let my cock slide out of her. I had become addicted to her pussy like some of the fae had become addicted to orc ale.

I gently propped her body up and let her lean on me as I carried her back to our room. I knew she couldn't sleep long. She had eaten and drank. I would need to be take her outside to use the restroom, since I did not have a bathroom built for her yet.

I had many things to do in the cabin, still, to make her comfortable in her new home.

I already had the logs prepared and outlined outside where a new bedroom and a bathroom would go. It would be large and spacious so she can bathe privately indoors.

I will not have my female bathing naked in any spring. No one will see her naked, not even the animals. They do not get to look at what is mine.

Jealousy rose inside me just thinking about those stupid fart squirrels... wait... skunks.

I opened the door to our bedroom. It smelled of us. We slept a long time after our first joining. I don't know if it had been a day or more. With our souls being intertwined, being weaved by a thread I have often heard about from the different kingdoms, I am sure we slept for at least two days.

That had to be why she was stronger, as well. I knew different species take on their mates' qualities, so they are better paired. My little fairy must have some of my strength now, and that was how she could push me off. She would also have better immunity to sickness, live as long as me, no longer age and of course, be immune to magic.

I would miss her pink hair, but she did not seem to mind it. My little fairy seemed content in my arms but if she wanted her hair to change colors again, I was sure her uncle would do his best to help with that endeavor.

I let my lips stay on the top of my female's head as I kept her attached to me and laid us on the bed. I didn't need to put the fur over my body to keep her warm. I was radiating enough.

My cock was still nestled inside her, but it was much tighter than before; she was tight when I first entered her. She had a powerful cunt. Was it due to our bonding?

Could my cock fall off from being inside her like this?

I groaned and secured her leg over mine to keep us comfortable. Really, if she had shifted when I carried her to our room, I was sure my cock would have stayed in the same place because she had bound to me so tight.

I yawned, the sound escaping softly from my lips, as I slowly pulled her in closer. The dim light of the room danced across her sweet and tender face, illuminating every delicate feature. I couldn't help but inhale deeply, catching a faint whiff of her intoxicating scent that smelled of home. The realization hit me like a wave crashing against the shore - I had found my miresa, my mate. The bond between us, as orc and human, was undeniable, radiating with a strength that seemed to intensify with each passing moment. I could feel it growing even now, a powerful force that connected us on a level beyond words.

What would my orgamo say when he meets her? I'd not had the chance to talk to him or my brothers to let them know that I even had a female.

And what of Thorn and his female?

There were many questions that I should seek answers for, but none of them mattered in that moment. My female and I were in our cabin, and I held her in my arms, creating a bond that would last forever.

It wasn't just me branding her, I realized, however. I believed her pussy had now branded me.

Chapter Forty-Eight

Calliope

My lady parts had *superpowers*. Superpowers I couldn't control, but they had dick-gripping powers. I hope it didn't do it all the time. I did like having Valpar be in control most of the time, but whatever the heck happened the last time we did it was freaking insane.

My vagina ate him!

Slurped him up like a person at a world champion hot dog eating contest.

I'd been awake for several minutes and I needed to pee, so badly. Valpar was still sleeping, and I was not convinced that orcs didn't have to sleep often, because most of the time he was sleeping. At least, I thought he was sleeping, until he wiggled his finger inside me and I squeaked in surprise.

"I know you are awake, miresa."

Oh, guess he was awake.

"Can you tell me why your fingers are stuck in my no-no place?"

His shaft slipped out of me at some point. My back was to his chest so we both must have shifted while we slept. However, he had two of his giant declawed fingers inside me, plugging up all his come.

"Making sure you didn't run off while I slept. You are an escape artist." He removed them and I groaned, feeling empty without his touch. Before I could protest more, the urge to use the restroom grew too strong.

"Gotta go!" I swiftly leapt off the soft bed, only to be halted by the sensation of a gentle, warm hand enveloping my arm, firmly tugging me back. I gazed up at him, my expression contorting into a scowl.

He shoved a tunic on top of my body, and as soon as my arms were in the sleeves I took off again.

"Miresa!" He yelled but I didn't stop.

Yup, gonna start trouble already, but I was about to pop.

I dashed out the bedroom door and jumped over a mess. I felt like I was faster, and this was going to come in handy when I was running away from a spanking. *But did I really want to run away?* I snorted and kept running. Valpar was hot on my tail as I heard his feet hit the soft ground.

"Calliope!"

Cheese and crackers. He said my name.

"I have to pee! Where do I go?"

Valpar let out a bark of laughter and shot out some directions. Before I knew it, I was behind a tree and squatting in the most unlady-like fashion, but who cared? We were in the woods and there weren't any pixies around here to make fun of me.

Once I let it go, I let out a sigh and could hear Valpar just behind the tree. He was covering his laughter with his hand, but I paid him no mind because this miresa had to go.

"Can you step back just a bit?" I said, still going.

He cleared his throat. "No, you don't know my territory yet and I haven't scouted to check for predators. You will not be out of my sight for long."

Well, at least he wasn't watching me go. That might be my hard limit.

Just then, I saw Valpar's head come around the tree. "Hey! No peeking!" He laughed and ducked his head back around the tree. It was so good to hear him laugh. He did not seem so uptight, like there was a tree stuck up his butt, anymore.

Once I finished, I saw that there was a closed wooden crate. I opened and saw there were cleaning supplies to clean myself up with. I patted the tunic down and came around the tree. Valpar had his arms crossed, leaning up against the smooth bark, and smiled.

"Feel better, little fairy?"

I snorted. "My bladder is itty bitty. There will be frequent trips to the bathroom, you know. I'll have to go by myself because I will not do number two in front of you."

Valpar frowned. "Number two?"

"Yeah, tummy dumplings."

Valpar made a face and shook his head. "I will construct our bathroom quickly. I have most of the supplies. I cannot have you coming out here at night. It isn't safe. There are large animals, and even ogres, that still roam the territory."

I shrugged my shoulders and when my eyes drifted from his, I noticed that he was very naked, and his dick did not look normal at all.

"Cheese and crackers!" I pointed to his shaft. "Valpar, I broke it!"

Valpar looked down and saw that his dick was no longer green with a purple tip, the entire thing was freaking purple!

I panicked and went to it, stroking it and cupping his balls. "Does it feel okay? Does it hurt? Do we need some ice? I can kiss it and make it better! Or I can massage it, to maybe get some blood flow back. I can't believe it; I broke it and I haven't had enough yet! Valpar, is it going to be okay!?"

Valpar looked as stunned as I was. He was looking at it not with despair or disappointment, though. His face morphed into that of pride?

"I think you branded me." He held onto his slowly rising shaft.

Okay, this was good. It was still working and getting hard.

"Marked you? I marked your dick?" I squeaked.

Valpar nodded, picked me up by my hips and settled me in the crook of his arm. "Yes, you marked me! Your cunt made me yours."

My lips parted as I tried to understand. This was totally weird and not anything like that of the Bergarians. There was biting and fudging. That was how you marked your mates over the wall.

With orc mates you just make the pussy big enough to take a dick, and then the women suck the dick hard enough with their lady parts to make it purple?

Alright, fair. Whatever.

"Okay?" I chuckled, as I placed both hands on the side of my mate's face and gave him a kiss. "That's weird. You really think that's how it is?"

"If not, you can suck my cock with your cunt every night until it is so." Valpar wiggled his eyebrows, and I felt my cheeks go pink.

"You can't say stuff like that." I swatted his shoulder. "People could—well, animals could hear. They would get so embarrassed."

Valpar chuckled but a boisterous laugh overpowered the sound. We both swung our heads towards the noise and saw a large male just twenty feet away.

As another orc emerged, my eyes widened at his imposing size. A massive sword rested on his back, while bags dangled from his hips. Leather cuffs adorned his muscular arms. I noticed striking white streaks in his hair, contrasting with his dark locks, and a thick braid cascaded down his back. His weathered skin bore countless scars. Wrinkles traced the contours of his face, revealing the weight of his years. I tilted my head, observing him intently as he approached, his steps deliberate and measured.

"Valpar, what have I taught you about not watching your surroundings?" The friendly laugh turned more serious, and my head jumped back and forth between the two like an awkward ping-pong match.

"Is this your dad?" I whispered to Valpar, but his grip grew tighter on me.

Valpar snarled and stepped back. "Stay back, she's mine."

The face of the male in front of me softened again, but he continued to come forward. "Figured you would be just as bad as Thorn. He's going through the same. Now let me see my new daughter before I die of old age."

I gasped and wiggled out of Valpar's arms. He growled at me, but once my bare feet hit the ground, I ran up to the male and stood in front of him with my hands behind my back.

"Little fairy, you get back here!" Valpar stomped forward and I could feel the heat radiating on my back.

"Hi! I'm Calliope. Valpar calls me by my nicknames, though. Either Little Fairy or miresa. I'm surprised he hasn't called me 'little shit' yet, though, because I've really been pushing his buttons, late—"

Valpar covers my mouth and groans. "Do not say such foul language, miresa, or I will correct it."

The warning in his tone made me pinch my thighs together and Valpar's dad— I believe his name was Azuk from when we talked about him weeks ago— snorted with amusement. Valpar's nose flared, and he swiftly picked me up and settled me in the crook of his arm.

"She's terribly small. Are you feeding her correctly?" Azuk asked, as he assessed me.

Valpar glared and covered me with his other arm. "She is fully grown and yes, I am feeding her. I have just branded her, and I need to feed her again."

These guys were talking to each other like I was a freaking puppy.

Azuk gazed down at Valpar and smirked. "I see she has branded you, too. Congratulations. Two orcs in the tribe have now been claimed. This is a special time for the entire tribe."

He isn't seriously looking at Valpar's thing, is he? That's totally gross.

"Stop looking at it and stop looking at my miresa!" Valpar snapped at him and turned me away.

I leaned up close to Valpar's ear and whispered, "He can still see your nice butt."

"Female," he growled, and his father chuckled deeply behind us.

Valpar wouldn't allow his dad to come into the cabin. He had to explain, again, to me that males don't appreciate other males in their territory, and

Azuk coming into his territory alone was enough to set him off. Especially, since we had just solidified our bond.

I let him do his thing. Valpar was tense as he gathered the food from the floor of the cabin and kept one eye on me. He was serious. He wasn't letting me out of his sight, and I would not push him right now.

I watched out the window while his dad was setting up a tent. It was enormous, just like the ones that scattered all over Uncle Osirus and Aunt Melina's courtyard and I watched how similar the mannerisms that Valpar and Azuk had were.

Azuk and Valpar were exactly alike. He was meticulously unfolding the tent, pushing away rocks and debris and scanned the surroundings for any sort of predators. There was a fire pit outside and Azuk was already gathering wood, when Valpar had finished salvaging what food was left from the crate and motioned for me to follow him outside.

Valpar had a cloth on this time, covering the new eggplant he sported.

I snorted. *Valpar had a purple dick.*

"You're staying overnight?" Valpar huffed and set the crate down. It was mostly bread, fruits and some veggies. There wasn't any meat, thank goodness because I think that would have gone rotten.

"I've spent time with Thorn, I think it's time to spend some with my seeded. Do you not want me here?"

Valpar was about to open his mouth, but I cut him off.

"We would love to have you! I want to hear all the stories about when Valpar was tiny!"

Azuk threw his head back, his belly— which was bigger than Valpar's— shook and he sat on the log next to the, now, roaring fire. "Valpar was never a tiny orcling. I remember Lash having a time getting that round melon out of her. I believe I had to pull him out by his head. That's probably why his face is stuck like that."

I turned around to look at Valpar, and he had a scowl on his face.

I patted my mate's cheek and snuggled closer into his lap. "Aw, his face isn't always like that. He laughs, too."

Valpar held me closer to his body and nuzzled his nose into my neck.

"Don't worry about him, little fairy, he is just angry I am here. Being newly branded will do that to an orc. I remember it like it was yesterday. I am still going to sit here and enjoy my time with my seeded and his new female, whether he likes it or not." Azuk pulled out an iron flask and took a big sip.

Valpar jutted out his chin, staring at his father intently. "Why are you so happy? Last time I saw you, you were ready to punch me in the face."

My mouth dropped at the accusation. This guy was like the Santa Claus of orcs. Why would he want to punch his own son?

Azuk just chuckled, his belly shaking. "That I was, but now I have something to look forward to. You have a female, your miresa, and soon I will meet mine, once again." He took another swig.

I darted my eyes back and forth, and Valpar's arms stiffened around me. His mother was gone. She passed away into the stars. What could Azuk possibly mean? He wasn't going to—

"Orgamo," Valpar rasped, "what are you talking about?"

Azuk remained silent, causing a sense of anticipation to hang in the air. Suddenly, he unveiled a hefty slab of meat. As the raw chunk spilled out from the bag, a nauseating churn rumbled in my stomach. The sizzle of the iron grill echoed around us as the meat hissed against the metal. Despite the unsettling sight, I forced my focus to remain fixed on Azuk.

Azuk gave the meat a crooked grin, the white wisps of his hair tickling his jawline that fell from his braid. "Because, soon I will meet Lash amongst the stars."

CHAPTER FORTY-NINE

Valpar

BEFORE MY ORGAMO COULD respond, four familiar fae emerged from the dense thicket at the edge of the wood. The subtle rustling of leaves accompanied their cautious steps as they ventured into the clearing, their delicate wings shimmering in the light. I didn't notice their presence before, likely too upset about my orgamo. Luckily, it was just my miresa's family. Each male clung to their female, their embrace exuding an undeniable sense of protection.

And they should—they were in my territory.

My orgamo leaned back on the log and assessed them. He had witnessed the king and queen through the war, and the treaties that they signed to maintain peace. He was grateful to the king for hosting such mating parties for our kind to find our mates.

"Come." My orgamo stood and gestured for them over with the wave of his hand. His face was back to its stern look, but that was his resting face, much like mine. He had been making extra effort to show a friendly face to my miresa.

They all joined us by the fire. I brought in extra logs from the Wood and set them down so we could all sit comfortably. I knew that for the king and the queen sitting on logs was not comfortable, considering their status, but that was how we lived, not with extra padding on our backsides and extra decorations in our homes.

For my miresa, however, I would make our cabin her own palace.

"Hi guys!" My female went to stand to greet her family, but I would not let her leave my arms. It was no ill-will against them. I knew they were good souls, but right now I could not let her leave me. Not when we had just bonded.

Osirus' smirk told me he understood, as well as Birch's, but I could tell Theresa was not as happy.

"Your hair is much silkier than I remember," Theresa said quietly. "It shines. It has never done that before."

My female gathered her waist-length hair and petted it, inspecting the color. It was the first time she'd been able to since waking up from the slumber that took away the magic keeping her memories hidden.

"Yes, it is nice. I will miss my pink hair, though. It doesn't feel like me." She studied it more and flicked it over her back. "When Valpar washes and braids it, it will make me feel more like me." She beams at me and the drums in my chest pound wildly, as my chest puffed up with pride.

I enjoyed taking care of her, and I was happy she was letting me.

My orgamo studied us and rubbed his hand over his chin. "Your hair is black, you mean it was pink before?"

"It was pink." My miresa's face brightens. "Uncle Osirus gave me pink hair as a gift, but now that Valpar and I are branded, I am immune to magic," my miresa said, her face brightening. "It wiped away all the magic that kept it pink so I can't have it anymore. It's okay though. I don't need pink hair to be happy. I have Valpar now."

She leaned her head on my chest and I petted it gently against me. I knew she missed her hair, and to hear her say she would give it up for me instantly gave me great satisfaction, but I wanted her to have both.

If there was a way.

"Valpar." My orgamo interrupted my thoughts. "Do you remember the fruit of the ishabie plant near the hunting grounds of manta? Where the large beasts roam?"

Of course I remembered, our orgamos told us to stay away from such a plant that it was extremely poisonous, and it could hurt our *malehood* if we went toward it.

I nodded in agreement, and he pointed his finger at me. "We will go get the fruit and bring it back here. We can make her hair pink again." He took a stick and stoked the fire. "It will be permanent, so little daughter, make sure this is what you want."

My mouth hung open, and I shook my head. "You said it was poison, that it would hurt our *malehood!* Why would I get her such a plant?"

Orgamo rolled his eyes. "It would hurt *your* malehood. It won't hurt hers. She has no male parts!" he scoffed. If she eats the fruit, her hair will turn pink. That is the poison. All of her hair will turn pink and there is no reversing it, not that we have found, anyway." He stoked the fire again while we all looked at each other in confusion.

"How do you know this is true?" Theresa snapped. "Why pink? And has someone taken this fruit themselves?"

Orgamo let out a loud chuckle until his stomach shook and tears came to his eyes. "Yes, one elder. Orcs have strong stomachs. We can eat anything. But, when Elmach ate of the pink fruit, the reaction was immediate. His entire head turned. His eyebrows, his chest, and even down to his shaft!" Orgamo snorted and wiped away his tears.

I shook my head. "Elmach has no hair—"

"—because he shaves it, you fool. I swear, is there fungus growing inside your thick skull?"

Ah, that made sense. I supposed a pink-haired orc would hurt his male-hood.

My female squealed and clapped her hands. "Really? So, if this plant works on orcs it will work on me too!" She clapped her hands and her family smiled at her. "I want my hair pink again. What do you think, Valpar?" Her long lashes batted against her face, and I huffed in agreement.

What my mate wants is what my mate gets.

We all stayed, gathered around the fire until the light sources fell behind the trees. My miresa had already fallen asleep in my arms, her head tucked under my chin, where she was always meant to be.

Her parents had already said their good-byes many times, but had yet to leave. I believed it was an Earth realm tradition because Birch continued to try pulling Theresa away, but she would shake her head, smile at my miresa and just stare at her, and continue to talk with us.

They had their own sleeping quarters just beyond the trees of my territory, along with the king and queen. The king and queen weren't there the entire time with them. They were spending time with Thorn and his female, Ellie.

They had their own celebration, their bonding ceremony. It included a tent just like my little fairy and mine at the Golden Light Palace. My seeded orgamo attended, and he said he could only stand for one party and not seeing mine was fine with him.

He knew in his beating drums that I had found my mate many moons ago. My ogamie came to him in a dream, told him all about it and said that soon he would be reunited with her, when the time was right.

I kept my worries away. We were spending time with my miresa's family, and I would not bring sadness to my miresa, but I would wait until she was asleep and her family was gone.

"Are you ready, my queen?" King Osirus stood and put out his hand for his mate. She stood, nodded, and grabbed his hand. "Good luck. I'm sure we will visit soon, Valpar." Osirus nodded to Birch who was pulling Theresa to stand.

"Just a few more minutes?" Theresa begs of Birch, but he shook his head and chuckled.

"She's fine now. She has a mate who loves her. She's going to be just fine, love." He tipped her chin with his finger and placed a kiss to her lips. "We will visit more after the baby is born, and I'm sure Valpar will bring her to visit once their bond settles."

I grunted, not bothering to get up and jostle my female. They all took one more look back before they disappeared into the dense forest, and my rigid shoulders finally relaxed.

I thought I was possessive of my female before the bond, but now that it was completed, I felt I may let no one touch her again.

My orgamo chuckled, the sound echoing through the air, as he deftly placed a jagged piece of wood between his teeth. With a determined twist, he extracted bits of food from the crevices in his mouth. "Difficult, wasn't it?"

I grunted, listening to the crackling in the fire.

"You are a good male. You were blessed. Even if you let your female get into situations you could have easily prevented."

I growled.

He was speaking of all the mishaps along the way. He heard most of the stories. My miresa talked about them animatedly. How she fell from the balcony when we first met, how she could evade me and sneak off into the night, and about my poor knot-tying. Yes, she put fuel to the fire on those. My orgamo laughed with her, but when she wasn't looking, I got a look of contempt.

Failure.

Yes, I knew I was.

"You are lucky to have her. She is a wild one." He stoked the fire. "Now that you are in the Wood, you will need help to watch her as you finish your cabin."

I perked my head up at that. Didn't he say he was ready to meet Ogamie? "Wha—"

"Hush, orcling. Yes, you are an orcling." He waved a stick in front of my face. "You possess a precious gift. I will help you, for a time," he sighed heavily, "to get your cabin ready, learn how to tie a proper knot to keep your mate in place, and orcling-proof your home." He put both his hands on his thighs and sat up straight. "Then I will go meet my Lash."

I shook my head. "What do you mean, go meet Ogamie? I don't understand, fully?"

Orgamo rubbed his hand up and down his face. "You understand, but you want me to say it don't you?" he huffed. "While you have been away, Zarfu, Eman and I have had dreams of Lash. She is our miresa in every way. We will have no other. She is ours and we will share her even in the stars, no matter how hard it is with our animalistic desires to not share her. It has been hard being apart from her, you know this."

I nodded and held my miresa tighter. My seeded orgamo and two other orgamos shared her. She chose them, but it was not chosen by the Moon Fairy. When the Moon Fairy came to the orcs so many years ago, she gave the orcs a choice, even the elders. They could remain with the females that chose them or have a new female all to themselves and to be bonded. My clan chose to stay with their ogamie and bond with her once they passed.

The orgamos would stay until they were no longer needed by their seeded, but I—I never thought it would be so soon.

"I'm not leaving yet, Valpar." My orgamo said. "You need me and your miresa needs me." He smiled down at my female. "I wish to know her before I depart this Wood. Zarfu did that before he left."

During our earlier conversation, my orgamo mentioned that Zarfu, Thorn's seeded, had passed to the stars. It wasn't peaceful. He helped fight an ogre, but his memory would live on, especially since he died a warrior's death. He was now with our ogamie.

I could not hold back the tears. I saw him as my orgamo, too.

"How long will you stay?" I brushed my claws through my little fairy's hair, unable to look at my seeded orgamo.

"As long as it takes. Do not worry, Lash will send me pleasant dreams. She wants me to do this for you both."

I hummed and pressed my forehead against my female.

"I am sorry you feel you must stay. But I am grateful you will stay longer to help. It is an odd feeling."

My orgamo huffed and pushed back the silver hair. "I don't know how much help I'll be. I've got a limp, and I'm not as strong as I was. My physical health deteriorates, but I have some wisdom. Besides, Lash would cut off my sack if I did not get to know our new daughter and tell her about what trouble the *little fairy* likes to get into." He eyed her and I gave off a growl.

Orgamo chuckled and shook his head.

It will be hard having my orgamo here while the bond strengthens with my miresa, but I will cherish the insults he has to throw at me until they are no more.

Chapter Fifty

Calliope

We embarked on a journey that lasted half a day, surrounded by towering, jungle-like leaves. The radiant light sources filtered through the dense foliage, casting gentle rays that danced between the leaves. The cool shade provided by the leaves shielded us from the scorching heat, allowing us to travel comfortably. As we moved swiftly, Valpar and Azuk's footsteps created a refreshing breeze that tickled my skin, keeping me pleasantly cool.

I shouldn't say the name Azuk anymore, though. He told me I was to call him Orgamo and nothing else. He called me *little daughter* because Valpar said he could not call me by his nicknames. At this rate, I would have so many names, I may not answer because there were too many to remember.

I sighed happily as I sat on top of my mate's shoulders. We were almost there, at least that was what they told me an hour ago. It felt like an hour, but he said it was only two minutes since the last time I asked.

I kept getting too excited as we traveled. Valpar would have to swat my leg while I sat on his shoulders, bouncing up and down happily.

Valpar said the smell was tempting him to take me behind a tree and rut me into the forest floor. He couldn't do that though, because he didn't want to take longer than he needed to, out here in the Wood. He said it wasn't safe, there were a lot of animals that I didn't know about.

I didn't think that was the case. I think he was worried I would wander off.

Which was smart, because there were so many pretty flowers and plants, and I wanted to look at and smell them all.

"It's just up ahead," Orgamo pointed with the walking stick. We've been in the blanket of the wood and the shade was giving way to a brightness I hadn't seen since we left the clearing of the cabin.

We couldn't bring Valpar's horse, because where we traveled the trail was small and the beasts that roamed manta would spook him.

As we entered the clearing, rustling grasses filled the air, surrounding us with their towering presence. In the center, an oasis emerged, its lush greenery and majestic trees resembling palm trees, adorned with peculiar pink coconuts. My jaw dropped in awe, as my eyes beheld creatures reminiscent of pictures I had seen of dinosaurs but adorned with fur, feathers and even hair.

"Woah." I gaped and Orgamo chuckled, stepping into the light sources.

"Come, we must be swift. We must leave this place before nightfall. This area of the Monktona Wood is dangerous when there are no light sources. You are never to come here alone. Do you understand, little daughter?"

Orgamo looked up at me and glared. He actually glared, and I nodded frantically because I didn't think I wanted to get on this male's bad side.

Valpar and I followed Orgamo through the tall grasses, careful not to make any sudden movements that might startle the strange creatures around us. They reminded me of huge, long-horned steers back on Earth. These were a deep blue, with long manes around their necks and piercing yellow eyes. They continued eating, but I couldn't help but stare at the creatures that Bergarian had yet to see.

As I gazed into the distance, the oasis was shimmering with beauty. A pond lay peacefully at its center, its waters glistening under the scorching rays of the sun. The sight of it was so inviting, its coolness would be a relief against the increasingly intense heat.

I wondered if we could go swimming.

As we approached the oasis, I could see colorful birds flitting between the trees, their calls different than anything I had heard before. The pink coconuts I kept eyeing swayed gently in the breeze, casting a rosy hue over the waters.

Pink was just the IT color.

Azuk cleared his throat. "I'm going to scout the east side. Make sure there aren't any predators."

I didn't pay attention, too busy staring up into the stark difference between the forest trees to this oasis. "Valpar, why is it that—"

Valpar rapidly turned me from where I was sitting on his shoulders, so his mouth was between my thighs. I squeaked in surprise, but he forced his hand over my mouth.

My eyes went wide and while my legs rested on his shoulders, his other hand came up and pulled my underwear to the side. His thick tongue parted my lower lips, and my body leaned back into the large boulder.

Valpar's tongue explored my folds with a hunger that took my breath away. I couldn't believe this was happening in the middle of the oasis and without any dang warning. But I couldn't deny the pleasure that coursed through my body, igniting a fire in my core that threatened to consume me.

I gripped Valpar's hair, pulling him closer as he devoured me, using my nails to scratch through his scalp. He groaned, tasting me like I was his favorite dessert. His grip grew tighter around my body as his tongue flicked and swirled, driving me to the brink of madness. I could feel the orgasm building inside me, a tidal wave of pleasure that I knew would sweep me away.

"You are to come on my tongue, little fairy." He spoke with a command I couldn't ignore, and my back arched, coming into his mouth.

The soft licks of his tongue cleaned me as his fingers gently stroked my clit, sending me over the edge yet again. My body shook and a loud moan tried to escape my lips, but he muffled it with his hand.

Since bonding, our pleasure was tenfold.

Not complaining, no ma'am.

Valpar pulled back, a satisfied smile on his face as he wiped his mouth with the back of his hand. "You're welcome," he said, clearly pleased with himself. I felt flushed and exposed, but also incredibly turned on.

"What about—"

"Later," he pressed a searing kiss to my cheek. "If I take you now, I will continue taking you many times over, and we cannot be left here in the dark when the night creatures come out," he said.

Well, this intrigued me more, but I also didn't want to get eaten...by a gigantic monster...like a monster to kill me, not to give me orgasms. I liked my big orc monster.

Orgamo pushed through the trees and stood with his walking stick, then let out a huff. "You didn't do it right. She should be almost passed out from exhaustion."

Valpar glared at Orgamo and shook his head. "You said not to rut her. She falls asleep faster with rutting."

Are they seriously talking about my post-orgasm sleeping habits?

Orgamo shook his head, walked past us and held out a rope. "Tie her waist so she doesn't get away while you climb the tree. Perhaps she will be too tired to untie it." He narrowed his eyes at me then at Valpar. "See if you can do that knot I taught you last night."

Wait a second, they had been working on new knots that I couldn't untie?

Those sneaky orcs.

Valpar tied a rope around my waist and then to the base of another tree. I was in the shade, and he laid out a blanket with food, water, and a pillow for me to rest.

I suppose this could be barbaric for him to tie me to a tree, but I have run from him a couple times. Guess I deserved it. I shrugged my shoulders and stared up at the tree, containing the fruit to my new hair color and smiled.

"You stay. You will not leave this blanket." Valpar put his hands on his hips, like a child wanting to get his way.

I crossed my fingers over my heart. "Promise. In fact, pinky swear!" I pulled his hand out and wrapped my pinky around his. "You cannot break a pinkie swear. I swear I will stay on the blanket."

Valpar shook his head. "What is the difference in a pinky swear?"

"Pinky swears can't be broken, duh." I sat on my butt and leaned back in the shade.

Valpar scratched his chin. "Should I have been doing these pinky-swears all along to get you to stay in place?"

I shrugged my shoulders. "Well, you never brought it up. It wasn't my fault."

Valpar sighed as we hooked our pinkies together and then he turned his back to me and helped his orgamo as they prepared to climb the smooth trunk of the tree. While it was smooth like a palm tree, it was extra thick and climbing it would be a challenge.

They couldn't just cut it down for the fruit, because it would be wasteful since we couldn't carry the wood back to the cabin, and we didn't waste things in Bergarian.

I hummed happily as I popped a piece of dried fruit into my mouth. I wiggled in my seat watching Valpar and Orgamo swear at each other, and Orgamo slapped his son's thigh in anger while he tried to climb.

It's really entertaining.

The bushes behind me rustled, and I jerked my head to look behind me. A quiet bleat that sounded very much like Simon came from inside the bush next to me.

I gasped, sat on my knees and parted the bushes. "Simon? Simon, is that you?"

Instead of seeing the white head and pretty eyes of my favorite animal, I was met back with a face nearly human. His nose was that of a goat, his eyes forward facing, and a goatee of facial hair. He had long white hair on his head, that was braided just like the orcs had done weeks ago.

"Oh, Simon, look how beautiful you are," I whispered, and my hand slowly approached to cup his face.

He jerked back, his eyes widened and he fell over into the bushes.

I guess the spell did not take away his fainting issues.

I checked on Valpar and Orgamo. Valpar was still climbing the tree, his loincloth blowing in the wind, and I was getting a magnificent view of his butt. Unfortunately, I couldn't pay attention to it, because I needed to check on Simon.

I leaned into the bush, making sure to keep my knees on the blanket.

I did not need to be breaking pinky promises. That would not be good for my butt, right now.

When I got down to pet Simon behind the ears, as he loved so much, he let out a small whine and I saw him coming to. "Hey bestie, it's okay. Nothing to fear."

He slowly came out of it, although, quicker than when he was in his goat form, and he looked up at me with such confusion, much like when he has fainted in the past.

"You fainted, it's okay. How are you feeling? Can you talk yet?" I kept my voice low as a whisper not to alert my orcs. I didn't think he was comfortable with them, yet. He kept looking at them funny, every few seconds.

Be bleated softly, his tongue lolling out of the side of his mouth.

"Can't talk yet, huh? It's okay, just keep practicing. Just know that they won't hurt you. Valpar would never."

Simon whined again and got back on his hands and knees to hide back further into the bushes. "Wait, are you just following us around? Why don't you stay with us?" I tilted my head and leaned further into the bush.

He grunted and shook his head.

Maybe he was still too shy about his body.

"Are you still my bestie, though? Will you still come say hi to me when Valpar isn't around? You know that isn't a lot, right?"

Simon gave me a soft look and leaned forward. His horns, which were the same as when he was a tiny goat, tapped my forehead before he retreated again into the brush.

"Calliope! What are you doing!" Valpar's voice cut through the silent moment Simon and I were sharing, and he scurried away.

I felt myself being lifted by my hips and soon I was hanging upside down. "I didn't leave the blanket!" I giggled and saw Valpar scowling.

"No," he mused and put me right-side up. "What were you doing? What is in the bushes?" he went over to look but I grabbed his face and gave him a kiss. "Just lookin', I was getting bored."

Orgamo stomped up beside us and held out the pink fruit in his hand. It was a cross between a dragon fruit and a coconut from Earth. It was soft, round and had a hint of fuzz on the outside. Orgamo took his two large hands and twisted, breaking it in half. On the inside there was a large seed, like you would see on an avocado and deep blue meat inside.

Valpar took his sharp claw and cut out a chunk of the meat, letting it sit on the tip of his claw. "Just a piece. That is all it will take. You ready?"

I nodded excitedly and reached out to pull it off his claw. Valpar frowned and pulled it away. "Have you already forgotten?" He lifted a brow.

Orgamo huffed. "You have not trained her well. You both need training." He stomped off and we were both left alone. I was laughing while Valpar scowled.

"Perhaps he should meet Ogamie sooner than later if he is making comments like that. I know how to take care of you."

"He's trying to help. Leave him be. I think he secretly enjoys it." I opened my mouth and Valpar placed the piece onto my tongue. "Besides," I mumbled with the fruit in my cheek, "maybe I should try and turn his hair white. It's a challenge I would take."

As soon as I swallowed, I felt a tingling in my scalp and between my legs, then a zap of electricity tingled all the way down my spine.

"Ooph!" I gripped onto Valpar and blinked several times. "Did it work?"

His smile was wide, and it looked like it hurt the way his lips stretched over his two very large teeth.

"There is my little fairy."

"Is it supposed to stand up like that?" Orgamo said from a distance. Like she got struck by lightning?

My eyes widened, and I put my hand on top of my head to feel my hair standing up. "Goddess, what happened?"

Valpar leaned his head back and laughed, then carried me to the refreshing pool. He sat me down and cupped the water in his hands. "It will calm down. I have oils in my bag."

"A-are you sure?" I pulled my hair down to look at it, but it was all frizzy and not soft and smooth like it was before.

Valpar continued to chuckle as he leaned my head into the pool, washing it and doing his best not to get my body wet. He dragged his bag over, pulling out glass vials that held hair oils and brushed my hair.

It didn't take long. He worked fast, and soon he had my hair braided in one long section, then put it over my shoulder. "We will leave it like this and let the oils work. Soon, it will be healthy and strong. Now we must hurry and return."

Valpar stood and packed his things as I turned to him, wrapping my arms around his waist. "Thank you," I said, rubbing my face into his chest. His arms wrapped around me, his cheek resting on my head. "Neither of you had to come all this way to do this—"

"It was our pleasure. You are family, part of the clan and tribe," Orgamo said, holding onto his walking stick.

Vapar lifted my chin with his claw and petted my cheek with the other. "I know you didn't need it, but I will do everything in my power to give you everything that you want, to make you happy. If that means turning your hair pink just to make you smile, I will cross mountains to make it so."

I smiled and pressed a kiss to his chest. "Yes, it really made me smile. I will always find ways to make you smile, too."

Valpar lifted me up and perched me on his arm. "As long as you listen to my rules, you will make me smile."

I rolled my eyes. "You know you like it when I break them, though. Keeps you on your toes and then we get to play. Wink, wink." I closed my left eye obviously several times.

Valpar's face turned a deeper green and I swear I might've seen some pink on those cheeks.

Orgamo's lips lifted into a smirk. "Hmm, maybe there is hope for the both of you."

CHAPTER FIFTY-ONE

Azuk

ROLLING TO MY SIDE, a soft groan escaped my lips as a familiar musk wafted through the air, instantly tickling my nose. It was a delicate scent, feminine and one that I had nearly convinced myself was Lash. With each night's slumber, its presence lingered, almost feeling too real. I could taste it on the tip of my tongue, its sweetness danced in my mouth and when it disappeared I would be left with loneliness.

Lash had infiltrated my dreams more frequently while I've been staying with Valpar and Calliope. They no longer needed me, yet both of them included me in their daily lives. More so my little daughter, than my son—but that was because he wanted all of his female's attention.

I longed for mine, and I could taste her. Every morning and night, between sleep and awake, she talked to me, telling me we would meet again soon. I longed for that day, and I waited anxiously until she would take me.

Instead of feeling the pain in my aching muscles and bones, I feel relaxed. Strange, but it could be the random teas that my little daughter has been making, trying to cure my ailments.

One time it did not fare well, and my stomach was tied up in knots for days.

I heard the flap of my tent open, and I groaned, my hand slapping on my face. "Little daughter, this old male needs to sleep. I am not young any longer. Go play with the whisps." I shooed her away, but the musk that normally faded by now became stronger.

I took in deep breaths, trying to breathe it in.

The bed dipped and I grumbled a curse.

The sultry voice, deeper than Calliope's, murmured, "There's my sleepy male." My eyes snapped open and were met with the captivating sight of a stunning orc female. Her long, flowing locks cascaded in a dark wave, while her beautiful yellow eyes held my gaze. No trace of exhaustion lingered below her vibrant green skin radiating health. A stark contrast to the worn-out Lash I last saw before she left me for the stars.

Am I dreaming?

Then, in a flash, I felt her delicate hand glide up my chest, sending a surge of electricity through me. As a bolt of lightning struck a tree, I jolted upright. There was no hint of pain in my bones, no lingering ache in my back. But those physical sensations paled compared to the overwhelming presence of my Lash sitting there before me. I could feel the warmth from her body on me. The touch of her velvety skin against mine sent me into a frenzy of emotions.

She laughed softly at my reaction, a musical sound that filled the tent and made my drums pound inside me. Her eyes sparkled in the dim light, reflecting the feelings swirling within me. I had missed her, and I had been so jealous that Zarfu got to her before I could.

Lash reached out to cup my face with her delicate hands, her touch sending shivers down my spine.

"It's really me, Azuk," she whispered, her voice barely above a breath. "We are together again."

Water leaked in my eyes as I gathered her into my arms, holding her tightly, afraid she would disappear once more. The scent of her hair seeped into my chest. It filled my senses with memories long cherished and dreams long forgotten.

"Lash," I murmured, unable to find any other words that could capture the depth of my emotions. "I thought I had lost you forever."

She pulled back slightly to look into my eyes, her gaze playful. "You were always the most dramatic of the three. I promised you we would meet again, Azuk. And here I am."

The weight of her words settled deep within me, bringing a sense of peace and completion I had not known since she left. We stayed like that for what felt like an eternity, simply reveling in each other's presence.

"Don't care, you are mine, ours now—" I corrected myself, remembering that Zarfu was around here somewhere.

Bassza, that means I am not—

"Shh." My miresa ran her claws through the loose strands of my hair. "Valpar and Calliope are fine. They will mourn you, but they know you are happier here. You have told them many times you wish to be here with me, haven't you?"

A low, primal growl reverberated deep in my throat, its rumble echoing through the air. "They do," I murmured, my hands smoothly gliding up and down her silky sides. My fingertips traced the contours of her wide, inviting hips, reveling in the gentle curve of her waist. The sight of her bounteous breasts, rising and falling with every breath she took, stirred a hunger within me. The scent of her skin, warm and intoxicating, filled my nostrils, heightening my desire.

I wrapped my arm around her back and pulled on the leather that she had tied around her to keep her modesty. I don't know why; there was no reason to be modest here, now that we were away from the tribe. I wished to keep her bare and ready for us always.

The leather dropped free and exposed her nips. They were beautiful.

I remembered back in the land of the living, when I had to share her with our clan, with Zarfu and Eman. I would want her covered. I would feel desirous rage that they saw her like I did. Now that we are here, I only felt the contentment that I had her. That I could share her because I cared for her as much as they did.

"I...love you." This phrase was used often by my little daughter and orcling. They used it as often as they could, and I came to realize it was a phrase that meant great emotion used in the form of words.

My miresa smiled at me, her hands cupping my face and giving me a gentle caress. "I love you too, my sweet orc."

I let out a huff of annoyance. "I am not sw—"

She pressed her lips to mine. My eyes widened in surprise. We have not done this before. Our tusks would get in the way. We often used our mouths in other places, but now she no longer had them, which I was only just now noticing. I was far too happy to see her eyes and her body. Now only smaller tusks, which sat inside her mouth, remained.

Her tongue swept over my lips, pushing against them, so I opened my mouth to feel her push her tongue inside. I groaned and pulled her close to me, having her straddle my waist so I could feel the wetness of her cunt.

Good, no undergarments.

"Azuk," she whimpered and pressed her tits into my chest. "I've missed your shaft inside me."

I groaned and fisted my hand into her hair, pulling her lips from mine. "May I claim you? Brand you in the way the Moon Goddess says?"

My Lash's cheeks turned a deeper green, and my cock filled with essence to the point of pain. Bassza, I'd missed her. Her smile, her laugh and the way she would shy away from me when I was brash.

"It's why you are here. We can bond, just like everyone else back in the Wood."

My balls filled with seed and hung heavily next to my leg. "I am going to brand your cunt. Zarfu better be taking a long walk."

I do not have jealousy that my female shares me with Zarfu and, soon, Eman. Not like I did once before. However, I would never have them near or in the same room while fucked her pale green pussy until it was puffy and coated in my seed.

Lash whined when I pushed her down onto the bed of furs and I latched my mouth around her tit. Bassza, she was sweet!

"I can't wait until it is your turn to brand me," I say, pushing my erection between her wet folds. "Going to fill you up then lock into your pussy so you can't move. Then, you will suck me deeper," I growled.

"Azuk!" She laughed and let out a squeal when I gripped her other breast in my hand.

"Never leaving you again," I whispered, putting my forehead on hers. She shook her head. "No, never."

EPILOGUE

Valpar

"Look at you, aren't you just the cutest little thing, ever?" My miresa cooed at Thorn's orcling and my hands balled into tight fists. If my jaw clenched any tighter, I just might break one of my back teeth and have to gum my food for the rest of my days.

My female took her finger and tickled the bottom of Kiah's foot. The orcling, with its wide, toothy grin, extended a small, clawed hand towards her. Its fingers were fat and chubby, and it had no control over its body. The orcling's eyes sparkled with excitement as it eagerly reached out, hoping to grasp my female's hand to hold her. The gesture seemed innocent and filled with curiosity. It meant he was a healthy orcling who was eager to explore, but I did not need him to explore what is mine.

"I think he is in love with your hair. I don't think he's seen the color pink before." Ellie, Thorn's female, laughed while she held her son.

There were plenty of colors in the Wood, but my female's hair was the most beautiful. Even the other orcs admired it, from a far of course. I intended to keep it that way. We did not attend the ceremony where Thorn and Ellie announced the name of their son, because I did not want her hair to take away from their moment.

At least, that's what I kept telling myself. Really, I did not want to share my female with anyone else. There had been no other pairings yet and it had been nearly six months. The other orcs were becoming restless, some even traveling into Bergarian alone and doing their own searches.

Those who stayed, I did not trust them being around my female.

Instead, I took my miresa to see Theresa and Birch for a visit, and she got to see her new little brother, whom they named Bramble. I supposed it went with his father's name. Those fae can be strange.

Ellie cradled the orcling in her arms while the females sat on a log outside of Thorn's cabin. The thing was almost too big for her to hold lovingly to her chest. Not that the blob wanted to stay there, anyway. He was growing fast, as most orclings did. I wouldn't be surprised if it started crawling by tomorrow.

I also did not like that my female was around all these tiny beings recently. It might give her ideas of having one of her own. I am a jealous orc, and I was still not ready to share her. Her body still captivated me, and I enjoyed her too much to give all that up so an orcling could suck at her tits.

Those were my tits!

"You know Starla, too?" My miresa brought me out of my thoughts.

Ellie nodded her head frantically. "Yes, she's a bar owner and a witch. She is the one that led me to honey buns here."

My brother, Thorn, rolled his piercing yellow eyes and let out an exasperated grunt. He crossed his thickly muscled arms over his broad chest, his biceps bulging as if to warn me off of his female.

I let off a grunt of my own.

The lines on his face deepened as he displayed his frustration. I felt the same sentiment toward this Starla.

That witch was trouble.

But wait a minute, did I hear correctly?

Honey buns? I snorted and covered my mouth from the laughter. Thorn glared at me, daring me to say something.

My miresa's smile grew. "That's crazy. Starla is a bar owner, too? She led me to Valpar. She acted like she was my fairy godmother and told me to go to the ball, and that is where I fell into Valpar's lap." She scratched her cheek and shook her head. "I don't think she meant for me to fall over the railing to get to him, but it all worked out."

I ran my hand down my face and groaned.

"Did you not smell your female close to you?" Thorn scoffed. "Did not feel her presence?"

"Says the orc who caught his female in a trap, with poison. You had to massage your female so she would even like you. Good thing it worked out, huh, *honey buns?*"

I could feel the tension crackling in the air as Thorn's growl reverberated through the air between us. His towering figure loomed over me, intimidating to most, but I refused to back down from my brother. With a determined glare, I squared my shoulders and puffed out my chest.

I knew that I possessed a certain level of skill that gave me the advantage in this confrontation. Years of training and honing my abilities had prepared me for moments like these. Thorn may have had the physical advantage with his height and strength, but I was confident that my experience and quick thinking would tip the scales in my favor. With every fiber of my being, I braced myself for the clash that was about to unfold, ready to show Thorn that I was not to be underestimated.

Bells ringing broke my concentration. It was a pixie, and I snarled, darting toward my miresa and wrapped my arms around her. The pixie sat on Ellie's shoulder and the tiny pixie cocked her head to the side.

Ellie gazed at me strangely and then to the pixie sitting on her shoulder. "This is Dewdrop. Is there a problem? Do you not like pixies?"

"No. I don't." I snapped. "The last pixie I dealt with tried to kill Calliope."

Ellie's eyes widened, and Thorn stood behind his female.

"As much as I don't like pixies, Dewdrop is fine," Thorn said and put his hand on Ellie's shoulder. "She's saved Ellie from an ogre once, so she's alright in my book."

I regarded the pixie, and my miresa patted my forearm. "It's okay. Just because there was one bad pixie doesn't mean they are all bad. Just like, if there is one terrible human it doesn't mean we are all bad."

She meant her life-giver. The sweetest gift given to me was born of a terrible woman. I sighed and released my hold. I pressed a tender kiss to her bruised shoulder, where I liked to continually mark her skin.

"I used to be able to understand them," my miresa said. "Just like Uncle Osirus." Ellie smiled and nodded.

"You could?" Ellie asks animatedly. "That's amazing. Do they sound just like us?"

She nodded happily. "They do. They are different, though. Their culture and everything, they act—like a hive, almost. They need to be around more of their kind—all the time. The one that Valpar is referring to was Karma—who got his karma." She snorted. "I think he was sort of a loner. I didn't see him hanging out with a lot of the other pixies. I wonder if they shunned him a little bit, and that was why he turned out the way he did. We will never know."

I huffed and ran my claws through my miresa's hair. "He still had a choice," I said. "He didn't have to be the horse-dropping he was."

"You mean flying glitter turd." My miresa corrected me.

He was made into a terrible ale. It was sweet as fuck I had to pour it out. My Orgamo spat it back in my face and cursed me for days.

Suddenly, Kiah reached out and grabbed a chunk of my miresa's hair.

My miresa giggled, took another lock of her hair and tickled the orcling's stomach. "Am I not paying enough attention to the baby?" she cooed, again. "Does the baby need all the attention?"

I let out a low growl and my hands balled into fists, again. I should not be jealous of an orcling. It was a tiny green blob that could not do anything.

"You are such a little man! I bet you are going to be knocking over some saplings soon, stomping through the forest and pounding on your chest. Be the next big orc—"

I snarled and ripped my miresa away from the orcling, and from my brother and his female. Ellie gasped and the baby reached out, waving his hands for my female.

"Mine." I gritted my teeth and threw her over my shoulder.

Kiah let off his own little growl and Thorn let out a bark of laughter. "What's wrong, jealous of an orcling?" He raised his brow and wrapped his arm around his family.

I roared at the couple and Thorn laughed more. I disliked how he laughed. He thought his orcling had won because my female thought him cute. That green blob cannot even wipe himself. His ogamie had to wipe his ass.

I stomped off into the forest, leaving our things by the fire. My female was going to know that she belonged to me, and she would not talk to any male, even if was a green blob.

"Valpar, what are you doing?" She giggled and slapped my butt when I got deeper into the forest. I stopped and my back straightened.

"Did you just slap my backside?"

She took her hand and rubbed it, patting it gently. "You were acting naughty in front of your brother and Ellie. You needed a spankin'."

Moon Fairy, grant me patience.

I slid her down my body so my shaft lined up with her belly and she could feel my length. I pinned her against the dragon-scale tree, a tree that would not move, too strong for me to rip down. Her eyes widened in shock and her hands grasped my chest for support.

"Why, hello there?" She bit her lip. "I haven't seen your little orc in about two hours."

"Calliope, this isn't a game. That little male was trying to—"

"To what, Valpar?" My female narrowed her eyes at me. "Tried to claim me? It's a baby, it's barely a month old! It did no such thing."

My clenched fist soared above her head, colliding forcefully with the sturdy trunk of the tree. The impact reverberated through the air, causing a cascade of delicate petals and vibrant leaves to descend. The gentle rustling and tumbling of nature's shower fell around us.

"Don't be foolish. He looked at me when he grabbed your hair. He was challenging me."

My female rolled her lips into her mouth and tried not to smile. I growled and pushed my shaft harder into her stomach.

"My poor orc," she finally said, and her fingers ran through my scalp. An involuntary purr rumbled through my chest, and I closed my eyes as I felt her get closer to that special spot. My spine tickled with anticipation as she got closer. "What can your female do to make it better?" She leaned closer and pulled my head closer to her lips. "Do you need to rut me, claim me right here, and show your dominance?"

My eyes popped open, and I growled, taking a deep whiff of her scent. "Yesss," I hissed.

"My handsome orc wants to brand me, doesn't he?" My female petted my hair until she tugged on my locks.

I growled again and hiked up both her legs. I could smell her arousal. She was already wet. My female was always wet for me, ready to take me. I didn't have to prepare her anymore if I needed her right at that moment. Just one look, one growl and she would be dripping.

I pushed the tiny dress to one side, knowing good and well she had no undergarments. We got rid of those wasted pieces of clothing long ago. We only wore any sort of cloth when we had to be in the presence of other creatures.

She let out a sharp breath, surprised by the sensation as my throbbing cock glides along her wet folds. A gentle touch against her sensitive clit made her gasp even louder. Leaning back against the sturdy tree, her head tilted, exposing her neck to the cool breeze. The tightness of her clothing barely contained her tiny breasts, which seemed to strain against the fabric.

I wanted to rip the fabric from her, but I did not bring extra and I would not have her wear Ellie's clothing. It had my brother's scent. I would not allow her to smell of him.

"Wider," I growled, speaking of her legs. So she wrapped one leg around me as I grasped the other to put atop my shoulder. It didn't quiet reach, but it gave me a perfect, wide opening to her dripping cunt.

Fuck, I loved her like this, so open, dripping, so willing to take me.

I almost liked it as much when we played games.

She had a wild imagination and at first I was reluctant to play these games—but they had been enlightening. I did not know rutting could have so many forms. This role-playing she liked to do on occasion was fun.

I slid my large purple head inside her, her cunt sucking me inside. I groaned, pushing in deeper.

"For a male trying to claim me, you are going awfully slow," she teased.

I growled deeply, feeling my blood boil at her taunt. I grasped her hips and slammed into her, causing her to cry out. "Is this good enough for you?" I snarled, loving the way her eyes widened and her nails raked down my back.

"Yes... yes, Valpar," she panted, her nails digging into me. "More."

I chuckled darkly, feeling the power coursing through me. I thrust harder and deeper. I had no qualms about forcing my brand inside her. Hard and deep, I listened to our arousals coat each other, I loved the sounds as our bodies slapped against each other.

Her cheeks were painted a beautiful pink and water rolled down her face. "I'm gonna come." Her head rolled to the side, exposing her pretty little neck again. I buried my face into it, taking in her scent and nipping at the skin.

"Cream all over my cock, milk me. Have your cunt suck me dry, little fairy." I watched while my shaft slid in and out of her body, disappearing and reappearing.

I felt her cunt squeeze me. It took all I had not to spill my seed. It was no use, it never was, and soon her muscles coaxed my shaft to lock inside her, sucking the life out of me and pulling ropes upon ropes of my seed into her womb. I let out a roar and it echoed into the Wood. I knew my brother and his miresa could hear, but I could not give a fuck.

That little orcling will know that his aunt is mine. Not his.

I groaned and put my forehead atop hers, letting myself fill her. Her arms wrapped around my neck, and I felt her tiny nails scratching my scalp.

"You know, you are kind of a hot mess," she said.

I huffed, and another spurt spilled into her.

"Seriously, can't take you anywhere. If any male looks at me funny, you gotta go fill me up with your stuff."

"You've never complained before, little fairy." My fingers ran through her hair while we waited for my brand to soften.

"No, just that when we have orclings of our own, you won't be able to get jealous like that."

I growled in annoyance. "Then, perhaps we won't have them for a while." I lifted my head and tilted her chin to look at me. "Unless you want them?"

My female shook her head. "Nah, I'm good. I'd rather visit and play with Mom and Dad, and Thorn and Ellie's babies for now. Don't you think? Besides, I'd like to know that Simon is going to be okay, too."

I let out a breath of relief. If my female wanted an orcling, I would gladly give her one. We would change our routine and make it work. I'd do anything to make her happy. I knew that she was still worried about Simon. The faun wasn't around often, that I could smell. From time to time, I could see patches of fur near our cabin. His scent had slightly changed, and I believed he had found the yellowcress root to calm his scent so he could not be detected.

He'd grown smart.

When I left my miresa alone, he'd visit her. It wasn't often I'd leave her, but when she slept after a good rutting, I'd leave her in our bed and tend our horse and garden. Simon would come from the forest and tap on the window with his claw, and my female would talk to him through the cracked window.

He never said anything back. I didn't know if he ever would.

Yells from Thorn's cabin reached our ears. "Are you coming for dinner, at least?" His voice carried through the trees.

My female squeezed my cock with her cunt, and I groaned when I realized my brand had softened and I could slide out of her.

She straightened her dress, and come dripped from her cunt, so I wiped it back up her leg and shoved it inside.

She squeaked and squirmed against my hold as I pinned her back against the tree. "It stays there."

My female huffed. "You are really going to let it run down my leg in front of them?" She waved her hand in the direction from where we came.

I smirked. "Yes. The orcling will know that smell. Besides, I'm sure Thorn does it to his female, too."

"Gods, that's gross. And so traumatizing for a child, Valpar. But, also hot." She giggled when I pulled my fingers out of her. "Maybe we can do the breeding game, again, after our visit?" she asked hopefully.

It was the games we played. She liked it when we pretended that I wanted to put an orcling inside her. She'd get so wet and needy when I tell her I wanted to have her belly swollen with our children. This game could last for days. She liked to do it when she was *ovulating*.

I scratched my chin and stared up into the sky. It was about that time again.

Which meant we were closer to her period.

I groaned and shook my head. I did not like this *period*. She'd get feisty and irritable and not be my little fairy. I'd just look at her to explain my love, while she would be in this pain she is experiencing, and that is not something I should do. She'd growl and hiss.

It was like she had turned into a rabid field mouse, ready to rip out my eyes.

My only defense was chocolate and lots of it. I would have to visit Sugha soon.

"Come on, Valpar, let's go eat. Then, we can go home." My female tugged on my hand.

Home.

The cabin that was once for a solitary existence. My miresa had transformed it from a pile of wood to a sacred space, filled with the warmth of love and the promise of a bright future. Where two souls finally merged together as one: the little fairy and the grumpy, possessive orc.

Want to read Osirus and Melina's story? What about Creed and his mate? Check out the next page to find their books!

Books by Vera

Under the Moon Series

Under the Moon
Clara and Kane's Story

The Alpha's Kitten
Charlotte and Wesley's Story

Finding Love with the Fae King
Osirus and Melina's Story

The Exiled Dragon
Creed and Odessa's Story

Under the Moon: The Dark War
Clara, Kane, Jasper and Taliyah's story

His True Beloved: A Vampire's Second Chance
Sebastian and Christine's Story

Alpha of her Dreams
Evelyn and Kit's Story

The Broken Alpha's Princess
Melody and Marcus' Story

Twinning and Sinning From Mutts to Mates
Dax, Dimitri, and Seraphina's Story

Under the Moon: God Series

Seeking Hades' Ember
Hades and Ember's Story

Lucifer's Redemption
Lucifer and Uriel's Story

Poseidon's Island Flower
Poseidon and Lani's Story

Thanatos' Craving

Thanatos and Juniper's Story

Saving Zeus—Coming soon!

Under the Moon: The Promised Mates of Monktona Wood

Thorn

Valpar

Simon—Coming Soon!

Sugha —-Coming soon!

Iron Fang MC Series

Grim

Hawke

Bear

Locke

Anaki— coming soon!

Visit authorverafoxx.com for updates and future books!